PRAISE FOR

SING FOR ME

"With *Sing for Me*, Karen Halvorsen Schreck takes readers far into the depths of the American Jazz Age—but with an emotional new twist. . . . Schreck is a masterful storyteller who will hook readers from the first page of this emotional story. Sure to be a fan favorite!"

—Julie Cantrell, *New York Times* bestselling author of *Into the Free* and *When Mountains Move*

"Karen Halvorsen Schreck's novel pulses with the notes of a smoky, Depression-era jazz club, the rattle of a downtown El train, and—most poignantly—the indelible spirit of a courageous heroine, Rose Sorensen. *Sing for Me* is a story of a woman who remains faithful to the passions that set her soul alight. Readers will feel the struggles of Halvorsen Schreck's fearless and persevering characters, and will be uplifted by the beauty of Rose's songs and spirit."

—Allison Pataki, author of *The Traitor's Wife*

"*Sing for Me* is an achingly beautiful story of longing and hope in the midst of what seems impossible. Karen Halvorsen Schreck reaches deep into the soul with prose that sings. Straightforward. Honest. Utterly compelling."

—Carla Stewart, award-winning author of *Chasing Lilacs* and *Sweet Dreams*

"A poignant, powerful, honest novel. Karen Halvorsen Schreck's prose and dialogue are pitch-perfect and Rose's story beautifully haunts this reader days after reading it."

—Rusty Whitener, author of *A Season of Miracles*

"*Sing for Me* is beautiful, pure, and passionate."

—Larry Woiwode, author of *Beyond the Bedroom Wall* and *Born Brothers*

SING FOR ME

A NOVEL

KAREN HALVORSEN SCHRECK

HOWARD BOOKS
A Division of Simon & Schuster, Inc.

NEW YORK NASHVILLE LONDON TORONTO SYDNEY NEW DELHI

BALDWIN PUBLIC LIBRARY

Howard Books
A Division of Simon & Schuster, Inc.
1230 Avenue of the Americas
New York, NY 10020

This book is a work of fiction. Any references to historical events, real people, or real places are used fictitiously. Other names, characters, places, and events are products of the author's imagination, and any resemblance to actual events or places or persons, living or dead, is entirely coincidental.

Copyright © 2014 by Karen Halvorsen Schreck

All rights reserved, including the right to reproduce this book or portions thereof in any form whatsoever. For information address Howard Books Subsidiary Rights Department, 1230 Avenue of the Americas, New York, NY 10020.

First Howard Books trade paperback edition April 2014

HOWARD and colophon are trademarks of Simon & Schuster, Inc.

For information about special discounts for bulk purchases, please contact Simon & Schuster Special Sales at 1-866-506-1949 or business@simonandschuster.com.

The Simon & Schuster Speakers Bureau can bring authors to your live event. For more information or to book an event contact the Simon & Schuster Speakers Bureau at 1-866-248-3049 or visit our website at www.simonspeakers.com.

Interior design by Jaime Putorti
Cover design by John Hamilton Design
Front cover bass player photograph © Corbis; singer photograph by John Hamilton

Manufactured in the United States of America

10   9   8   7   6   5   4   3   2   1

Library of Congress Cataloging-in-Publication Data
Schreck, Karen Halvorsen.
Sing for me / Karen Halvorsen Schreck.
pages cm
1. Women jazz singers—Fiction. 2. Faith—Fiction. I. Title.
PS3619.C4619S57 2014
813'.6—dc23   2013031090

ISBN 978-1-4767-0548-4
ISBN 978-1-4767-0552-1 (ebook)

For Greg Halvorsen Schreck
At dawning, midday, dusk,
and through and beyond the dark—
thank you

ONE

FEBRUARY 1937

I know something's up when Rob gives the DeSoto's steering wheel a sharp spin and we veer off the dark city street. There's no intersection here, no corner to round, not even a one-way alley to barrel down the wrong way. There's just a stretch of ramshackle sidewalk, over which Rob's rattletrap lurches, thin, patched tires thunking against the wooden slats. And a vacant, rutted lot—we hurtle across this, too, car bottoming out, axles grinding, seat springs twanging. And a looming blackness that suddenly engulfs us like the mouth of a vast cave.

Rob brakes abruptly, and we skid to a stop.

Only now do I think to grab the dashboard and hold on tight. My heart thuds in my chest. A moment ago, we were, in a series of twists and turns, driving south. Now we're facing east. State Street, Michigan Avenue, Lake Michigan, the invisible line of the far horizon—all are somewhere ahead, beyond my ken. From somewhere behind, from the West Side of the city (where

Mother, Dad, Andreas, and Sophy sleep in their beds, I hope and pray), something rumbles. A gathering storm.

"Are we lost? Or have you gone bananas?" I say this to Rob as calmly as I can, which is to say, not so very calmly.

My cousin doesn't answer. He doesn't need to, what with the way he lets out a wolfish howl as the ground begins to tremble, and the car, and now I might as well start trembling, too, because it's one of those nights. Rob's off his rocker. Forget his promises; Rob's promises are mostly whims. I should know this by now. I never should have climbed out my bedroom window and down the fire escape to sneak out with him. I should have been a good girl, followed the rules I've been taught since I could toddle, the rules I try so hard to follow.

I clap my hands over my ears at the sound that's closing in on us now. No rumbling storm after all, nothing so tame as thunder and lightning. A metallic monster roars overhead. There's a flash of white light, and another, shot through with blue. Fiery sparks rain down, illuminating rusted steel girders rising on either side of us, curving tracks above, grinding wheels.

Of course. I lower my hands, relieved. Not a monster. Just the elevated train. We're parked in the El tracks' shadow.

I should have known this, as the El passes right outside our apartment's bathroom every hour on the hour, shaking cracked windowpanes, stirring water in the toilet. Nearly three months, we've lived where we live now; still the train startles me every time it rattles by. Saddens me, too. *Angers* me. How far my family has fallen. Whenever I consider the cold, hard fact of our perilous state, I try to remember what Mother says and says and says: "All will be well. God is with us." I try to believe her.

I can't believe in much of anything right now—I can't even

think. Not with Rob howling back at the El in rage or rapture, I don't know which. Some little thing vibrates and goes *ping* inside my skull. My left eardrum, maybe. I punch Rob's shoulder.

"Stop it!"

Rob's shoulder is plump, like the rest of him has gotten this last year since his father died and everything went wrong in his life, as he sees it. In this regard—the everything-is-wrong regard—Rob and I have a lot in common these days. All the more reason why he should have followed through on what he promised and done something right.

I give him another sock. "Be quiet!"

Rob quiets. We sit for a moment as the El rumbles away. Now I can hear the soft *swish, swish* of Rob's hand, rubbing where I punched.

"That hurt, Rose."

"You're not the injured party here." I let out a loud sigh of frustration. "You know what I wanted tonight, Rob. I didn't want any hijinks. I just wanted to hear some good music. You promised."

"It'll be your birthday present, three weeks late," Rob promised. (This was at the sociable after church last Sunday.) "You've been twenty-one for nearly a month already." (As if I needed reminding.) "There's no reason why you shouldn't be able to enjoy what the city has to offer—in moderation, of course. Everything in moderation." Smirking, Rob dumped more sugar into his cup of coffee, and stirred it with a spoon as he stirred my wishes and dreams with his words. "*Trust* me, Rose. I'll take you exactly where you want to go. Chicago is your oyster."

I've never tasted oysters. I don't desire to—just the raw thought of them makes me almost gag. But that doesn't mean I hesitated much when Rob offered me the city on a half shell.

I told him I wanted to see Mahalia Jackson, the gospel singer down on the South Side, whose voice nearly brings me to my knees when I listen to her on the radio. Mahalia Jackson's singing is flat-out gorgeous, as deep and expansive, stormy and serene as Lake Michigan. (I'd say the ocean, but I've never seen the ocean.) The way Mahalia Jackson takes liberties with the likes of "Amazing Grace" and "At the Cross," the way she sustains notes when anyone else would run out of breath— well, she leaves me breathless. I've seen only one picture of Mahalia Jackson and the sanctified gospel choir that sings with her, on a poster that someone tacked on a telephone pole outside the Chicago Public Library. *Come Sing and Worship with Us! All Nations and Races Welcome!* The words floated above their heads like a kind of halo. In their satin gowns, the choir—men and women both—glowed and shimmered like the stars I don't see very often anymore, now that we live surrounded by so many buildings and streetlights. And with her shining smile and radiant eyes, Mahalia Jackson was the brightest star of all.

All I want to do is sing like Mahalia Jackson. I can't, obviously. For one thing, I haven't got her voice. My voice is its own kind of good, I've been told by a few dear ones who'd probably say that if I sounded like a donkey braying. But my voice is not the kind of voice that brings a person to her knees. My voice is too high and too thin; it breaks under pressure. If there was a hope on this cold, gray earth of my voice growing stronger, becoming, in its own way, really good, maybe even great . . . well, I'd have to sing, wouldn't I? I'd have to have the time. The place. The chance. But except for the occasional offertory solo at church, there's no hope of that. Pretty much since I graduated

from high school, I've either been working—cleaning apartments and houses, mostly—or tending to Sophy. I'm doing what
needs to be done. Following rules, not breaking them. Keeping
my family afloat, or, at the very least, helping them bale out the
waters of ruin that threaten to submerge our little ark of survival.

"Tonight isn't hijinks, Rose," Rob says. He's still rubbing his
arm. "Tonight is *living*. And there'll be some high-caliber live
music, I promise."

"You *promise*." I scowl, never mind that my cousin probably
can't make out much of my face in the darkness. "We're nowhere
near Mahalia Jackson's church, am I right? You never intended
us to be, did you?"

"Who put a bee in your bonnet?"

"You did! I wish that train had stopped. I'd have gotten right
on board and gone to hear her sing all by myself."

Rob snorts. "Not half likely. You don't know beans about the
city."

"You're so . . . bad!" I practically spit the last word.

Rob laughs. "You wouldn't know bad if it jumped up and bit
you."

"Don't underestimate me."

Rob suddenly goes serious. "I don't underestimate you, Rose.
You underestimate yourself."

This hits me like a slap. I can't think of what to say, which
makes the bee in my bonnet buzz with even more ferocity. If I
could sting Rob, I would.

"The night is young, Rose, and so are we." My cousin's voice
drips with sultry innuendo. "And the waiting world is wanting
and wanton." Then, with a snap of his fingers: "Hey! That's

catchy. Make that your number-one single, why don't you. Bet your bottom dollar it'll hit the top of the charts."

"I don't sing songs like that." Through gritted teeth, I say this. "You know that, Rob. I don't even *sing*, hardly."

My cousin throws back his head and laughs harder than I've heard him laugh in a long time. "Tell me another one, why don't you," he says when his laughter finally subsides.

Forget sting. I could kill him. Not exactly the Christian thing to do. Perspiration beads on my upper lip. I run my finger under the collar of my dress. It's mid-February, below freezing, and I'm sweating like it's mid-July. My coat smells faintly of wet wool. A horrible, damp animal odor. I shrug off my coat and fling it in the backseat.

"Take me home, Rob. Right now. Then you can do whatever you want."

The car's close air stirs as Rob jerks his hand over his shoulder, a vague gesture at something I can't see. "What I want—what *you* want, even if you won't admit it—is just over there. Waiting."

"Want schmant. I *need* to go home before I get caught."

Rob bwacks and cackles. "Chicken."

"Home." My voice rises with desperation.

"So you can play nursemaid to your sister, housemaid to your folks, and just plain dumb to your brother? No. You are not going to spend another Friday night rotting away in that hovel you call home. I'm broadening your horizons, musical and otherwise. Consider it my good deed for the day. Heck, consider it my good deed for the year, Laerke."

At the sound of my nickname, my fury cools a degree. *Laerke* in Danish means the same as *lark* in English: a sweet-singing songbird. Rob's the only one who calls me that. Besides

Sophy, Rob's the only one who really goes on about my singing anymore. Mother's too worn out to think about such things. Andreas is too busy thinking about himself. Dad just doesn't care—not about anything but money and Sophy. Only Sophy and Rob beg to hear my renditions of this song or that. But this or that doesn't give either of them—especially Rob—the right to tell me what I want or need.

Again, I say it: "Home."

Rob drums his fingers on the steering wheel and waits.

"It's creepy here." I add a little quaver to my voice. "We could get mugged. Or worse. You read the papers. You remember last week, in a place just like this under the El, a man was murdered. The *Trib* said he might have been a member of Frank Nitti's outfit—"

"Oh, buck up! This neighborhood is safer than the one you live in."

Rob digs for something beneath the driver's seat. There's a crack and the smell of sulfur. A flame flares from a long wooden match—the kind Dad uses now to light the old oven in our kitchen. As Rob grins at me through the warm glow, the buzzing bee of my fury fades away completely, and I remember why I love him so, why I love only Sophy more in this whole wide world. And it's not just because the two of them still ask me to sing. My cousin Rob, with his round gray-green eyes, curly golden hair, and deep dimples—he knows everything there is to know about me, the good, the bad, and the ugly, and still he's as loyal as they come. He might get me in trouble, but he'd never hurt me. Not on purpose.

Rob reaches into the backseat now, the match's flame wavering, and retrieves a big paper bag. He shakes the bag's contents onto my lap. I gasp as out spills a sapphire-blue dress, the kind I never thought I'd be able to have, especially not now. In the match's glow, I can make out the flowing butterfly sleeves, the lightly padded shoulders, the narrow waist, the long, sweeping skirt. It's the latest style, which I've only seen worn by the mannequins posed in the windows of Marshall Field's, or on models photographed for the *Trib*'s fashion section. The fabric is so soft and silky that it might as well be water, moving between my hands. Maybe it's rayon, the newest sensation. I've never worn anything made of rayon before. And there's a zipper running up the side. Zippers have been hard to come by these last years, now that Mother makes most of my clothes. She says sewing zippers is too much trouble.

The match sputters out. Rob strikes another against the side of the box. I lift the dress close to the soft circle of light.

"Where on earth?" I brush a sleeve against my cheek. "This must have cost a fortune." Or what my family calls a fortune now. Five dollars at least.

Rob shrugs. He pokes at a silver satin purse lying on the seat beside me, which must have spilled out of the paper bag with the dress. "Look inside."

I unsnap the purse's mother-of-pearl clasp, and there, nestled in the black velvet lining, are two matching mother-of-pearl barrettes, a tube of lipstick, a pot of cream rouge, a black eyeliner pencil, and a round white cardboard box with the words *Snowfire Face Powder* inscribed in scrolling letters across the top.

"It was a gift set, Rose, a real good deal. I got it just before Christmas. I've been saving it for you ever since—for tonight."

"But . . ." I blink. "I don't wear makeup."

"Right. And you don't sing songs like that."

"I *don't*."

"Well, as of tonight, you *do*, Laerke. Really, truly. No denying it."

I bite my lip. "If Mother and Dad ever found out we were even having this discussion—"

"And my mother, and Pastor Riis, and the entire population of the Danish Baptist Church, not to mention all the Scandinavian immigrants in Chicago, fresh off the boat or the farm . . . wouldn't you be the talk of the town then, Rose, a real scandal? Wouldn't that be *fun*?"

"No. That would not be fun. That would be bad."

"Which would be good, as far as I'm concerned." The flame sputters out. Rob lights another match. He frowns, looking me up and down. "You can't go out on the town resembling a missionary to the heathen. At least, not with me."

For the first time, I take in what Rob's wearing: a silvery gray double-breasted suit made of soft, supple wool. I've never seen him in a suit this nice before. The heavily padded shoulders, also the latest style, make him look a lot more muscular than he is.

He notices me noticing. "Pretty snazzy, huh?" In the flickering match light, he cocks the rearview mirror, then cranes his neck to check the knot of his tie, which is the same gray-green as his eyes.

"You look very handsome. Now please tell me how you managed to come up with these duds on a secretary's salary."

Rob sighs, and out goes the match. He lights another. "I've been saving. Working all the time like I do, you got to save for something special."

I finger his cuff. "Still, this plus the dress—"

Rob clucks his tongue. "Stickler for details, aren't you. Well, if you must know, I found the dress and the suit at a pawnshop. Not a big surprise, right, with so many stuffed shirts going belly up since the Crash? Anyway, who cares how I got it? It's an investment for my future. I'm going to be one of those stuffed shirts one day and buy lots of suits like this—even better. Just you wait, I'll be the best-dressed lawyer in town. Oh, Rose." Rob's voice goes soft. "I want this, see? I want to live a little." He clears his throat and firmly says, "You will, too—especially once you've given it a try."

"Last time I checked, I was alive," I mutter. But I can't help but think maybe Rob's right. I'm twenty-one, for heaven's sake. I might as well be in my sunset years, for the way I spend my nights.

"You're alive if living is cleaning up other people's messes and taking Sophy out for walks." Rob confirms my thoughts, but the bee buzzes in my head again.

"You talk about Sophy like she's a dog!"

Rob ducks his head, appropriately embarrassed. "You know what I mean, Rose, and I don't mean that." Gently, he takes the dress from my hands and drapes it across the backseat beside my ugly, stinky coat. "Now get changed."

A startled laugh escapes me. "Where?"

"There." Rob jerks his thumb at the backseat. "When you're done, you can use the rearview mirror to doll yourself up."

I shake my head hard. "I'm not doing any such thing."

Rob levels a look at me. "You *are* doing such a thing. Or I'm telling about those songs. Your singing."

My so-called singing. It's what I do when I'm alone, or I think I'm alone, only to discover Rob sitting outside my window on the fire escape, listening, his eyes wide with astonishment and delight.

I slam my fists against my thighs. Rob catches hold of my hands and stops me from doing it a second time.

"Listen, Rose. Listen to me now. I'm on your side. You know that. Tonight is only for your own good."

"You wouldn't tell. You promised." My voice cracks and falters. "But promises, promises. That's you all over, right?"

"Come out with me and have a good time." Rob tucks a lock of my hair behind my ear. "It's just music, Laerke, music that's made for you. A little good music never hurt anybody. And you know, if you'd just let 'er rip and sing what you really want to sing, your voice could . . . well, who knows what might happen! You've just got to believe, Laerke. You've just got to get past the past, your fears, your family."

"I Got Rhythm," "Pennies from Heaven," "Puttin' on the Ritz." Songs of the world, not of the church. Songs that are wrong. These are the songs I love, in a different way than I love "Amazing Grace" and "At the Cross," but deeply, so deeply, as deeply as Mahalia Jackson must love singing gospel. These are the worldly songs I sing that I shouldn't, leaving Rob wide-eyed with astonishment and delight.

I want Rob to keep my secret. I want to hear some music. Most important (at least, this is what I tell myself), I don't have another way home.

I climb into the backseat and begin to change.

TWO

Minutes later, I'm a different girl. A girl Dad would call a tramp. A girl I'd avoid if I saw her on the street. Too pretty, I'd think. Too racy. Too rich. Too much like someone I guiltily wish I were, lying in bed in the dark with Sophy asleep beside me. And now in the dark, here I am. Here she is. That very girl in a dress that surpasses my dreams. I created her by match light. I saw her in the rearview mirror. Brown eyes accentuated by black pencil at eyebrows and lids. Cheeks rouged to shimmering pink and powdered with Snowfire. Lips lacquered until they're be-still-my-beating-heart red. Wavy, shoulder-length hair swept up into a simple twist and secured, except for a few tendrils, with mother-of-pearl barrettes.

I'm jittery with amazement and guilt. Putting on "face paint"—that's what Mother calls it. It came so easily to me. I must be looking at too many magazines when I should be getting what Mother needs for Sophy at the pharmacy. God forgive me.

"Minxy!" Rob says, God forgive him. "Course I always knew

you had a special allure, Rose. Now, come on, let's go." He blows out the match. When I reach for my coat, he says, "Leave it."

Is pretty always this cold? That's what I wonder as I emerge from the DeSoto into the wintry night air. The rough wind bites my bare throat. It flutters the butterfly sleeves, exposing my arms, and wildly whips the dress's hem until it's a blue froth at my bare ankles. (Rob made me take off my old stockings; he almost made me go barefoot, rather than let me wear my scuffed Mary Janes, but I put my foot down there, so to speak.) I'm shivering uncontrollably now. The wind nearly blows me back into the car.

But Rob slips off his suit jacket and throws it over my shoulders, then grabs my hand and drags me from beneath the El tracks, across the vacant lot, down the wooden sidewalk, and round the corner to where East Thirty-Fifth Street hums with lights, traffic, and people—black people, mostly—all of them wearing coats, many of them wearing fur coats, laughing and talking as they hurry past.

Back to the question I asked when Rob took his little detour under the El tracks. "Where are we, exactly?"

Rob licks his lips and smiles like he's tasted something sweet on the bitter air. "Bronzeville."

Well, that explains it. Bronzeville is the heart of Chicago's black community, home to the very rich and the very poor, and to many in the middle. I've heard Dad speak with grudging envy of this neighborhood's thriving businesses—the banks and beauty colleges, the department stores and movie theaters, the hospitals, and the offices of the nation's most influential weekly newspaper, written for those who inhabit this community and others like it, the *Chicago Defender*, which speaks not of "col-

ored" or "black" people but of "the Race." At least that's what
Dad says, his voice heavy with judgment and foreboding.

I blink into the wind. It must be close to eleven now. Once a
month, Mahalia Jackson and her gospel choir do a special Saturday program that lasts late into the night, sometimes into the
wee hours of the morning. I could be hearing that good gospel
music right now, but instead I'm standing here. *Here!* Yet I've
never been more awake in my life. Or felt more alive.

A car passes by, and from the half-open passenger's side
window comes a sharp whistle.

"That was directed at you, my dear," Rob says. "Some University of Chicago snobs out slumming, I'd venture to say. At least
they know a pretty girl when they see one."

Dad would be horrified if he knew I was being perused in
such a manner. Mother, too. And Pastor Hoirus and the entire
congregation of the Danish Baptist Church. And me. I pull Rob's
jacket closer around my throat, tighter across my chest, covering
the far-too-low-cut neckline of this astonishing dress. I want off
this street. I want inside just about anywhere. Teeth chattering, I
manage to ask, "Where now?"

Rob smiles slyly. "Guess."

I look around. Where could all these people be hurrying to?
A picture show is letting out of the Grand Theater across the
street, but the box office windows are curtained, so it's closed
now. At the end of the block, bums huddle around the warmth
of a smoldering ash can. My throat tightens at the sight; just last
week, Dad said we weren't so far from that kind of life. He was in
one of his moods, but I can't shake his words from my memory.
Some of the men are in tatters, but others are more nattily
dressed. It's a slippery, swift slope to poverty, so the saying goes,

and as my dress and Rob's suit prove. One swarthy white man wearing a red-and-black plaid hunting jacket and matching cap wields drumsticks. He's rapping a beat against the side of the ash can. He's got rhythm, that's for sure. Another, more ragged man, a black man with thinning gray hair, is playing the harmonica. I can't make out the melody, but something sure is setting the men's feet tapping, keeping their blood flowing in the cold.

I nod in their direction. "If that's the big musical attraction, I'd say we're a little overdressed."

"Not quite." Rob takes my elbow and turns me toward a metal door. A delivery entrance—that's what it looks like. Then I see the wooden sign across the top, the words painted there in red block letters: CALLIOPE'S.

Rob draws me toward the door. "This is *the* place, right up there with the best clubs in town. The Sunset Café, the Royal Gardens, the Apex Club, and Calliope's—people come from all over to hear music at places like this. Last time I was here, I met a man from France. Another time, a woman from Cuba. And then there was this fellow from India. You should have seen the cut of his jacket—the strangest little collar, but swellegant, I gotta say." Rob's voice rises with excitement. "Oh, Laerke, you'll love it here. The musicians may not be Mahalia Jackson, but they're their own kind of heaven-sent."

With that, he opens the door and pulls me inside.

Here's what I know about bars, clubs, dens of iniquity: nothing.

Well, I do know this. I know that up until just four years ago, in 1933, a place like Calliope's wouldn't have existed. Not out in the open, anyway. Prohibition would have pushed it underground.

A place like this would have only been found behind a locked door guarded by thugs with guns. Rob and I would have needed a password to get inside. We would have needed to know someone, the wrong kind of someone. We would have put our lives on the line—or, at the very least, our clean police records.

Prohibition never should have ended, that's what Mother and Pastor Hoirus say. Teetotaling temperance. That's what's best for everyone. Dad remains quiet when this subject comes up, but then, Mother's the Baptist. Dad just drops us off at the church entrance and picks us up when the service is over. And he frequently smells like he's had a little nip of something Mother would like to prohibit in between.

Regardless of Mother's and Pastor's wishes, temperance is clearly a thing of the past. That's the first thing I realize, taking in this place. The smell! No, Dad carries the smell of liquor; this place reeks. It reeks of all that's spilled and sticky beneath my Mary Janes. Stale beer, musky whiskey, fruity wine. And all these cigarettes, wafting around my head, and something even more foul that's wafting . . . cigars! Stinking, hazy wreaths of smoke fill the air.

Rob has brought me to a crowded, noisy, boozy club, and people that aren't him are pressing up against me, pushing me this way and that, nearly knocking me off my feet. I'm stumbling now, snagging the beaten-down heels of my shoes on the hem of my beautiful dress. I can't breathe. I can't breathe! In front of me, a woman throws back her head, laughing, and a heavily scented lock of her fiery orange hair—lilies? gardenias?—catches in my mouth. I drop my silver satin clutch. The lights spread and smear like melting butter. The woman's hair slips from my mouth as my legs buckle. I'm going down.

Someone grabs my arm. Rob hoists me up with one hand; with the other, he waggles my purse before my eyes.

"Music swept you off your feet, huh?"

"Music?" I gasp for air, sounding dull and dim-witted. I take the purse from Rob. The silver satin still looks clean. There's that.

"Listen, Rose!"

All I can hear is the sound of me catching my breath. And now laughter, shouting, clinking glasses and bottles . . . I hear all this, too.

Rob peers at me. "You look pale, even under all that makeup. Don't worry, though. You still look pretty."

"I'm not worried." This comes out faintly because it's a lie. I try to conjure the sound of Mother's voice: *All will be well. God is with us.* Instead I hear something else—a reedy piping from somewhere across the crowded room. Lilting notes, a hint of melancholy weaving sinuously through the chaos. It's a clarinet—an instrument I've heard a lot on the radio at the Jewish deli where I get the dark rye bread that Dad likes best. The clarinet's music makes me think of a wizened man, making his spry way through a difficult world, sometimes stumbling just to get a laugh—or maybe it's the deli's owner I'm thinking of, because Mr. Kalman is a lot like that, making his way from day to day. Mr. Kalman sometimes sways to the sound of the clarinet coming from his radio. He moves like a cobra, hypnotized by a snake charmer's flute, swaying like I'm swaying now.

"You hear it, don't you?" In his excitement, Rob gives me a little shake. "I told you this music is out of this world. And the band's not even warmed up yet. Heck, they're not even all on-stage."

Rob takes his jacket from my shoulders and puts it on. Runs his hands quickly through his hair, taming his curls. Settles the jacket more securely into place to cover his potbelly. Smiles his charming, impish smile, and, smoothing my butterfly sleeves into place, says, "There, now. Perfect. Listen, wait right here, okay? There's someone I have to find. You'll be *amazed* who else is here, Rose."

I blink. Someone I know? Someone who knows me? I reach for Rob's sleeve, trying to hold him back. "Don't go!"

But he's gone.

Alone in the crowd, I sway with the push and pull—not so much cobra now as flotsam or jetsam. I look for the stage, but all I can see are the backs of people's heads. But I can hear. Oh, I can hear the clarinet lilting up and down a scale. And there's a low thrum—a bass fiddle being plucked. Two musicians, warming up. Will anyone else join them?

"Excuse me, please." The man's voice is low and husky. Even Mother would have to call his tone gentlemanly, never mind that the words were spoken in a bar.

I turn to make way for the man with nice manners, who is right here, standing so close because he has no other choice in this crowd. I meet his eyes, black and almond-shaped with long, thick lashes. I take in his tawny skin, his carefully groomed and glistening black hair.

A black man is standing in front of me, so close I feel warmth emanating from him. His scent is warm, too. It's a light, bright scent—from cologne, maybe, or fine French soap—that reminds me of nothing so much as sun-warmed lemons. The man must have been trying to get past me to somewhere else, but now he stands very still. As close as can be, he stands, looking into my eyes. And never mind what's right and wrong, assumed or forbidden, he doesn't seem the least bit concerned about the fact that I'm a white woman and he's a black man. A handsome man. A very handsome man who also happens to be black. As close to me as can be.

My skin prickles with some emotion I can't put a name to. *Fear.* I try that on for size, but it doesn't fit. *Embarrassment.* Nor that. *Recognition* is the word that comes to mind, though that's not a feeling, is it? It's an experience. I'm having an experience of recognition, standing face-to-face with this man. An experience that makes sneaking out of the apartment and setting foot in this club seem like minor experiences by comparison.

The man looks swiftly away from me, then back again. Surprise—no, astonishment flashes across his face. *Yes, it's her. She's still here.* He recognizes me, too. He bows slightly. *Hello again*, he might as well be saying. He's wearing a tuxedo, I realize, as he runs a long, dark finger under his crisp white collar. He swallows. The muscles of his throat, his Adam's apple, rise and fall beneath his skin. *Beautiful.* My mouth has gone dry, my face hot. "Oh," I say for no reason I can think of, no reason at all. Pink must be flooding my warm face. Or maybe my face is the same color red as my be-still-my-beating heart lips, as my heart, for that matter, which is thudding so hard now in my chest it's all I can do to keep from looking down to see if this far-too-low-cut neckline is rising and falling with each beat. But his gaze holds mine. I don't look anywhere but into his eyes.

"My," I say, which seems to mean nothing and everything at the same time.

He nods, agreeing. "Yes," he says, confirming once and for all. He leans closer yet, so that his lemon-scented warmth becomes summer's heat. "Miss . . . ?"

How can he be so brave, so bold, so foolish, so familiar? How can I be so glad that he is all these things, and surely more?

"Sorensen," I say.

"Miss Sorensen." He nods again, his thanks this time, and his nose nearly bumps against mine. Then—impossible though it seems in this crowd—he slips easily past me. As he does, his elegant fingers graze my left wrist. *Summer's heat.* His touch burns even after he disappears into the crowd. I stare after him, though there's nothing to see but other people.

And this is when the mixed-up nature of this place finally reveals itself to me, and I suddenly understand the *how* of him. There are as many black folks as white folks in this club. Some of them are sharing tables. One couple—a white man and a black woman—are sharing a drink. The man holds the thin green straw as the woman leans close to sip from it. Another couple, a black man and a white woman, test out dance steps together.

I taste waxy lipstick, then the iron tang of blood. I'm biting my lip, and far too hard. I clench my hands instead.

My parents have always made sure that we stayed out of colored neighborhoods. We'll take the long way if we have to, to pass such places and their people by. On the rare occasions when Mother sees a black man approaching, she makes me cross over to the other side of the street. If Dad sees such a person, he's likely to do the same, and then make an ugly joke at the person's expense.

I duck my head so swiftly that the mother-of-pearl barrettes loosen in my hair. I can set them back into place, but I can't shake off this sudden sense of shame.

Someone bumps into me with a grunt. Another pair of hands gives me a solid shove, and a man growls, "Move it or lose it, twit." So much for good manners. So much for waiting for my cousin. So much for being inhibited by so many things, but especially, in this moment, by my shame. It's time to get out of the heavy traffic.

Using my silver satin purse as a small shield, I push and shove my way to a row of tall stools flanking a wall. Miraculously, a stool is empty. I carefully smooth out the back of my dress and perch on the cushioned seat. I can see the stage from here. There are the musicians, gathering beneath the spotlights, and among them—well, there he is. I'd recognize him anywhere. The man who knows my name though I don't know his. The man whose brief touch still lingers, hot on my wrist.

He's a musician.

He's testing out the keys on an upright piano. His fingers fly up the octaves, the notes flaring like the flames on Rob's matches. Now his fingers descend, the notes cascading like drops of water. The man's younger than the other band members, not much older than me, probably. But he's playing like a seasoned professional.

There are four men total in the band. Two of them black, two of them white. That must explain the band's name, the Chess Men, stenciled in black letters across the white face of the bass drum. A portly white bassist twirls his fiddle in a neat circle, then dips it low as he might a female dance partner, teasing laughter from the audience members flanking the stage. And the ash can drummer, the swarthy fellow in the red-and-black checkered hunting jacket (swapped now for a black tuxedo, though he still wears the red-and-black checkered cap on his head), he's up there, too, hunkered down behind his drum kit. He flings off his cap now, and his bald head shines pinkly in the spotlights as he whisks a brush across a snare. And there's the licorice-whip-thin clarinetist, with salt-and-pepper gray hair and skin nearly the ebony color of the instrument he's playing.

And there's the man I'd recognize anywhere.

"Smoke Gets in Your Eyes"—that's the song he's playing. One by one, the drummer, the bassist, and the clarinetist join in. The song's a hit this winter. I hear it all the time, wafting through other people's open windows, and up and down store aisles. Though a cigarette will never touch my lips, still I sing this smoky song when I'm alone, or I think I'm alone, only to find Rob listening at the window. I close my eyes now, and I hear the forbidden melody clear as can be in spite of the noise all around:

> *They asked me how I knew,*
>> *My true love was true*

"Know this one?"

My eyes fly open. It's Rob, holding two glasses filled with ice and water.

"I think I may have heard it before." My attempt at nonchalance comes out forced.

Rob winks and hands me a glass. I am thirsty, I realize. Not only has all this smoke gotten in my eyes, it's coated my throat, too. I take a long drink, then sputter and spit as the liquid sears the roof of my mouth, my tongue, the back of my throat, the pit of my stomach.

"Whoa! Take it easy on that gimlet. They go heavy on the vodka here, light on the lime."

Rob's laughing. Now his laughter splits in two, and through the blur of my watery eyes, I see who's standing beside him.

Zane Nygaard, the Great White Hope of the Danish Baptist Church. Zane, the fellow every fellow wants to be. The fellow every gal wants to date, including me when I let myself think that way, which is rarely. Zane, with his strong Viking features, his wavy, white-blond hair, his ice-blue eyes, his perfect physique—except for his bum left leg. Afflicted with polio as a child, Zane's got a slight limp, but somehow he makes that limp seem jaunty, an asset to his style.

And now here Zane is, not a fantasy at all but as real as Rob, as real as the man (whose name I wish I knew) at the piano. Zane's father, Dr. Erik Nygaard, is my dad's current boss, the man who "saved" us by giving us a roof over our heads when we were practically out on the streets. But salvation doesn't come free, not from Dr. Nygaard, at least. We keep that roof over our heads in exchange for nearly every hour of Dad's days and nights. (Dad and Mother tried to find less taxing work. But people with more schooling and better skills were snapping up the jobs they might have gotten when times were easier.) An apartment superintendent's job is never done, especially when he's managing the ten large buildings owned by Dr. Nygaard and his wife, the formidable socialite Mrs. Pernille Nygaard.

The job of the girl who cleans those buildings is never done, either. And never mind how I look tonight. That girl is me.

I muster a smile for the son of my boss.

"Well, if it isn't Rose Sorensen," Zane says, taking a long, slow sip from the amber-colored liquid in his glass as he evaluates my dress and the makeup on my face.

It isn't, I consider saying. *This is some other girl. You've never seen her before, and I haven't, either.*

But then, because Zane and his parents hold my family's lives in their hands, I decide it's better to match him at his own confident game.

I lift my chin in the air. "Indeed it is. I am. She's me."

Here's what I realize as I watch Rob and Zane exchange barbs, drain their glasses, and go for seconds, while I get thirstier as the ice melts in my gimlet, but still I don't drink it.

We're all where we shouldn't be tonight, Zane, Rob, and I. Rob's not drinking water. Zane's not drinking ginger ale. I'm not . . . myself. We've all broken rules. We've all got something on one another. We'll keep one another's secrets, because we have no other choice.

Clearly, Rob and Zane have run into each other at Calliope's before. They share stories about other nights, drinks, bands, and orchestras. But this quartet, they agree, is the best, even without a singer. Forget what most other people are listening to. Forget boogie-woogie. Forget swing. Tonight's kind of jazz, played by small ensembles like the Chess Men, is *IT* with a capital *I,* capital *T.* It's solid. It's swell. Better than solid and swell, it's against the rules in most clubs. Even here, the Chess Men are allowed to play only when other bands cancel (like tonight, and even with tonight's cancellation, they're waiting until it's almost after hours to play). Or they play after hours when the all-white or all-black bands are done playing. Or they'll play off-nights between sets of all-white or all-black bands.

"Why?" I ask.

Rob gives me an isn't-it-obvious look over the rim of his glass. "They're *mixed*, Rose."

I shift on my stool, suddenly uncomfortable. I'm tired of talk. I'm just plain tired. I want to close my eyes and listen to the music. The Chess Men are almost finished warming up; I can tell from the way they're watching the crowd. Now the man who knows my name gets up from the piano and moves toward the center of the stage. Standing there in the footlights, he gives a sharp whistle. The crowd quiets. Rob and Zane yammer on. People stare in our direction. In a moment the man who knows my name will be staring.

I elbow Zane, give Rob a swift kick with the blunt toe of my Mary Jane. They grimace when they see other people are looking. But now everyone turns toward the stage again, and Rob, Zane, and I do, too.

In the bright glow of the footlights, the man rocks back and forth on his heels, as if in time to a song nobody else can hear. His hands are clasped before him. His head is bowed. For the life of me, it looks like he's praying. Then he lifts his eyes and says, loud and clear, "Thank you."

"Thank *you*!" a woman shouts back from the crowd.

He gives a professional nod. "You're most welcome. I speak for the Chess Men when I say how glad we are to be able to play for you tonight. All things being equal, we'll do three sets, with a short break in between each."

He put special emphasis on the word *equal*. Now he looks pointedly at a table of dark-suited white men, sitting just a few feet away from Rob, Zane, and me.

"As some of you know," he continues, "all things are not always equal." His gaze sweeps the room again. "A few weeks ago, our vocalist left us for another band. Opportunity came knocking. We understand. That happens sometimes. But now we're in a bit of a fix. We need to find another singer, pronto." He levels another stare at that table of men. "The powers that be hath ordained it."

"You're just not pretty enough," one of the men says loudly.

He gives another nod. "I'll be the first to agree."

"You are *more* than pretty enough!" a woman calls from a back corner. There's laughter, until he raises his hands and quiets the room again.

"The bottom line, my friends, is that we've been told we need to find a vocalist by next week or we'll be looking for another club. As you all know, that club may be hard to find. So we're holding auditions this Tuesday night. We've put an ad in tomorrow's paper, and we'll spread the word. But if you'd be so kind as to point any ladies with fine voices in our direction, we'd be much obliged."

"You want my opinion, the only reason they're being forced to find a singer is because they're a mixed band," Rob whispers to me. "A woman buffers the tension, you know what I mean? If they were all white or all black, they wouldn't need to worry so much about offending."

"And the fellow who owns this club and his bigwig backers would be more confident they'd have a full house," Zane adds. "Some folks here don't really care about the music. Just like the fellow said, they just want to feast their eyes on some sweet young thing."

"*Thing?*" I give Zane a look and then turn toward the stage again.

He is back at the piano, raising his hands to the keys.

"If the Chess Men find the right gal, there'll be no stopping them," Zane says through a mouthful of ice. "It won't matter what color their skin is. They'll be playing every venue in town."

A low minor chord sounds as he presses down on the keys.

"I've got it!" Rob slams his glass down on the table, startling me and a few other people close at hand. "This Tuesday, Laerke. We're coming back! I'll see you up on that stage, mark my words. You'll be doing what you were born to do, and you'll be making money doing it. What more could anyone ask? This is your chance!"

"This is *not* my chance." I mutter this, leaning close to Rob so he can hear. "Not a chance in heaven."

Another minor chord, closer to middle C.

"Who cares about heaven? I'm talking about right here and now."

"That's blasphemy, Rob." So why am I fighting back a smile? "Now, once and for all, be quiet. Please."

The chords shift tentatively upward. Zane leans close to Rob and says something that makes Rob laugh. I stand up, scoot my stool to the other side of them, sit down again. Now I can really listen. I can really see. I can ignore Zane, and Rob, too.

The drummer's brush whispers across the snare. The bassist plucks an answer. The clarinetist weaves it all together. The Chess Men are playing "Cheek to Cheek," another of the songs always pouring out of other people's open windows. The man at the piano leans deep into the keys. "Heaven, I'm in heaven." I breathe the words, catch my breath. *You'll be doing what you were born to do, and you'll be making money doing it.* Would that be so bad? Yes, as I've been told all my life, it would—if it meant doing this, singing these songs, the ones I listen to on the sly, though I know I shouldn't. The ones I can't get out of my head. The ones I know by heart.

But suddenly it's like I'm hearing this song for the first time. Beat by beat, note by note, the Chess Men are transforming Fred

Astaire's suave single into a rapid-fire number. People are dancing. Really dancing. I can't keep up with what's happening before
me—the whirling and twirling these people are doing, like der-
vishes. The band plays at a feverish pitch. The man's hands blur
on the piano keys. The man's hands . . .

My hands are shaking. I turn to Rob. "We really should go
home." I stand to make my point.

"Not yet."

I catch a glimpse of Zane out on the dance floor, glowing in
the smoky, hot light, twirling a beautiful girl like she's less weighty
than a yo-yo at the end of a string.

"Guess I'll take a cab." My voice sounds shrill.

"With what money?" Rob drains his drink. "*Enjoy.* We'll be
leaving soon enough."

I take a deep breath and sit back on my stool. The Chess
Men are slowing the song down finally, winding it down, down,
down. *Dancing cheek to cheek* . . . People are doing just that as he
shapes minor chords to end the number.

"Incredible," Rob says with a sigh.

The notes of another familiar song change the mood of the
room. I know this song, too, God forgive me. It's "You're the
Top," light and lively, just the way it sounds on the radio. Only
better.

"Wanna dance?" Rob asks. "It's calmer now."

I shake my head until a lock of my hair tumbles down and
grazes my shoulder.

Rob shrugs. "Me neither. Not really. Wouldn't want to get
my new suit all sweaty. But when I'm a lawyer I'll dance the night
away. Why not? I'll have plenty of suits to choose from the next
day. Just you wait, Rose. Wait and see. You'll be dancing, too."

Maybe Rob goes for another drink. I don't know. Perched on my stool, I lose sense of everything but the music. The only time I keep track of is the beats from measure to measure. Now it's four-four. Now I could waltz—one, two, three, one, two, three— if I was the kind of person who waltzed. Now, with all the crazy syncopation, I don't know what time it is. I don't care. I sing along in my mind, and since I don't know the words to this song, I make up my own.

"Oh, Laerke." Out of nowhere, Rob is leaning close to me. "I don't care what you've been told all your life. I don't care what you think. You have a gift from God. And this music—it's a gift from God, too."

"I didn't—" My hand flies to my mouth.

Rob laughs. "Yep, you sang. Loud and clear."

I cast a quick look around. "Did anyone else hear?"

Rob shakes his head. "Too noisy. Anyway, nobody here cares about the things our family cares about. If people dance crazy, if a girl sings like a house on fire, it doesn't matter. That's why I love it here. That's why I never want to leave." Sighing, Rob flashes his watch, and I see the time as clear as can be. Nearly two in the morning. "I guess we have to leave soon, though."

I know how Rob sounds when he's beyond sad. I heard it in his voice last summer, when he called me on the phone to tell me that a steel beam had split his dad's head in two, falling from the wavering frame of one of those new skyscrapers in the Loop. Poor Uncle Lars. He didn't know anything about construction. He was just desperate for a job since his printing company folded. At the funeral, Rob didn't cry. He shook with rage because even in the casket you could see the raw blisters left on Uncle Lars's hands from hard labor, and the permanent stains on his fingertips from printer's ink. "All that work. What good was it?" Rob asked. He really wanted me to tell him, but I couldn't think of what to say. *He kept his family afloat.* I could have said that, and it would have been true, but it wouldn't have lessened the loss. I hear traces of that loss in Rob's voice now. Rob is grieved that the night has to end. His every grief taps into that big one.

In less than four hours, I'll be up with Sophy and it will be Saturday as usual. I should be worried about being able to do the work I'll have to do, the work I was born to do (forget what Rob says). But right now, I'm only concerned for my cousin.

I put my hands to Rob's full cheeks and plant a kiss on his forehead. I'd kiss all our sadness away if I could. Instead, I say what Rob wants to hear.

"Thank you for tonight."

As we leave Calliope's, I don't let myself look back at the man playing the piano, the man I'd recognize anywhere, the man I'll never see again.

THREE

So this is what they mean by the morning after.

Not that I drank more than an accidental gulp of that gimlet. But I can barely keep my head up, for the weight of it. I didn't get a few hours of sleep. I got none. By the time I'd shed my magical dress in the backseat of Rob's car, and changed back into my everyday wear (leaving the dress, purse, and makeup in Rob's safekeeping), snuck through the alley and up the fire escape, climbed through the bedroom window, and settled down by my sleeping sister, I was wide awake. I couldn't even keep my eyes closed. Now it's seven in the morning, and I'm so weary my bones ache.

"Tuesday," Rob said as I got out of his car. "You'll audition, and then we'll stay and hear the Chess Men play. You just have to sneak out. I'll be waiting right here to take you."

"No," I said.

But I want yes. Not yes to any old audition. (Never mind the money I could earn. Never mind it.) Just the ability to listen to the Chess Men's music again. I want yes to that.

Instead, I've got this. The morning after and Sophy in the bath, the water already cold, and me sitting beside the tub, bathing my sister, keeping her safe like I should.

Sophy sighs, happy to be here, happy to be with me, happy to *be*, and my heart aches, remembering who she is, who I am, who we are together. I take a deep breath, my inhalation mirroring her inhalation, as if we're one being, as sometimes I believe we are. I force a smile, because a smile makes everything feel better, I've been told. Never mind music or what I want. I'm holding Sophy the way I do, the way I have to. I'm keeping her safe like I should, like I should have last night, when I was nowhere near.

"Sing."

Sophy's voice startles me, which startles her. She twists in my arms. I hold her tight to help her settle down. Mostly this works. It works now. She settles down. The water ripples around her. If I weren't tired to the bone, this moment might be peaceful.

"Sing," she says again, not quite clearly, never quite clearly, but I understand her. I understand my sister better than I understand anyone, better than I understand myself. Better, yes. Sophy often seems like the better part of me.

"*Sing.*"

Sometimes she seems like the better part of me, the girl I should aspire to be—like someone in a Bible story, a child whom Jesus didn't choose to heal, for there must have been those children in the crowds, reaching for the hem of His garment, never quite touching. Mustn't there? *Why Sophy?* I want to ask, and sometimes I do. *Why not me?* The better to teach us on this earth. (That's how Mother sees it; Dad has no answers.) The better to show us the way. Which Sophy does most of the time. Mostly she's that kind of girl.

"Rose! Sing!"

But sometimes, like right now, Sophy is just a typical kid, wanting her way.

"Patience," I mutter to her, to myself.

Impatient, Sophy chops the water with her hands until her breasts bob on the scummy surface. At fourteen, she has bigger breasts than me at twenty-one. She could be mistaken for a calendar girl (God forgive me). If her shoulders didn't curve in so. If her spine didn't twist. If she didn't have cerebral palsy. If she wasn't an invalid from birth.

God forgive me.

"Sing!"

Once in a blue moon, Sophy's able to say more than one word at a time; once in the bluest moon of all, she stutters out a sentence. But usually not when she's whining.

Blue moon
   You saw me standing . . .

The man who knows my name. Last night he saw me just like that.

"We're not going anywhere," I say to my sister. "We've got plenty of time for a song."

Sophy jerks her narrow, lathered head, insisting. "Now!"

"I'll sing, for the love of heaven. Just give me a minute, before soap gets in your eyes."

"Sin!" Sophy catches her breath and tries again. "Rose! Sing!"

Sophy thrashes. She could drown herself, she's that strong,

flinging herself about, all because she said the wrong word—the very wrong one. *Sin*. And because in this moment, as in nearly every moment of her life, her desires are frustrated, her wishes out of her reach.

"It's all right." I blink water from my eyes, hold my sister tighter yet. I'm drenched. I might as well have gotten into the tub with her. *Not her fault, not her fault.* "It'll be all right, sweetheart."

But Sophy jabs her elbow into my jaw. She scratches my arms (time to trim her nails), and it's not all right—not at all. And it could get worse. Now that's she's been roused there's risk of a full-blown seizure.

I lock hold around her chest and she howls.

"Hurts, Rose!"

She goes quiet then; the fit passed as quickly as it came. We're breathing hard, in perfect time. The water is even murkier than before.

"Ouch," Sophy whimpers.

"You're fine." I sound snappish. I'm not, though. I'm not angry. I'm just anxious, fearful for her health, her survival.

But her breathing is slowing to normal. That's a good sign.

I study her skin. I'm always checking, afraid of hurting her, trying to help. But I'm the one who's scratched and bruised now, not her. All that's different now about Sophy is that she's tired, exhausted. And her middle looks puffier than usual. Usually her belly dips down, a shallow bowl between her sharp hipbones. She must have taken food when Mother fed her breakfast.

"You're fine, Sophy. See? I told you it'd be all right."

Just look at the water slicking the floor, the small white tiles fairly gleaming in the sunlight. I can't let go of her to wipe it up. One of us will probably fall, struggling out of the tub.

"Sing."

I have to laugh. She never gives up, this one. Laughing, I grope for the empty jelly jar on the floor, dip the jar into the bathwater, tip back Sophy's head, and begin to rinse her hair.

I sing:

Shall we gather at the river,
  Where bright angels' feet have trod?

When I'm singing, and Sophy is calm, I can rinse her hair with my eyes closed—the task is that familiar. So I rest my tired eyes.

Shall we gather at the river,
  That flows by the throne of God?

I was eight and Sophy was barely one the first time I bathed her. We were still living in northern Wisconsin then, outside the little town of Luck. This was on Aunt Astrid's farm, before our move to the fancy suburb bordering Chicago, and our house there, with its indoor plumbing, electricity, stained-glass windows, heavy oak trim, butler's pantry, two staircases, and five bedrooms, so that everyone, even Mother and Dad, could sleep alone. This was before the Crash and the hanging-on, until the hanging-on left us hung out to dry.

This was before, in the quiet heart of the country.

Mother boiled water on Aunt Astrid's monstrous stove, then poured the water into a dented tin washtub. I don't remember testing the temperature, or wet heat on my skin. I only remember skinny little Sophy descending through the steam, and me steadying her as she entered the water. And Dad hollering, in the mix of Danish and English he spoke at that time, and still sometimes does, when he's in a rage: "Tekla! Have you lost your mind?"

Mother took a long look at me. Her eyes were weary, her arms hung limply at her sides. She looked at me, for the first time, as if I were more comrade than daughter.

"Quiet yourself, Jacob," she said. "Rose is able. She's her sister's keeper."

Mother smiled at me in that special way she used to smile all the time before Sophy was born. Maybe being able would earn me more smiles, I thought, as Mother left the room. "Back soon," she assured me at the door, nearly giddy, this little breather like a holiday. I held on to Sophy. Held on and on. Able felt scary, alone with my sister.

Then one-year-old Sophy tried to tilt her face toward me. She tried to smile. I tried to smile back, and in spite of my fear, in spite of the past and my terrible mistake, in spite of myself, I began to sing. I sang "Row, Row, Row Your Boat," "My Bonnie Lies over the Ocean," and "Shall We Gather at the River." I made my baby sister laugh, rocking her in time in my arms. Singing, I made her happy.

I open my eyes. She's happy now.

"All done." I squeeze water from the ends of her hair. Her beautiful hair, white as cotton, glossy and fine as milkweed when dry, goes silvery, wet. She rests her head against my arm. Her eyelashes spread like fans over the dark circles under her eyes. She must have had another restless night, haunted by dreams and a bed sore we can't seem to heal. Maybe she was haunted by my absence, too. I pray—oh, I pray—that my night out had nothing to do with her disrupted sleep. I stroke her narrow head, wipe away the drops of water that trickle down her face, her delicate features. Yes, she is an invalid, palsied. But right now, and at other moments like this, when she's not grimacing or having a fit, she's also the most beautiful person I know.

A gift from God. A gift better by far than music. Better by far than the notes that cascaded from the piano keys last night. Better, far, far better, than his touch.

Sophy laughs like she can read my foolish thoughts. Sophy sounds like a bird when she laughs. She should have wings to fly away, I think, and then I think, *far, far away, away from me*, and I feel so bad.

"Girls?"

Mother peers around the bathroom door. Mother hasn't had a bath herself for several days. She hasn't taken the time. And she's been saving the little warm water there is for us. Her bobbed hair hangs lankly against her strong jaw. Her hair is usually the same brilliant white-blond as Sophy's, but you wouldn't know it today; it's that dark with grease and sweat. Sweat stains the neck of her blue dress, too, which droops on her frame. She's been scrubbing the kitchen, ceiling to floor, cleaning as she's done practically every day since we moved into this place. It's as if she's exorcising demons of misfortune or the downtrodden spirits of previous residents. And when she's not working here, and I'm at home with Sophy, she's working elsewhere for the Nygaards. Just look at her poor raw hands.

She comes into the bathroom. There's so little room between the tub and the door, she has to ease herself in sideways. She looks down at Sophy and me. Then her eyes—a stormier blue than Sophy's—widen. Mother screams. The sound ricochets off tile and porcelain and bounces around the bath.

I cry out, too, for now I see what Mother sees. Blood, twisting like a red silk cord in the gray water.

Sophy is bleeding from some hidden place.

My sister whimpers. She sounds like a small animal caught in a trap, wounded and afraid. Mother and I go quiet at her bleating, remembering ourselves—who we are, and who we care for, and how we care. I tighten my hold on Sophy. She's trembling. I'm not able to stop it.

"What's all the noise?" Dad stands just outside the bathroom door. "Five minutes and I'm off to work. Can't I have my coffee in peace?"

"Jacob." Mother hurriedly drapes a towel over Sophy; the towel, instantly sodden, melds to her body. "Wait."

"I'll be late, Tekla." Dad starts to retreat, but Mother grabs his arm and yanks him to a stop. Dad nearly slips—the water spread that far—but then he catches his balance. Dad always catches his balance. He's a small man; the top of his balding head barely grazes Mother's chin. He can move with the grace and agility of a cat when he wants to, which is most of the time, even when he's carrying buckets of paint and plaster, or ladders and scaffolding, or Sophy.

Mother leans over and murmurs something in Dad's ear.

"Bleeding?" Dad barely whispers the word, but I hear the horror in his voice. There's panic in his eyes, which turns to blame when his gaze lands on me. I shrink down as if I can grow smaller, so small I disappear. Dad can sit Sophy on the toilet; he can wipe her bottom when she's done. He'll accept

Sophy under any condition—naked, dressed, fitful, messed. As for me . . . I'm not someone fragile that Dad cherishes. I'm just someone who takes up the little spare time and energy he has left.

"Hurts." Sophy jams her fists into the towel across her belly. I catch her wrists to keep her from hurting herself more. Her breasts may be a woman's, but her wrists are a little child's. Whimpering, she pushes down against my hold, but I don't let go, even as I understand. It's like a message in the water.

Sophy's time has come.

As never before, she's going to need me.

"She's too young," Dad says.

He paces the drafty living room, stirring the air. Still chilled from bathing Sophy, I huddle on the love seat. I tug an afghan over my damp dress, tuck my bare feet beneath the cushions as Dad stalks past. Someone is whooping it up on the street below. Dad strides to the window. Even this upset, he's graceful. He's vain about his grace, Mother says. He's vain about his lean good looks, too, and the wavy chestnut hair he's so angry to lose, and his once carefully purchased, now carefully patched clothes. He looks dapper even in his coveralls, which are blindingly white now, at the start of the day, and will be blindingly white tonight, when he returns after long hours of apartment painting and re-pairs. He is that particular about cleanliness. He snaps the cuffs of his shirt into place and glowers down on whatever is going on outside. This window is his post when he's home. He served as a sentinel in the Great War; now he guards his family. Sucking his teeth in disdain—whoever is below isn't a threat, apparently, just *common*—he draws the heavy velvet curtains closed, shutting out the light and the outside world as best he can.

Mother and Dad took these curtains from our previous house and hung them here, though the curtains are twice as wide and long as these windows. They took the lamps, sconces, chandeliers, rugs, and furniture as well. One by one, we sell or pawn these things when the pantry is bare. As for those things that are left—well, there are still plenty. We're constantly scraping our shins on chairs, impaling ourselves on table corners, or stubbing our toes against unpacked boxes. There is no room to push Sophy's adult-sized wheelchair around the apartment, so we leave it in the foyer and carry her, or ease her into her now-cramped child-sized chair if we're feeling too tired. There is no formal dining room, so the largest chandelier hangs above Mother and Dad's bed, and there is no entryway, either—just a door that opens onto a corridor—so the smaller chandelier graces the alcove in the kitchen. It's apartment living, train car style, with the few rooms strung one after another down the hallway.

In one of these—the bedroom Sophy and I share—Sophy lies sleeping now. There's a hot-water bottle nestled between her hips, and, beneath her lingering bedsore, a sheepskin pad. My mother and I wrapped old towels around her to staunch her flow.

"Sophy's fourteen, Jacob." Mother lowers herself onto an ottoman.

Dad flings himself into the chair behind Mother, jostling the needlepoint pillow there. He grabs the pillow and balls up his fist. But instead of hitting the thing, he hugs it tight.

"My little girl." His voice goes wistful, the kind of voice he'd call weak in a man.

"Who will grow bigger still," Mother says.

Dad glares. "What are you getting at?"

Mother doesn't answer.

"Sophy belongs with us!" Dad flings the pillow aside. "You saw Donald. Where they put him."

Mother saw, and Dad saw, and I saw, too. This past fall, the three of us visited the place where the Larsens put their son—their Donald, who is only a little older than Sophy and similarly impaired, and who lives now in a redbrick building that rises out of nowhere smack-dab in the middle of cornfields. "Sophy could live there, too," Mrs. Larsen had said enthusiastically to Mother after church one day. "She and Donald could keep each other company." It was a two-hour ride to the institution, the last hour down dirt roads. Bare cornstalks rattled all around us in the wind. The place looked as pretty as a castle until we went inside. After our visit, it was hard to know what to say to the Larsens. How could we reveal what we really thought about the patients lining the halls, propped in wheelchairs or lying on dollies? The smell? Dad still refuses to speak to them, though Mother says they're hiding their suffering, the pain they feel about Donald's absence from their home. We must show the Larsens compassion, Mother says. So she and I do our best to do just that—though Sophy will never be Donald's companion in that place. Not if we can help it.

"My back hurts, that's all, Jacob," Mother says now. "These stairs—I'm not sure how much longer I can carry her up them."

Dad glares at me as if I'm at fault for this.

"Rose helps all she can." Mother's voice is soft but firm. "You know, Jacob, how much she cares for Sophy, on top of all her other work. Rose works as hard as we do."

I could sing. I could make money doing that. This flashes through my mind unbidden.

Mother takes a deep breath, emboldening herself. "I know you don't like to trouble the Nygaards, Jacob, but perhaps we could ask them to let us move to a ground-floor apartment. It would be such a help."

"Speaking of hard workers, did I mention that I ran into Nils Hoirus on the street yesterday?" Dad is looking at me, pointedly ignoring Mother, making it clear that asking isn't just a bother, it's a humiliation. "Nils is still a clerk at the National Tea, but he said he's in line for the assistant manager position. That fellow has promise, Rose. Works hard, saves his pennies. He said he's going to change his name from Nils to Neil first chance he has. 'I don't want a name that makes people think of nil, of nothing,' he said. 'Not when I'm going to make something of myself!'" Dad claps his hands—a single, sharp crack of approval. "Whatever he calls himself, he'll provide well for his wife, and care for her family, too. He's the best of the old country, right here in the new."

I shift on the love seat, not just cold now but uneasy, too. I've known Nils since we moved to Illinois and started attending the Danish Baptist Church. He's like a brother to me. No, easier than a brother—easier than my brother, at least. When we were kids, Nils and I teased each other mercilessly, made each other laugh, played hard. I still consider Nils one of my oldest friends. But his feelings for me seemed to have changed in the last couple of years. And it's not just me who's noticed. It's Mother and Dad, too.

"Nils is hoping to get together with you, Rose," Dad says. "He spoke of a Saturday night—not tonight, but sometime in the near future. Do you have plans you can think of coming up?"

"No."

"I didn't think so." Dad stands and goes to the bayonet he brought home from the Great War, his cherished souvenir from when he was young and heroic, a trusted soldier. He pulls a handkerchief from his pocket and begins to dust the bayonet, as he often does when he's anxious. And he's often anxious, so he often does. It always seems to reassure him. It seems to reassure him now. "I knew as much. I told Nils so."

In these last months particularly, Nils has started looking at me almost like I'm bedazzling, bright and shining, glorious with possibility. Sometimes I find it flattering. But other times, when I'm feeling contrary, I feel burdened by his new attention. On those days I'd like to shine a little less brightly. My glow, I fear, eclipses the person I really am.

But who am I, really? After last night, I wonder.

"This reminds me, Rose," Mother says with forced cheeriness. "I was hoping you and Sophy would make a trip to the National Tea later today. We need a few things—flour, oatmeal, and the like. I've made a list. The fresh air will do Sophy good, and you know how she likes that store."

Like the rest of us, Sophy doesn't simply *like* the National Tea; she's loyal to it. Sophy, Andreas, and I were raised on tales of the store's founders, the Rasmussen brothers, Danish immigrants who established their business in Chicago at the turn of the century. Within twenty years they were raking in the millions. Even now, with the economy what it is, the National Tea Company is one of the country's largest grocery operations, with stores all over these forty-eight states. Nils is lucky to be a rising star there. And with his Danish heritage, his star will shine all the more brightly.

"If you see Nils, say hello," Dad says.

Nils has a way of slipping me sweets now. On my twenty-first birthday, he gave me six white roses, freshly shipped to the National Tea. Those roses were just about the most beautiful gift I've ever received—and the one and only gift I've received from a man other than a man in my family. Even now, remembering their petals, soft and cool against my cheek, I breathe in deeply. If only the scent lingered on the close air of this room. A man like Nils might very well shower his wife with roses. And the stems of those roses surely would be stripped of thorns.

I promise Dad I'll say hello to Nils. I promise Mom that I'll make sure Sophy has a chance to say hello to him, too. I leave them both as satisfied as they can be now, with the velvet curtains still drawn.

FOUR

Bundled against the bright, cold day, Sophy and I make our way toward the National Tea. It's tricky, pushing Sophy's rickety wheelchair up icy curbs and down them, over frost heaves in the sidewalk, around potholes in the streets. Far trickier than navigating the well-shoveled walkways and plowed roads that framed the blocks around our Oak Park house—though, of course, there were curbs to manage there, and everywhere people stare, or look right through us. Being ogled or being invisible—Sophy and I can never decide which is worse.

She is quiet now as we pass through Garfield Park's wrought-iron gates; so quiet, I wonder if she's nodded off in her warm cocoon of blankets. I've chosen this route because it provides a shortcut to the store. But for Sophy, Garfield Park is more than a shortcut. With its famous botanical conservatory and lagoon, the park is her favorite place in this neighborhood. I'd hate for her to miss a visit.

I glance over her shoulder, checking, but she proves to be

awake and watching. She's thoughtful, that's all. With all that's happened to her today, I can see why.

Perhaps the sights and activity will distract her. Sunlight glints on the curved glass roof of the Conservatory, and even with the steam coating the windows, the shapes and colors of the flowers and tropical plants inside create a kind of kaleidoscope for our eyes. This late in the morning, skaters skim and twirl, their blades making brilliant patterns across the frozen lagoon. Children hurtle on sleds down the little hills all around. If they are too poor to have sleds, which most of them are, they ride battered baking sheets and old tires. Some of the boys wear the fur-lined jackets and leather bomber hats that are so popular. The girls, in their simple wool coats and knit stocking caps, look vulnerable to the cold by comparison. There's a snowball fight on the softball field, and couples stroll, huddled close, around flower beds accented only by rose cones, barren shrubs, and small, strategically placed conifers. From this distance everyone looks like they're exactly where they want to be, coming and going as they please. Everyone looks so happy.

I grit my teeth and push hard against Sophy's chair. It's proving harder to conquer the park's snow- and ice-crusted path than it was the sidewalk and street. The chair jounces and tips this way and that.

Sophy cries out as we pass close to a team of Holsteins at work, pulling a man on a snowplow. The horses are working nearly as hard as I am. I toss my head like I've got a mane to ripple in the wind, stomp my feet like they're hooves, let out a high whinny, and wrest a laugh from Sophy. Then I hear someone calling my name.

"Rose! Wait!"

My cousin Julia and her fiancé, Paul Schmidt, are scrambling on their skates up the side of the lagoon. She calls my name again, and waves. They make a handsome pair, those two, skittering on the jagged toes of their blades toward us. Julia, the youngest of three girls, carries herself with the lively confidence of the favored child—even when she's stumbling and clinging to Paul's arm, as she is now. Her auburn curls tumble from a cap the color of cranberries—a color that brings out the flush in her heart-shaped face. She is joyful. She is with the man she loves, the man she will marry in August on another picture-perfect day, I'm sure. And now: icing on the cake! Here come her favorite cousins!

"I was just thinking about you. I evoked you!" Julia calls.

She only wants to share her joy with us. She only wants us to be joyful, too. That's Julia. Plain and simple, easy-peasy. She met Paul at the Fannie Mae Candy Factory, where they both work. Paul waltzed over to her at the end of her first shift and invited her out to dinner. Nine months later, they were engaged. "You'll meet your match, too," Julia keeps telling me. "You just need to get out more!"

She sounds a lot like Rob, only her idea of getting out is quite different. When Julia gets out she follows all the rules. She'd delighted by the fact that I'm about to see Nils.

They're upon us, Julia dropping down on her knees and catching up Sophy's mittened hands, Paul giving me a brisk, efficient hug, and then the two of them switching places in a clumsy little dance. Julia clings to me, relieved to have support on her skates. Over her shoulder, I watch as Paul tries to shake Sophy's hand and then, confused at how to negotiate Sophy's stiff limbs, steps back. Ankles wobbling, Paul glances longingly over his shoulder at the lagoon while Julia chatters on about the beautiful day, her frozen toes—"Frostbite! I'm sure of it!"—then on and on about their wedding plans.

Finally she runs out of steam. Breathlessly she asks if I'll come shopping with her. "I need help deciding about my dress," she says.

"Sure," I say.

"How about this Thursday, or the next? The stores are open later on Thursday night. Sophy, you could come, too." Julia glances down at Sophy. "Would you like that?" Julia gasps. "Oh, honey! What's wrong?"

I look down to see my sister silently crying. Already her wet cheeks are chafed by the wind.

"We *want* you to come shopping with us, Sophy," Julia says.

Sophy wrenches her head toward me. "Tea?"

The National Tea, she means. With my gloves, I pat her face dry. She needs some privacy in which to compose herself. I turn the wheelchair away from Julia and Paul.

"We're on an errand." I'm as good as Mother at forcing resolute cheerfulness into my voice. "We'd better get going."

Paul takes the hint. He slips Julia's arm through his and starts drawing her back to the lagoon.

"See you soon, then, Rose? You and Sophy, too?" Julia asks, tottering along.

I nod. "We'll be at church tomorrow."

Julia shakes her head. "I'm going with Paul's family. We're taking a drive around his parents' neighborhood afterward. His mother says that the apartments in their part of the city are more affordable than almost anywhere else. And it's a nice, clean neighborhood, too! We're thinking of making our first home there."

"Sounds nice." I can see Julia's future as clearly as I see her moving toward the lagoon with Paul now. Nice and clean. Easy-peasy. That's Julia's future.

"'Til some night soon, then—this Thursday, maybe, or the next definitely," Julia calls. "Parting is such sweet sorrow!" With a wave, she turns away, then quickly back. "Wait! Can't do this Thursday! We're having dinner with some of Paul's friends. So a week from this Thursday, okay?"

I holler okay.

"Promise, Rose?"

I holler my promise, and then, as Julia and Paul glide away on the ice, I bend over Sophy. She's crying even harder.

"Sweetheart! What's the matter?"

Sophy shakes her head.

"Try and tell me. Just try." I pat her cheeks dry again. "Sophy, you're going to be raw with windburn. Please stop!"

She closes her eyes. Tears slide from beneath her lashes.

"Are you hurting?"

She hisses through her teeth, her easiest way to say no.

I have to get her out of the cold. A seizure in the cold would be . . . well, I won't let that happen. I step behind the wheelchair and start pushing. Hard, harder I push. We go fast—nearly too fast on icy patches—toward the park's exit. The sound of traffic rushing by on the boulevard grows louder. We are nearly there when, surely to Sophy's surprise and almost to mine, I turn the wheelchair into the shelter of a gazebo. Brown tendrils of dead ivy twine thickly through the gazebo's latticed walls, sheltering us from the wind. Compared with the wide-open park, this little dank place is toasty.

I crouch at my sister's feet. "Please tell me what's wrong."

"You." She ducks her head, hiding her expression as best she's able. "Tell."

"Tell what?"

For a moment, nothing comes out of Sophy's mouth but the throaty sounds she makes when she's struggling to frame her thoughts with language. She memorizes all the baseball stats each spring with Dad. She can chime in on key words when Andreas reads from the Bible. She remembers whole passages from novels by James Fenimore Cooper and Rudyard Kipling (someone in the family reads to her nearly every night). Her speech just can't keep up with her mind.

Finally she gets control of her tongue and says what she wants to say.

"No husband, children." More sounds, and then, "For me."

I suck in a breath. While Mother and I were settling Sophy down for her nap, swaddling her in old towels, nestling a hot water bottle between her hips, we took turns explaining what was happening to her. We told her about her time. I told Sophy nothing was wrong. This just happens to us girls. Mother took it a little further, mentioning God's words to Eve in Genesis, the harsh consequences of forbidden fruit, plucked and briefly savored. The curse, the pangs of childbirth, far outweighed by the joys of children. When we were finished explaining, Mother and I left Sophy to rest while we went into the front room and talked with Dad. We didn't think to ask if she had any questions.

Wind rattles the vines. Wind seeps between the leaves.

I never imagined this far into Sophy's future. Her womanhood. Her grief.

"I'm sorry," I say.

She nods. Though her expression is still pained, she is

calmer now, quiet and thoughtful again, not crying. We should press on. We should see the kinds of things she likes to see at the National Tea. We should find some distraction.

I grip the wheelchair's handles and push Sophy out of our shelter. Surely the temperature has dropped in these last minutes. The air cuts to my lungs as I huff and puff, steering Sophy in her chair through the park's gate.

There across the street is the National Tea. It will be warm inside. I will find a treat for Sophy, something she loves. She loves tapioca pudding. I will treat her to a little carton of that.

I bend down to tell her this. To reassure her, without explicitly saying so, that there are other joys in life besides songs you can't sing.

Besides husbands and children you can't have, I mean.

I trundle Sophy into the National Tea and park her chair at the front counter. I pull Mother's list—*Just a Few Staples*, Mother has written across the top—and the nub of a pencil from my coat pocket. I add to the list: $^1/_8$ lb of prepared tapioca without raisins. This would barely be a taste of pudding for me; it will be just enough for Sophy.

One of the apron-wearing boys behind the counter takes the list and runs off to collect the items. There are so few things we can afford now, so I know each and every item by heart. Oatmeal, milk, butter (only a little, but we'll make it stretch, though this is *not* the Danish way), eggs, flour, coffee, potatoes, split peas, a ham bone.

"Warming up?" I lean close to my sister. She doesn't smile or kiss the air, but she does seem to be taking careful note of the stocked shelves, the displays of daily specials, the newfangled appliances. *A gas oven! Who ever heard?* We'll talk about things like this when we get home. It will give us something to say.

"Hello, Rose."

I turn to see Nils, smiling shyly down at me. He's dressed like he's already an assistant manager: neatly pressed black pants and green apron, a white shirt, a black bow tie, black suspenders. The only part of him that's out of place is the shock of his honey-colored hair falling boyishly across his blue eyes.

"Hi." This was where we stood when he presented me with the roses. The other employees and the customers applauded us both. I feel nearly as confused now as I did at that moment. Nils does that to me—this change in him that yields this change between us.

"I spotted you from the office." Nils shoves that shock of hair into place and nods toward the back of the store, where a long window spans the top half of the wall. The store manager is at work there, riffling through a sheaf of papers. Nils lifts a hand to him, and the store manager lifts a hand back.

"I'm glad you were able to come out," I say. "It looks busy back there."

Nils nods. "Mr. Block has asked me to help with the book-keeping. I have a head for figures, Mr. Block says. He's the man-ager, you know."

"That's wonderful."

Nils blushes, then ducks down and gives Sophy a gentle pat on the arm. "Hiya, kiddo." By the time Sophy has said her own hiya back, his hair has fallen into his eyes again. Now up he comes, the long, tall length of him, shoving back that shock. When he takes his hand away a sheen of pomade glistens on his palm. Beneath that sheen I glimpse the shadow of newsprint.

Nils fancies himself a future member of a Chamber of Commerce, perhaps even the mayor of a small town out West one day, so he pores over the *Trib* whenever he has a spare moment, studying up on business and politics.

Silence stretches. Nils is looking at me that way again. I might be the sun, moon, and stars combined. A girl could get used to the expression on his face. But now Nils glances at Mr. Block and winces. Mr. Block is eyeing him, tapping the face of his wristwatch.

"Break's over." Nils takes a deep breath. "Listen, Rose, I got a coupon for a two-for-one dinner at Old Prague. I've yet to eat there, but I've heard it's good. They have three meat specials. You can have your choice of pork, duck, beef, chicken, steak, or sausage . . . any three, with side dishes, soup, salad, and dessert. And coffee. I would love to have you as my guest at Old Prague this Saturday. Not *this* Saturday. Not tonight. I have to work late. Next Saturday, I mean." He pauses for a breath. "What do you say, Rose?"

"Why," I say, "thank you. That sounds lovely." And it does.

"We're set, then." Nils holds out his hand with all the professional formality of an assistant-manager-to-be. We shake as if we've just made a deal. Only Nils squeezes my hand so tightly that I can feel the blood pulsing at my fingertips. I can almost feel his pulse, too.

He lets go of my hand and gives Sophy a quick peck on the cheek before he turns away. I watch him walk toward the back of the store and Mr. Block. Loping down the aisle like that, he looks like the high school basketball player he once was. He was the star of the team his senior year. I was proud of him then. I'm proud of him now. Any girl in her right mind would be proud of him.

FIVE

We sit in our usual spot at the back of the Danish Baptist Church. Here, Sophy has room to stretch out, which is necessary, because when she sits in her wheelchair for too long—these services can sometimes be close to three hours—her arms, legs, and back cramp up. If Sophy has a spasm or a seizure, she's less likely to interrupt the worship. Most important, as Sophy sees it, people can visit with us as they enter or exit the sanctuary. People can linger, leaning over the back of the pew. This is the highlight of Sophy's week, and Mother's. And mine.

Forget Tuesday night. Forget Calliope's and the music and the man who knows my name. And this isn't the time to be thinking about Nils, either, though he is just across the sanctuary, glancing my way.

I look down at Sophy. Her head is a warm weight in my lap. She is draped in her white, Sunday-best afghan, crocheted by Mother when Mother could afford to buy silk thread. Poking out of the bottom edge of the afghan are Sophy's feet, which rest comfortably in Andreas's lap. At six feet six inches, Andreas

looks quite the giant looming beside her—a gentle giant cush-
ioning his little sister's feet. A fair giant with a fleshy nose. Last
summer, when Andreas worked on Aunt Astrid's farm, he got so
sunburned that his nose swelled up and turned strawberry red.
It stayed that way. Dad sometimes calls him W. C. Fields, which
drives Andreas crazy, I can tell. (W. C. Fields bills himself as a
drunk, and Andreas would remain a teetotaler under torture.)
But Andreas is too mindful of the Ten Commandments to talk
back to Dad, or even calmly tell Dad how he feels. With his full-
ride scholarship to Moody Bible Institute, Andreas is nothing if
not Commandment-abiding. He is steeped in the Commandments of the Old Testament and the Beatitudes of the New. He
can memorize whole books of the Bible, and he even knows his
favorite passages in Hebrew and Greek. Andreas can recite the
doctrinal stance of any Protestant denomination, and he evange-
lizes with the best of them. In fact, he recruited many of the
newest members of our church. He'll certainly be a wonderful
pastor. He might even be a missionary. Just look at him, taking
notes on Pastor Riis's sermon in the margins of his church bulletin. It's hard to see where the bulletin's type ends and Andreas's
careful writing begins.

I glance down at my own bulletin, which rests open on Sophy's middle. Shows how closely I've been listening—I have to
read the sermon's title to remember Pastor's topic for today: *The
Call to Service.*

"'As they ministered to the Lord, and fasted, the Holy Ghost
said . . . '" Pastor Riis pauses for emphasis. He plants his hands
on either side of the pulpit and bows his head. Pastor is nearly
eighty. His wide, deeply lined face is covered with liver spots.
His voice, however, has the strength of a robust man in the

prime of his life. "'Separate me, Barnabas, and Saul for the work whereunto I have called them.'"

To my right, Mother stretches her legs into the aisle. Balancing her Bible on her lap, she underlines the passage Pastor just read. She is wearing fur-lined winter boots. The seams are splitting at the toes. We could never afford to replace those boots now. Or the fur coat, draped so elegantly over her shoulders. She makes a little note in Danish in the margin beside Acts, chapter thirteen. I can't read what she's written; her script is too small, and it's gotten horribly messy, what with the arthritis affecting her hands. As for the verse in Acts, I recognize none of the Danish words.

If I took that singing job, would I be able to buy new boots for Mother? Maybe not fur-lined ones, but sturdy, with treads to keep her steady on the ice? Say I was able to squirrel away a dollar a week. (Cleaning, I'm lucky if I can pocket anything.) How many weeks would I have to sing before Mother could have warm, dry feet again? How many weeks would I *get* to sing?

I press my lips together tightly, lest the wrong kind of singing slip out. It's one thing to dream of singing for provision. It's another thing altogether to dream of singing for pleasure. Besides, sometimes I am able to sing for pleasure. For God's pleasure, and for the pleasure of this congregation, and for my pleasure, too. I'll be singing the offertory next week, for instance. I'm on the schedule. They're counting on me. I must choose a hymn.

Pastor Riis is elaborating more fully on the Scripture passage now. The Holy Spirit is the Great Executive of the Church, Pastor explains, laying plans and taking measures to carry them out. To do so, the Holy Spirit must select men, set them apart, and send them forth.

And women, too, I suppose.

"It is of the utmost importance that we have a call," Pastor Riis says. "We were born to serve God in a way that He has ordained for us."

I've accepted my calling: my sister. As for my singing . . . I wasn't born for it, and Sophy almost died because of it.

My singing almost killed her.

I try not to think about that winter night in Luck, Wisconsin— fourteen years ago just like yesterday—but I can't stop myself. I never can.

Rob was there that night, too, and Mother and Dad, and, of course, Sophy. But Rob is the only one among us who directly refers to the event.

You know, if you'd just let 'er rip, your voice could very well bring people to their knees. You've just got to believe, Laerke. You've just got to get past the past.

I was seven years old that winter night. But I remember every breath, taken and not taken. Every moment. I could tally them all. I could arrange rooms in my mind to exactly mirror the layout of Aunt Astrid's weathered farmhouse. I could traverse them mentally, taking in the place. But I don't. I go straight to my mistake, and the room that contained it. I go to the drafty upstairs bedroom where Sophy, newly born, lay in a cradle and under diminutive flannel blankets that until a few moments prior had belonged to my doll.

My doll lay on the floor, her yarn hair caught beneath Dad's boot.

It had been a long, cold night at the end of a long, cold day at the end of the series of long, cold days that contained Mother's labor. After delivering Sophy six weeks early, Aunt Astrid and the doctor were suddenly somewhere else. Rob was staying out of the way, watching from a shadowy corner. Mother lay in the bed, frighteningly silent and still. Dad kneeled over my doll's cradle. He touched the deep indentations in Sophy's skull, where the doctor's forceps had left their mark. "She's breathing now," Dad was saying, and in the next moment, "Oh, no. Oh, daughter, breathe. Oh, apple of my eye, light of my life, *live*."

Up until that night, I had been the apple of Dad's eye. Now this blue-tinged baby had taken possession not only of that distinction but also of my doll's cradle.

"Help her," Dad cried, even as, with his finger and his thumb, he pried open Sophy's fingernail-thin lips. He bowed low and covered her tiny mouth with his own. He blew air down her throat, into her lungs. Moments, breaths, passed. Then Dad sat back on the heels of his boots, ripping strands of hair from my doll's head.

"She's all right," he said, gasping. "She's all right now, Tekla. She's breathing again."

Mother didn't respond.

I wanted someone's attention, preferably Dad's, with Mother the way she was and Rob a shadow in the corner. So I knelt beside the cradle. I leaned over my newborn sister. I began to sing. I sang *la, la, la*, and *lu, lu, lay*. I sang pretty nonsense. I tried to be the apple of Dad's eye, the light of his life.

Instead, I woke the baby. Sophy, scarcely bigger than Dad's hand, arched her back, rocking my doll's cradle. She writhed, twisting the little blankets that Mother had stitched from Dad's old handkerchiefs, which had been stitched from his even older shirts.

"Stop it, Rose! Don't you see what you're doing? Stop sing-ing! Be quiet!"

Dad blamed me for Sophy's first fit.

Months later, and repeatedly throughout the years since, Mother, in her own way, blamed me, too. "Who knows what caused Sophy's trauma? The forceps, maybe. Or maybe it was that episode she had just after her birth. If she'd just stayed sleeping, she might have gathered the strength she so badly needed to restore her health. But once that episode started, there was no turning back."

Stop it, Rose! Don't you see what you're doing? Stop singing! Be quiet!

There was no turning back.

Somehow over the years I remembered my voice, approach-ing song as one might approach a wild animal. Sophy, during her baths, was the first person to hear me softly sing. Later, Rob. Then Mother heard me, and she told Pastor Riis, who asked to hear me, too, and when he did, he called the choir director, Mr. Helt, long dead now, who gave me a hymnal and asked me to sing "Away in a Manger," and then proceeded to give me free lessons, twice a week, for several years. Mr. Helt was a kind old man with crooked, broken teeth who was prone to cry when a song touched his heart. I learned to ignore his weeping; I simply did what he told me to do and kept singing, even as the tears rolled down his fleshy cheeks. I learned to drop my jaw, control my breathing, extend my range, transpose a song. Under Mr. Helt's tutelage I learned my deep love for songs written in a minor key.

It was Christmas Eve when I sang my first solo in church. I was nine years old, still getting used to Oak Park, still missing Aunt Astrid's farm, and the praise I received afterward made me feel finally at home. By the time Mr. Helt died, I couldn't imagine living anywhere else, singing anything other than hymns and sacred songs. I was fourteen. I was sure of the way the world worked, and of myself in it. And then one day only a few years later, I heard as if for the first time the music in alleys, on streets, from open windows, in shops. I couldn't get these new songs, these worldly songs, out of my head; they held me in their sway. I started singing them when I thought no one else was around, only to look up and see Rob and, sometimes, Sophy, watching me wide-eyed, open-mouthed, delighted and amazed.

Only Rob and Sophy have known about the wild animal, the late-blooming love that lurks inside me, deep beneath the surface of my every night and day. As of Friday night, Zane has a hint, too. But I think of all the people I know, only the man at Calliope's, the man who knows my name, might truly understand what this love means to me and why, try as I might, I just can't turn away from it. I just can't let it go.

I have taken hold of a lock of Sophy's hair. She winces; as my thoughts got the better of me, I twisted her hair too tightly around my finger. Quickly, I let the little lock fall free. Quickly, quickly, I stroke her hair just the way she likes it. We're moving into the altar call now. As the organist softly plays "Just as I Am," Pastor Riis describes our human condition.

"Come, all who are heavy laden. There's no better time to give your life to Jesus. Accept His life-giving salvation and be received in baptism."

"Bap—" Sophy clears phlegm from her throat. I hold out a handkerchief and she spits into it, then hoarsely whispers, "tism."

There's urgency in her voice. I smooth her hair, trying to calm her, but she bats my hand away.

"Easter!"

"Yes, you'll be baptized this Easter, Sophy," I whisper. "Hush, now."

Sophy's expression relaxes. A man I've never seen before stirs in the pew across the way. Now he stumbles up the aisle toward Pastor.

"He looks like he's just off the bread lines," Mother murmurs. "At least he'll receive spiritual food today."

"Coffee," Sophy says meaningfully.

There's always food at coffee hour. She wants to make sure he receives some of that, too.

Mother nods and smiles. "I'll invite him downstairs."

I open the hymnal to number 348, "Just as I Am." I'm adjusting the hymnal so Sophy can see the words when Mother nudges me. I look up to see mustachioed Mr. Lund, who's an usher today, beckoning to me from the end of the pew. "Go," Mother says, so I ease myself from beneath Sophy. Mother slips into my place as I step into the aisle, still holding the hymnal.

"Pastor asked that you lead the congregation in song, singing every other verse of the hymn as a solo," Mr. Lund whispers through the long white strands of his mustache.

Mother nods at me. She likes it when I sing in church. I like it, too, when I've had a little time to prepare. Good thing I know "Just as I Am" as well as I know the alphabet. I wouldn't have opened the hymnal if it hadn't been for Sophy.

Mr. Lund steps aside, and I walk down the aisle and up to the podium. I raise my hands to lead the congregation in the first verse of "Just as I Am" and then see Rob sitting in the second row.

"Tuesday night," he mouths. "Calliope's."

Worldly songs. Those are the only songs I'm thinking of now.

I bring my hands down and, God bless the congregation, they sing the right words:

Just as I am, without one plea,
But that Thy blood was shed for me,
And that Thou bidst me come to Thee,
O Lamb of God, I come, I come.

A hymnal is open on the podium. With the words in front of me like this, I can sing the second verse alone, as Pastor Riis requested:

Just as I am, and waiting not
To rid my soul of one dark blot,
To Thee whose blood can cleanse each spot.
O Lamb of God, I come, I come.

I've nearly pushed the other songs out of my mind. It's my soul that's aching for that music, my soul that I have to cleanse.

Though Pastor and the man are still praying, the hymn is done, so the service is as well. Mother beams at me. Nils, too. I manage not to look at Rob, who will only remind me of my blotted soul. I walk right past him down the aisle toward Mother and Andreas, who holds Sophy in his arms. Perhaps Nils will follow us down to the basement, and he'll look at me like I'm all bright, celestial elements combined. Perhaps when that shock of hair falls in his eyes, I'll be the one who reaches up and pushes it back into place.

"Rose Sorensen!"

I stop in my tracks at the sound of Dr. Nygaard's voice.

"Come here, please."

I turn back to the front of the sanctuary, where the Nygaards await me. Dr. Nygaard, a swarthy, bearish man, is tapping the head of his cane against the palm of his thick hand. The tapping beats out a warning: *Do as I say or else you may not have a roof over your head.* Mrs. Nygaard, a willowy woman, preserves her energy by leaning languidly into her husband. Her buffed nails flash as she drums her fingers against his arm.

"Alas," Dr. Nygaard says when I stand before them. "We've learned that the man in 2B, 546 Marquette left his apartment in a state of filth." With the handle of his cane, Dr. Nygaard scratches meditatively at his chin. "We have a new family moving into 2B first thing tomorrow morning. I'm loath to ask you to do this on a Sunday, Rose, but we must have the place cleaned today."

"This family would be living on the streets if we hadn't provided a place for them," Mrs. Nygaard says coolly. "So we might consider it an act of service. You've been to our Marquette building before, haven't you, dear?"

I nod. Their Marquette building is just off Maxwell Street, near Jane Addams's Hull House. It's not the safest neighborhood by day. After the sun goes down, I don't want to be there alone.

"Here are the keys." Dr. Nygaard holds out a set. "You'll find cleaning supplies in the janitor's closet. There is no electrical hookup yet, so you'll need to hurry in order to do what needs to be done while it's still light out. I'm afraid you may not even have time to put on your work clothes."

I smooth my last best skirt.

"We could drop you off on our way home, I suppose . . ." Mrs. Nygaard's voice fades unenthusiastically away.

"I'll take the El," I say.

SIX

There's a crowd outside Hull House—families lined up for medical attention, food, and heaven knows what else. Could be us someday if things keep going as they are, Dad once hinted, grimly polishing his bayonet. People are speaking Italian, Russian, Yiddish, and others have accents that I recognize as Irish. There are black people waiting outside Hull House, too, and people speaking quietly in Spanish, newly arrived from Mexico, I'm guessing.

I wend my way through the crowd and down peddler-packed Maxwell Street to Marquette. There's number 546. The bottom floor is a butcher shop, the front window of which is filled with plucked chickens and a single, spectacularly large goose. (What Mother once upon a Christmas could do with a goose!) Beside the window is the narrow, locked door that opens to the steep stairs that lead to the apartments jammed into the building's second story. I fumble with the keys, fit the right key into the lock. The foyer is barely big enough to turn around in. There is the door to the janitor's closet. I open it.

Cockroaches scatter beneath my feet.

In three trips I carry up: two buckets, one filled with clean water, the other with water and vinegar. The jug of vinegar, in case some mess demands undiluted application. A basket of rags, several of which I recognize as scraps of the rose-patterned bed-sheets from my childhood. (Back then everything of mine seemed covered with roses.) A broom, dustpan, and mop. A bin for trash. Three scrub brushes with the metal bristles all but worn away. A wooden stepladder.

When these things are clustered on the floor outside apartment 2B, which is at the shadowy far end of the hallway, I muster my courage and unlock the door.

It's a studio apartment. One room. At least there's that. I won't think about the fact that a family will be living here when there's barely enough space for a single person.

As Dr. Nygaard warned, there's also no electricity. The shades are drawn over the main room's two windows. The light is amber-colored at best. Sepia-toned to muddy brown in corners. I hear the sound of many little, brittle feet, skittering away into hidden parts of this small place. I have had dreams like this after a day of cleaning. Dreams of such light and such skittering. Tonight I most likely will have these dreams again.

The place smells of something rotten. Something dead.

I swallow hard, pray harder. I pray about calling and service. I pray about my life, Sophy's life, Mother's, Dad's, and Andreas's, too—all of our lives held in precarious balance. I pray that God weaves a net beneath us all. Then I choose my best weapons against the unknown—the mop and the broom—and step into the apartment.

The little brittle-footed creatures have gone into hiding, so that's a mercy. But the smell. The smell is out and about, taking full possession of the place. As does the garbage on the floor—newspaper, wax paper, unidentifiable bits and smears of dried food, open tin cans, and what looks to be the leavings of an animal.

Gagging, I stumble back into the hallway, where the close air is at least not putrid. Before I bring in the rest of the cleaning supplies, I tie a scrap of old, rosy bedsheet around my mouth and nose. I must look like one of those people suffering through the Dust Bowl storms. If they can endure, so can I.

Back to work.

First thing I do is open the windows as far as they will go. They've been painted sloppily shut—Dad would never have done this; it must have been the work of the Nygaards' previous su-perintendent—so I have to bang on them. Finally they give and lift. The cold air outside smells of the garbage cans lined up in the alley just below. Which is to say, in comparison to what I smell inside, the air smells fresh and fine.

With the broom and the mop held aloft as a defense against rats or mice, I begin searching out the stinking thing. I think (though I can't be sure, because the smell pervades the room) that the stench is caused by the rotting fish lying on a shelf in the warm refrigerator. From the long whiskers and sharp teeth, it appears to be a catfish, perhaps pulled from the filthy Chicago River. Its empty eyes stare balefully at me as, using the broom handle, I nudge the carcass onto a piece of newspaper that the tenant so thoughtfully left behind. I toss aside the broom. Hold-ing my breath and the catfish, I run to an open window and drop the catfish into an open garbage can below. Then I plunge my hands into the bucket of water and vinegar and, to the best of my ability, wash them clean of *eau de rot*.

Now I can really start cleaning, working from top to bottom as Mother taught me. Using the stepladder, I wash the ceiling first. Then the walls. Then the windows, which means having to close them. Closing them forces me to open the door to the hallway. Never mind who sees me cleaning. I need to breathe. Once I've opened the windows again, I decide to leave the door open, too. It helps with circulation. It's cold in here now because of the draft, but the fresh air is life-giving. I clean the small kitchen and the smaller bathroom. Time is flying, and I'm not nearly finished. Never mind that I'm tired, I must work fast, faster.

I try to pretend I am a machine. I try not to think or feel.

This doesn't help.

I start to sing.

This helps.

Singing "Bringing in the Sheaves," I pick up the litter from the floor. It takes a good while, especially since I have to keep emptying the trash bin into the garbage cans in the alley. *We shall come rejoicing, bringing in the sheaves.* I don't toss the litter out the window, because the wind tunneling through the alley would blow it hither and yon. I walk the bin down the stairs, empty it carefully, return for more. Seven times I do this before the floor is finally free of litter. Now, to sweep. Sweeping, singing, I think of Mahalia Jackson. Hers is a voice that holds hundreds of years of hard history, trials and labors beyond any I can imagine, any I'll ever know. I'll never sing like Mahalia Jackson, but I can sing inspired by her.

I clear my throat and test out my best, lowest register. My voice isn't nearly as low as Miss Jackson's, or nearly as rich and lush. But warmed up like this, I'm surprised by the notes I'm able to reach. Mr. Helt would be proud. My voice doesn't falter or break. I can sustain the song:

> *Amazing Grace,*
> > *How sweet the sound . . .*

I sweep back and forth, back and forth, the broom's straw bristles against the stained-wood floor my steady accompaniment:

> *I once was lost*
> > *But now am found . . .*

There's no blot on this music. It's spotless, as is my soul when I sing it. And if I keep up the effort, soon this place will be spotless, too.

I make bold and ask God to bless Miss Jackson, wherever she is, however she is, whatever she is doing on this day. Then I tuck the hem of my last best skirt up into my waistband. I pull off my shoes and stockings, get down on my knees, plunge a rag into the bucket of vinegar and water, and start to scrub the floor.

Before Dad came to America, he was a cabin boy on a Danish ship, and then a sailor. Though Mother winced, he's told us stories of swabbing the ship's deck, the raucous songs they used to sing. The only sea chantey I know is "Blow the Man Down." Swabbing, I sing that:

> *Yo ho, blow the man down . . .*

Because I am alone, and because this is the most fun I've had all day, I pull out all the stops. Forgive me, God (and, by extension, Mother), but I really let 'er rip:

> *Give me some time*
> > *To blow the man down . . .*

"Miss Sorensen."

As clear as a ship's bell, my name sounds in my ears. I look up, frightened. Too late, I remember to yank down my skirt's hem.

He's standing in the open doorway. I'd recognize him anywhere.

"How on earth?" I hear myself say.

"My question exactly," he says.

He's not wearing the dashing tuxedo of Friday night. He's wearing a simple brown suit, a white shirt, a brown tie with thin gold stripes. The suit's cut is a few years out of date, and there's a sheen to the fabric that shows the wear that comes when cloth is at the cheaper end of the spectrum. But he's neatly put together. There's not a wrinkle from collar to cuff. That's true of his white shirt and his striped tie, too.

He either takes very good care of himself or there's someone in his life that does.

"Your voice." He starts to say something else, but then he simply smiles. It's like a light has been turned on inside him, and that light fills up the room.

I can feel his warmth again, though he is standing some feet away. I can feel his warmth, and now I am warm, too, in spite of the draft from the window that stirs my hair.

Am I looking at this man in exactly the same way that Nils looks at me? I look quickly down into the bucket of dirty water. "I didn't realize anyone was listening or I would have kept my singing to myself." I can't see my reflection for the water's cloudy surface.

"Keep your singing to yourself and you'll deny the rest of the world a lot of happiness."

I look up and his smile fades at my expression.

"I don't sing for the world. I sing for God." My hands are tight fists. "I sing at church."

"God is bigger than church, don't you think?"

I feel a sudden, sharp need to stand up and defend myself. But my bare legs are soaked, my skirt the worse for wear, and I have no desire to look foolish. So I stay where I am and hold my head high.

"Why are you here?"

He takes a step back. I suppose he doesn't want me to feel threatened. No wonder. Just last week I read a story in the *Trib* about a lynching. Something about a black man daring to consort with a white woman, and the consequences of that. If this news story is crossing my mind, I'd venture there are many more crossing his.

But he doesn't shrink into himself, as some men might. He stands at his full height. His gaze remains steady, though it's cooled, regarding me, like I'm not who he thought I was, or I'm someone else, someone all too familiar. I drop the rag into the bucket and wrap my arms around myself to keep from shivering.

"I haven't been following you, Miss Sorensen, if that's your concern," he says quietly. "Sunday afternoons I help out the folks over at Hull House. They have a music program for the kids there. I teach piano lessons. Sometimes I lead their children's chorus. One of the boys I teach lives just down the hall. He's been getting into trouble lately, falling off the straight and narrow. His mother asked that I walk him home after practice. So I did. And I heard you singing. Now here we are."

We look at each other. Here we are.

My face is burning hot. But he's blushing, too. A color deep as ripe cherries rises beneath his dark skin.

How can a man this familiar make my thoughts, not to mention ordinary conversation, so unfamiliar? More to the point, how can this man be so familiar?

The radiator clangs, interrupting the growing quiet. I need to say something.

"That's kind, what you did. For that child," I say.

The color has crept down his throat; the flush accentuates the neat knot of his tie. He presses the back of his hand to his cheek as if testing for fever, then manages a shrug. "I wish someone had done the same for me. I might have been a different boy. As it is, I'm glad to be alive and able to help."

Again, the quiet. Again, the clang.

"If you don't mind me asking, Miss Sorensen, what brings *you* to this part of town?"

I owe him an honest answer. I gesture at the bucket of filthy water, the rags on the floor, the state of things. "This is my job. I clean up other people's places. I didn't always, but now I do, and I will for some time to come, I imagine."

His expression softens again. I am as suddenly, inexplicably happy as I was a moment ago defensive.

"With a voice like yours, why are you doing a job like this?" he asks.

I sit back on my heels. "I don't have a choice."

"Miss Sorensen, everyone has a choice."

"I don't."

He takes a deep breath. "All right. I've got to say it." He gets down on his knees, too. I don't know whether he's going to make an appeal or he's trying to see me eye to eye, or both. It doesn't matter. Here he is, right in front of me. He clasps his hand before him as he did when he stood at the microphone on Friday night. Lets out that breath. "The Chess Men need a singer. We need her bad. You'd be perfect."

I hug myself tight, tighter. *Blot. Spot. Soul*, I think. But then, God help me, I think *yes*.

"No," I say. "I can't."

"Why?" He unclasps his hands, and I remember his touch on my wrist.

I say, "I told you why."

He shakes his head as if I did nothing of the sort. "Miss Sorensen, I love church. I love God. But I believe God made me a musician as well as a believer, and I believe God makes as many kinds of musicians as there are songs to sing. There's not sacred music and worldly music. There's *good* music. All good things come from God. That's what I believe."

"You believe a lot of things."

He nods in all seriousness. "I do. For instance, I believe you loved the music on Friday night, worldly or not. I *saw* you, Miss Sorensen."

I don't deny my love. I don't confirm it, either.

"It's *good* music," he says. "And you were born to sing it."

I reach into the bucket, pull out the rag, start swabbing the floor again. "You sound like my cousin Rob, saying crazy things like that."

"It's not crazy. It's good sense. The Chess Men need a singer. You need to sing."

And suddenly he's singing in his low, husky voice:

And if we ever part, then that might break my heart

He laughs then, slapping his leg as if he's just made the perfect argument and he's delighted with it.

"You know that song?" he asks, still laughing.

I nod. I haven't seen the picture in which the song is featured, *Shall We Dance* (the picture just came out, and anyway, I don't go to the pictures), but I know from the radio that Fred Astaire sings it. And, yes, I know the lyrics, too.

"'You say tomato, I say *tomahto*,'" I mutter, swabbing at the floor.

"That's the ticket!" He slaps his leg again. "We may have been making different music lately, but it's all the same good thing. And there's money to be made, Miss Sorensen, if that makes any difference to you. Who knows? You might even make more than you do cleaning. I'd lay odds on you making as much."

I won't look at him. I wring water from the rag, further dampening my already damp skirt. "This is my job."

"This job makes you happy?"

What's happy? I don't say, swabbing the floor.

"Because if it does make you happy, we could work around your schedule," he says.

"Please don't make fun at my expense." I glance over my shoulder at the window. The sun is lowering in the sky. Dusk is descending. The cold wind is rising. I need to finish here.

"I'm not making fun. I'm dead serious."

My eyes are stinging, and it's not from the vinegar. "I'm not that kind of girl."

Suddenly he draws back from me, catching his breath as a thought strikes him. In a quiet, harsh voice he says, "It's because I'm black, isn't it?"

I look up at his tone, stunned. "No!" But partly it is, I realize as tears spill from my eyes.

He's looking at me as if he's never seen a woman cry before. Slowly, tentatively, like I just might bolt and flee, he leans forward, gently presses his fingertips to my cheek, and brushes the tears away.

His touch again. A fire that doesn't hurt, that only lingers, warming me.

"Forgive me, Miss Sorensen," he says. "You've given me no cause to think that, let alone say it."

"Do you know Mahalia Jackson?" I sound like I can't sing a note, the way my voice breaks.

"Not personally. We don't *all* know each other, you know." He gives me a gentle smile to show that he's not being mean. "I know her voice, though."

"I love her voice. I'd give almost anything to sing with her."

"Well, I'd give almost anything to accompany her. So we have that in common."

My tears are still wet on his fingertips. He doesn't seem to want to wipe them dry. He looks down at them, and I wonder, from the puzzled expression on his face, if my tears feel strange against his skin. A white woman's tears.

The radiator clangs, and we both jump. We look at each other, and then in spite of ourselves, because of ourselves, we laugh.

"Listen to us, talking on and on when we've got work to do," he says.

"*We've* got work to do?"

He bites back a smile. "I'll make a deal with you, Miss Sorensen." He takes the rag from my hands. "I'll help you clean for another song." He swishes the rag in the bucket and then twists out the excess water. "Where should I start?"

"I didn't say—"

"You didn't say I couldn't help." He gives the rag a twirl.

"I didn't say you could. And I didn't say I would, either. Sing, I mean."

"One thing at a time." His smile again. That light. "Should I keep working on the floor?"

Before I can stop myself, I've looked at the noisy radiator. I've been dreading the grim, gritty work it will be, digging all the dust and grime from between those coiled iron pipes.

He follows my gaze. "Guess I'll start there."

"Wait," I say. "What's your name?"

"Theo." He smiles his light. "Theo Chastain."

"You can call me Rose."

"Rose." He nods like my name makes sense. And then he gets to work.

Together it takes us only a little over another hour, and the place is as clean as it's going to get. Theo helps me carry the cleaning supplies back down to the janitor's closet. Two trips it takes with his help. Out on Marquette again, we find the street and sidewalks empty, which I know relieves me, so I imagine it does him, too. Still, if we linger, we might be seen. I don't know what might happen then, and I'd rather not know. Most of Chicago—most of the world—is not Calliope's.

"No song?" His hands are clasped, as is his way. I give him a look that makes him heave a great sigh of defeat. He supplies my answer. "No song."

"I warned you."

"Another time maybe." He looks thoughtfully past rooftops at the sooty sky. "Perhaps Tuesday night at seven o'clock?" He looks back at me. "You know where I'll be." He takes a piece of printed paper from his pocket and scribbles something across the top. "If you come on Tuesday, you'll hear 'Blow the Man Down' like you've never heard it before, Rose, played especially for you. And if by any chance you decide to sing along . . . well, you'd be doing the Chess Men a mighty big favor." He holds out the piece of paper. "I live with my mother and sister. I'll tell them to take a message if you call and I'm not home."

I take the paper from his hands.

"Please come on Tuesday, Rose. Please."

"I'll try," I hear myself say.

I watch him walk away. He glances back and sees me watching, and his smile broadens. I smile back.

When he disappears around the corner, I look down at the paper. He's written a phone number across the top of the page. Below this is a sketch of a spired church. The African Methodist Church, it looks like from the type set beneath the picture.

It's a bulletin from this morning's service.

Like me, Theo was wearing his Sunday best because church came first. Then Hull House. Then the two of us together again. A miracle.

As I walk toward the El, the streetlights flicker on. I start to count the lights. Then I count my steps. Then I'm counting the hours until Tuesday night—not because I'm going, just because I can. I have a choice, just like Theo said, and I choose to count the hours. Once I've counted them, I start to count a different kind of time passing. It's four-four time, the meter to *tomato, tomahto, potato, potahto.*

I'm boarding the El train when I remember the song's title: "Let's Call the Whole Thing Off."

But that doesn't keep me from tucking his number into my pocketbook and clutching my pocketbook tightly beneath my arm so I don't have to worry so much about losing it. That doesn't stop me from hearing, again and again, the music of his *Please.*

SEVEN

It's nearly five o'clock on Tuesday evening when I finish cleaning stairways and foyers; nearly six when I'm finally home. Rob will pick me up in less than half an hour. "That's my girl!" he declared when, after much thought, I called him yesterday to say I'd like to go to the audition. "Not that I'm auditioning," I told him (and myself). "There will be plenty of other singers for the Chess Men to choose from. I'm just going to listen—and if by any chance no one else shows up, well, then maybe I'll help out. Maybe. Just until they find the right person. I don't want them to lose their chance to perform."

Rob snickered at that. Snickered! "Right," he said. "Your motives are pure. I understand, Rose." I managed to ignore his knowing tone.

Now I need to freshen up fast. But first I must make some kind of excuse to Mother. The truth is impossible.

I find her in the kitchen. She gives me a frantic look and gestures expansively at the bags of flour, sugar, and cinnamon, the brick of butter, the bottle of oil, the mixing bowls spread across the table, the baking pan resting on the stove.

"It might as well be Christmas! We're having *brunsviger!*" Mother exclaims. "When I saw Nils at the National Tea today, we started talking about good food—Danish food. I asked him if he likes brunsviger as much as we do, and next thing I knew he'd purchased the ingredients for me, and next thing after that, I'd invited him over for dessert. He said he was tickled pink at the thought of brunsviger, which I think, Rose, is really the thought of you."

"Mother!" I imagine Nils, collecting and paying for things that are by no means staples, things that are in fact rare treats these days. I imagine him handing these things to Mother with a shy duck of his head, that shock of hair falling into his eyes.

If it were any other night but tonight.

Mother smiles at me. "Nils is generous. Quite the fellow. Now"—she flaps her hands—"go clean up, then bring Sophy back with you. You know how she loves to help. Hurry, Rose! He'll be here shortly."

"I have other plans—"

But I don't get the chance to finish. Mother darts at me. "Change them! I've already told your father. He's on his way home." She turns me right around and pushes me down the hall to the bedroom, where Sophy sits in her chair by the window. Then, like that, Mother's gone. I can hear her in the kitchen, unwrapping the wax paper from the precious brick of butter.

Sophy gives me a bright-eyed, questioning look. "Hurt?"

I look down. I'm clutching my chest. Mother's strong-arming left me breathless, and now that I'm breathing again, my heart does ache. No wonder. My heart's divided. The thought of a night with Nils is comforting. It would be so easy to stay here with him. We are easy together. Nils and I like the same, delicious food. We share many of the same memories. What are Theo's memories? What kind of food does he like? And how have I become a person who sneaks around, doing things she's been raised not to do, enjoying—no, embracing—things she's been raised to reject?

I tell Sophy that I'll be right back. I go to the telephone that rests on the little table in the hallway. I dial Rob's number.

When my cousin realizes it's me calling, he interrupts my hello to say he's on his way out the door.

"I can't go." Quickly, I tell him what's happened. And then: "Dad will be here any minute."

That's all I needed to say. Rob doesn't respond, but I know he understands.

"Well." I put my hand to my chest. My heart aches again. "Mother needs my help now."

Rob says, "I'll be by at our usual time."

I blink. "Our *usual* time?"

"Like last time. Late, after everyone else has hit the sack. So you can't take advantage of a once-in-a-lifetime opportunity to audition with one of the best up-and-coming groups in town. Calliope's will still be there. We can at least enjoy the music."

From the kitchen, Mother yells my name. She is not the yelling type.

"I'll be outside your place at eleven o'clock. I'll wait for ten minutes. If you haven't climbed down that fire escape by that time, I'm going to knock on your door and wake your parents up. We'll see what happens then."

"That's blackmail!"

"See you soon."

He hangs up the receiver. I stand in the hallway, considering Rob's threat. My mad, maddening cousin. But then again, he's right, isn't he? I have a choice. I don't have to call the whole thing off. Just part of it. And if Mother and Dad don't know that I sometimes listen to that music in a place like Calliope's—well, what they don't know won't hurt them. Will it?

I set the receiver back into its cradle, go to the bedroom, freshen up fast, then carry Sophy into the kitchen and settle her as comfortably and securely as possible into her child-sized wheelchair.

"The topping, please. Get to it, sweetheart." Mother, kneading the brunsviger's thick, doughy batter, nods at the necessary ingredients. I start mixing cinnamon into brown sugar, and next thing I know, I'm thinking of Theo—his hands holding a remnant of my childhood, the rose-patterned rag, the contrast between the faded pink-and-white cloth and his beautiful dark skin. Applying the whisk in smooth strokes, I remember the curve of Theo's back as he bowed over the radiators. He took off his suit jacket and tie, working, and beneath his neatly pressed shirt, I saw the shape of his ribs, his shoulders. He rolled up his sleeves, and I saw his arms, the muscles there. When he turned and caught my eye, he blushed again. His high color, his sweet confusion, his eyes . . . I am remembering all this. If I let myself, I'll remember more.

"Hurry!" Sophie says.

Blinking, I look up at her. She frowns, impatient with the way I'm dawdling, whisk in hand.

"He'll be here soon." Mother cracks the oven door and checks the temperature.

Nils. *He* is Nils. Nils will be here with me tonight.

I grip the whisk tightly and with a few sharp flicks of my wrist finish mixing the topping. Now I help Mother pour the batter into the large baking pan and press it flat to the edges. Then I spread the topping across the top of the batter with a spatula.

"My turn," Sophy says, and it is. It's one of those rare, special times when Sophy can feel helpful in the kitchen, when she can feel helpful anywhere at all.

I set the pan before her on the table, then kneel beside her. She kisses the air—*I'm ready*—and I lift her arm, gently straighten her curled fingers, and ease her forward so that her hand hovers just above the pan. "Now?" I ask. Sophy kisses the air again. I lower her hand until the tip of her index finger pokes a hole in the topping. Sophy laughs, a throaty chortle of pure joy. I help her give the unbaked cake another poke. Again and again she pokes at it, until the raw brunsviger is dotted with impressions of her fingertip. Into these, the rich topping will melt, spreading through the batter as the cake bakes. This is what makes brunsviger so delicious. Even now Sophy's hand is a delicious, gooey mess, ready to be savored. I lift her hand to her mouth, and hold it there while she licks the batter from her fingers. Mother puts the pan into the oven. Soon the scent of baking brunsviger will waft through the air. I can barely wait. And in a few hours, I'll be sneaking out to Calliope's again. I can barely wait for this, either. I am tense with waiting.

We hear it then, the knock at the door. I jump, jarring Sophy's hand against her teeth.

"Ouch!" She narrows her eyes at me.

"Sorry!"

"He's early." Mother smiles. "Don't worry so, Rose. You'll be fine."

"Will I?"

Fumbling, as I never do, I grab a damp tea towel and wipe Sophy clean. Then I take a deep breath, fling the towel on the counter, and go to open the door.

We sit on the love seat in the front room, Nils and I, balancing our plates on our laps. It is just as I knew it would be with him. It is easy, enjoyable, a confirmation of who we've been raised to be. Nibbling at the last crumbs of our brunsviger slices, we talk on and on about the Danish food we love—the desserts, of course, but other dishes as well. He builds an open-faced sandwich this way; I build it that way. *Tomato, tomahto.* At the next church sociable, we agree to build sandwiches for each other and test which method is truly better, which results are more delicious. Now we are on to American food. I tell Nils about Dad, just off Ellis Island, making a beeline for a drugstore to taste his first ice cream soda. It's still Dad's favorite treat, and I've inherited his passion for cold, creamy, sweet drinks, along with his love of pretzels and caramel apples. Nils prefers Cracker Jack and hot dogs. These taste best at Wrigley Field, he says. When he asks what sports I like, I have to admit: none in particular. Sophy's the baseball fan. Like Nils, she has a head for sports and numbers and sports' numbers. I don't have a head for any of these things, I admit. I prefer words. I took Latin in high school and loved it for the way the words sounded. If I could learn Italian, I would. It's like music. No wonder why the Italians love opera so much. And pictures—I like pictures, too. It's been a long time since I've been to the Art Institute. I'd like to go again. Nils says he'd like to go, too. We could go together. We agree we'll do that soon.

"But music, that's what I love best," I say.

Nils nods, and his hair falls into his eyes, and I find myself leaning toward him. "There's nothing like a rousing chorus of 'A Mighty Fortress,'" he says, pushing back his hair even as I'm raising my hand to do the same. I quickly sit back, though I don't think he realizes what I was about to do. He crosses one long leg over the other, getting more comfortable. "I love those great old hymns," he says. "Though some of them have questionable origins, you know. 'A Mighty Fortress' was originally a German drinking song—the tune, that is."

"Oh?"

"In fact, Mr. Block was telling me the other day that his church doesn't allow music during the services for just that reason," Nils continues. "Mr. Block says the focus is wholly on Scripture, teaching, and prayer. It's a purer form of worship, he says. Which makes me think. What is the purpose of all the hymns we sing, Rose? Prayer? I don't think so, at least not for me. By verse two, my mind is wandering—unless you're the one singing, of course. But if you're not singing, well, then, I'm a goner. It only takes a word from Pastor Riis to bring me back again, but I'm concerned that I wander at all. 'If your hand offends your brother, cut it off.' Isn't that what it says in the Bible?"

"Something like that." If our church banned music from its Sunday mornings, I would ban our church from my Sunday mornings. I would join another congregation. Not Mr. Block's. Not for all the bricks of butter in the world.

Nils looks at me intently. "I'm thinking of asking Pastor Riis about it all."

"You should."

"I will."

The ticking of the clock on the mantel fills the room. The gas fireplace flares and fades, glittering black glass coals reddening and darkening.

Second helpings. That's what we want.

Saying just that, I take Nils's plate and go to the kitchen.

"Well?" Mother says as I cut us each another big piece of cake. "How is it?"

Sophy scrutinizes me from her wheelchair.

"Delicious," I say.

Mother laughs. "Nils is delicious?"

"Mother!"

The back door swings open and Dad bursts into the kitchen, bringing with him a blast of cold air and the scent of smoke. He's been smoking on the back porch again. Or maybe he was sitting on the narrow stairs that lead up to it from the back alley. Those are his two options if he wants a cigarette close to home. Mother hath ordained it. Can't say I blame her. Still, Mother frowns even though Dad has followed this, her singular rule.

Dad ignores her frown. "Nils is still here?"

I gesture, plate of brunsviger in hand, down the hallway. "I'm about to bring him seconds."

"Good," Dad says.

Nils and I dig into round two, and our conversation shifts to our shared longing for spring flowers and summer warmth. If he can take the time away from work without leaving Mr. Block in a lurch, he plans on visiting his grandparents in Iowa over the Fourth of July. They are growing frail, and he wants to help them with some big tasks. "Batten down the hatches, so to speak, so they don't have to worry about paying someone to do what they used to do without batting an eye," he says. "And they have some things they brought over from Odense that they want to tell me about. I'm their only grandchild, so I have to carry on the old stories. I plan on writing them down before I forget."

He asks about my long-term plans, and I tell him about Sophy's baptism on Easter, Julia's wedding in August. "She wants me to help her find a dress," I'm saying, when Nils softly says, "Rose. Hold still." He reaches out and gently plucks a crumb of cake from my lower lip. Then, as if I'm a small child, he pops the crumb into my mouth. "Now, then," he says, and he leans close, leans closer—

"Watch out, young man. You'll be peeling grapes and fanning her with palm leaves next."

Nils's eyes widen, as do mine, and he leans away from me. Just behind us stands Dad, a plate of brunsviger in his hand. Nils swallows so hard that I hear him gulp. "Mr. Sorensen," he says, "you know I'd never—"

Dad waves Nils's words away, and sits down in the chair opposite us. Dad's talking the economy now, and soon Nils is, too. And then they're talking FDR in the White House and Hitler in Europe and Stalin in Russia. They're talking the future in general, and Nils's future specifically, and, without saying so, a possible future for me. Dad, in his own way, is watching over me, I realize, playing the sentinel again. Dad is making sure things don't go in a certain direction. He is making sure things go exactly where they should, the way they should. I should be grateful. I guess I am.

When Nils looks over and gives me a shy, apologetic smile— *Sorry about this. Please forgive me. I'm just trying to be respectful to your dad*—I am indeed grateful. What a good man. Any parent would want him for their daughter.

It is just after nine when Nils says he must go. "I have to be up early. Tomorrow's going to be a long day," he explains. "Mr. Block offered me overtime if I'll help him finish last year's taxes once my other work is done."

Dad, still with us, though reading the newspaper now, nods his approval.

I walk Nils downstairs to the foyer. There, hat in hand, he leans close enough to kiss me on the cheek; then, like the kids we once were, he gives my ear a gentle tug instead. We laugh, relieved to be ourselves again, alone.

"Dad talked your head off," I say.

Nils claps his hat on his head as if to prove that this isn't the case at all. "I'd probably do the same. Wouldn't want any daughter of mine getting in too deep too fast. Not that we would have," he adds quickly.

He reminds me about our dinner at Old Prague this Saturday night, but I didn't need reminding.

"I'm looking forward to it," I say, meaning every word.

And then he's gone, and, with only two more hours until eleven and Calliope's and Theo, I wonder what I really meant, what I really mean at all.

The dim glow of the streetlight illuminates the front seat of Rob's DeSoto. I jump inside, shut the door, take off my sleet-drenched hat, kick off my already sodden shoes, and nestle my feet beneath the car's blasting heater.

Rob smiles an I-knew-it-all-along smile. "Right on time."

I nearly fell descending the slick fire escape—the city is icing over—and almost turned back. But then I remembered Rob's threat. Theo's "please." My choice. And I kept going.

Rob gives a Tarzan yell.

What does it mean that this time I join in? What does it mean that it feels so good not to be singing or talking or silent, but just to be plain old loud?

Whooping it up, we drive past Garfield Park, dark and forbidding at this late hour on a Tuesday night.

"Watch out!"

My Tarzan call shifts to a warning as a shape lunges from the thick trees that border the park's fence. The shape lurches across the sidewalk and staggers in front of the DeSoto. A ragged young man. No, a gang of ragged young men. Rob brakes just in time, and the ragged young men make it safely across the street.

"Nogoodniks." The relief in Rob's voice doesn't hide the fact that even he is unsettled. "You've got to watch out for punks like that, Rose. They're giving thugs like Frank Nitti a run for his money, at least in this neighborhood. Vandalism, looting, mugging, you name it. That's what I've heard."

"I'll keep my eyes open."

"Doesn't help when they're drunk as skunks, of course."

I'm remembering Calliope's two-drink minimum and, last time, the liquor hot in my mouth, throat, belly.

"You bring me water tonight, Rob. That's all. And if you can't keep control of yourself, I promise you I'm walking home."

Rob grimaces, his plump face souring to a scowl. "I'll be good."

I run my hands over my plain-Jane gray skirt, nervously smoothing the wrinkles there. Again my coat smells like wet dog. It would be a terrible thing to walk through the wee hours of the morning in this grim, late February weather. I hope I don't have to. I wouldn't make it home if I tried. I'd have to find some safe place to hole up until I had the company of early-morning commuters on the El. I'd get home after Mother, Dad, Sophy, and Andreas were awake. What would happen then?

Rob jerks his thumb at the backseat. He must have noticed my shabbiness, too, or caught a whiff of my coat. "Why don't you climb on back and change into your dress now? That way we won't waste time later."

I do as he suggests. It's easier tonight, even though the car is moving. Shows what a little practice can do. You'd think I'd transformed myself in close quarters many times, not just once before. I know the way the beautiful blue dress works now. I slip into it like it's a second skin. Back in the front seat, I apply the makeup as we wait for traffic at well-lit intersections. This time I recognize the young woman looking back at me in the rearview mirror. She smiles.

We enter Bronzeville, but Rob doesn't turn off onto a side street to park. He pulls right up in front of Calliope's.

"Aren't you going to find a better place to leave the car? I don't think this is legal."

"On a night like this, I'll take advantage of valet service," Rob says.

"You and whose wallet?"

Rob laughs. "Guess I haven't told you my good news, huh? I got a real job, Rose, the job I've been waiting for."

"Rob!" I give him a swift hug. "What is it?"

"Legal assistant."

A red-jacketed valet dashes from Calliope's toward us. Rob

leaps from the car, takes a ticket from the valet, and runs around the front of the car to open my door. This time he doesn't say a word when I wrap my ratty old coat around my shoulders. He must know that I really do need some protection against the cold. He holds out a hand, helps me out onto the street, and escorts me up to the door of the club.

"I'm really going to do it," he's saying. "I'm going to start night school this summer. I'm going to be a lawyer."

"I'm happy for you."

"I'm happy for you, too. You're *here*."

And we're inside.

I can't see the Chess Men for the crowd. But I can hear them. Not as well as I'd like to because of the noise, but well enough to know that they are playing a song I don't recognize. I'm on my tiptoes, trying to get a glimpse of the stage, when Rob flings his arm around my shoulder and pulls me close. He's trembling with happiness and enthusiasm for this night, for his future. I haven't seen him this way since his father died. And as for me, well, Rob's right: I'm *here*. I'm almost as happy as he is.

Until the crowd shifts and I see a lovely woman in a long crimson gown lean against the piano and tip a microphone toward her lips. Theo nods at the woman. It's a nod that says *sing*. Notes cascade from Theo's fingers, and the woman parts her lips and her voice rises and drifts intoxicatingly through the crowd and around me:

I've got you under my skin.

The woman has a smoky voice that's as beautiful as she is, with her coils of golden hair, her glossy, sparkling lips, painted just the color of her dress, and her dark, pencil-thin eyebrows that arch expressively on the word *you*, making me believe she's got Theo and the other musicians, she's got Rob, and she's got me, too. She's got each and every one of us here at Calliope's. We're hanging on her every word, her every note:

I've got you deep in the heart of me.

The Chess Men have found their singer. And she's gotten under our skin.

EIGHT

"Ladies and gentlemen." Theo joins the singer and speaks into the microphone. "Miss Lilah Buckley. The newest addition to the Chess Men. It's been suggested that we call her the Queen, the strongest player on the board. Let's give her a big—"

Theo doesn't need to tell the crowd what to do. The applause in Calliope's is more explosive than I've ever heard it. Lilah Buckley presses her palm to her lips and flashes the perfect crimson shape of her mouth at us all. When the applause finally subsides, she sashays with long-limbed grace from the stage.

Theo has loosened his bow tie and his tuxedo shirt collar. He leans into the microphone again. "We'll be taking a short break now. But don't go too far. We'll be right back."

The other members of the Chess Men start to leave the stage, but Theo lingers at the microphone. He shields his eyes with his hands and scans the crowd. I'm glad Rob and I worked our way over to a free table at the edge of the audience during the last number. It's dark where we are. Theo glances my way, then past me. With the spotlight in his eyes, he doesn't see me sitting in the shadows. He turns away and leaves the stage.

I let out a breath I didn't realize I was holding and notice that Rob has vanished, too. I'm alone at a table for four. I'd feel uncomfortable, I suppose, if I were able to feel anything but numb confusion.

What did I want? What did I expect? More important, why does it seem that not just this little corner of the club but the whole world is in shadow?

A chair scrapes against the floor. I look up as Zane sits down across the table from me. From somewhere inside my numb, confused self, I draw a smile. I give it to Zane.

He doesn't smile back. "I'm sorry, Rose. I didn't know they'd found a singer already, or I would have told Rob, who would have warned you."

"Warned me? Why?" I muster a shrug. "The Chess Men needed a singer. I'm glad they found such a good one."

My words sound wooden, even to me. Little wooden blocks, falling *clunk, clunk, clunk* on the table between us. Nothing musical about them at all.

Zane reaches down and hitches his bum leg under the table, away from the people surging past. "Buckley's a good singer, all right. An amazing one. But from what I've heard, she's also . . . complicated."

"Aren't we all?"

As if in answer, Rob, precariously balancing three drinks, approaches us. I pull out the chair beside me, and Rob sits down.

"Water for you."

Rob sets a glass in front of me. I stare at it for a moment, the ice melting like dreams there. I pick it up. Take a sip. Water, indeed. It loosens the knot in my throat.

"And for you, not water." Rob sets another drink before Zane. Rob doesn't choose to comment on his own drink. He takes a gulp, bangs the glass down on the table, and grabs my hand. "Compared to you, Laerke, she's a crow."

"Don't."

"I'm not kidding!" Rob squeezes my hand. "That throaty voice just doesn't compare."

Zane shakes his head. "That throaty voice is memorable. Who are you kidding, Rob? Rose isn't a fool. She knows a good thing when she hears it. But Rose is a good thing, too. She's her own good thing."

Rob leans over and touches his forehead against mine. "Now, that's truth with a capital *T*. You just have to believe it, Laerke." He draws back, clinks his glass against Zane's, then mine, and takes another drink. In another gulp, he's drained his glass.

I tell Rob to take it easy. Even Zane tells Rob to take it easy.

"I'm celebrating my new job, remember?" Rob slugs back some ice, noisily chews, and swallows. "Here's to the future!" He clinks his empty glass against mine. "You have a future, too, Laerke. You wait and see."

The Chess Men are back onstage. Lilah Buckley is not.

The clarinetist fiddles with his instrument's reed. The drummer taps his finger repeatedly against the taut skin of his snare. The bassist plucks at strings, adjusts the tension. Theo positions and repositions his hands on the piano keys, but he doesn't press down.

"Remember what I said?" Zane gives me a meaningful glance. *"Complicated."*

Rob and Zane go to the bar. I sit alone at the table. The crowd is growing restless and noisy, but I stay still and quiet, waiting for the music.

Finally Theo lifts his hand and plays a single note on the piano that no one can hear above the rising din. He plays the note again. The audience gets a little quieter. When he plays the note a third time, I am able to make it out. It's a rousing sound now, a call to action. The other Chess Men watch Theo closely. He plays the note yet again, and this time he puts a bit of bounce into it. There's something hopeful about the sound, the action. It catches everyone's attention. The Chess Men settle into their instruments. They talk back to Theo's single note. There's the whisper of the drummer's brush against the snare. A lingering tone from the clarinet. The bassist plucks a pattern that stitches it all together. And suddenly the music expands. A singer would be nice, but she's not necessary—at least not right now. The Chess Men are carrying the melody just fine by themselves.

"I'm not going to sit this one out." Rob is just returning to the table, but he doesn't bother to sit down. He sets his half-empty glass by mine, then weaves his way onto the dance floor. There's a flash of strawberry-blond hair as a woman whirls into his arms. Away they go into the crowd.

Zane, back as well, asks if I'd care to dance. When I decline, he turns to another woman sitting just behind him. She nods her curly head and they're off, the drag in his step only adding to the distinctive grace with which he sweeps her in a circle.

Is it my imagination, or has Theo seen them, and in seeing them, seen me? He's looking in this direction.

And now his eyes meet mine. His hands falter on the keys. My hands tremble in my lap. His lips shape my name. Not Miss Sorensen this time, but Rose.

Rose. He says my name again.

I want out of here.

There before me, painted on the wall just to the side of the stage, is an arrow pointing toward the ladies' room.

Somehow I make my way between tables and chairs, people and more people. I reach the sign. I follow the arrow down a dark, empty corridor to the ladies'. I push the door open, and Lilah Buckley stumbles into my arms.

Even in the dim light, I can see that her eyes are glittering with something besides excitement. Her beautiful face is wet—not with tears but with sweat. She looks through me, pushes past me. With her hands pressed to the walls on either side, Lilah Buckley slowly makes her way down the corridor, keeping a difficult balance. The back of her lovely crimson gown is drenched, dripping, as if it's been dragged through a puddle or fallen into the toilet.

She can't go onstage like this. She'd embarrass herself. She'd embarrass the Chess Men. For her sake, for their sake, for Theo, I say her name. But Lilah Buckley continues her unsteady progress down the corridor.

I rush to her side, touch her thin arm. There are bruises there, on the inside. She stops walking, but she doesn't turn to look at me, even as I babble about her state of disorder. She leans toward the stage and the spotlight's glare, moth to flame.

"Miss Buckley, your dress. It's—"

"Fix it."

The Queen, the strongest player on the board, has given an order to a lady-in-waiting. Me.

I obey. I bend down and lift the hem of her dress. I wring water from it until a small puddle pools at my feet, and then I smooth out the train. The wet stain is still apparent, dull, dark brown, just the color of dried blood, compared with the original crimson sheen.

"Maybe we should tie it up. Just a bit," I say.

Her eyes are closed, but she nods. Only her hands pressed against the corridor's walls keep her from falling.

I knot up the back of her dress and the sides; the front, too. The knotted portions lift to the middle of her calves, hiding the creeping stain. Otherwise, the length of the dress drapes elegantly, just touching her slim ankles. She is wearing golden sandals. Her toenails are painted a red so deep it's nearly black. The audience will savor this glimpse of what was previously hidden.

But there are bruises there, too, on the inside of her ankles, creeping up her calves. What if the audience sees those?

Lilah Buckley doesn't care, or she doesn't think to care. She mumbles her thanks, wavers, then takes another step forward, and another. In this way, step by faltering step, she weaves her way toward the spotlight.

I stand, knees cracking, and watch her go. When she turns and disappears up the steps that lead to the stage, I return to the ladies' room.

It's not a class act. It's cramped, dark, and dank; it smells of ammonia and worse. A quick look tells me that the toilet is clogged. Iron stains the sink. Cigarette smoke clouds the mirror so I can't get a good look at myself. I can, however, hear the music faintly through the bathroom's heavy door. Lilah Buckley is singing now. Her deep voice is breathtakingly unpredictable in its harmonies, yet she's hitting every note just right, perfectly complementing the rest of the band. A genius. That's what she is. One of those rare, once-in-a-generation voices. Right up there with Billie Holiday. Right up there with Mahalia Jackson, though Mahalia Jackson's star shines in an entirely different constellation.

I see the needle on the floor beside the sink then. And, beside it, the syringe.

I have a sense of what this means—but only the vaguest sense. Rumors and whispers.

Those bruises.

I feel sick.

I lean over the sink, turn on the tap. Rusty water chugs out. Filth swirls—black flecks of dead bugs and who knows what else. I bow my head, the better to concentrate on the music. A few minutes pass as the water gushes, cleansing the pipes. I clear my throat, clear it again. The only music I can hear is the water, splashing cleanly now into the sink. I start humming. I plug the drain and plunge my hands into the cool, rising water. Words fill my head:

I'll fly away
in the morning . . .

This comes out of nowhere, out of me, this hymn. It was inspired by a slave song, Pastor Riis told us when we sang it a few Sundays ago. I can almost taste the words, smooth and succulent as a peeled and pitted plum, sweet gold pouring out of me, filling this dank room like light. I swirl the water in the sink, and the feeling of sickness subsides.

I sing the song again, remembering the first time I tasted sound. It was a few years before Sophy was born. It was spring.

A window was open in Aunt Astrid's kitchen. Somehow I was perched on the sill. My bare feet dangled against the house's rough wood siding. I opened my mouth and breathed in the spring air. It tasted good—wet and clean. Birds sang in the tree before me, and their sounds began rolling from my tongue. *Chick-a-dee-dee-dee, chick-a-dee-dee-dee. Cuckoo, cuckoo.* Bird-songs perfectly echoed, note for note, refrain for refrain, until it seemed the birds were singing back to me. I wanted to climb the tree and join them. I wanted to pour my voice into the bright blue bowl of sky. I wanted to fly away.

For months afterward, Mother has told me, I sang bird-songs. Then I filled the house with nursery rhymes and hymns. Then Sophy was born, and I sang for her. And then I sang only for her, and for Rob, and for God. And then Theo heard me sing.

The bathroom door bangs open, and I splash the front of my blue dress nearly as badly as Lilah Buckley soaked the crimson back of hers.

The cigarette smoke has cleared. I glance in the mirror and glimpse a flash of strawberry-blond hair. It's Rob's dance partner, blotting her damp face with a dainty handkerchief. She flicks on a switch I didn't see, and the bathroom is illuminated with lambent, amber light. Must be a short in the wiring. Rob's dance partner and I blink at each other through the flickering glow. She's about my age, maybe a year or two older. Her bright green dress brings out her green eyes, which are topped by brows the same brilliant color as her hair. She has freckles, a pert nose, a Cupid's bow mouth. Her hair is done up in the latest fashion. Carefully crimped, the shining locks curve in gentle waves against her cheeks. I didn't think to pin up my hair tonight. My wet hands drift self-consciously to my own brown bob, bluntly cut by Mother with our kitchen sheers. I drip more water on my dress. There's no towel with which to dry my hands. At a loss, I plunge them into the sink again.

"You sounded so pretty, singing away in here." Rob's dance partner smiles. "I could hear you through the door. Guess you didn't know you were that loud, huh?" She presses her handkerchief to the back of her neck. Her smile turns rueful. "Aw, your dress got all wet. Sorry about that."

"It's all right." Flustered, I search for something to say, mumble, "That was my cousin you were dancing with."

"Huh. He's a good dancer. Said he's looking for fun, nothing more, though. Aren't they all?" The woman snaps her gum. "You okay, kiddo? You don't look so hot."

"I'm fine."

"If you say so." She sidles past me, inhaling sharply at the sign of the offending toilet. "Oh, well. Nature calls." Without further hesitation, she goes into the stall and closes the door.

I pull the plug on the sink. I do not let myself look down at the needle and the syringe on the floor. I watch the last of the water swirl away, then press my cool wet hands to my throat, which still feels warm and full from singing. In the coming early morning, I will sing again for Sophy. I will sing in a whisper so as not to wake her. If she is dreaming bad dreams, I will sing her dreams sweet. I will remind myself that I can still, always, at least do this. I can sing the way I should sing, to whom I should sing, the songs I should sing.

The stall door bangs open. This woman must have a penchant for dramatic entrances.

"I love this song!" she exclaims. "They're playing it on the radio all the time now. But no one plays it like the Chess Men." She hums along to another song I don't know. She's flat on every note, which makes the sound endearing. Humming, she gives me a friendly wink. "Ready to head back out there? Your cousin is saving me a seat. Bet he's got one for you, too."

Before I can answer, she links her arm through mine. "I'm Dolores Pine, by the way."

I tell her my name, and we're out the door.

Dolores and I make our way through the dancers. I don't look at Theo as we pass in front of the stage. I keep my eyes on Rob and Zane, who are sitting at our table again. Zane holds his head in his hands as if it's a heavy weight. As Dolores and I approach, Rob pats the empty seat beside him. I sit down. Rob smiles blearily at me. Dolores sits next to Zane, who doesn't look up.

Dolores jerks her thumb at Zane. "What's up?"

Rob shrugs. "Not him, that's for sure. Something come over you that last dance, Zane?"

"My leg hurts. That's all."

Zane says this to the table. His pant leg is hiked up to reveal the metal brace that sheathes his thin, pale shin. I've only seen his brace once or twice before. Usually he's careful to keep it covered.

Dolores clucks her tongue. "Maybe you should rest up a bit?" She grabs a nearby empty chair and drags it over to Zane. "Why don't you put your foot up? Take the weight off. It might help."

"I can take care of myself." Zane looks embarrassed. For the first time, I realize that he has something in common with Sophy. He wants his condition to be accepted, not coddled. "I think I'm calling it a night," he mutters.

"I can see why, what with the way Buckley's singing now!" Rob leans into me. "Oh, I wish it was you up there, Rose. You wouldn't put me through this, would you?"

Dolores says, "I heard your cousin singing in the bathroom. That voice of hers is something else."

"Sure is. And this is jibberish." Rob glares in the direction of the stage.

Lilah Buckley is singing skat. I've only heard one other person sing this way, Louis Armstrong, and I only know it's called skat because the radio announcer said so. Once, during a recording session, the announcer said, Armstrong dropped his lyrics on the floor. The record producer encouraged Louis to keep on singing without the lyrics, so he sang the chorus in nonsense syllables. He improvised the sounds with perfect timing, using his voice like an instrument. "Scat gives a song *flavor*," the announcer said. "When it's good, it releases emotions so deep, so real, they're unspeakable."

I think that's exactly what Lilah Buckley is doing right now. Accompanied by the Chess Men, her nonsense sounds make perfect sense to me.

"Bleet, blat, bloop." Mimicking Lilah, Dolores leans across the table to give Rob's wrist a reprimanding tap. "You still owe me a drink for that dance, buddy. And here I thought you were a gentleman, true to your word."

"Jiminy. Where are my good manners?" Rob stands unsteadily and heads to the bar. Zane lifts his head from his hands, gives Dolores and me a curt nod, and limps to the bar, too.

Dolores frowns after him. "He's hurting."

"He usually doesn't complain. It must be bad."

Then the thought flashes through my mind: if Zane is leaving, maybe I could go with him. I'm more than ready to go to bed. I'm more than ready to sing to Sophy. I stand, crane my neck, search the place. No sign of Zane. I drop back into my chair. Never mind. It would be out of his way to take me home. And with him feeling so awful, it wouldn't be fair of me to ask him for a ride.

Rob returns to the table and clinks his fresh drink against Dolores's. Lilah Buckley has shifted from rapid skat to a slow ballad, yet another song I don't know. I listen to her voice, strong and powerful, fragile and broken, all at the same time. Theo's playing responds to her, encourages her, lifts her up, as do the rest of the Chess Men.

Beneath all this courses the ongoing current of Rob and Dolores's slurred exchange. Rob is speaking of his dreams, his new job, law school, a practice of his own someday, and the money that goes along with it. Dolores is speaking of her dreams, her new job—against all odds, she's just finished school and gotten her first full-time nursing position at Mount Sinai Hospital. A family—they'd both like to settle down and have one of those, one day. Rob wants a single, perfect child. Dolores wants many. She doesn't care if they're perfect or not.

What do I want? I can't think for the music, which is winding down now. Which is ending, it appears. Theo is at the microphone again, bidding us all good night. Lilah Buckley has already left the stage.

"Good riddance," Rob says drunkenly. He lifts his glass to his lips. Before I can stop myself, my hand shoots out. I snatch the glass and dump the liquor on the floor.

"Hey!" Rob blinks, astonished.

"You've had more than enough."

Rob glowers. "If you're so sure about that, guess you'll need to find another way home."

"I'll do that."

I stand, grab my coat from the back of a chair, and move through the crowd. I am going to put one foot in front of the other until I come to an El stop that will take me where I need to go.

At the door, I glance back at the stage. This time, Theo's the one watching me walk away. I gasp as he waves. "Wait!" he calls into the microphone. And then he whistles the opening measures to "Blow the Man Down."

I clench my jaw, suddenly, inexplicably furious. I turn toward the door. *That was between us. That was not his to share.* One foot in front of the other, I walk right out of Calliope's. It's the darkest hour of an early February morning, and a cold sleet is falling. I can hear the distant rattle of the El. I will head in that direction and find some sheltered place to wait until it is safe to ride.

"I guess you turn into a pumpkin at the stroke of midnight?"

Dolores. She's followed me. Rob stands swaying behind her. Others are stumbling out of Calliope's, too. Dolores wraps her arms around a lamppost and sways back and forth as people surge around her.

"She turns into worse than a pumpkin. She turns into a prune. I mean, a prude." Rob fumbles in his pocket. He draws out the valet ticket, looks dazedly around. "Who gets this?"

I point at the valet, huddled in a nearby alley. Rob waves the ticket, and the valet dashes over, takes it, then dashes off.

Rob grins. "This is living. My ladies, your coach approacheth."

Dolores laughs, swinging around the lamppost again. "Our coacheth, you mean."

Rob joins in laughing, his breath a puff of smoke in the cold air. He gives me a quick look and explains. "Dolores needs a ride home."

"I'm not riding with you, Rob." I look at Dolores. It takes her a moment, but finally she registers me. "And you shouldn't, either," I tell her.

Dolores swings around the lamppost again, laughing.

I shake my head. "Listen, though, Dolores, if he starts driving crazy, you ask him to pull over, you hear?"

She doesn't seem to hear. She swings and swings and swings.

I am walking toward the distant rattle of the El when someone catches hold of my arm. I turn sharply, ready to tell Rob or Dolores to let me be. I'll be fine.

But it's Theo, standing there.

"Rose."

My name on Theo's lips doesn't sound like my name on the lips of anyone else.

People are watching us. Dolores and Rob are watching us. A black man and a white woman. A black man gently holding a white woman by her arm. *Us.*

The look Theo gives me is tender and sad. And something else. His dark eyes flicker with something like desperation.

"Where are you going?" he asks.

Cautiously, carefully, like one of us might break, I remove my arm from his hand.

"Home."

"How will you get there?"

"I'm working on that."

"Hey!" Rob stares at Theo with something like awe, but there's fear is in his eyes, too. "You're coming with me, Rose."

Theo glances at Rob. His brow furrows. To me, he says, "I have a car. Let me take you home. We can leave right now."

"Whoa there." Rob is still slurring his words, but there's a sharpness to his tone now. "That's my cousin you're talking to. You may be a great musician, sir, but I'll be the one driving her home."

Dolores gives one last, big swing. "Oureth carriageth awaiteth!"

The DeSoto idles at the curb. The valet dashes over and hands the keys to Rob. Rob tips him a shiny silver quarter, then jingles the keys at me. "I'll let you do the driving if that's what it takes, Rose."

I remind Rob that I don't know how to drive. "And right now, you don't, either," I say.

"I'm a great driver. Great a driver as that one is a great musician." Rob lurches toward his car. "Fine. Take care of yourself, then, Rose!"

Rob gets behind the wheel, and Dolores slouches into the seat beside him. Theo and I watch as the car tears away from the curb and careens down the street and around the corner.

I want to get home to Sophy. I want to get home to her now. I turn to Theo. Quietly, so no one else can hear, I say, "I'll take that ride."

Theo's eyes widen, but then he nods. "Best you meet me around back."

He turns on his heel and goes quickly into Calliope's, ignoring the women and men who tug at his jacket, ask him for a drink, ask him for an autograph, ask him for more.

I hesitate only a minute. Then I walk past the valet and down the dark alley around to the back of the club, where Theo already stands waiting by his car.

NINE

I focus on the cold. The sharp wind gusts and propels me toward Theo's car; it keeps me from hesitating. This man helped me clean an empty apartment, I tell myself. This man makes music I'm struggling to live without. This man is a gentleman. A gentle man. I trust him to drive me home.

I open the passenger's side door. I am about to get in when Theo holds up his hand. *Stop*, his hand says.

I stop.

"Backseat, Rose. Better safe than sorry."

I shut the door and get into the backseat. Theo slips in behind the steering wheel. He closes his door and turns to look at me.

"I'm the chauffeur. You're the passenger. Got it?"

"Are you sure about this? I can find another way—"

"I'm sure. I'm not foolish, though." He claps a newsboy's cap on his head, tugs it low over his eyes. "The wrong people see us at this time of the morning in what they think is a compromising situation, your life could be ruined and I could be dead. We can talk, but only when we're driving. Not when we're stopped at an intersection, not when we get to your place, wherever that is. Where is it, by the way?"

I tell him my address.

"Near Garfield Park?"

I nod. He faces forward again and we're on our way.

We don't say a word, even as we turn onto Lake Shore Drive. Rob has never taken this way—at least not when I've been with him. There are no stop signs or streetlights, I can't help but notice. Maybe that's why Theo picked it. Driving along like this, we can talk freely. Now if only one of us would think of something to say.

The slope of his shoulders is more noticeable than on most men, but of course I'm not going to say that. I suppose it's from all those hours of bending over, leaning into the piano keys. His hands on the steering wheel—the quick touch of his fingers, tendons rippling as he steers us into the slow lane—his elegant hands are strong and agile from all those hours of playing, too.

At this rate I'll never be able to say anything without embarrassing myself. I look out the window at the dark expanse of Lake Michigan.

"Lilah Buckley is an old friend of Bill Pritchett's. Bill's our drummer," Theo says suddenly. "Bill came to us yesterday and said Lilah needed the gig. Needed it bad, the way we needed a singer. A year ago she was on her way up, moving with the likes of some really big swing bands. She's not soaring so high anymore. Not in that way, at least. When Bill said she'd work with us—she wanted to work with us, needed to—well, we could really only say yes. She could change our . . . trajectory. And there aren't many women, especially white women, who would sing with a mixed band." He glances into the rearview mirror, and his eyes meet mine. "You wouldn't." His gaze is back on the road again, but not before I glimpse the disappointment there.

I sit up straighter in my seat. "I never said I would."

"If you'd auditioned you might have changed our minds about Lilah. No, don't deny it, Rose. You're that good."

Is it possible to fly into a million pieces? I think it is. I grip the edge of the car seat and hold on tight. "You have your singer, Theo."

"I said no at first."

"What?"

"When Bill told us about Lilah, I said no."

"Why?"

"I wanted to see if you would show up after all. I wanted to play 'Blow the Man Down' and hear you sing that song like it's never been sung."

We listen to the slush shushing beneath the car wheels, the windshield wipers doing their steady best to keep things clear.

"Yes was the right thing to say." My voice is so quiet I almost don't hear it. But he does.

"I let the fellows persuade me. They reminded me of the cost if we had no one at all. It wasn't just me that would have been out of a job, and they all have families to support. Wives and kids. But then tonight the way she was, and it was only the first night . . ." Theo sighs, and his sigh is weary. "Lilah does things I'm not going to mention, Rose. Not to you or my mother or my sister, either. She does things I pray every day not to do. I pray for Lilah, too, truth be told. She's a good person underneath all the tracks. If she lives long enough, she'll come through to the other side. I'll be honored to meet her there and lend a helping hand. Until then, as the fellows put it, 'The Chess Men will keep her working and she'll keep us working.' And I'll keep praying for us all."

I stare out at the lake. Something flashes in the distance—a bright point of light. A lighthouse, perhaps, guiding a slow-moving barge safely toward morning.

"Lilah is meant to be with you. With the Chess Men, I mean."

"By which you mean you aren't."

"I'm not called to this, Theo."

The nape of his neck brushes against his collar as he slowly shakes his head. "That's like saying you're not called to love."

"Don't say that!" I look toward the lake until my eyes burn. It is all I can do to keep from looking, looking, looking at him.

Some minutes pass, slush shushing, wipers swiping, the silence between us crackling with implications. We turn off the drive onto streets peppered with stoplights and stop signs, intersections where people stand, waiting and watching as we drive by. Now, for our own good, for our safety, the silence is something neither of us breaks. I close my burning eyes, opening them only when we pull up in front of the apartment where my family lies sleeping if I'm lucky, since the horizon is already paling in the east.

I get out of Theo's car and shut the door. He leans across the front seat and looks at me through the sleet-streamed window. He raises his hand, more like a blessing than a wave. He leans across the seat and presses his hand to the window glass. His hand is so close. I could press my hand to the window, too. Palm to palm but for the glass, we could almost touch. I could reach for the door handle. I could climb back into the car with him. I could sit beside him in the front seat, fearless.

But he draws back his hand. He leans away, drives off before I can do anything at all.

I trudge through icy slop to the fire escape and climb the slippery steps. Through the bedroom window, I see the shape of Sophy on the bed. I open the window and steal inside. Strip off my beautiful dress and hide it at the bottom of a drawer. Drape my ugly coat over the chair. Put on my nightgown. If I'm lucky, I'll have an hour of sleep. Then Wednesday will be here, and my workday will begin.

I ease my way beneath the covers. I would like to curl close to Sophy's warmth, but I'm afraid my chill will wake her. So I balance on the edge of the bed.

My face is wet with something besides rain. I touch my cheek and realize I'm crying.

Now, if I only understood why.

"There's something I want to show you," Nils says.

We are sitting in Old Prague, nipping at silver bowls of orange sherbet, plates of three meats and potatoes pushed aside. The food was delicious. Our conversation never flagged. But now there's a polka band playing in a far corner of the restaurant, and it's hard to hear each other for the *oomp pa pa, oomp pa pa* of the accordion and horns.

"Are you ready to leave?" Nils practically has to shout to be heard. When I nod, he goes and pays the check. Outside Old Prague, he says it again, with more fervor. "There really is something I really want to show you."

A view, I'm thinking. Perhaps the view of the skyline from Adler Planetarium Point. It's a clear night. Tall buildings will glitter against the sky. After all the noise of the restaurant, we will sit quietly together and watch for shooting stars. We'll make silent wishes. I'll try to guess his wish. He'll try to guess mine. Maybe we'll guess right and, if not, maybe we'll tell.

"Let's go," I say.

It's only when we're in his car and driving away from the planetarium, not toward it, that I ask Nils what he wants to show me.

"It's a surprise back at my house. But don't worry, Rose. My parents will be home. I'll leave my bedroom door open. . . ." He falters, embarrassed at the implications of this.

"I trust you, Nils," I say.

Is it possible that only a handful of nights ago I was driving with Theo on roads not so far from here? Is it possible that I can sit in the front seat now, but not then? Is it possible that I can drive to Nils's house, go into his bedroom, and no one will think the worse of me, not even Dad?

It's more than possible. It's the way things are.

And really, truly, Nils in the driver's seat and me riding beside him feels very much like the way things should be. Julia would certainly think so. This past Thursday night, I met her at Marshall Field's on State Street, and we looked at wedding dresses. I asked Julia all the right questions, and she talked on and on about her plans with Paul as we oohed and aahed over the different styles on display in the Bridal Salon. She tried on her favorites then. We determined that these sleeves best suited her, this neckline, and this fabric, train, and veil, and I realized that my mouth was literally watering with desire for a wedding dress of my own someday. In that mirrored fitting room, I wanted Julia's life. Afterward, we agreed we were hungry (so *that's* why my mouth watered, I told myself). We treated ourselves to hot fudge sundaes in the Walnut Room. Beside the burbling fountain there, I told Julia about tonight's date with Nils. It was her turn to ply me with questions then, and as I answered them, a future with Nils became even clearer in my mind. "If it weren't for Paul, Nils would be my top pick," Julia said. I bridled a bit at that. "Oh, I think Nils trumps Paul any day," I said. "Just joking, Julia!" I added quickly. But I wasn't. I'm not. Nils does trump Paul.

His house, a little brick bungalow, is in close proximity to our apartment. He parks in the alley and opens the car door for me. I get out. I take one last look at the stars, which are shining tonight with surprising clarity, for once not overshadowed by the city lights.

I can't think of a wish that is worth trying for, beyond my wish to let this night continue to be a nice one. So I wish for that. And I follow Nils inside.

From the entryway, I can see Nils's mother and father in the living room, hunkered down in chairs on either side of a radio.

"They just brought it home," Nils whispers to me. "They've been saving for it for longer than you can imagine."

"Oh, I can imagine," I whisper back.

Mrs. Hoirus presses her finger to her lips as Nils and I step into the room.

"Dear Lord," a man says.

Nils's father raises his hand in a military salute to greet us. A veteran of World War I like Dad, Mr. Hoirus's salute is his standard greeting. But Mr. Hoirus isn't the one calling on the Lord.

"On this Saturday night, we come together to worship you."

Nils's parents are listening to a church service on their new radio. It's a big model in a wooden case, and I can make out the numbers on the glowing dial. They're listening to WMBI, Moody's radio station. Nils and I wait, heads bowed, until the congregation choruses amen. Then Nils points down the hallway toward where his bedroom must be. "Be right back," he says quietly, so as not to interrupt his parents' listening. Mrs. Hoirus nods; Mr. Hoirus issues another salute. Nils has never been the kind of son to trouble his parents.

We're walking down the hallway when I hear another voice, this time reading a passage from the first chapter of Mark. This voice stops me in my tracks.

"'Behold, I send my messenger before thy face, which shall prepare thy way before thee.'"

"Andreas!" I'd know my brother's voice anywhere, of course, but it's the fervor undergirding his words that has stopped me in midstep. It's still hard for me to believe that this passionate, committed, deep voice belongs to my brother, once a shy, soft-spoken boy given to daydreams.

"'Prepare ye the way of the Lord, make his paths straight,'" Andreas reads.

"That's Rose's brother!" Nils calls to his parents. "Can you believe it?"

"Really?" Mrs. Hoirus hoots, giving a little clap of her hands. "Andreas on Moody Radio! How on earth did he get the chance?"

Nils beckons me back into the living room. Mr. and Mrs. Hoirus don't turn down the volume on the radio, so I have to raise my voice to explain that Andreas has read Scripture on the air at this service one other time, too.

"Such an honor," Mrs. Hoirus says.

I nod. "I just hope he remembered to tell Mother and Dad that he was reading. Last time he forgot."

"He's preaching in church tomorrow, isn't he?" Mr. Hoirus asks.

"I think so." I remember now. I did overhear Andreas telling Mother and Dad about this. And I'm singing, too, I realize. I still haven't chosen my song.

"We'll have to make sure and go early to get a good seat," Mrs. Hoirus says.

She and her husband are leaning toward the radio again. Someone else is speaking now. Nils leads me back to the hallway and to his room. He flicks on the light and I stand in the doorway, blinking. I don't know what I was expecting to see, but it sure wasn't this.

The walls of Nils's room are covered with insects. Framed wooden boxes that contain rows upon rows of exotic butterflies, spiders, beetles, and other bugs—winged and wingless. I've never seen the like of most of them before.

Nils grins. "I love surprising people like this."

"I'm surprised, that's for sure." I almost expect the butterflies to flap their glorious, iridescent wings, equally startled. Without thinking, I sit down on Nils's narrow single bed, then quickly stand up again. "Where did you get all these—what do you call them? Specimens?"

"I call them wondrous." Nils's grin widens. "Guess where they came from."

"I can't."

"Try."

I walk over to a wall and peer at the hairy body of a tarantula bigger than my hand, bigger than Nils's hands, bigger than Theo's, even. The tarantula is the size of a dinner plate.

"You traveled the globe without anyone knowing."

Nils laughs. "Now, when would I do that? And why, when the globe comes to me?"

I turn to a many-legged insect nearly as long as a ruler. "So how?" I shiver. "Where?"

"There are benefits to my job besides a paycheck."

"Benefits?"

"You've never unpacked a crate of bananas, have you?"

I turn to Nils. "You found these at the National Tea? Oh, my heavens. I'll never walk through those doors again."

"Don't worry. I comb through the produce so carefully there's not a chance that one of these fellows makes it from the packing crate to the floor. You see this one?" Nils strides over to a rust-colored beetle with ferocious-looking pincers. "He crawled out of a bunch of grapes. I'm not kidding." He adjusts the frame, moves to the next display. "I keep glass jars and a bottle of formaldehyde in the back room at work so I can capture my finds before they suffer damage or perish in the cold. Just this past fall, I started tracking the delivery trucks so I could be even better prepared when they arrive, and that led me to the trains pulling into the yards from Central and South America. The engineers and dock workers got to know me, and next thing I knew, they were letting me have free rein of the freight cars. Some of the fellows down there have even started saving specimens for me. At the oddest hours, that's where you'll find me, scouring crates and barrels for beauties like these." He taps the glass sheltering a luminous green moth, and adjusts this frame as well. "I guess you could say this is my passion."

"I guess so."

"Truth is, I always wanted to be a scientist. If I could do anything in the world, I'd be a lepidopterist. I'd study moths and butterflies." Nils is quiet for a moment, gazing at the beautiful creature. Then he turns resolutely toward me. "But that's just a passion, of course, and passion won't put a roof over your head." He shrugs. "We do what we have to, right? And when we can, if we can, we find ways to do what we want."

Nils reminds me of Dad, and Mother, too, working so hard to get ahead, stay afloat, survive. And Nils reminds me of myself as well, doing what I have to, not what I want.

Nils might be able to spend the rest of his life like this. But can I?

TEN

Last night's Scripture reading has influenced Andreas's message this morning.

"John the Baptist might seek refuge at the Pacific Garden Mission today. Then again, Jesus might be found there, too."

A framed painted portrait of Jesus hangs on the wall behind the pulpit where Andreas stands. This Jesus has long, radiant hair and a serene, sad expression. His fair skin is smooth and clean. He doesn't look at all like the type who'd wind up at a mission.

Andreas's suggestion makes me a little uncomfortable, truth be told. I'd venture to say that more than a few other members of the congregation feel the same. Nils, for instance, sitting with his parents across the aisle from me. What strange specimen is this? Nils seems to wonder, leaning forward, scrutinizing my brother.

If Andreas senses the scrutiny, he ignores it. He says that we live in fear of the John the Baptists in our midst, the John the Baptist in ourselves. "We must cast aside our fear as Jesus cast out demons," Andreas says.

Something tickles my back, startling me. Thank goodness Mother is holding Sophy today, or I would have jostled her mightily. I turn around. Rob stands behind me, impishly grinning, wiggling his fingers near my throat now. And who but Dolores Pine stands by Rob's side. Dolores is dressed in a prim blue cotton dress that's stiff with starch. A long black coat drapes her shoulders. A dusty black hat with the wide brim that was so popular balances precariously on her head. Dolores must not go to church much, if at all, if she thinks she has to dress like someone's grandmother in order to be welcome here. I hold out my hand to her, and she grabs it like a lifeline, clutching my fingers so tightly that my knuckles grind together. Her mouth twitches in a nervous smile. She wears no makeup, and her freckles seem to float on the milky surface of her pale skin.

Andreas says, "Maybe it's time we examine our fears, so we can prepare the way for Jesus."

"Time you examined your fears, Laerke," Rob whispers in my ear.

Dolores lets go of my hand and slides into the pew beside me; Rob follows her. Mother nods hello. Sophy cranes her neck to see what's happening. Spittle has collected at the corners of Sophy's mouth, but Dolores doesn't seem to be put off. She gives Sophy a little wave as I clean her mouth with a handkerchief. Sophy blinks hard at Dolores, her way of waving back.

"'Like a voice crying in the wilderness'—a John the Baptist voice. This is the voice for which we need to listen. We need to stop running away from the blessed voices in the wilderness all around us."

Dolores fishes a pencil from her pocketbook. She scribbles on her bulletin, shows it to me.

Your brother?

I nod.

She scribbles some more.

Rob said he was a wonderful preacher.

I nod again. She scribbles again.

I've never been to a Protestant church. (Raised Catholic.) Glad I came.

I take the pencil and the bulletin and, careful not to bump Sophy, I surreptitiously tuck the bulletin down on the pew between Dolores and me. I write in tiny, cramped letters so Mother can't see: *How did you get here?*

Dolores's turn.

Rob invited me. He took your advice on Tuesday night and had a little nap in the car. I must have dozed off, too. Whoops! Our woozy ride home turned into breakfast at a diner. Drank lots of coffee. Talked lots. Subject of church came up. Rob's no saint, but that doesn't mean he isn't concerned for sinners like me.

Dolores smiles drolly, then sits back against the pew and listens to the rest of Andreas's sermon. Soon she's as caught up in what my brother is saying as the rest of us. When Andreas says, "Amen," Dolores chimes in immediately and loudly, "Amen!" She blushes prettily as she realizes we are not that kind of church. But Andreas nods in her direction.

"'A voice in the wilderness,'" Andreas says. "It startles us, shakes us up, wakes us up. Just like this young lady's 'Amen.'" Dolores stares at him, her eyes widening as he raises his hands. "Let's try it, brothers and sisters. Try it with me. Echo that life-changing voice. Lift up your amen!"

A few of us, Dolores and myself included, haltingly lift up our amens. Rob turns and gives Dolores a smirk, but she doesn't see. Amen said, she is absorbed in the work of her hands now. Her fingers are quivering as if her nervousness hasn't abated in the least, but still she manages to fold a delicate paper bird out of a page from the bulletin. Leaning across me, she flutters the bird before Sophy's eyes. When Sophy smiles, Dolores perches the bird on Sophy's lap. The folds of Sophy's dress make a nest for the little paper thing, and Sophy kisses the air.

It is the offertory now, and though I have been fretting all morning, still unsure of my song, I know in this moment exactly what I'm going to sing.

I take one last look at the little paper bird in the nest of Sophy's dress, walk to the front of the sanctuary, stand before the congregation, and close my eyes.

> *Come Holy Spirit, heavenly Dove,*
> *With all Thy quickening powers,*
> *Kindle a flame of sacred love*
> *In these cold hearts of ours.*

At coffee hour, Mother, Sophy, and Andreas talk with Rob and Dolores in one corner of the church basement while Nils guides me to another. "Wonderful singing," he says. "You're by far my favorite soloist."

I'm about to murmur my thanks, but he's caught my hands in his. "Guess what?" he exclaims. And then he's telling me about a phone call he received early this morning from the train yards. An engineer found a tarantula even bigger than the one Nils has in his collection. "Mammoth" is how Nils describes the spider. He's going down to the yards today to collect it.

"You want to come along for the ride?" Nils asks. "I'll buy you lunch."

"Lunch sounds nice. A ride, too. But do I have to touch the thing?"

"Wouldn't let it near you."

I laugh. "Are you protecting me from it or it from me?"

"What do you think?" Nils flicks his eyebrows, teasing as he used to when we were kids.

"That's not a proper answer!"

Before Nils can supply one, Rob strides up to us. Rob is wearing his nice suit again, and the gray-green tie that matches his eyes. He'd look quite dandy, except that a shirt button has popped open at his belly. I reach out to button it, but Rob bats my hands away, and sheepishly does it himself.

"Wonder how long it's been like that." He snaps his jacket into place. "Better?"

I nod.

"Good." Rob glances over his shoulder at Dolores, who is talking quietly with Andreas now. When Rob turns back to me, there's the sheen of perspiration on his upper lip. He likes Dolores, I realize. I'm glad there's someone new in his life that he seems to really care about. It may mean his grief is lessening, and if his grief lessens, he may stop drinking so much.

"Listen, Rose," Rob says quietly, "Dolores and I are coming over to your place for lunch. Your mom just invited us. But Dolores will feel uncomfortable without you, she says. In fact, she's asked that I take her home if you're not there." Rob grasps my hands in passionate appeal. "Please, Rose, don't tell Dolores I told you this, but something about Andreas really makes her skittish, and Andreas will be at lunch, too." Rob lowers his voice and leans close so only I can hear. "I think my mom will like her, Rose. And if my dad were here, I think he'd approve, too. She's a little wild, sure, but she doesn't want to stay that way. We've got that in common, and a lot more."

I can't imagine Rob's parents would approve of a girl he met at a bar—a Catholic girl, at that. But Rob seems so smitten that I don't say this.

"I'm sorry, but Nils just invited me to lunch," I say instead. When Rob frowns, I explain more about Nils's invitation, hoping that a trip to the train yards will appeal to Rob's sense of adventure. But at the word "tarantula," Rob rolls his eyes.

"Please. A spider?"

"*Tarantula*," Nils says.

Rob gives an exasperated sigh. "There will be other spiders, Rose. Nils, take a rain check, will you? Please? Just this once?"

"Well. If it's that important." Nils gives me a long look. "I guess it would be pretty unfair if I had you all to myself two times in twenty-four hours." He casts Rob a sideways glance. "And, yes, there will be other *spiders*."

Rob slaps Nils hard on the back. "Thank you! Knew I could count on you, buddy."

Nils shakes his head. "Rose is the person you really should thank, Rob."

I could just about hug Nils for saying that, but of course we're surrounded by other members of the Danish Baptist Church. So I ask him to call when he can and tell me about his new specimen instead.

—⁓∾⁓—

On the way home, Mother tells me that we are going to be busy next weekend, helping with Zane Nygaard's birthday celebration. We'll spend much of Friday and Saturday in Hyde Park, cleaning the Nygaards' house, and serving at the party as well. Mother studies her swollen knuckles. She picks at the raw skin around her cracked nails. Her long, lost hope, never realized, was to be a name on the Nygaards' guest list. She probably never dreamed she'd be cleaning and serving for their guests instead. "Oh, well," Mother says, tucking her hands into her coat sleeves. "We'll have our own little celebration today."

Lunch proves delicious—*farsbrød*, with a dill sauce ladled over the meat loaf. Nils, Mother tells me on the sly, was generous again last time she went shopping, this time tucking a package of dried dill into her bag. She asked him to come to lunch today, too, but he already had other plans. *A date with a tarantula*, I think, smiling.

The meal tastes almost like old times, and the conversation is almost like old times, too, with all of us chiming in, sharing stories. All of us except Dad and Andreas, that is. As usual, Dad is solely focused on his food and his thoughts. Andreas is silent, too, closely watching Dolores, probably assessing her potential for evangelism.

The conversation takes a new turn when Dolores asks about our neighborhood. Dad glowers at his food. Andreas assesses. Mother stays quiet, too. *(If you can't think of anything nice to say, don't say anything at all.)* It's up to Rob and me to find something nice to say. We describe the beauty of Garfield Park. "We must go there!" Rob says, and Dolores says she'd like that—perhaps some Saturday when she's not working. She's working a lot these days, she explains. As a new nurse, she has to take the shifts nobody wants, and cover for other nurses when they're home sick or taking a holiday. She's working a lot of overtime, too, just to scrape together a little extra change.

"What about your family?" Andreas asks abruptly.

Dolores pushes a potato around on her plate. When she finally looks up at Andreas, she is as sober as I've ever seen her. "My mother is dead. My father is a drunk. My brother is off I don't know where. I'm on my own. I rent a room at the YWCA. I pay my own way in life, thank you very much."

Andreas is the first one to break the quiet. "Sounds hard. And lonely." His voice is low and compassionate, and to my surprise, tears brim in Dolores's eyes.

"It is."

"But you make the best of it, don't you?" Rob says brightly. Dolores blinks away her tears, and then falteringly agrees that she does.

"And with all the hours I'm working, I'm finally able to get a thing or two I've needed for a very long time." She smiles shyly. "I'd been wearing the same gloves for so many years, there were holes in nearly every finger. Just last week I went to Field's and bought myself a new pair. They were a floor sample, a little the worse for wear. But with that and the sale, I got them nearly for free."

Mother sighs. "I've not been to Field's in so long. Is it still the same?"

To Mother's delight, Dolores describes recent renovations to the store.

Mother chimes in then, talking about the frequent trips we used to make there. "I loved to look at all the beautiful things—the displays, the Tiffany glass ceiling. And lunches in the Walnut

Room with Rose and Sophy. Those were some of my favorite times." Mother's face brightens with a new memory. "And speaking of gloves—one particular day, I was wandering through Accessories, and I was smitten with a pair of lace gloves from Belgium. They were as delicate and dainty as anything I'd ever seen. I asked if I could try them on, and the clerk couldn't hide her disdain. 'But, my dear,' the clerk said, 'those gloves are *imported*.' Well, I didn't miss a beat. 'But, my dear,' I said, 'so am *I*.' I didn't even bother to try on the gloves then. I simply bought them. I could do that kind of thing then." Mother gives a pained laugh. "I've still got those gloves tucked away somewhere. I'm saving them for something special someday, for myself or Rose or Sophy."

For a moment no one says a word, then Dad roughly pushes back his chair. "Enough of this talk," he says, and mutters something about second helpings.

So second helpings work their way around the table. We eat and chat about other things, until finally everyone's napkins are folded and laid carefully beside their plates. We are evaluating the cleanup when Andreas suddenly leans forward.

"You haven't told us yet, Dolores. How did you meet Rob?"

"And Rose!" Dolores says. "She was there, too!"

I go stone still. Rob levels Dolores a look. Dolores snaps her mouth shut. Her eyes dart from Rob to me, then back to Rob. He must have warned her not to breathe a word about Calliope's in my family's presence.

"You tell, Rob." Dolores sounds panic-stricken. Andreas gives her a close look, as does Dad. "I'd love to hear your version, Dolores," Mother says quietly.

Dolores stares at Rob, her eyes wide with appeal. "Go on, Rob."

I feel sick. All this delicious food is going to come right back up again. I take a sip of water. Barely able to swallow, I give an audible gulp.

"Well, let's see." Rob runs his thumbs between his plump stomach and his straining belt. His lips are drawn into a thin, tight line. I remind myself that Rob loves a challenge, especially if there's risk involved. He takes pleasure in convincing people that he's right. No wonder he wants to be a lawyer. Oh, please let him present a convincing case now.

"How can I say this?" Rob clears his throat. "I guess I'll just say it. Rose and I met Dolores under questionable circumstances."

"Pardon?" Mother says.

Dolores sinks down in her chair. I clutch my stomach.

"Tell!" Sophy says.

"Patience." Rob gives Sophy the gentlest of reprimanding looks. "Rose and I went out to a jazz club, truth be told. That's where we met Dolores."

Dad stands abruptly, knocking over his chair. I hear my voice as if from a great distance, saying Rob's name as a question. And then: "What are you saying?"

Ignoring me, Rob gives my parents his most charming smile. "I haven't always been the most convicted of Christians, I know. Not like Andreas here. But Rose and I were talking, and we both felt like we needed to see how sinners live, what their temptations are, in order to better share the Gospel. So we went to a club. We learned a lot."

At this point, good manners are the least of my worries. I rest my elbows on the table, hide my face behind my hands. My forehead is slick with cold sweat. For a moment, no one says a word. The only sound is my stomach churning.

Rob clears his throat. "Andreas, you were talking about this to me just the other day—the fact that our methods of evangelism often fall flat because we don't really understand how others live, their loves and habits. In fact, you were saying something like that in today's sermon, weren't you? All that about John the Baptist at the Pacific Garden Mission. And Jesus, too. Isn't that what you were saying, Andreas?"

Before Andreas can deny or confirm anything, Dad says, "That's a bunch of hogwash."

Dolores gives a high, nervous laugh. "It worked, though, Mr. Sorensen. I'm Exhibit A. If Rob and Rose hadn't come to the club, I never would have come to church, heard Andreas preach, and shared in this delicious meal." She leaps to her feet. "Now let me do something for you. I'll clean up the kitchen."

"Sit down." This is not a polite invitation from Dad. This is an order.

Dolores sits down.

Dad stands up. His hand is on my arm, near my wrist. I can't think of the last time he touched me. I try to remember. Which is why it takes me a moment to realize that he's holding on too tight. I look up at him. His eyes are dark with rage.

"Dad," Andreas says.

"Jacob," Mother says.

"Uncle Jacob." That's Rob.

Sophy hisses no.

Dad doesn't look at anybody but me. "You should know better."

Someone says something I can't make out. I think it's Rob, but I don't know for sure, because the room has tunneled to the darkness of Dad's eyes.

"Men sow their wild oats," Dad says, in answer to whatever someone—Rob?—just said. "Women become tramps."

That's not what happened to me. Not at all.

I can't be looked at this way anymore. This look will snuff out the little light that is me. I turn my head away from my father, and he does something with his hand on my arm. I hear a yelp. The yelp came from me.

Sophy hisses. She hisses louder, and louder yet, until finally Dad releases me. Where his hand was aches. I hear his quick footsteps on the floor. Then the kitchen door swings open and bangs closed.

"He's gone," Dolores whispers in my ear.

I look up. Mother, Rob, Sophy, and Andreas are staring, stricken, at the remnants of our lunch—the crumbled bits of meat, hunks of potato, shreds of carrot on our plates, the congealing grease and sharp flecks of seasoning on the platters.

That's not what happened to me.

I stand and run from the kitchen. There are my coat and pocketbook, lying on my bed. I put on my coat, grab my pocketbook, head to the front door.

"Rose! Where are you going?" Mother calls from the kitchen.

I don't answer. I hear Rob say that I must be going after Dad. I must be going to explain.

Let them think that.

I open the door and run down the stairs.

ELEVEN

Head bowed against the cold, I run toward the only place I can think to go. I run to Garfield Park and take shelter in the Conservatory. Clutching my aching arm, barely seeing the lush plants and trees, I wander from glass room to glass room until I find myself standing at the edge of a pool. Pennies glitter at the bottom.

There's a penny lying on the walk beside my feet. I pick it up and throw it into the pond with a wish that splits itself in two and refracts with the ripples in the water.

I wish I could sing. I wish I could talk to Theo.

I remember then. Theo wrote his phone number on the bulletin for the African Methodist Church. I put that bulletin in my pocketbook. I'm carrying that pocketbook now.

I don't know Nils's number. That's why I'm not calling him. That's why. And the fact that Dad would want me to do that, given the choice. Dad would expect me to do that. Dad knows me so well.

Men sow their wild oats. Women become tramps.

But that's not what happened to me—not Friday or Tuesday night. And it didn't happen last Sunday, either. (Was it only a week ago today?) When Theo heard me singing and found me on my knees, he was only a gentleman and I was only a lady. Together, we were only doing a job.

I push up the sleeve of my coat and there is the shape of Dad's hand, darkening as a bruise. His fingers wrapped around my arm. His palm pressed down. Dad knows me well, all right. He knows me right down to the bone.

I consider the Danish Baptist way. The oldest daughter, big sister way. The Rose Sorensen way.

I take a detour off the only way I've ever known and find myself back at the entrance to the Conservatory. The entrance feels arctic after the tropical warmth of the Conservatory's inner rooms. The cold air settles on me like a weight. Far weightier is the truth, which is what I will live for from now on, never mind where it takes me.

There is a pay phone in the corner of the entrance. I go to it. I fumble with the clasp on my pocketbook, dig inside its cluttered depths. Beneath three handkerchiefs—because of Sophy, I always carry more than one—a comb, bobby pins, and barrettes, and a small jar of Vaseline, I find my coin purse and the bulletin from Theo's church. I take out a nickel, lift the phone's earpiece, plug the nickel into the phone, dial the numbers on the bulletin, and listen to the ringing at the other end of the line.

A girl answers. "Hello?"

I stare at the phone as if the machine itself had just spoken.

From behind me, a man clears his throat so loudly that I jump. I glance over my shoulder. The man is waiting none too patiently to use the phone. He twirls a finger in the air: *Come on, speed it up.*

"Is this the Chastain residence?"

The girl, who has a soft, southern accent, says it is.

"Is Theo Chastain available?"

"One moment, please."

A clunk as she sets the receiver down, then the sound of her feet pattering off to some distant part of where Theo lives. A murmured exchange. More footsteps, heavier this time. Theo's footsteps.

I can hear my heart beating, the blood surging in my ears.

"Hello?"

Why did I never notice that Theo has a southern accent, too? Perhaps it grows stronger when he is in his own home, among his own people? Rob once told me that many of Chicago's best musicians traveled up the Mississippi River from New Orleans to Chicago. I wonder if this is true of Theo. There is so much I want to ask him, so much I want to know. I want to know his truth.

"It's Rose," I say.

Silence. He doesn't remember me, or he doesn't remember my name. Either way, he doesn't remember.

I swallow the pride, or whatever the emotion is, knotted in my throat. "Rose Sorensen. The girl you found cleaning. You drove me home last Tuesday night after—"

"Rose. I know who you are."

Worse, he remembers me and he wishes he didn't. At least that's what his clipped tone suggests.

How foolish to call him. How pushy. How unladylike. *Men sow their wild oats. Women become tramps.*

The man behind me harrumphs again. It's time for me to hang up.

But Theo asks if I'm all right before I can. His voice cracks with worry.

I say that I'm all right, though I'm not, not at all.

"Don't misunderstand. I'm glad you called. But . . ." Theo sucks in a breath. "To heck with this. Where are you, Rose?"

I tell him.

"Stay put. I'm coming to get you."

He says it shouldn't take him more than twenty minutes to drive to where I am. I should stay inside the Conservatory, where it is warm. He'll find me.

He finds me where it is warm, sitting on a stone bench nestled in ferns.

Snow has started to fall. I am watching it sweep and swirl across the peaked glass roof arching above when I hear his footsteps sound against the stone path that winds ever closer. A burbling stream of water interrupts the path, and now I hear Theo hesitate as he judges the distance between stepping-stones. He crosses the stream in a leap. I could never make that jump; his legs are so much longer than mine. But if Theo took my hand I would be less uneasy navigating the stones.

This is what I am thinking as he rounds the bend in the path to where I am, where we are.

Abruptly, he stops walking. We consider each other. This glass room, with the storm whirling all around, suddenly seems a snow globe—a whole world containing just us two. Too quick a gesture, a slip or a sharp word, and our world might shatter.

"You found me."

Theo nods. He is bareheaded. His black hair glistens wetly where the snow has melted. The shoulders of his long gray coat are wet with melted snow, too. The toes of his galoshes stained with salt.

He made his way through worsening weather to me.

He puts his hand to his hair and looks at his wet palm. "I left so quickly, I forgot my hat." He blinks as if dazed. "I never go out without a hat."

My own hat lies on the bench beside me. I pick it up, but Theo doesn't sit down.

Others are coming down the path toward us. They round the bend—a man and a woman. A white man, a white woman, holding hands. Holding hands, they must have stepped on stones to cross the stream. The man, who wears a hat (though in this warm room, sweat has started to bead on his forehead and upper lip), warily regards Theo.

Theo turns his back on me and takes a few steps down the path. He bends over a silvery fern. Gently, he lifts the fronds and examines them. He seems to be contrasting the plant's upper surface with its hidden underside. If I didn't know better, I'd think Theo was a botanist, doing a bit of field study on a Sunday afternoon. Perhaps he does have an interest in botany, as Nils has an interest in insects. Another question to ask.

The woman, who is wearing a rust-colored coat with a fox-fur collar, has drawn closer to her companion. Now she clutches her companion's arm and whispers into his ear. The man frowns, nods. He turns his wary gaze on me.

"Everything all right here, miss?"

Theo combs his fingers between the fern's fronds. He could be soothing the plant. Or saying good-bye to it, to me. For now he moves farther away down the winding path.

"Yes." I sound irritated. I'm not. I'm nearly breathless with panic. Theo could keep winding away from me, winding his way to wherever he came from, leaving me behind.

"Hon, you're sure you're okay?" The woman asks this in a hushed voice, the voice of a confidante. *We are women. We are white. You can tell me.* She lifts her hand—the hand that is not clutching the man's arm—and touches her fur collar. I see the fox's little head now. Its pointed snout and the glittering black beads of its eyes. She pets it. "You're not being . . . bothered?"

"Not at all." I muster a sickly smile.

The couple moves on, each glancing back—ever wary—once they are safely on the other side of Theo, who is bowed over some other low-growing plant now. No, the couple isn't wary. They are tight-lipped with anger. This anger isn't about little old me. It's about them. I sense this from the way they put their heads together as they walk, from their offended whispering, pitched just loud enough to be overheard. *You never know. . . . Things aren't what they used to be. . . . All kinds . . .*

Not a month ago I would have appreciated the couple's concern for me, even their anger at who is increasingly able to go where. I would have found it comforting. I would have mentioned it to Mother, maybe even to Dad, as a sign that it really is all right for me to go out on my own. This may not be Oak Park, but even here in this neighborhood people will watch out for me. There's a reason why angels are so often strangers in the Bible. There are angel-strangers all around us, even here. I would have said these things in defense of my own freedom.

Then again, until recently I wasn't thinking about my freedom, or lack thereof. I'd never climbed down a fire escape, escaped into the night, heard music like I've heard, called a man who wasn't my cousin or brother or father on the phone, called a black man.

"Theo."

He still has his back to me. His hands hover over the plants as if they are instruments he'd like to play. But he doesn't touch them. Perhaps he thinks they are too delicate for his touch. I don't agree. His hands only make things more beautiful.

I am standing just behind him now. I don't remember walking up to him, but I don't let that worry me. I watch his bowed back rise and fall with his breath. His breathing quickens; he must know that I'm close. Or someone is. Still, he doesn't turn around.

"Let's go." My whispered words are barely audible. I don't touch Theo to make sure he's heard. I don't hold his hand or clutch his arm. I am not the woman in the fox-fur collar and he is not the man in the hat. We are not that couple. We are not a couple. We are us. I whisper again into the swatch of wool between his shoulder blades. I whisper straight to his heart. I whisper the truth. "I'll follow you. I'll keep a safe distance."

He leads me down the winding path. And then we're outside, walking through the cold and the falling, drifting snow. A safe distance separates us. When we reach his car, I know just what to do. I get into the backseat. He uses his coat sleeve to brush snow from the windshield, then he opens the front door and sits down behind the steering wheel. He drives us slowly through the storm, past coffee shops and restaurants and bars. Some of these are open in spite of the weather. We could duck inside a coffee shop, drink something hot, maybe share a piece of pie, warm up a bit, talk. I could ask him all the questions I want to ask—*Are you from New Orleans? Are you interested in botany? What were you like when you were a little boy?* If we weren't who we are.

As it is, we don't even mention the possibility of stopping.

For a long time, we don't say a word. Finally I remember that not all cafés and restaurants look the same.

"We're driving in circles."

"I don't know where to go."

Theo sounds lost, almost frightened, like he's spent his life running and now he finds himself cornered.

What I've always felt for Sophy, and only for Sophy—fiercely protective—suddenly stirs inside me for him. There's nothing logical about this feeling. It's pure, hot emotion, a sharp contrast to the cold snow falling thickly all around. The streets and sidewalks are blanketed in white. There, at the end of the block, is a coffee shop we've passed three times already. As we approach it now, a waitress in a pink uniform walks to the door. Theo slows the car as if he's actually considering the possibility that we might be welcome there. But the waitress flips the sign from *Open* to *Closed*. The lights inside flicker and dim. She disappears into the kitchen, and now the place is dark and empty.

The streets and sidewalks are empty, too, except for the rising drifts. There is no one to blame, no one to do battle with, because everyone knows the only place to be on a night like this is home.

"Let's go home," I say.

Theo slows the car and glances swiftly over his shoulder, his eyes wide with surprise. "Your folks wouldn't mind having me?"

I look at him. He knows the answer. His eyes narrow under the weight of it—the truth, cold and hard. Quickly, he turns his gaze on the road again, as he should in these conditions. We pick up a little speed until the car shimmies on a patch of ice, and then we slow down. Everywhere now the signs read *Closed*. The world goes whiter as I wait for him to come to the only possible conclusion.

After a few more slow trips around the block, he finally does.

"My mother cooks a fine Sunday supper. You'd be welcome."

I accept his kind invitation.

A feast. That's what Mrs. Chastain has prepared. The round table in the center of the kitchen seems to strain beneath the weight of steaming platters of fried chicken and corn bread, surrounded by bowls heaped with green beans, baked beans, and a white porridge that Theo calls grits. My mouth waters at the sweet and smoky smell. How can I be so hungry after the big meal Mother served? The cold can do that, I guess. I press my hands to my stomach to keep it from growling. Doesn't work. Theo looks at me and smiles.

He's been smiling since we arrived here, bolstering me with encouraging looks. The whole long, snowy drive—nearly an hour it took us—we barely spoke. He seemed to be concentrating on the roads and the weather; I didn't want to distract him. The roads were practically empty, thank goodness. As the car skidded from one lane to the other, so did my mind from one thought to the next. *I am here in a storm because of Dad—those things he said, this ache on my arm. Theo is here because of me. Here we are together, braving this cold night. There is no going home, not for me, not with him. I can only be a guest now. A guest in Theo's home and, because of Dad, a guest in my own.* Just when the quiet seemed unbearable, unbroken only by the sound of the tires against the road, the windshield wipers against the glass, the tumult in my mind, Theo began to whistle. He seemed to be whistling against the storm, against every unpredictable danger. The high, bright sound, as lilting as any flute, saw us safely to a narrow Bronzeville street crowded with six flats. Still whistling, Theo parked before one of these, turned off the engine, got out of the car. Even as he came to open my door, my heart sank. I might be willing to be a guest here, but would they be willing to have me? The sidewalk was icy, the snow thick. In spite of Theo's whistling and his hand at my elbow, steadying me, the way was hard.

It didn't get easier. Not immediately.

Theo's sister opened the door to the first-floor flat. At the sight of me, her hand flew to her mouth. A moment later, she lowered her hand and, in that soft southern voice that I first heard over the phone, introduced herself as Mary. Then she ran down the hall to warn the rest of the family of my arrival. I know she warned them, because when Theo introduced me, each and every person—his three cousins, his uncle, aunt, and grandmother, all visiting for the day—was as composed as if I'd been expected.

When Theo took me to the kitchen to meet his mother, Mrs. Chastain was composed as well. She was a wide wall of composure. I had to hand it to her—hand it to all the Chastains. If Theo, or Mary, or the three cousins, uncle, aunt, grandmother, or Mrs. Chastain, for that matter, had showed up without warning at my family's apartment, my family would have been anything but composed.

"My, my." Mrs. Chastain smoothed her green plaid apron over her dark green dress. "Who do we have here?"

Spruce tree, I thought, taking her in, and her voice made me think of the spring-fed lake tucked deep in the spruce woods that border Aunt Astrid's farm. The lake's surface was always completely calm; I could only imagine all that was going on in the depths beyond my understanding.

Theo told his mother my name. And then: "She's the singer, Mama."

I'm the singer.

"Well, then." A slow smile softened Mrs. Chastain's expression. Her gray hair was pulled back into a bun—a spruce touched with frost—and as she nodded, the bun bobbed. "Perhaps we'll have some music later."

I took a deep breath and held out my hand to Mrs. Chastain. I intended to say "Nice to meet you," or some such thing. But "Thank you" is what came out.

"Why, you're welcome." Mrs. Chastain took my hand in hers. "Goodness." She rubbed my skin briskly. Her strong, calloused fingers came near the bruise but never touched it, for which I was grateful. "Theo, is the heater out on the car again? Child might as well be made of ice."

Suddenly she went still. She'd seen the bruise, and from his quick intake of breath, so had Theo.

"Some ice, please, son." Releasing my right hand and taking my left, Mrs. Chastain nodded toward the icebox. "I'm sorry, Rose, I know you're cold, but it still might help."

Theo got busy at the icebox. With a pick, he chipped away at the block of ice, filled a tea towel with bits and pieces, folded the towel. Then, with his mother's help, he wrapped the towel around what ached. The frigid cold seeped into the bruise, down to the bone.

Now the towel has been set aside, the ache has lessened, and my way with this family is nearly easy. We are finally seated in a tight circle around the food-laden table. Theo gives me another smile, then bows his head as his uncle prays a long blessing over our repast. At amen, Mrs. Chastain starts the passing of bowls and platters.

Every taste is new to me, and as good as it looks and smells. Better. I clean my plate. When the food is passed again, I take seconds. It's only when I've eaten the last bite of this helping, and I'm as full as I've ever been, that I realize I haven't said a word. I haven't really been listening to the conversation, either, though it's been going on all around me, along with much laughter. I glance around, wondering if anyone has noticed my silence. Mrs. Chastain nods approvingly.

"Full up?" she asks.

"Yes, thank you. It was all so—"

I belch. I clamp my mouth shut, embarrassed. No, mortified.

But everyone is laughing, and Theo is laughing hardest of all. He mops his eyes with his napkin and laughs harder. I can't help but laugh, too.

Suddenly Theo pushes back his chair. "Mama, leave the dishes. I'll do them later, I promise."

I follow Theo and his family into the front room. There, Theo sits down at a battered upright piano, and the rest of us gather around. Mary is beside me. She must be about Sophy's age, I realize, what with the way she's clearly not a girl anymore, but not quite a woman, either. She is going to be a beauty, that's clear. She already is, with her honey-colored skin and her golden brown eyes, her slim figure and soft curves. She has Theo's elegance and dignity, which is their mother's elegance and dignity. I smile at Mary. Instead of covering her hand with her mouth, she smiles back.

Theo plays a few chords. The piano is terribly out of tune, but Theo's touch brings out a jangly beauty. He's playing "Take My Hand, Precious Lord," Mahalia Jackson's song.

Theo's uncle throws back his head and lets loose singing, the cousins join in, the aunt and grandmother, and finally Mrs. Chastain and Mary, too. Mary sways in perfect time to the slow, steady rhythm that Theo has set. She slips her arm through mine, and I sway, too. I'm being rocked; that's how it feels. I'm being cradled by this hymn. I close my eyes and join in the singing.

Theo is playing the last note of the last verse when I realize how quiet the room has become. My voice is the only voice I hear. I open my eyes. Theo's cousins, his uncle, aunt, and grandmother—they're all watching me. Mrs. Chastain's hands are steepled at her lips. She seems to be praying. And Mary—well, Mary is still rocking, as am I.

"I'm sorry," I say.

Theo looks at me. "For?"

"Singing."

Mary stops rocking.

Mrs. Chastain opens her eyes and regards me. "You know better than that, child. Now, then. I fed your body. You feed my soul."

The others murmur their agreement. Mary whispers something into Theo's ear, and he smiles and nods.

"Perfect," he says.

TWELVE

Next morning, Dad and I pass in the hallway. His gaze skims the bruise on my arm. He looks only at the floor then. At this moment he isn't at all a vain, handsome man. He is aging, aged, as if in the past twenty-four hours decades have gone by.

"I would never hurt you, Rose."

"But you did."

"I didn't intend to."

I think about chains. How hard it is to break them.

"I'll never touch you again," Dad says.

This I believe. For one thing, I won't let him. For another, he never has, much. It's Sophy he touches, and he's only a loving father holding her.

I walk past him to my bedroom, close the door, and get ready for work. In this way, it's just another Monday. In so many other ways, it's not.

I clean and clean, one apartment after another in a building down the street from ours. And while I clean, I sing all the songs I want to sing, from "Amazing Grace" to "Zing! Went the Strings of My Heart." The doors are closed, and the windows, too. I sing as loudly or as softly as I want. At the end of the day, floors and walls are spotless, windows and mirrors are shining, yet my thoughts and feelings still split and shimmer like ripples across the surface of a pool when not just one penny but many have been cast into water. There's no single wish, no calming my mind. The only thing I know is that I will find a way to see Theo again. I will go to Calliope's and listen with my whole heart. And with my whole heart I will continue to sing the songs I want to sing, if only while I'm cleaning.

As soon as I'm home, I give Rob a call.

"Tomorrow night is Tuesday," I say.

He agrees that it is.

"I'll meet you at our usual place and time."

"Is this about your dad, Rose?"

Anger stirs in me. I clench my hand around the receiver, and the anger becomes determination.

"No. This is about me."

Once more, it's a cold, stormy night—not snowing this time, but sleeting. Once more, I change clothes in the backseat of Rob's car.

When we arrive at Calliope's, Rob makes no mention of valet service. This relieves me, as any sign of levelheadedness on his part always does. He drops me off at the club's door and then drives off to park. I don't relish the thought of entering the place on my own, but then I think of Theo and the music, and I step inside.

I come to a dead stop as the door closes behind me. The

place is emptier than I've ever seen it. There are men drinking at the bar, talking with the bartenders, and people are gathered at tables. But there's no press and pull of the crowd, because there's no crowd. With more than enough room to walk around freely, I can see the stage fine even from way back here.

Perhaps Rob and I got the night or time wrong. Or something has happened—my heart quickens—perhaps to Theo. Only one of the Chess Men stands on the dimly lit stage—the portly white bassist. He draws his bow over a block of rosin. His brow is furrowed; he looks anxious, too.

I don't know what to do with myself while I wait for Rob. To put it another way: I know what I *don't* want to do. I don't want to sidle up to the bar and spend my little bit of spare change on a soda, all the while negotiating the glances and advances of strangers. I don't want to sit myself down at a table, dreading the moment when the brashest stranger joins me. I don't want to fend someone off.

I look away from the bar before the men there have a chance to see me looking. There's a coatroom I've never noticed before for the crowd. A girl sits on a stool behind the half-door. Bored, she blows a stream of cigarette smoke at the ceiling.

I go to her, take off my trusty old coat, hold it out. She looks at my coat as she might look at a piece of refuse, drags on her cigarette, then grinds out the lipstick-stained butt in the ashtray on the table beside her. Blowing smoke, she takes my coat and hangs it up. She sits down again and looks off into the distance.

"Hey, you! Blue Dress!"

I turn. From the stage, the bassist is pointing his bow at me.

"It's about time!"

The bassist is all but shouting. The coat-check girl scrutinizes me. The men at the bar and the bartenders, too.

"Hustle on over here, Blue Dress. Hurry!"

The bassist beckons with his bow. To ignore him would only draw more attention, so I make my way to the stage. This close, I can see the rosin dusting the tips of his calloused fingers. I open my mouth to ask what he wants from me, but before I can say a word, he swings his bow to the side, points behind the red velvet stage curtain.

"This is the quickest way. The others are waiting. Let's go."

"But—" I glance quickly around. Still no sign of Rob.

"No 'buts.' We expected you two hours ago." In a mincing, falsetto the bassist says, "'Look for the brown-haired girl in the knockout blue dress.'" He scowls. "We'd about given up on getting knocked out, I gotta say. As it is, you may have killed our chances tonight, being so late."

I gape at him. "I'm not that girl."

The bassist doesn't seem to hear. "Lilah said you were good. She also said you could be unreliable." He regards me from beneath his thick eyebrows, which are as red as his hair. "Not as unreliable as she is, though, since you did ultimately show up, and you appear to be clean and sober."

I shiver at the memory of the needle and syringe. "Is Miss Buckley all right?"

"She's safe. Getting help, she says." He leans down and sniffs my hair. "You *are* clean and sober, right? You look it, you smell it, but like my ma always said, looks and smells can be deceiving." The bassist beckons again with his bow. "Never mind. Don't answer. At this point it doesn't matter, does it? Come on. The others are waiting."

"'The others'?"

He gives me a hard look. "Listen, either get to work or get lost, Blue Dress. Too much is on the line here to mess around."

I follow the bassist backstage to where Theo and the rest of the Chess Men sit in a small, cramped room, waiting. Theo looks up from the keyboard he's chalked onto a tabletop, and his eyes widen at the sight of me in the doorway.

"Better late than never." The bassist's voice is grim as he ushers me inside.

The licorice-whip-thin clarinetist looks up from the reed he's whittling down to size, the bald drummer from the wooden crate against which he's tapping his sticks. Theo's hands come down hard on the chalked notes, smudging them.

"Well, if it isn't the mysterious Elaine." The clarinetist runs his reed back and forth across his dark cheek as if testing for rough edges.

"I'm not Elaine," I say.

The bassist turns on me, reminding me of nothing so much as one of Aunt Astrid's big bulls, suddenly riled. "Why didn't you say so?"

"I said so," I say.

Theo stands and goes to the bassist. "Jim." Theo sets his hand on the bassist's shoulder. "Calm down. It'll be all right."

"It better be," Jim mutters, shaking off Theo's hand.

"So." The drummer taps his sticks lightly, nervously on the crate. "Elaine or not, can you sing? That's all I care about."

"Oh, she can sing, all right," Theo says.

The clarinetist laughs. "Well, well. Get a load of you, my man, going all dreamy-eyed."

"I didn't come to sing." I edge closer to Theo. "I came to listen."

Theo says, "You came to sing." His fingers brush against my arm, and I know it's not an accident. None of this. Not his touch—the warmth of it, radiating so close to where Dad hurt me, soothing that lingering pain. And not my being here, either. "God knows, you came to sing," Theo says, confirming my thoughts.

"Yes," I hear myself say.

Theo draws in a deep breath and turns to the other men. "This is Rose Sorensen, fellows." His hand isn't touching mine now, but he's standing so close I can feel the air thrumming warmly between us. We might as well be two magnets. "Now that we've taken Miss Sorensen by surprise," Theo continues, "let's give her a chance to get comfortable, okay? A few more minutes of waiting won't hurt anybody. Then we'll get started. Rose, do you need something? A glass of water?"

"'Get comfortable'?" Jim slams his block of rosin down on the table. "We got a slim chance here, and the clock is ticking, Theo."

Theo doesn't take his eyes from me. "Water?"

I shake my head.

"Anything?"

I shake my head again.

"Okay. You think you can sing for us, then? Any song you want, Rose. You pick."

I swallow hard. "First tell me what's going on."

"I told you!" Jim's face has turned nearly as red as his hair.

"Tell me again." I look at Theo. "You tell me."

So Theo does. They learned early this evening that Lilah was in such a bad way she was unable to perform. She'd found someone to replace her—a real professional who could nail the gig, no problem. Blue dress. Brown hair. Elaine. But Elaine never showed, even as the crowd gathered, and Calliope's owner and his backers got madder and madder. "I tried to reason with them," Theo says, "but they said they were taking a risk on us as it is. 'Come back when you've found your girl,' they said, and then they docked us our pay and said this was our last chance. And because the crowd wanted something different than we could give—well, a lot of folks went elsewhere, including the boss and his friends."

"We're dead in the water," Jim says grimly.

Theo shakes his head, determined. "Not necessarily. Not if we come back better than before. We won't get paid tonight, but we can get one last chance." Theo turns to me, lifts his chalky hands in appeal. "Pretend it's just me here, Rose. Sing for me."

Heat creeps up my cheeks. *What's happening here? Something, everything, anything might happen.*

Quickly Theo says, "Or if that doesn't work, pretend it's just your family. Sing for them." He claps his hand to his forehead as if suddenly struck by something. "For pity's sake, Rose, sing for *yourself.*"

I close my eyes.

Sing for me.

The voice in my head might be Sophy's, Theo's, or mine. It might be the voice of God, for the way it works on me. Eyes still closed, a hymn takes me over and I'm singing:

My life flows on in endless song;
Above earth's lamentation . . .

In my mind's eye, I see Rob, standing by his father's casket. Dad, driving away from our house in Oak Park for the last time.

Mother, helping Sophy through one of her seizures. Sophy, crying in the shelter of the gazebo in Garfield Park. Mrs. Chastain and Mary, and the rest of Theo's family. Theo at the piano. Mahalia Jackson and her choir. I sing on:

> *All things are mine since I am His—*
> *How can I keep from singing?*

When the hymn is finished, I open my eyes to see Theo, his smile like light.

Jim claps his hands together one, two, three times, stirring up a thin cloud of rosin dust. "You're in, Blue Dress."

"Where you been hiding, anyway?" the clarinetist asks.

"Does it matter?" The drummer gives a quick roll of his sticks against the crate. "She's here now."

Theo beams at us all. "Rose, this is Jim." The redheaded bassist salutes me with his bow. "Dex." The clarinetist nods in my direction. "Ira." The drummer gives me a blue-eyed wink.

I clear my throat. Talking proves suddenly harder than singing, for all the emotions I'm feeling. "Nice to meet you all."

The Chess Men, in one way or another, say it's nice to meet me, too.

Theo flexes his fingers, suddenly all business. "Jim's right. The clock is ticking." He takes a piece of chalk from his pants pocket and starts marking out a fresh row of keys. "I can't do much with a tabletop, Rose, but how about if the other fellows accompany you on a quick rendition of 'Blow the Man Down'?"

I laugh, and the muscles in my throat relax. I'm singing. No one is the worse for it. People are happy. And there's talk of paychecks in the future if we get tonight right.

The door bangs open. "Rose!"

I turn to see Rob, standing in the doorway, his coat half on, half off.

"I've been looking all over for you!" Rob sounds as disgruntled as he looks.

The Chess Men go very quiet and still. Perhaps they think Rob is my boyfriend. Perhaps members of the group have encountered more than a few irate boyfriends in their time. I glance at Theo, whose gaze darts from me to Rob and back again. Last time Theo saw Rob, Rob was about as drunk and unfriendly as Rob gets.

I go to my cousin. "You got your wish."

Rob raises an eyebrow. "What's that?"

"You won't have to climb a fire escape and listen outside my bedroom window to hear me sing tonight."

"Laerke!" Rob throws his arms around me.

I hug him back, then push him playfully away. His shirt is unbuttoned at his belly again. I button it, adjust his collar. "Why don't you go freshen up a bit more while I practice?" I say.

He glances down, grimaces at his general disarray, then gives me a swift peck on the cheek and hurries off to get snazzy.

I turn back to the Chess Men. Dex slips the reed into the mouthpiece of his clarinet, blows a few notes, testing, then whips through "Blow the Man Down." When Theo gives the downbeat, Ira taps out a quirky rhythm on the crate, Jim plucks a few low answering notes on his bass. I join in. I sing the first verse a few times as they work on synchronizing the easy, rocking rhythm. Each time through becomes more playful than the last. Sophy would love this, I think, as we wind down "Blow the

Man Down" and bust out into "The Very Thought of You." Sophy would kiss the air.

Halfway through our third song, a hollow-chested man in horn-rimmed glasses pokes his head into the room. "What's the news, fellows?"

Theo proudly introduces me as the new singer and then says, "Rose, this is George, the stage manager."

George looks me up and down over the rim of his glasses. Seen one vocalist, you seen them all, his expression implies. He turns to Theo. "You want I should go out and find the boss?"

Theo looks at the rest of the Chess Men, who nod.

"We'll try out a few numbers on the small house. Then, unless we say differently, yes, please do that," Theo says.

We run through "The Way You Look Tonight" until I've got a pretty good sense of the tempo and mood they want to work with. When I forget the words, Theo hands me the sheet music, telling me that this crowd won't mind. "They're here for the liquor, not the Chess Men," he says.

At one point, Dex stops in midsong and lowers his clarinet. "This beats all, Rose." He snaps his fingers. "Like that, and you're hep to us. How do you figure?"

I don't look at Theo. "I've been listening."

This seems to satisfy. We jump back into the song just as the door opens again and George says that the few folks left are about to leave for good.

Theo looks at me. "It's now or never."

You shouldn't listen to music like that. I hear Mother's voice, and Dad's voice, too. *Boys sow their wild oats. Girls become tramps.*

As the other Chess Men gather their instruments and jostle

their way toward the stage, Theo holds out his hands to me. "You're sure you're ready?"

Dear God. Am I?

And I believe I hear the answer: *Dear Rose. Yes.*

We are alone now, Theo and I. I rest my hands in his, so warm and steady compared to mine.

"Ready as I'll ever be," I say.

Somehow I'm onstage with the Chess Men.

The stage is hotter than I expected. Dustier. It smells of rosin, wood, and brass. For better or worse, it smells of humanity. After the dim, cramped practice room, I can't see for the spotlight. But I can hear. Oh, I can hear. The few people lingering at the bar are talking and laughing. Glasses clink. Chairs scrape against the floor. The sheaf of sheet music rattles in my hands. Time to bring in the sheaves, all right. I tighten my grip, but that doesn't stop my trembling. The paper feels pulpy from the sweat that slicks my palms.

Theo murmurs in my ear. I have no idea what he's saying, but the familiar sound of his voice comforts me. He steers me toward the microphone. Now I see shapes that must be the people out there. Not much else. Once in Oak Park I had a dangerously high fever, and shapes that I knew must be Mother and the doctor moved about my bedroom. It was disturbing then; it's disturbing now. I keep my gaze up. I stare at the exit, the door opening there, closing again.

You want this. Stay.

Theo says into the microphone, "I'm delighted to introduce Miss Rose Sorensen."

My name ricochets like a bullet around the room.

From the bar, a man grumbles, "Where's the Queen?" The question is echoed by a woman.

"The Queen's taking a holiday." Theo speaks boldly, like this news is exactly what everyone wants to hear. "Her last proclamation was that her loyal subjects show Miss Sorensen some respect." Theo smiles at me as only he can. "Miss Sorensen?" He steps back from the microphone, making room for a singer—the singer, me.

I step forward. In the glare of the spotlight, the microphone is a presence, big and bulky, almost a barricade. Theo watches me closely. He lifts his hand; he's about to touch me. He catches himself in time and lowers his hand. "You okay?" he whispers.

I manage a nod.

Into the microphone he says tonight's first number is my call. "Miss Sorensen, what'll it be?"

The sheaf of sheet music trembles. I couldn't read the lyrics if I tried. What song do I really know by heart? What song can I sing like I was born for it? What song do I sing nearly every night to Sophy? What song will save me?

"Amazing Grace." The microphone captures my voice and lets it fly around the room. It's like I'm everywhere at once. Anyone can grab hold of me or push me away. But this song that I know so well—this song I was raised on—it will bind me together.

The few people left don't like it. There's a smattering of hisses and boos. "Don't tell me we've got us a Holy Roller," a woman says with a snarl. I want to shrink down into myself, become invisible. I've only ever felt this way before with Dad. With Dad, it was bad enough. With a roomful of shapes that are strangers, it's a nightmare.

A hand slaps the edge of the stage. In spite of myself, I look down. Thank heaven I do. It's Rob. His gray-green gaze pierces even the spotlight's glare. "Sing, Laerke." He mouths the words, but I can make them out. "Sing!"

At the sight of my cousin, the nightmare ends and I am restored, ready again. Those strangers out there, they're not so different from me. They may not know it but they need music in their lives, too.

I turn to Theo. He is telling the crowd, yet again, to give me a chance. "Respect," I hear him say. He is calling me a lady. He is comparing me, in the most surprising way, to that famous beauty of ancient Greece, Helen of Troy. "You know how Helen of Troy's face launched a thousand ships? Well, Miss Sorensen's voice might just do the same. Who knows? You might just go to battle to defend her singing. I know I would."

My hand slips through Theo's arm, and I lean into him. Somehow this has happened. We are arm in arm. I am leaning into him. In my gratitude to him—for who he is, for what he has done for me, for what he is doing now—I have expressed my affection on a stage before strangers. The audacity of my act seems to stop time. We might as well be statues, Theo and I. I'm not a betting woman, but if I were, I'd bet that everyone else has gone as still as we have.

Mixed couples might sit at tables or dance together in Calliope's, but they stay in the shadows or lost in the crowd, doing so. A fling, they might be having, a passing fancy. Not this. A public statement.

I look up at Theo. His expression is unreadable. It could be: *What's happening here?* Or: *Here's what I've been waiting for all my life.* Or: *So this is how it ends.* From behind us, one of the Chess Men makes a low sound in his throat. A warning sound.

I have to do something. I have to undo this.

I look at Theo again—his beautiful, familiar, dark face—and it comes to me. I've been through this kind of thing before with Sophy. When people tease Sophy as if she's some kind of broken doll, what do I do? I hold my head high as Mother and Dad taught me to. I push through.

I push through now. I do not let go of Theo's arm. I must not. I hold on to Theo's arm as tightly as I've ever held on to Sophy. Gratitude and affection between two people like us must be made to look like an everyday kind of thing. There's nothing to be ashamed of, nothing to fear. If you, Joe Schmoe or Jane Doe, are upset or enraged, that's your problem. You've never stood where we stand now. You've only watched from the shadows. Your loss.

"'Amazing Grace,'" I say into the microphone. My hand is still on Theo's arm. I'm remembering something I learned on Aunt Astrid's farm: when you look away from an animal, the animal thinks it's dominant. I don't dare look away from the people before me. I tighten my grip on Theo's arm, and then I release him. I pray he understands that this is my signal for *now or never, let's push through*. Theo understands. Without a word, he goes to his piano, sits down, and plays the first notes of "Amazing Grace." His fingers render sounds as haunting as anything I've ever heard. Time starts again, and it has the signature of a ballad, for this is what "Amazing Grace" is, I realize. It's a story, just like every other ballad. A love story about God.

I close my eyes and sing the song with all the love I can muster.

We draw the first verse out, Theo and I, delivering it slowly and sweetly. *I once was lost, but now I'm found.* I'm found now, singing. Ira joins in on his snare; his brush whispers across the drum's taut skin, sounding very much like soft wind in thick leaves. Jim begins plucking his bass, and the low notes throb as steadily as a strong heartbeat. Finally Dex sounds the clarinet, weaving longing-laced harmony through my melody:

> *We've no less days to sing God's praise*
> *Than when we'd first begun.*

The last words of the last verse. In no time at all, these words are upon us. I can't bear to open my eyes when I've finished singing them. I want to stay wrapped up in the music, which moves through the air all around me as Dex, Jim, Ira, and, last of all, Theo work their way to an end. Theo's last note lingers in the air long after he's played it. Only when it fades away do I open my eyes and blink into light that glows around the dark star of the microphone. People are staring at me through the light. I can feel them staring. The silence is so thick now that it wraps around my throat like a noose. I am no Queen. I am a white woman who touched a black man onstage. I am trouble. I am in trouble. I'd run, but the noose holds me here. *Lynching*, I think, and I know I should pray. *Oh, God* is all I can muster. *Oh, God* will have to suffice.

There's a sharp report—a sound like a shotgun. Another sharp sound and another and too many to count. People are clapping. Clapping hard. They are cheering and shouting for more. Rob is clapping, cheering, shouting loudest of all.

Theo doesn't give the people time to grow quiet. His hands come crashing down on the keys, and the next thing I know he's set sail on the first verse of "Blow the Man Down." Here's another side of God, another graceful way to sing, to swing. Theo's hands are lightning, as are the hands of Jim, Ira, and Dex. It takes me more than a few measures to figure out how to join in. But once I do, I'm hurtling along on a madcap voyage, a deluge of notes splashing and crashing all around me. And from "Blow the Man Down," we move on to another kind of watery song: "Pennies from Heaven" rains down on Calliope's, and two couples begin to dance.

This night is a dream, one song after another, until the first set is done, and we take a break.

"How do you feel?" Theo asks me in the dim little practice room. It must be obvious how I feel from the way the Chess Men are smiling at me. *I once was lost, but now I'm found.* I feel wonderful. No, better than wonderful. I feel whole.

"Good," I say.

Theo pulls out a chair, and I drop down into it.

Dex runs a hand worriedly through his salt-and-pepper gray hair. "She's tapped out."

Theo nods, his gaze soft with concern. "You're not used to this, Rose. Performing takes it out of you, even when you've been working toward it."

"George found the boss and got him here in time to hear the end of the first set." Jim downs a glass of water and then grins. "The boss wants to hear more. That's a good sign."

"Can you keep going, Rose?" Cradling his clarinet like it might break, Dex softly asks this. Dex is the shy one, I'm realizing. For all his talent, you'd think he was the one who'd never been onstage.

I lean toward him, the better to give a reassuring smile. "I'll be ready to go back out when you are."

"I'm glad," Dex says.

Theo beams at me.

"We want you back. You're our gal, Blue Dress," Jim says.

Ira adds, "Until Lilah gets her act together."

Everyone except Theo nods in agreement.

"You're important for Lilah, and Lilah's important for you. I understand." And I do understand, though my heart aches to admit it.

Back onstage, the ache is alleviated. I'm singing again, and they're backing me up, and I'm listening, too, when Jim, Dex, Ira, and Theo take turns playing solo. With every note, I learn something now. With every number, more people walk through the door and gather around the stage. I give my all. By the end of the third and last set, the Chess Men and I are working together as one instrument. At least that's how it feels to me. And from the expressions of astonished joy on each of their faces, I think it feels that way to Dex, Ira, and Jim, too.

Though he doesn't say a word, I know it feels that way to Theo. It's all I can do to look away from the light of his smile. But it's rude to ignore this applause, so I turn to the crowd and bow.

At the end of the night, Rob finds me backstage. He flings his arms around me. "You did it!" Rob's voice quavers with emotion. "If you can do this, you can do anything, Rose!" I thank my cousin. I babble something even I don't understand, about family and courage and the birthday gift he gave me, the gifts he's given me over the years—his promises that are whims, his Tarzan calls, his dreams—and how it took someone special, someone like him, to make me sing—

Rob stops me right there, literally clapping his hand across my mouth.

"*You* did this, Laerke. You are the one who got up there. You shared your voice. You made the brave choice."

Ira, Dex, and Jim are backstage now. They grin at me, nod at Rob. A white towel flashes as Ira mops the sweat from his brow. At some point he must have taken off his tuxedo jacket and rolled up his shirtsleeves; the veins in his arms bulge from the hard work of drumming. Dex drops into a chair and starts cleaning the inside of his clarinet with a brush. Jim squats down by an open kit bag, digs out a jar of salve, opens the jar, and dunks his thumb inside like Peter Pumpkin Eater pulling out a plum. Only Jim just pulls out his thickly coated thumb and tenderly massages the salve into the tip. The callus there has split, and so has the nail. Guess plucking away at a bass for hours can do that.

There's a movement at the door, and Theo enters, his smile lighting up the room.

"What a night!" He's about to say more, but then his bright smile fades. He's seen Rob.

But Rob's eyes are clear tonight. He holds out his hand to Theo, and Theo takes it. They shake hands, man to man. The way Rob might shake with another white man, or, I suppose, Theo might shake hands with another black man.

Rob says, "She's my cousin. You'll take good care of her?"

"I will," Theo says. The other Chess Men say they will, too.

"I'll take good care of them, too," I say, which makes everyone laugh, even me. Tired and giddy with laughter, I lean into Theo again. His hand touches the small of my back, supporting me. *What's happening here? Something's happening.* His touch is tender. I don't want him to take his hand away.

Rob goes to the door. Only when he's in the hallway does he look back. He clasps his hands together and raises them to his chin in an appeal that surely extends to me and may extend to God. The gesture takes my breath away; it's something a much older person would do—someone from our parents' generation, perhaps, or, more likely, our grandparents'. "Be careful," Rob says over his clenched hands. "Be careful together." And then he's gone.

Theo is beside me. That's what turned Rob into our grandfather.

The other Chess Men are packing up their instruments now. Theo busies himself organizing sheet music into folders. He takes notes on tonight's playlist, and jots down ideas for what Friday might hold. He says good night to the others, then turns to me. He doesn't ask if I need a ride. He simply nods. *Yes, I'll take care of you.* I follow him from the room, keeping a safe distance as we wend our way out the back door and into the alley, where his car waits.

We are silent the whole way home, him in front, me in back. Only when Theo pulls up in front of the apartment does he speak.

"So, Friday?" It is still dark, but the streetlight illuminates his face. He looks weary, yet hopeful. "You'll be our vocalist again?"

I nod, and there's his smile.

"Could you arrive a little earlier on Friday, though—say, eight? It would be good if we could put in a little more practice."

"Eight is fine by me."

Theo's smile fades as he glances warily at the apartment building. "Are you sure it will be fine with your family, though?"

I tell him not to worry. I'm not sure how, but I'll make it fine.

THIRTEEN

Wednesday and Thursday pass as Wednesday and Thursday will. Friday is on the horizon. When I finally sleep on Thursday night, I dream that I am running through dark streets in my blue dress, running and running, trying to get somewhere—where I don't know, but I know it's a place as important as my life. Someone is chasing me; I hear footsteps not so far behind. Someone will catch me if they can, stop me if they do. I run harder. I am almost there. Then a hand comes down on my shoulder.

Someone is shaking me awake. It is dark and cold. Friday—it's Friday. I was supposed to arrive at Calliope's at seven. If it's this dark, I must be late. I must have taken a short nap after work, and it turned into a long one.

"Rose."

Mother's voice. Mother's hand on my shoulder, drawing me from my dreams.

"What time is it?"

"Nearly six."

I breathe a sigh of relief. I can make it to Calliope's by eight.

"Wake up, Rose." Mother raises her voice. "Sophy, you, too. We have to get some breakfast into you both."

I'm aware now of Sophy's warm weight in the bed. Sophy never takes naps in the late afternoon or early evening. If she does, she won't sleep at night. She mumbles something into her pillow. Something that sounds like a version of "not hungry yet."

I rub my eyes, confused. "Breakfast? Don't you mean dinner?"

"Not unless you want to have dinner for breakfast. I've got oatmeal on the stove. Come on." Mother gives me another shake. "Hurry now. We can't be late."

Nearly six in the cold, dark morning. That's what time it is. The day still stretches before us.

Sophy groans.

"Late for what?" I dread the answer; it's lurking like a shadow at the back of my mind.

"The Nygaards, sleepyhead! Zane's party." Mother clucks her tongue. "I told you about this after church last Sunday, Rose. Remember?"

"I guess I forgot."

Mother heads for the bedroom door. "Bring only a work dress today, Rose. Tomorrow you'll pack a nicer one for the party. Quickly now!"

Mother hurries from the room. A snore escapes from Sophy. Clearly, Mother's words had no effect on her. On me, they had plenty. Wide awake, I sit bolt upright in bed. If I know Mrs. Nygaard, she will have us cleaning until late tonight to prepare for her party, and tomorrow, the party itself will go late into the night. I will not make tonight's eight o'clock rehearsal and performance. Or tomorrow night's, either. And if I don't show up at the performance, the Chess Men will never perform at Calliope's again.

I need to come up with a good excuse to slip away.

I go to the closet, rifle through my small collection of work dresses, pull the cleanest one from its hanger, and put it on.

If only excuses could be found in closets.

In spite of the cold, we're sweating, Mother, Sophy, and I, pressed so close together at the back of the El car that the heat we gathered during our dash to the station continues to intensify. Mother has taken the seat by the window. Sophy sits on her lap, her back braced against the glass. I sit beside Mother, with Sophy's legs stretched across my thighs. So far, so good. Sophy hasn't had a spasm we weren't able to control. The wheelchair stands in the aisle beside me; I hold tightly to it to keep it from rolling off down the aisle. Once, on a trip like this, the wheelchair got away from me; it banged into a conductor, nearly knocking him off his feet, and he asked us to leave the train. Learned my lesson that day, standing with Mother and Sophy on the El platform in the pouring rain.

Mother's breathing hard—too hard. I suck in a slower, deeper breath for her, and for Sophy, too, just in case. And for myself.

Still haven't come up with a good excuse.

At least we're on the right train, barreling inelegantly toward posh Hyde Park and the Nygaards' mansion. At the El station, two trains passed above us while we waited for the kind stranger in the brown, grease-stained coat who helped us carry the chair, then Sophy, up two flights of stairs to the platform. The next train that came was packed with people. Finally this one arrived, and there was a car that wasn't so crowded. We could leverage ourselves inside and down the aisle. Now Sophy is nodding off; Mother, too. I stare out the window, too tired to close my burning eyes. Buildings flash past, and the people below, the cars and trolleys, and time. Tonight—what might have been, what might still be—feels as distant as last night's dream.

The train lurches in a new direction. If I'm correct, we're nearing Bronzeville now. I search for landmarks, but nothing catches my eye. The sidewalks are filled with people bustling off to punch the clock. Not a white person to be seen at this time of day. Once this would have disconcerted me. Now I only hope to catch a glimpse of Theo, or Mary, or Mrs. Chastain.

The train banks abruptly east toward the lake. Sophy and Mother sleep on. In spite of her frailty, Sophy's legs are growing heavy. I adjust her weight and rest my head on Mother's shoulder.

A rotten stench startles me upright. I must have nodded off, too. We are passing close to the stockyards now. The odor brings tears to my eyes. I cup my right hand over my nose and mouth, my left hand over Sophy's. This smell, if anything, will surely upset her, and when she's upset, she's at risk for something worse. When Sophy and I give muffled groans of discontent, Mother's eyebrows draw together in irritation. From behind the sleeve of her coat, she reprimands us. We should count our blessings, she says. Dad could be working in a slaughterhouse. Or I could. Or Mother herself. We could be meat packers instead of what we are.

"What are we, exactly?"

Mother gives me a sharp glance. "We are clean folk with good manners. We don't bring this smell into our home."

With her voice still muffled by her coat sleeve, she reminds me that before she met Dad she was housekeeper for the mayor of Luck, Wisconsin. She learned about the finer things of life doing that job. Dad learned about them as a sailor, exploring port cities. They've passed this knowledge on to their children. We should always remember, never forget, the fine things we've learned, Mother says. We have surrounded ourselves with them in the past. We will surround ourselves with them in the future.

I interrupt her. "Sometimes the fine things in life are different for different people. A stockyard worker might think his life is just fine. Who's to say it isn't?"

"If the stockyards are so fine, then why are we trying not to breathe this very air?" Mother's tongue works at her cheek, prodding the back molar that has been troubling her so. "I imagine there are many down in the yards who would trade much more than a day's work for a trip to the dentist."

Sophy and I exchange grim looks. We didn't realize that this trip would also include a dental visit to Dr. Nygaard—an additional benefit of our employment we've yet to take advantage of. Makes sense, I suppose, that our checkups should occur this weekend. Dr. Nygaard's office is in his house. Mother's teeth, and Sophy's, too, need attention. As for me, I like sweets well enough. It's only a matter of time before my own teeth are in trouble, too.

We rattle on. The air improves as the train moves forward, but it's some time before Sophy will let me lower my hand from her nose and mouth. Finally the train grinds to a halt. We are in Hyde Park. I push the wheelchair aside and slide from beneath Sophy's legs. Mother manages to stand, too. Hefting Sophy in her arms, she staggers to the door of the train and out onto the platform. I'm right behind with the wheelchair. The platform's wide, wooden boards tremble beneath our feet as the train thunders off. Mother settles Sophy into the wheelchair, then catches her breath and balance. I look around, hoping, but there is no kind man in a brown, grease-stained coat to be seen. In fact, the platform is empty.

"The stairs." Mother points. "We can't wait around for help that won't come."

I wheel Sophy to the stairs. There, Mother and I weave our arms together and make a place for her to sit. A princess chair, Dad named this configuration of our arms. We wrestle Sophy forward and scoop her up. We manage to carry her down thirteen stairs, navigate the landing, and carry her down another flight of thirteen. At the bottom Mother and I collapse onto a bench with Sophy still wedged between us.

"The hardest part is almost over." Mother is trying to be reassuring, I know, but given the household tasks that await us, her words fall flat. She adjusts Sophy's hat and coat, murmuring, "There, there." Mother gives me a look, then, and I know what I must do. I can feel Sophy's worried eyes on me as I climb back up the stairs. I can feel her eyes on me as I push the wheelchair down twenty-six stairs, twenty-six jarring bumps to the sidewalk.

"Hardest part, over and done with." I add my reassurance to Mother's. Again, it falls flat. I still haven't thought of an excuse to escape, after all. Thinking of an excuse is proving to be the hardest part for me.

We head into Hyde Park. What was a cold, gray morning has turned drizzly. Mother reminds us that we only have a few blocks to walk, and then she sets off down the sidewalk. I trudge along behind, pushing Sophy. The wheelchair spews slush on my shoes. Icy water runs down the back of my neck.

By the time we arrive at the ornate wrought-iron fence that guards the Nygaards' enormous brownstone, my feet and ankles are sopping wet. Mother straightens her hat, marches up the walk and past the bronze lions that roar silently on the front porch. I stay with Sophy on the sidewalk. Mother raises the knocker and lets it fall with a thud against the massive door.

The door swings open. A slight, silvery-haired man dressed in full butler's livery stands at the threshold. He scowls at the sight of us. Mother bravely wishes him good morning; still he looks down his nose at us.

"You were expected at the back entrance."

A flush saturates Mother's throat and cheeks. She apologizes, and asks for the butler's help carrying Sophy inside. The butler's training gets the better of him and he complies, negotiating another princess chair with Mother. Sophy grimaces. Me, too. When Sophy is awkwardly in their arms and finally inside, I start to wrestle the wheelchair up the front steps. But the butler pokes his head out and gestures toward the back of the house, the door there.

Down his nose he looks. "Mind the rules, you."

The back entry leads to a mudroom. I park the wheelchair there and go inside to the kitchen, which is blessedly warm and empty. There are freshly baked rolls cooling on the counter. It seems hours since that oatmeal. I lean over the rolls now, breathe in their buttery scent, and my mouth waters.

Footsteps sound at the kitchen door. I whirl around, expecting to see the butler. Instead Mrs. Nygaard stands before me, a drooping calla lily in her hand.

"Well, well." Her voice is languid and cool. "I see you've made yourself right at home."

Her sarcasm is not lost on me. My ability to respond to it, however, is.

She turns on her heel to leave the kitchen, tossing the faded flower into the garbage bin as she goes. "Follow me," she says without so much as a backward glance.

I follow.

My first job, Mrs. Nygaard reveals, is to clean the ashtrays. They had a smaller get-together last night and are still cleaning up the mess. "There should be fifteen," Mrs. Nygaard clarifies. "About two in every room on the first floor. You can worry about the second floor later."

I blink at her. Good Danish Baptists don't smoke. But then good Danish Baptists don't find excuses—or desperately try to find excuses—to slip away to Calliope's, either.

The corners of Mrs. Nygaard's mouth tip down in her version of a smile. "You needn't worry, Rose. The ashtrays are for our guests, not us." And she drifts off to another part of the house.

What Mrs. Nygaard neglected to mention, I realize shortly, is that ashtrays—at least the Nygaards' ashtrays—can prove difficult to locate. I find them in the strangest places, places I'd never have thought to look and might not have found if it hadn't been for Sophy. While Mother polishes silver, I wheel Sophy about the first floor of the house, and we turn ashtray hunting into a game. Sophy seems to have a sixth sense when it comes to finding them. *Look under that settee*, her eyes tell me, and there, sullying the carpet, lies a crystal bowl of lipstick-stained butts. *Now behind that game table*, Sophy says with a jerk of her head. *On that marble mantel. Beside that toilet.*

My fingers are gray and chalky by the time we've worked our way through all the rooms. All told, we've stacked thirteen ashtrays on the kitchen counter.

Mrs. Nygaard, who is discussing the party menu with the

cook, frowns at the stacks. "You're missing two." Mrs. Nygaard
has high cheekbones and pale, thin lips she shades with coral-
colored lipstick. Her eyes are the very color of the ash that coats
my hands. Her blond hair crowns her head in a cap of chic coils.
I always think she's beautiful until I take a second look, and my
gaze snags on the hook of her nose. And now the smoldering
ash of her eyes. "Please do locate them," she says. "Then use a
toothbrush and vinegar and make them gleam."

Sophy and I finally find an ashtray beneath a teacup on a library bookshelf. The last one caps the head of the marble angel
guarding the doorway to the conservatory. The game isn't fun
anymore. Sophy seems tired and sad. I balance the ashtray on
my own head, mimic the angel's pose, and manage to wrest a
smile from her. To make her laugh, I do a little dance, one I saw
at Calliope's. Dancing, I can't help but sing:

Forget your troubles
  Come on get happy

Sophy looks past me, and her eyes widen. She stops laughing. I turn to find Zane standing just behind me. He's wearing a
white shirt and vest, white slacks, white shoes. He holds a tennis
racket.

"Working hard, Rose?"

"Yes." I take the ashtray from my head and slip it into the
pocket of my apron. I smell like ashes. Sophy smells like ashes,
too. Zane smells like bay rum. He studies Sophy and me. His
eyes are nearly the same gray as his mother's, but they have a
warmer cast.

"Sorry," he says.

"About what?" I keep my voice nonchalant. Acknowledging humiliation only makes it worse. I've learned that.

"This." Zane gestures at the rooms all around, then points the round head of his racket at his chest. "You should be our guests, not our—"

I hold up my hands—*stop!*—because I can't bear to see myself and my family through Zane's eyes.

"We better get back to work." I wheel Sophy in her chair away from Zane.

I'm halfway down the hall when I hear Zane's uneven step, the drag of his right foot across the floor. I turn back to him. "Is there something you need?"

He shrugs. "I was wondering if Sophy might like to escape, that's all. Our neighbors the Sloanes have an indoor tennis court, and they've invited me to play. Their house is just a stone's throw away. They're a lovely elderly couple. I imagine you'll like them just fine, Sophy, and I know they'll like you." Zane pats his racket against his right leg. The gesture reveals how thin and frail his thigh is. "Neither Mr. Sloane nor I are up for much of a contest, so the game won't go on for too long, I promise you. Then we'll have something to eat and drink, and enjoy their new record player. They have quite a music collection. Everyone from Mozart to Mezzrow."

Envy courses through me. But then I see Sophy's sparkling eyes, her sweet, happy smile, and my envy abates. When has she ever really escaped in her life?

"You'd like that?" I ask her.

She kisses the air yes.

"It's settled, then, " Zane says. "Least I can do is make one person happy while everyone else is working to make me happy."

He seems to know where the butler has stashed Sophy's coat. He heads off to retrieve it and returns quickly, having done just that.

"Keep her safe," I tell him, buttoning Sophy's coat.

"Sure thing."

Zane sounds so cavalier, I can't help but worry. I watch as he pushes her away. Then they are gone, and I am left with two ash-trays and a handful of hours until eight o'clock.

I work like the dickens, washing, dusting, polishing. By lunch-time, even Mrs. Nygaard is impressed with all I've accomplished. The cook serves Mother and me split pea soup and a few of those delicious rolls. As we eat at the kitchen table, Mrs. Nygaard re-veals what's left on the to-do list for today. There are rugs to be beaten, bathrooms to be cleaned, and ovens to be scoured. Table-cloths, napkins, and hand towels to be ironed. Lightbulbs to be changed, candelabra to be arranged. We must finish the first floor today so we can come back early tomorrow and address the more public rooms on the second floor, then set up for the party.

"And our appointments?" Mother asks. "For our teeth?"

Mrs. Nygaard frowns. "Oh, yes. He told me to tell you. At the end of the day when everything's been accomplished, that's when he can fit you in."

My heart sinks. The day just got longer.

The doorbell rings and Mrs. Nygaard goes to receive a deliv-ery. Mother has more silver to polish in the dining room, so I quickly wash up our lunch things. I'm cleaning the sink when I notice a phone mounted on the wall before me, and beneath it the directory for the Danish Baptist Church.

In the past month, I've acted without permission and broken the rules more so than ever before in my life. I do so again now. I dial Theo's number—a number I know by heart. The Chastains' phone rings and rings, but there's no answer. My heart thuds in my chest. Time is wasting. Help, I pray, and another idea strikes me. I wonder, dialing Rob's work number, which I also memorize fearing a situation just like this, if these new impulses of mine are born of choice, or if they're becoming pure habit, or if they're gifts from God. I swallow hard, press the receiver to my ear. Then there's the operator's voice on the other end of the line. She says she'll have Rob paged. After a few minutes, he comes to the phone.

"Mother? Are you all right?"

"Can you talk? I'll be quick, I promise."

Rob draws in a sharp breath. "Rose! What on earth are you doing, calling me here? I've only been at this job a few days!"

"I'm sorry. I wouldn't have called if it wasn't an emergency."

I tell him then where I am, where I want to be tonight, and how important it is that I get there. "If you ever want to hear the Chess Men play again, you'll help me," I say. And then I ask Rob for a ride.

"How are you going to get out of there? I highly doubt the Nygaards have a fire escape. And how in God's name are your mother and Sophy going to make it home without your help?"

My knees go weak. How could I have been so thoughtless, or thoughtful only of myself—where I needed to be and how I needed to get there.

I lean against the wall, try to get my balance. And then I see the boxes of candles for Zane's cake, all lined up in a neat row on the counter, and I know the answer.

"Just be here by seven and I'll be waiting at the corner, I promise."

"You owe me a song, Laerke." Without further ado, Rob hangs up the phone.

"I'll pay up. Don't worry," I say to the buzz of disconnection.

I find Zane and Sophy in the library, safely returned from their escape. Sophy's cheeks are still pink from the fresh air. Zane has positioned her wheelchair by a large window, and together they watch a cardinal feasting at the birdfeeder just outside. I go quickly to them, and only the flash of red glancing past the glass and their startled gasps reveal the stillness that I've disturbed.

"I have to ask you something, Zane." My words are garbled; I'm talking all in a rush.

Sophy glares.

"I'm sorry." I press my hand to my throat. I can feel my blood surging there, the rapid throb of my beating heart. "I'll leave you in peace, quick as can be. I just need to ask—Zane, can you do me a favor? Can you drive Sophy and Mother home tonight? I have somewhere I need to be."

Zane's eyes widen at my tone. He understands. With a reassuring glance to Sophy, he draws me from the room. In the hallway, we exchange whispered words about where, and when, and why. Again, he promises he'll keep Sophy safe, and Mother, too. I thank him, thank him, thank him. And then I get back to work.

I fly through Mrs. Nygaard's list, tackling rugs, bathrooms, and ovens, while Mother does the ironing. It's seven o'clock by the time I've changed all the lightbulbs. Mother is still working on the candelabra. I return to the library and find Sophy sitting by a crackling fire now, tucked under a soft blanket. Zane has taken good care of her over the course of this long day. I touch

her shoulder, rousing her gently. Blinking sleepily, she smiles up
at me. She finds a way to tell me about the birds she saw at the
feeder and in the trees, the winsome squirrels, the swift fox, the
rabbit that just managed to escape him. Spring must be on its
way, I tell her, if there was a rabbit. Her smile widens. But then I
tell her that my work here is done. "I'm going to leave now," I say,
and her smile fades.

"Tell me," she says, and the why is in those words.

I hesitate. There's no time for the truth, I decide. The truth
would take too much explanation. Anyway, I'm not sure how
Sophy will take it when it comes. And the truth will have to
come. I've never been able to keep secrets from Sophy for long.
When I tell her my secret, the truth, I want to be able to stick
around. She might need me.

For now, I'll try out my excuse on her.

"Nils called . . . And this way, with Zane's help, you and
Mother will be able to get home a little earlier. It'll be fun, riding
home in Zane's car, Sophy. And heaven knows it will be nice to
get a little extra sleep before tomorrow."

"Fancy car," Sophy says.

I nod. "You better believe Zane's got a fancy car."

"Oh. I believe."

Her dry tone makes me laugh. But then her expression goes
sober.

"Nils." She draws out his name as if she's testing it for believ-
ability.

"Yes, Nils. You know how Mother and Dad feel about him." I
force out the half-truth. No, call it what it is: the lie.

Sophy screws up her mouth, doubtful and confused, but
then she says okay. "Have fun," she tells me.

Guiltily, I hurry from the room, find Mother, and tell my tale again. It feels no better that Mother practically shoos me out the door, saying she'll make my excuses to Mrs. Nygaard. "We'll be fine with Zane. You be home early enough to rise and shine, Rose!" Mother calls after me. "And make sure and thank Nils again for all his lovely gifts of late. The dill, the butter—you know."

I know. And I will thank him. First chance I have, tonight or tomorrow, I'm going to call Nils and thank him and apologize for turning him into a good excuse. The best of excuses, that's what he is, and of course he's so much more than that. He's the best of Danish-American men. I'm going to tell him so, and ask his forgiveness, and together we'll make a plan to really and truly do something special soon. Adler Planetarium Point on a starry night. We could do that. Or the train yards and freight cars where insects are aplenty—that, too. Whatever Nils wants, we'll do it. We'll go there. And if he asks to come to Calliope's and hear me sing, well, that would be wonderful, too.

I grab my coat and pocketbook, fly past the startled butler, and out the front door—yes, the front door! Down the sidewalk I go to the corner.

Long minutes pass during which I wait beneath the streetlamp.

Then there's a rumbling of gears and the rattletrap DeSoto with Rob inside rounds the corner, and now I'm inside the car, too. Never mind that I'm wearing an old black work dress. I've made my escape.

FOURTEEN

It is just after eight when Rob drops me off in front of Calliope's, then drives on to park the car. The place is already crowded and noisy. From so far back, I'm unable to catch even a glimpse of the stage. I make my way forward until I'm just behind the first row of tables, and only then do I see: the stage is empty. The opening band must be taking a break between sets, mingling with the crowd. Here's my opportunity to get back to the little practice room. I weave my way past one person after the next, hike up my black dress, clamber over the footlights, and duck behind the red velvet curtain.

But the little practice room proves empty.

"Just what do you think you're doing here?"

I spin around at the sound of a man's accusing voice. George, the hollow-chested stage manager, stands in the doorway.

"Backstage is off-limits—" He stops abruptly, and peers over his horn-rimmed glasses at me. "You're that singer from Tuesday night."

I nod.

George smirks. "Didn't recognize you in that getup."

I look down at my dress. I hadn't noticed the bleach stains and dirt on the black fabric before this moment. It's worse than I'd imagined. No wonder he didn't recognize me. The fact that I don't have on a smidgen of makeup probably doesn't help matters, either.

I run my hand through my hair, smoothing stray strands into place. "Where are the fellows?"

George shrugs. "Thought maybe you could tell me. Theo said they'd be here by now, practicing."

"Have they been late like this before?"

"Never. And wouldn't you know it? Tonight of all nights. The other band's bus broke down, so they're stranded in the middle of God-knows-where Kansas. Thought maybe you all could cover. The natives are getting restless out there."

"Theo and the fellows will show up soon. I'm sure of it." I sound surer than I feel.

"They better. There's a lot of hungry musicians out there right now, drowning their sorrows at the bar, begging for a chance to play. The boss is keeping his eyes peeled for the best candidates." George's glasses have slipped too far down his nose; he pokes them into place. "You all may be good, but that doesn't make you irreplaceable. Look at Lilah. Even Lilah wasn't irreplaceable. My advice, missy, make some phone calls, track your mates down. You've got twenty minutes to report some good news. Otherwise I'll get someone else to cover for the God-knows-where band, and if that someone happens to make the natives happy, and the boss, too—well, I might just ask them to play the night away. And things won't end up well for you, if you know what I mean. The Chess Men have already pushed the boss a little too far as it is."

George turns and goes. Twenty minutes and counting, and he'll have consulted with his boss, scouted the bar for hungry musicians, and picked the best of the lot.

I start searching the room for a phone. When I find it, I'll try Theo's house again. Maybe someone will be home by now—Mrs. Chastain or Mary, but not Theo, because he will be on his way here. He has to be on his way here. Mrs. Chastain or Mary will simply tell me how long it will be before he arrives. They'll tell me Dex, Ira, and Jim are with him. They're running late, that's all. They'll be here in plenty of time.

That's what Mrs. Chastain and Mary will tell me.

But there's no phone to be found in this little back room.

I run out into the club. In my hurry crossing the stage, I bump against the microphone. It's on. The rasping sound of my shoulder against it bounces around Calliope's. People look, look away. In this dress, I am the girl who does the cleaning. Fine by me. One benefit of wearing an ugly, dirty dress and looking unkempt (to put it nicely) is that you can slip through the crowd like a shadow. Shadow-like, I make my way to the bar. It takes some time to get a bartender's attention. I have to shout to be heard. He points at the coatroom. Apparently there's a phone back there.

I duck and scurry my way to where the coat-check girl sits behind her half-door. Tonight her blond hair is curled, the scrolls and loops as elaborate as fancy frosting on a cake. She exhales and a cloud of cigarette smoke engulfs me. I peer through it and over her shoulder and, yes, mounted on the far wall of the coat closet is a phone. When I ask to use it, the coat-check girl holds out a hand, palm up. I don't have a thing to give her for a tip. Not a penny or a piece of candy or a stick of gum. When I tell her this, she shrugs. "Sorry. Them's the rules." I say *please please please may I*, *please*, until she says, "Shut up, or I'm going to have you kicked out."

I shut up. I shadow my way backstage to the empty practice room again. I could take this as a sign from God: *You shouldn't sing these kinds of songs.* Or worse: *You shouldn't sing at all.* I could go home, lie down, give up.

Or not.

Or I could cover for the Chess Men, and I will, because they wouldn't be late—not if they could help it. Theo and the others are only late because something has gone very wrong.

A weight like a cold stone settles heavily in my chest at this thought.

The microphone was on. All I have to do is walk up to it and sing.

The weight grows heavier.

Just that little thing all by myself. That's all I have to do.

"Ha." My voice seems to float in the air before me, small and lonely. "Ha!" Louder this time. I believe in my voice, I remind myself, and others are relying on it. I say this to myself until the weight in my chest lightens. Just barely it lightens, but I can take a deep breath now and that helps.

The mirror hanging by the door helps, too, once I've forced myself to look into it. With the mirror's help, I try to make myself passably presentable. I take my hair down from its messy bun and run my fingers through it until it frames my face well enough. With a relatively clean towel, I rub my cheeks until they turn pink. My eyes are wide and bright with excitement—with fear, truth be told. But no one needs to be told that. Let the people out there simply see my eyes, wide and bright. As for my dress . . . well, there's not much to be done with it except brush away the dirt with the towel.

I am brushing at my sleeve when, reflected in the mirror, I catch a glimpse of something sparkling bright as a diamond on the top shelf of an open locker behind me. I go to the locker. The sparkling bright something is nearly hidden behind wads of dirty socks and T-shirts. Intent as a magpie, I reach for it. It is thin and cold and hard to my touch. I pull it out. It is a belt made of rhinestones. A belt as bright as diamonds that is surely Lilah's.

When Mother and Dad were first married and lived in a little house in Luck, the diamond fell from Mother's wedding ring. It was a little diamond—nothing more than a flawed chip—but it was the only valuable thing Mother owned, the testament of her husband's love, and she searched for it for days that turned into weeks. The space on the silver band where it had been gaped at her, day in, day out, as nagging and worrisome as a missing tooth. Months passed. The whole season of winter passed. Then early one Monday morning, she stood at the sink doing dishes, looking out at the clean laundry drying on the line. A breeze snapped the sheets and shook the blades of grass below, on which dew sparkled. One drop in particular sparkled more brightly than all the rest. The wind stilled, yet the tiny drop sparkled on, brighter than ever. Strange thing was, the sun had gone behind a cloud. Mother stared. Blinked. Gave a yelp and ran outside, her soapy hands dripping. She knelt down over the bright drop of dew and found her lost diamond. "A miracle," she said. "Just when I had all but given up hope."

I cinch Lilah's belt around my waist and turn back to the mirror. What it does for my black work dress isn't a miracle, exactly. But it's close enough.

I go to the door, open it. George isn't standing there, waiting for a report, but in two shakes of a lamb's tail, he will be. My twenty minutes are up.

I take a step forward. Feels like I'm diving off a cliff, diving into shallow, rocky water, as I walk onstage. The place is as noisy as it's ever been, and the lights are as bright, for which I'm grateful. With the microphone in front of me, I can almost pretend I'm still a shadow. Only the diamond belt has enough pizzazz to catch someone's eye. George's. He's standing at the foot of the stage, staring up at me.

"What do you think you're doing?" he says.

This is his job, I guess, to keep tabs on who's where and why. I lean away from the microphone so it won't pick up my voice. "Singing."

"Where's your backup?"

I don't answer. Whatever I say, it won't make a difference to George. He'll let me stay up here and do the best I can alone, or he won't. I lean back into the microphone again.

"Nice belt!" a man hollers from the audience. Someone laughs, and others join in.

In readying myself, I didn't plan what song to sing. Now, not a note or verse is coming to me. I close my eyes, trying to clear my head and still my mind.

"Great. Another off night at Calliope's," a man snaps.

A woman says, "I'm heading for the Sunset Café. Anyone care to join me?"

And then: "Laerke! Open your eyes!"

I look down to see Rob, standing by George at the foot of the stage.

Rob folds his arms across his chest and takes the strongest

stance he can. "You owe me a song, remember? 'Happy Days Are Here Again!' That's my request. Sing it. Now, Laerke. Now."

I want to close my eyes again. Like a little kid, I want to lose myself in delusion: *I can't see them, they can't see me.* But in so many ways, for so many reasons, I'm not a kid anymore. So I keep my eyes wide open. I look right at Rob. I sing for him:

> *The skies above are clear again*
> *Let us sing a song of cheer again*

If I were bathing Sophy, if I were holding her, calming her, keeping her safe, I would sing this song simply and sweetly. I would strip away embellishment, cast off showy impulse. I would open my heart to her. Let the music carry us someplace deep inside ourselves, a safe and sound place that endures even as cold seeps through windows and passing El trains rattle glass, endures even when Dad is angry and hurtful, and Mother is weary and haggard, and the cupboards are all but bare. I would sing us safe and sound, and ready us for whatever is next. Heaven on earth, or as close as we can get, that's what I would sing. I would sing us whole and able, even as we know all too well that we are broken. I would sing us free of our struggles and grief, even as we are aware that these experiences are inevitable, maybe even necessary. These experiences are, after all, what make us fully human, our true selves, receptive to blessing and healing and song.

I sing that way now, and Rob hears me. I owe him this; we owe each other a great debt. We're family, after all. We give and take, offer and receive. Tomorrow may be as hard as yesterday, but tonight Rob will have this song to remember. My gift.

I have to come to the end of it now. Quiet, eyes wide open, I smile down at Rob, who smiles up at me. Almost, I have forgotten that we are not alone. But then Rob starts to clap, and lo and behold, George joins in, and the next thing I know, other people are clapping, and those who aren't are waiting and watchful, not booing me off the stage. And here is a woman, and there, another woman, wiping tears from their eyes.

"Sing another, sister," a man calls from the back of the crowd.

I catch my breath. The man, hidden as he is, just might be an angel, for he has shared a vision. Never mind race or creed, status or religion. The strangers in this room are not strangers. They are my brothers and sisters. We are children of God.

I look out at the crowd and see family in need. I sing for them as I'd sing for Rob or Sophy. That gaunt woman whose makeup doesn't hide the bruise at the sharp line of her jaw—I sing her safe and sound. That man whose arrogant stance is belied by the rosary he worries between his fingers—I sing him heaven on earth, or as close as he can get. The elderly lady who's trying to look young, the young man who's trying to look old, the old man who's trying to stay alive, the middle-aged man who's drinking himself to death—I sing for them, one song after another. When someone shouts a request, I sing it if I'm able. If I don't know the lyrics, I promise I'll learn. "Give me another suggestion," I say, and I sing that instead.

After seven songs—none of them from the hymnal, but all of them feeling as sacred as can be—I realize that my mouth is going dry. I have maybe one song left in me to give, and it has to be a simple song, a small song, a fleeting birdsong that lingers in the air long after this bird has flown:

Just as I am
    Without one plea

I realize that I'm singing this sweet hymn as I finish the first verse. I'm not singing it as an altar call, not tonight. I'm singing it as a way of saying thanks. There is something of God in each and every one of these people, and for this reason, and this reason alone, they have accepted me just as I am, alone on the stage, but in their company.

I finish the song and leave the stage as quickly as I stepped onto it. Just as I am, I go back to the little room, where I find Theo and the other Chess Men, waiting.

They applaud with the audience, long and loud.

"What happened?" My legs feel leaden as the last bit of energy drains from them. I collapse into the nearest chair and take the glass of water Theo offers. Over its rim I see Ira's split lip. The blood crusting Dex's nose. And Jim, whose face is really a mess. Theo is the only one who appears unharmed, but when he sits down beside me, he winces, clutching his ribs.

"We got jumped." Dex opens his clarinet case and checks the instrument inside.

"What! Why?"

Theo gives a one-shouldered shrug. Again, that painful wince. "Wrong place, wrong time."

His grim tone stands in sharp contrast to his offhand remark. Adrenaline courses through me, and I stand up again. I find the towel I used to clean myself up and hand it to Jim, who is testing the strings of his bow even as his lip and forehead ooze blood. Then I hurry to the bathroom, collect towels there, run them under the questionably clean water, and hurry back. Ira, Dex, and Jim gratefully take the towels and start tending to their injuries. Theo, in my absence, has gotten a glass of ice from the bar. He wraps a towel around the ice, opens his shirt, presses the towel to his ribs, and I see the bruises there, purpling angrily against his dark skin.

"What place? What time?" I ask.

Dex takes a brown glass bottle from a cabinet. "Some guy called, said the manager at the Green Mill wanted to talk to us about a possible North Side gig. We went all the way up there, parked where he told us to, in the alley behind the joint. We weren't twenty feet away from the car when it happened." Dex douses a towel with what's in the bottle—rubbing alcohol, from the odor that pervades the room—then strides over to Jim and swiftly presses the towel to the gash on his forehead. Tears spring to Jim's eyes, but he doesn't say a word. (Jim's the garrulous one. He still calls me Blue Dress, though I've ask him to call me Rose.) "We were set up," Dex says, pressing harder, his black hands stark against Jim's pale, bleeding face. "There are more people who don't like us mixing things up than there are people who do. I'll find some tape to get you through the night, Jim." Dex continues as if this were all one seamless thought. "But after we're done here, we're getting you to the hospital. You need stitches."

"I should have known," Theo says. The ice is melting quickly against his skin. He looks at the towel like it's what did him wrong, then flings it hard against the wall. Roughly, Theo buttons his shirt again. "I *did* know. Some things never change. I just let myself forget that. I *wanted* to forget that. And look where my foolishness got us."

Theo's voice is so low that it's almost a growl. I remember what he said about the chains that made him a prisoner, not a man. *I won't be a prisoner to the color of my skin or the world we live in—not the way I was, not anymore.* That's what he vowed.

But it seems like tonight he was that prisoner again. Or he feels that way. And now he won't look at me. He won't look at anyone. He keeps his eyes trained on the floor.

The door to the room opens and George pokes his head in. "Are you going on, or what? Because I've got some other guys lined up. They're waiting by the stage, straining at the bit. I say the word and they'll take your place."

"We're going on," I say.

"Five minutes or forget it," George says.

Then it's just us, and we sit in silence, and I can't believe we'll ever be on any stage again. Theo doesn't look up from the floor. Ira presses his fingertips to the bruises circling his eyes. Dex takes the towel from Jim's face, and he and Jim regard the blood-stains there.

Moments pass that feel like hours. Then, without another word, they're up and gathering their things. I step outside into the hall while they change into their tuxedos, and one more long moment later, we're on.

This time I bring along a glass of water, and when that glass is empty, George delivers me another. Once people stop making cracks about the tough guys on the stage, we make good music. Occasionally I turn to see the pain on Jim's face, and the way Theo holds himself so stiffly at the keyboard. Or the lights hit Dex or Ira just so, and I realize they're in worse shape than they appeared to be in the dim light of the back room. Between the second and third sets, Jim, Ira, and Dex pop aspirin and change bandages. Icing his ribs again, Theo says he won't be able to drive me home at the end of the night. He has to take Jim to the hospital, and he thinks maybe he should get checked, too. Reassuring him that I can get a ride with Rob, I pass the bottle of aspirin his way.

We keep the third set short. Jim is looking ashen; he has to sit a couple of numbers out. In spite of the fact that Dex did his best to tape up Jim's wounds, the blood keeps seeping through the gauze. And Theo isn't playing nearly as well as usual. The last number of the night, he asks for a request from the audience, and Rob shouts, "How about another take on 'Just as I Am'?"

No one protests, so we jazz the hymn up and we wind it down, until practically everyone in the room is singing "Just as I Am." Some people are anything but sacred in their intentions, but others are clearly transported by the song; some even seem to be prayerful, singing. I keep my eyes on them. When the last note is played, Theo promises the crowd we'll be back tomorrow night.

Only then do I remember Zane's party, and the fact that I may very well have to come up with another good excuse to-morrow night to get away. And I remember Nils—the explanation I still owe him regarding tonight's excuse—and I feel guilty all over again.

Backstage, I'm tucking Lilah's rhinestone belt away where I found it, when Theo passes around the night's pay. A whole five dollars for each of us! I allow myself, if only briefly, to feel a little bit better. And then the fellows are talking about something I've never heard them talk about before. A recording! Someone came up to Dex after the last set—a producer—and we might have a shot at a record. That's where the real money is, and a real future.

I can't fathom it. But the five dollars—it's something to hold on to, and I do. I clutch the wrinkled bill tightly and hold it close to my heart. When I'm able to give it to Mother, and she's able to accept it, knowing how I earned it—that will be a happy day indeed.

FIFTEEN

Somehow we are on the El again, Mother, Sophy, and I, rushing through another cold, early morning. Today, as if in honor of Zane's party, the sky is cloudless. Stark sunshine glances sharply off buildings and pavement. I squint against the light, submit to it, close my eyes, and doze. Only a handful of hours ago I was onstage at Calliope's. Now Pastor Riis stands beside me there. An organ has replaced the piano, and Theo is playing a melody I'd know anywhere. He gives me a nod. I turn back to the microphone and start singing "Just as I Am." There's a movement at the back of the crowd. A young woman with bright blond hair, cigarette in hand—the coat-check girl!—comes forward for an altar call. She kneels before the stage and Pastor Riis says her name.

"Nils."

I awake with a jerk. *That's a boy's name, not a girl's* is all I can think. Blinking, I turn to Mother. Today, as yesterday, Sophy sits on Mother's lap. Not minutes into our journey, Sophy fell asleep, too. Looks like she's staying that way. Lucky girl. I press my hand to my mouth to suppress a yawn as Mother repeats herself in a whisper. I'm half asleep, but I believe she just asked me if Nils is helping with the Nygaards' party today.

Wide awake now. "Sorry?"

"Last night. Did he say he was coming?"

My good excuse has caught up with me and turned into a bad lie.

"No," I say. "He didn't mention it."

Mother frowns. "Mrs. Nygaard had a fellow cancel. She asked if Andreas could help with some of the heavier work, but Andreas is preaching at a rally in Lincoln Park tonight. I suggested Nils instead. She said she was going to call him first thing after Sophy and I left. Oh, dear. I wonder if she decided on someone else. I know how much Nils likes to earn extra money when he can."

Never has sunlight seemed so harsh. It must be revealing my every flaw and indiscretion.

"Nils didn't say a word." In the thicket of lies springing up around me, this, at least, holds an element of truth.

Mother sighs. "Well, I guess we'll just have to wait and see who she found. I was hoping you'd have someone you'd enjoy working with today."

"It would be nice."

There. The whole truth and nothing but the truth, if lamely said.

He's here.

I hear his laughter before I see him—a clear, bell-like sound that chimes with memories. I'm standing in the Nygaards' kitchen, and Nils is in their dining room, but we could easily be children again, playing hide-and-seek in the church basement, or skipping stones across the surface of Lake Michigan during a junior high picnic, or caroling together, back in high school again. At happy times like these, Nils's laughter made me all the happier. Apparently his laughter has the same effect on the Nygaards' butler, for now he's laughing, too. From the sound of things, the two of them are working together in the dining room, adjusting the leaves in the table. "I think we've reached our limit," the butler says, and Nils says something else to make him laugh.

Mother, who is positioning Sophy close to the kitchen radiator for warmth, looks up at me and smiles. "I'm so glad Mrs. Nygaard did as she said she would. But why on earth didn't he tell you last night?"

Like that, my happy memories vanish. I shrug and head toward the door to the dining room.

"Don't you want to take off your coat first?" Mother asks.

Pretending I don't hear, I flee the kitchen. I must get to Nils before Mother does. I must prune this growing thicket—at the very least, the rapidly rising tangle between Nils and me.

I'm not a foot into the dining room when the butler swallows his laughter and gives an order. "There's another table that needs to be expanded to seat ten in the parlor. You two can see to that."

"With pleasure," Nils says, as always, respectful of authority.

He opens the parlor door for me and ushers me inside, whispering, as he does, so that the pleasure is indeed his. My cheeks burn. Nils blushes, too; he clearly regrets being so forward. But that's not the cause of my embarrassment. Guilt. That's the cause for me.

Nils is a wonderful man, not a good excuse.

We clear a lamp and assorted china figurines from a large mahogany table, then stand at either end and pull until it separates into two parts. "A table divided shall not stand." Nils breaks the strained silence with this little joke, and now I am remembering another time: the two of us acting out a scene from *Romeo and Juliet* in our high school English class. *Two households, both alike in dignity/In fair Verona where we lay our scene,/From ancient grudge break to new mutiny,/Where civil blood makes civil hands unclean.* We shared the role of Chorus. It was all we could do to get through the opening lines of the play with straight faces.

Nil has located table leaves in a closet. He tucks a leaf under each arm and lugs them over. Together we wrestle the leaves into place. In minutes, we've wrestled two more. That should do it, we agree. We adjust the rest of the furniture accordingly. Nils smiles. "We make a great team," he begins, and before he can say anything more I tell him.

"I lied, Nils. I said I was seeing you last night so I could go to a jazz club."

His smile fades. The way he looks at me, you'd think we'd never hidden and sought, skipped, caroled, or chorused. You'd think we'd never laughed together. You'd think I was a stranger.

"I don't understand." He gives his head a rough shake. It's like there's an insect buzzing too close—not a rare specimen but an irritating distraction, a fly or a mosquito, perhaps. His shock of hair falls into his eyes and, rougher still, he shoves it aside and looks at me. "You said you were seeing me so you could go where?"

"Calliope's. It's a club. You can hear music there. Live music."

"Where is it?"

Honesty is the best policy. "Bronzeville."

Nils is standing by a divan. He sits down hard, then, remembering he's on the job, stands up quickly. "What do you mean, 'live music'?"

"Jazz. The musicians play jazz." This comes out in a most unmusical croak. "And I sing there sometimes, too."

"Oh, really."

I take a step toward him. "I wish you'd come with me sometime." *But Theo*, I think. Confused, I push the thought away. "I could go to the train yard with you, and you could come to Calliope's with me. That's a fair exchange, don't you think? You'll be amazed, Nils. Not at my singing—I mean, you know what I sound like—but at the rest of the musicians." I feel desperate to explain. "If the music were an insect, it would be the most beautiful, iridescent butterfly you could ever find."

"Not a moth? Not a beetle?" Nils steps around me and walks toward the parlor door.

"Nils." I follow him. "Wait."

He opens the door, turns toward me. "I need to find Mr. Poole."

This must be the butler's name. "But—"

"We have a job to do, Rose." He looks at me, then his face softens. "I'm sorry. You took me by surprise, that's all. It's not that you used me as an excuse. I'd do just about anything for you, you know that. It's what you used me as an excuse for. I don't understand why you'd want to go to a place like that to listen to music like that. For pity's sake, I'm meeting with Pastor Riis after church tomorrow to ask about the purpose of hymns! I'm concerned, Rose. Very concerned."

"Let me explain about hymns. Let me explain about everything," I say.

He gives another hard shake of his head. "We have a job to do, Rose. We need to get to work. I'll feel better when things are under control. Tonight, maybe you'll let me drive you and your mom and Sophy home. That's what I was hoping, anyway. I could come up for a cup of coffee. Maybe we could talk more about this then."

I tell him I'd like that. Then I remember that I won't be going home with Mother, Sophy, and Nils tonight. I'll be going to Calliope's.

I catch hold of his arm. There's nothing light about my touch. Desperate again, my words come out in a rush. I beg him not to tell Mother what I've told him. For that matter, don't tell anyone. I'll explain to my family, I promise, as soon as I'm able. They'll understand. He'll understand. Just, please, as a favor, play along for now.

Nils watches me for a moment. "No one's getting hurt, right? Especially you?"

"No! Everything's fine! I'm better than fine!"

"I guess I can keep your secret, then. For a little while."

He forces a smile. I wish it inspired one in me. But I'm too busy thinking of Theo and the others last night, bruised and bleeding.

"No one's getting hurt," I say. Another lie. "No one will get hurt." Plagued by guilt again, and doubt, too, I somehow make this sound like a promise.

Not an hour later, Mother tells me that Rob called the Nygaards' house and left a message for me. His mother is sick. He'll have to stay with her tonight. "Though why he thought you needed to know this, I have no idea," Mother says.

I know why. In just a few hours, I'll have to find another way to Calliope's. Another way home for Sophy and Mother. I'll have to find another way to lie.

Once upon a time, I might have said that Zane's birthday party was in full swing. Now that I've been to Calliope's, I have to say this party's got no swing. Not seven o'clock at night, and most of the guests are yawning, having consumed a rich dinner. After an ardent conversation among some of the women about the latest bestselling novel, Margaret Mitchell's *Gone with the Wind*—"*I've never read the like! Such a fascinating portrayal of plantation life.*" "*I know. All those slaves! So loyal!*" "*And the passion! It kept me up nights, I'll tell you!*"—the conversation falters. Each and every person, even Zane, looks bored. No wonder so many of the guests rely on cigarettes for something to do. If come nine o'clock tonight, they're all still this bored, maybe one of them will take me to Calliope's. Maybe someone else can take Sophy and Mother home.

I'm just about desperate enough to ask.

At least Sophy's not in the midst of all this smoke. She's safely tucked away in the kitchen with Mother, who's arranging twenty-five candles on Zane's cake. Nils is in the kitchen, too, washing his way through stacks of dishes. Only I am out here in the midst of the revelers, strolling from library to parlor to game room and back again, pushing a tea cart on which stand pots of coffee and tea and stacks of cups and saucers.

"Miss!"

I start. I'd been wondering which guests might consider the favor I need to ask. Who at this party besides Zane would venture to the west side of the city? And as for the south side—well, life on a plantation in the pre–Civil War South is one thing. It's *Gone with the Wind* in more ways than one. Life in Bronzeville is another thing altogether. It's right over there, just a few miles away, and I believe most everyone here would like to keep it as distant as antiquity.

The young lady who Missed me lifts a finger to attract my attention. "Here."

I push the tea cart across the library to the window seat where she sits with a young man.

"I'm terribly thirsty."

I study her, this young lady. She's elfin, a wisp of a waif in a green velvet dress, with a pert nose and a long, slender neck that seems even longer and more slender because her black hair is twisted up in a high French knot. A high school friend did my hair up like this once, back at our other house. She and I were just going out for ice cream, but we pretended we were on our way to a cotillion. We'd read about such events in novels.

"I said I'm thirsty," the young lady says.

She sounds worse than a child, which is how I realize that she is one. She's probably younger than Sophy. She purses her lips at the young man who sits beside her. He's about Sophy's age, too—just a boy, really. He rolls his eyes, understanding his friend's predicament. *Help these days!*

"Cold punch. That's what's called for," she says.

I bob my head as Mrs. Nygaard directed me to do when presented with a request, then trundle the tea cart off toward the kitchen. I've been avoiding Nils all day—or he's been avoiding me. Regardless, we've caught only glimpses of each other. So now I fix a smile on my face in anticipation of encountering him with Mother and Sophy also present. All must appear as it should be between Nils and me.

But when I trundle the tea cart through the kitchen door, I see only Mother, setting the last candles into place, and Sophy, sitting in her chair. There's the sound of footsteps descending the cellar stairs; perhaps Nils heard me coming and fled. If I'm feeling concerned about giving myself away, surely he is.

I pull the kitchen door closed behind me. "The cake looks delicious."

Mother goes to the sink and washes her hands. "Only the flowers to add now." Drying her hands, she nods at a bowl of purple and orange blooms on the table. "They're edible."

I can't imagine the taste of flowers, but I believe her. In this house, anything is possible, except a ride to Bronzeville. I go to the counter where the punch bowl stands and ladle some into a pitcher. I am setting the cup on the tea cart when the kitchen door swings open and Mrs. Nygaard makes her entrance.

"It's time," she announces.

"Already?" Mother looks startled. "I thought you said eight o'clock. I'm sorry, Andrea. I'm not quite finished decorating—"

Mrs. Nygaard cuts her off. "Given the circumstances, I prefer that you address me by my surname, as I've repeatedly asked you to do."

Sophy hisses softly so that only I hear. I hope only I hear. I hope that Mrs. Nygaard continues to act as if Sophy doesn't exist. There's frosting on my sister's upper lip. Mrs. Nygaard won't like it if she sees that Mother has been treating Sophy to tastes.

"I'm sorry. I keep forgetting." Mother twists her hands together.

Mrs. Nygaard purses her lips in irritation. "The flowers, please."

Mother gets the bowl and starts carefully arranging the

blossoms in little clusters on the topmost tier of the cake. She cleans as she decorates, working carefully from top to bottom. But apparently she isn't working fast enough. Mrs. Nygaard snatches the bowl from Mother and, in a flurry of purple and orange, tosses blossoms hither and yon over the frosting.

"There." Mrs. Nygaard sets the empty bowl on the table and pats her hair into place. "Now, then. Zane has made a request, one that surprises me, I must admit, but here it is. Zane wants to hear Rose sing."

My hand is at my throat. I swallow hard and lower my hand. It takes some effort to keep from yelping. "Really?" This comes out in a kind of squeak.

Mrs. Nygaard regards me. "Really."

"I don't know," I say. "I'm not prepared."

Mother says, "Take off your apron, Rose."

Numbly, I obey. I'm wearing another black dress—this one provided by Mrs. Nygaard. It's a little nicer and cleaner than last night's, but not much. I run my hands down the skirt, smoothing it. Really, there's no need to worry, and certainly no need for a sparkling belt. This isn't a gig, after all. It's a favor. No, an obligation.

"'Happy Birthday'?" I ask. "Is that what he'd like to hear?"

"I assume so," Mrs. Nygaard says dryly.

Mother quickly adds, "Just don't make a spectacle of yourself, dear."

"Indeed. Don't do that." Mrs. Nygaard presses her fingers to her temples. She appears to have a headache. "Sing the song through once, then lead our guests as you lead the congregation."

"You're singing, Rose?"

I whirl around at the sound of Nils's voice. He stands in the cellar doorway. He must have come up the stairs without my hearing. His gaze is troubled.

"Again?" he asks.

"What do you mean *again*?" Mother says.

"He's talking about church. It's been almost two weeks since I sang in church, Nils." Somehow I am smiling. "But we're not talking about church. We're talking about right now, Zane's party, 'Happy Birthday.'" Dodging the tea cart, I rush to the door. "Where shall I stand to sing, Mrs. Nygaard?"

She frowns. "Wait a moment." She points at Mother. "Light the candles." Points at Nils. "Bring the cake into the library when the guests join in singing." Points at me. "Come."

I follow Mrs. Nygaard into the library, where she positions me by the door. Word must have spread; the guests have all gathered here. Dr. Nygaard sits in the warm glow of the fire. Zane stands beside him. Zane knows what's coming, it's clear from the way he flicks his eyebrows at me. And suddenly I'm glad to sing for him. It's the least I can do, given the way he helped me out last night, driving Sophy and Mother safely home. I can wish Zane all happiness with this song.

I flick my eyebrows back at him, a signal that all is well.

Mrs. Nygaard raises her hands, quieting the conversation. "As you know, it's my son's special day. But then, every day is my son's special day as far as I'm concerned."

Polite laughter fills the room. Zane hides his face in his hands and then looks up, grinning. He appears at ease with this attention. He appears entitled to it.

Mrs. Nygaard looks at me. "Now," she says.

I sing "Happy Birthday." I sing with all my heart, thanking Zane, blessing this new year of his life as best I can. I work my way through the song. Zane is smiling, happy. I lift my hands so that others will sing along. But no one does, and I want Zane happier yet, so I sing the song again, solo. I improvise a little to keep it interesting. Lift my hands higher, and sing it a third time, slower, so people can join in if they like. Join in now. But still, it's only me, my voice filling the room.

Zane beams at me. At least there's that.

This time, when the song is finished, I am finished, too. Silence takes up the space where my voice just was. I glance over at Mrs. Nygaard. She is rubbing at her temples again.

"That's certainly not the way you sing in church," she says.

I've changed, I realize. The nights in Bronzeville are changing me, and my voice. Calliope's is changing me. The Chess Men are changing me. And Theo. My singing is changing for the better, I think. I hope.

Silence expands all around. I clear my throat to break it. Lift my hands again. "Please," I say. "Together. Let's sing."

Before anyone can so much as make a peep, someone starts to clap. It's Zane. Others join in. The applause grows. People stamp their feet. The elfin girl nods proudly at me, like I'm something she created. "Brava!" someone shouts. And others shout, "Encore!"

"Rose?" Mother says.

She stands in the kitchen doorway. Nils is there, too, holding a cake on fire. That's how it appears to me at this moment. The candles' waxy scent, the lingering odor of sulfur from the many matches Mother must have struck to light the many wicks, wafts toward me. The cake wavers in the heat; Nils sweats from it. But though the green wax is dripping onto the white frosting now, Nils doesn't carry the cake to Zane. He stands staring at me until Mrs. Nygaard tells him to hurry, hurry, hurry. Mother tears her gaze from me. She heads back to the kitchen as Nils bears the cake over to Zane. After a few attempts, Zane blows out the candles. Applause fills the room again. By the time Nils has set the cake on a side table, Mother has returned, pushing the tea cart, which now holds dessert plates, forks, and napkins.

"Shall we hear another from our guest singer?" Zane asks as Mother pushes the tea cart over to where Nils stands, cutting the cake. Nils pauses, knife in hand, and gives me a wary look, as does Mother. They needn't worry. I am finished being the unpaid entertainment for the evening. I am finished revealing my secret passion.

I start to shake my head, but then I glimpse Mrs. Nygaard's scowl. Dr. Nygaard plants his hands on his knees and leans forward in his chair. If I decline and anger them, what will happen? I think of our family's past and our future. I think of Sophy in her wheelchair, sitting close to the kitchen radiator for warmth.

"What would you like her to sing?" Mrs. Nygaard gives Zane a bright, forced smile, but people think she is putting out a general call for requests. "'Danny Boy,'" someone says. And others: "'Greensleeves.'" "'America the Beautiful.'" "'Keep Your Sunny Side Up!'"

Zane looks at me. "You choose, Rose."

Fine. Let everyone else think I'm singing for our supper. The truth is, I'm singing for my sister.

I close my eyes and pretend I'm surrounded by the Chess Men. I can almost believe I hear Theo's fingers lightly flying over the piano keys:

My heart is sad and lonely
For you I pine, for you, dear, only

The last verse of "Body and Soul" finished, there's not a moment of silence. The room erupts. For a moment I keep my eyes closed, taking it all in—the applause and whistles. People are asking where I perform, when I'll perform again.

"She doesn't perform. She sings in church," Mother says.

I open my eyes. Mother is handing around plates of cake. She passes by me to retrieve more servings from Nils. As she does, she whispers, *"Skam dig."* I don't know much Danish, but I know this. *Shame on you.*

Cake is being eaten. Presents will be opened. There are dishes to be done.

I go to the kitchen, roll up the sleeves of Mrs. Nygaard's black work dress—the bruise Dad gave me has gone greenish—and plunge my hands into the water in the sink. Sophy watches me from her chair.

"Sing," she says.

The sound of water sloshing reminds me of all the times I've bathed her. I sigh. "'Shall We Gather at the River'? Or 'Washed in the Blood'?"

Sophy laughs like I've made some kind of joke. "Body. Soul," she says.

I turn back to the sink. Grimly scrub at a glass. "I just sang that one, Sophy. And you know Mother doesn't like those songs."

Sophy slams her feet against the chair, startling me. I turn sharply toward her, my hands dripping soapy water on the floor. Her lips are pursed in a pout. She reminds me of someone. The elfin girl demanding cold punch—that's who Sophy reminds me of at this moment.

All in a rush I'm tired, very tired, of taking care of other people. And I still don't have a ride. Not for me or Mother or Sophy. I still haven't gotten what I need. What *we* need, I mean.

"I don't want to sing right now," I say. I plunge my hands back into the dishwater. I rinse the glass clean. I wash all the glasses that still need washing. Mother and Nils are bringing in the dirty dessert plates now. Mother won't talk to me; she hardly looks at me. Nils asks only if I need any help. No, I tell him. I'm fine. Mrs. Nygaard will have something for him to do soon enough, I'm sure.

And I'm right. Mrs. Nygaard calls Nils and Mother into the other part of the house and sets them to work there. I'm left to tackle the kitchen alone, with Sophy for company. But Sophy, exhausted from the day, is soon asleep in her chair. I work quietly, quickly, plate by plate, fork by fork, setting Mrs. Nygaard's kitchen right again.

But what will happen if I leave before the job is completely done? I'm not worried about myself. I'll endure whatever consequences come my way. But Mother—what might she suffer at the hands of Mrs. Nygaard if I leave things less than perfect?

By nine o'clock the party is over, the guests are gone, and the kitchen is clean. If I run for the El now, then I could make it to Calliope's on time. But where would that leave my mother and sister?

That's what I'm wondering when Zane bursts into the kitchen, holding two coats, his and mine. "Come on!" He grabs my arm and tugs me past suddenly-wide-awake Sophy to the back door. "I just threw everyone for a real loop." He's practically crowing this news. "I told my parents that all I really want for my birthday is to go out on the town with you. I said there's a singer I've been dying to hear who's finally performing in Bronzeville, and tonight was my only night to hear her. I didn't say it was you, of course. I simply hinted that you and I might be an item. You should have seen the looks on their faces, Rose! I mean, *I* know Nils is your fellow, but for tonight, let's say what we have to, to get where we need to go. Agreed? I'm suffocating in this house. I need to get some fresh air and really *celebrate*. And as for you— well, you know what you need to do."

I shake my head. "Mother and Sophy—"

Zane shoves his arms into his coat. "Stop worrying. I've taken care of that, too. Poole's got it all worked out with our chauffeur. Sophy and your mother will be luxuriously transported to your place. There are just a few more things to tidy up, and Nils will help. The work will be done in no time."

Somehow I'm wearing my coat. Zane must have worked some other magic, slipping it onto me without my knowing.

Now he opens the door, and Sophy's voice pierces the air.

"Singer? Me, too?"

I turn to her. From her chair by the stove, she stares at me. Her expression is troubled, forlorn. She wants to escape again. She wants to celebrate with Zane. She wants to hear a song.

"Great idea, Sophy!" Zane glances at me, checking for my okay. "Let's get you bundled up for the drive."

The wind rattles the frost-covered windows. It's bitterly cold again. There might be another storm brewing. It wouldn't be safe taking Sophy out on a night like this. If Mother ever found out, she'd really and truly never forgive me. Heck, I'd never forgive myself if something happened to Sophy. That would be pain from which we'd never recover.

"I'm sorry, sweetheart," I say. "Not tonight. You could catch your death."

Her pained expression makes me want to weep. To keep from doing just that, I bolt from the kitchen. Zane steers me toward the garage, where his sleek car awaits us, already running, warmed up by Mr. Poole.

That night, singing my heart out, I pour all the pain of Sophy's expression into the sad songs. I pour all the joy of her afternoon escape into the happy ones. I wish, oh, I wish she was here.

I wonder at the music in my life. I look at Theo, his hands on the piano keys, and remember Nils, a butterfly in his hands, and I wonder about these men, too. What is my calling? Who is calling to me? How will I answer? I wonder all these things and more.

Zane I don't wonder about one bit. He's flirting and dancing the night away. When I catch his eye, he pounds his fists against his chest, yet another Tarzan-in-the-making. I'm glad for him. After the iron lung of his childhood, it's no wonder he wants to celebrate his birthday with wild abandon.

I fill my own lungs with air and sing another song. Once I was a lark tangled in a thicket, trapped for so long that I'd forgotten I had wings. Then a fierce storm stirred the branches. When the storm quieted, I glimpsed light, an opening to the great beyond. Perched on the edge of the only world I'd known, I spread my wings. I discovered I could fly.

That's the story behind the song that I'm singing. And the song that I'm singing opens a whole new world.

It's not my new world my sister wants, I realize. She wants—she *deserves*—her own.

SIXTEEN

The ride to church is silent. Dad broods. Mother broods, sometimes dozes. Sophy dozes, sometimes broods. I stare out the window at the feeble sun creeping between buildings. No one has said a word about last night—my night on the town with Zane, as I suppose it's understood. In fact, no one has said a word to me at all. When it comes to Dad, this isn't surprising. But extended silence from Sophy and Mother fills me with concern. Sophy is still angry that I wouldn't let her come along last night because of the bad weather. Mother is still upset that I know such worldly songs. And not only do I know them, but I know how to sing them well.

My thoughts turn in circles around my concerns until we pull up in front of the church. Dad helps Mother and me lift Sophy up the front steps and into the sanctuary. We settle into our back pew. For oh, so many reasons, we got a late start this morning; there was no time to load the wheelchair into the trunk. We'll have to navigate the service and coffee hour as best we can without it, and without Dad, of course. Dad's already on his way out the door. Andreas might be able to help when the service is finished, if he's not too busy praying with people. Then again, Andreas is preaching today. He's giving the altar call. He'll no doubt be busy.

The Nygaards are nowhere to be seen. I didn't expect to see Zane up and about this bright and early. He was glad to let Theo drive me home; he headed off to yet another bar. But Dr. and Mrs. Nygaard never miss church. Perhaps they're doing their own brooding at home.

I spot Dolores now, seated near the front of the sanctuary. She attended last Wednesday night as well, and the Wednesday before that, as she said she would, though she sat near the back and slipped away before Rob or I could talk to her. There was the same guest speaker both nights—a Danish Baptist missionary who has served in Ruanda-Urundi and hopes to enter its northern portion within the next two years. To Sophy's delight, the missionary opened the first of his talks by reading excerpts from the poem "The White Man's Burden" by Rudyard Kipling. The missionary exhorted us to take up the burden and exile ourselves to serve the great need abroad, to wait:

> *On fluttered folk and wild—*
> *Your new-caught, sullen peoples,*
> *Half-devil and half-child.*

Once I would have appreciated this poem, too, but it doesn't settle well with me now. I keep wondering what Theo would think of "the White Man's burden." Often enough, he and the other Chess Men talk about Africa. "The cradle of civilization," someone will say. "The cradle of jazz," someone else will say.

"Same difference." Someone else will say that. And then Theo will play a spiritual on the piano, and Dex will weave in a jazz riff, and the heavenly and the worldly will be one and the same, harmonious. Until something comes over Theo, some sadness that makes him lift his hands from the keys and hold himself tight, and Dex stops playing, too. "What's wrong?" Jim once asked, setting aside his bass, going to the piano and planting his big hand on Theo's shoulder. Theo didn't answer. He shrugged off Jim's hand, suddenly as angry as I've ever seen him. *Chains.* That was the word that came to my mind. But I kept quiet. I didn't go to Theo or try to ease his pain. It's not my place to do so. Not yet.

Sophy still recites bits and pieces of that Rudyard Kipling poem from day to day, aided by anyone in our family with the time and patience to follow along in his *Collected Works.* I've helped so often that now I can recite the poem, too. I guess that's another reason it's become what I remember most about the missionary's talks, along with the guilt suffered by Mother because we were unable to give money to the Ruanda-Urundi effort. After two nights at Calliope's, I now have ten dollars tucked under my pillow. When the time is right, Mother will be able to do with that money what she likes. (When will the time be right? That's the question.) If Dad allows, perhaps she'll give some to the missionary. It will feel like a luxury, being able to give again. A luxury afforded by my singing. Perhaps that's how I'll start the conversation about my work with the Chess Men. *We can tithe again now.* When the time is right, that might be a good approach.

Rob slips into the pew beside me as the organist plays the opening to the first hymn. "How did it go last night?" he whispers. I start, afraid he'll be overheard, jogging Sophy's head in my lap. Sophy glares until I apologize. I glance at Mother. She's busy scrounging for a handkerchief in her pocketbook, so I lean close to Rob. "Great," I whisper. "But Mother knows something's up."

Rob grimaces, and his worry only heightens mine.

The congregation stands to sing, except Mother, Sophy, Rob, and me. Rob and Mother take hymnals from the rack and find the right page. Rob holds his hymnal so Sophy and I can see. Together, Rob and I sing the hymn. Sophy chimes in on this word and that. Mother, never much of a singer, follows along, mouthing the words silently. "'The Lord God made them all,'" we sing. The Lord God made this music and that music, too. The Lord God made Nils, sitting across the aisle, steadfastly not looking at me. The Lord God made Theo, who is surely sitting with his family at the African Methodist Church. The Lord God made the Chess Men, and the audience at Calliope's last night, the bartenders, the coat-check girl, George, and the boss, whoever the boss may be. The Lord God made the time that stopped while I sang and all those people became my brothers and sisters, my nearest and dearest, the way the people in this pew are, the way everyone in this sanctuary is, including Dolores and Zane and his parents, too. We are all God's children. I sing for us now. I sing to high heaven. I sing because I'm called to do so, and the Lord God stops time until we finish the hymn.

In his sermon, Andreas speaks about our fascination with the world. He talks about the crowds flooding movie theaters to see Charlie Chaplin's first talkie, *Modern Times*. "In these modern times, shouldn't we be looking at our sinful hearts instead? There is no glitter there, or glamour, either. There is only despair." He speaks of the dark heart of Ruanda-Urundi, where our missionary friend fearlessly journeyed. "There are sullen people, half-devil and half-child, right here in Chicago, too," Andreas says. "Just look at the hoodlums and harlots roaming our streets. You don't have to go to Africa to find ignorance and despair." Andreas looks right at me. "You just have to go to Bronzeville. Or you might consider looking in your own backyard. Or at your heart."

Mother told Andreas about last night. The song I sang at Zane's, and where I went afterward.

I don't hear the rest of the sermon. I don't know what Andreas says that prompts Dolores to go forward during the altar call. I only know that she is saved, and, in Andreas's eyes, I am lost.

We don't stay for coffee hour. Mother says Dad will be waiting outside in the car. Fine by me. Andreas is lingering at the altar now, but my brother and I would surely cross paths at coffee hour. If we did (when we did), he'd make it his mission to save me from Bronzeville. *Your new-caught, sullen peoples,/Half-devil and half-child.* That's who I am now.

Nils still won't look in my direction.

The car reeks of cigarettes and something else—whiskey, I'm guessing, from the array of liquors I've smelled at Calliope's. Dad's been at it again. I keep my eyes on the road and hold tight to Sophy. The ride home from church proves as silent as the ride there, only this time no one dozes. If Mother told Andreas, she must have told Dad, too. I hold Sophy tighter, and my coat sleeve creeps up to reveal what's left of Dad's mark. I once saw a man with jaundice; my bruise has turned just that dull yellow. The pain is faint unless I press down, which sometimes I do as a reminder. I press down now. I won't let him hurt me again.

We park in the alley behind our apartment building and take the back stairs up to our place. Dad carries Sophy. Mother and I follow. Inside the kitchen, Mother drops into a chair by the table. Dad lowers Sophy into her lap. Mother's eyes are bloodshot. How late did she stay at the Nygaards' last night? Quite late, the purple shadows beneath her eyes suggest. I sit down in the chair beside her and gently rub her bony, knotted shoulders while Dad circles the kitchen.

"I spoke with Dr. Nygaard early this morning," Dad says.

Mother winces at my touch. I lighten up.

"You've nothing to say?" Dad glares at me. I look back at him; I struggle to keep my gaze steady and calm. He wheels away and strides to the kitchen window, stares out at the curve of the El tracks that bank past. Even from where I sit I can hear the tracks faintly humming. A train is fast approaching.

"The Nygaards offered Mother a job as their full-time housekeeper. She's accepted," Dad says.

Sophy hisses her no. The humming grows to a rumble. The El is less than two blocks away. I can see the engine's blunt, cold face. The dishes and bowls stacked in the open cupboard tremble. Glasses and cups skitter toward the cupboard's edge. If these things aren't pushed back far enough when they are put away, they will fall off the edge and shatter on the floor. We learned this the hard way. Whoever put them away last must have forgotten.

I rush to the cupboard, quickly push back the glasses and cups. I reposition plates and bowls, too. This is Mother's only everyday set. I must make sure nothing is broken.

The El train blasts past, shaking crockery and glass. From where Dad stands at the quaking window, he should be able to see every person on board, their unconscious gestures and private moods. When people don't think they're being watched, so much is revealed. I learned that living here, watching out these windows. And then I started climbing out one and down the fire escape, and I wasn't only watching anymore. I was in the thick of it.

The train thunders on until the sound fades. Dad turns back to us. "Starting tomorrow, Rose, you will stay with your sister during the day, and in the evenings, too. Your mother will be too tired to do so. Andreas is too busy, as am I. And the Nygaards have said that your mother must spend the night at their house when they entertain—sometimes the night before a party, sometimes the night after a party, sometimes both. They entertain frequently, as you know, so you'll be Sophy's only real companion then."

Sophy hisses again, and Mother holds her closer, tells her to hush.

I hear myself ask if Dad's trying to kill his wife.

Dad gapes at me.

"Because that's what's going to happen." I'm the one pacing now; I'm the one circling the kitchen. "They'll work you to death, Mother. You know it. Dad, you know it, too. Heck, Sophy knows it. Mother can't be the Nygaards' full-time housekeeper. She won't be. I won't let her."

"I don't have a choice," Mother says wearily. "You don't have a choice, Rose."

"Your mother's right." Dad's voice is harsh. "Your shenanigans at Zane's party did not endear you to the Nygaards. We may appreciate Zane's sudden interest in you, but they do not.

Dr. and Mrs. Nygaard want you out of sight, out of mind. They're none too happy with us for another reason as well. Because I've told them you need to be with Sophy, they'll have to pay another girl to take over your cleaning duties, daughter."

Daughter. What should be an endearment, a testament to our bond, makes me feel demeaned. He says it like I'm a little child. Or, worse, like he owns me. I touch my bruise again, press down until the dull ache rises to meet fingertips. *Say it*, I tell myself. *Say it now.*

I say, "I can make more money in one week than Mother and I put together."

Dad laughs. I can hear his thoughts, and they aren't anything like music. *You, daughter? What could you possibly do besides care for your sister, or get married and care for your sister.*

"With the money I'll make singing, Mother can stay home with Sophy. She won't have to work at all." I say this, too.

Mother bows her head. Her lips move in prayer. Sophy watches Dad and me, wide-eyed.

"What's that?" Dad's voice is too quiet.

"I said." I draw in a deep breath. "I'll sing. I'll get paid to do it, and I can still be with Sophy during the day. We'll get by. We'll more than get by—we'll do better than we're doing now."

"You can't sing," Dad says.

I don't have the freedom, he means. Come to think of it, he may mean I don't have the talent, either. Since he doesn't come to church, he's rarely heard me sing.

"I can. I'll show you." I fly to the bedroom, take the five-dollar bills from beneath my pillow, and fly back to the kitchen. I hold up the money. It is all I can do to keep from waving it in Dad's face. "Ten dollars. I made this in two nights, singing."

"Is that what you call it? *Singing?*"

Dad's innuendo isn't lost on me. But instead of shaming me into submission, it has the opposite effect. I turn to Mother and Sophy. I press the money into Mother's hands. I speak only to her.

"I will give you everything I earn. That'll be fifteen dollars a week, Mother—and that's just for starters. There'll be more. And we'll have Dad's salary on top of that. We'll pay our bills. We'll—"

"If your mother doesn't take that job, the Nygaards will surely fire me, too," Dad says.

I turn to him. His face is twisted with anger—and with something else. Fear. Having failed once, we may fail again. We may fall even further.

"Do you see what you're doing to our family, Rose?" Mother's voice breaks in desperation. "What you're doing is wrong. All we have left is our reputation, and you'll ruin that!"

Sophy hisses at Mother, Dad, and me. She hisses until she's spitting, saying no with all the force she can muster. *Stop arguing*, she's trying to say.

"Hush, Sophy. Calm down," Mother says.

Sophy hisses at her. She turns to me, wild-eyed. "Sing," she manages to say. "Rose, sin—"

Sophy jerks in Mother's arms, and the spasms start. Again and again, Sophy's body jerks, and Mother can't hold her, and I can't, either, and she falls to the floor with a sickening thud. Dad lunges for her heaving body as her back arches, her body pitches. He catches hold of her legs. Should we hold her down? Should we let the fit run its course? Different doctors say different things. Dad is trying to keep her from hurting herself against the table leg, and somehow I am on my knees, too, sliding my arms between her head and the floor. Silver flashes; Mother is holding a spoon. She thrusts the spoon into Sophy's mouth, presses it against Sophy's tongue. This is one thing we know, one thing we have learned the hard way: at these moments, Sophy can easily bite her tongue; she could bite through it, bite it off if we're not careful. She could die.

"I'm here, right here, Sophy. Mother and Dad, too. We're right here beside you. It's all right. You're all right. You'll be all right. We're right here beside you."

I say all this—or maybe it's just a silent prayer—until Sophy goes limp on the floor. Her head is heavy, her hair matted and sweaty on my arms. Time stops. She's as limp as the rag doll whose cradle she slept in as a baby. Mother, Dad, and I are stone statues. We stare at our beloved Sophy in terror. Our beloved Sophy, only a breath from death.

But no, there's a pulse at her throat. And her breathing is steadying, though still shallow and quick. She remains with us.

Tears stream down Mother's face and mine. Tears stand in Dad's eyes.

We caused this. Our fighting.

Together, Dad and I lift Sophy into Mother's lap. Sophy's skin is cold, cold, cold, clammy and pale, almost translucent. Almost she's a ghost. But she's not. She's my sister, alive, but nearly in shock. I run to the linen closet, and return to the kitchen bearing a blanket. I wrap the blanket around her thin, twisted body. Mother hunches over her, holding her close in the nest of blanket. *As a hen doth gather her brood under her wings . . .* If this verse were a song, I would sing it for Sophy and Mother now.

Dad's hand strokes Sophy's hair just the way she likes it. "Light of my life, apple of my eye," he murmurs. Then he looks at me, and his eyes turn cold. "She needs you, and you say you have better things to do."

He says this, then gets to his feet, not graceful at all, but a bent, broken man who smells of whiskey and cigarettes. With the halting steps of the aged, he goes to the kitchen door, opens it. He stands there for a moment, a small man looking out at the bleak winter day. Then he is gone, and I'm a little girl all over again, a bad girl who nearly killed my sister, doing something I shouldn't have done.

I slam my fist down on my bruise, but it doesn't hurt enough. I'm still bad, and Mother is still bowed over Sophy in her nest. Mother is watching Sophy, guarding her, keeping her warm beneath her wings. I'm not needed here anymore. They've forgotten I'm here at all.

I get to my feet.

Dad went that way, so I won't.

Where will I go?

As a girl, I might have turned to Julia, but our lives have taken different paths. As recently as last month, I might have called Rob, but escaping with him won't serve me now. There's Nils, but Nils won't look at me.

Theo.

I go to the phone in the hallway. But when I call his house, no one answers.

There's just me.

I go to the bedroom, shut the door, crawl under the covers. I'm still wearing my coat, but I might as well be naked. I'm that cold. I curl into the smallest ball my body can make. *I once was lost.* I want to sing myself to sleep, but I can't remember the rest of the words.

I wake to find Sophy beside me in bed. We're lying face-to-face, nearly nose-to-nose. She is watching me closely, the way I've so often watched her over the years. Her cheeks have color again. She is warm. I'm warm, too.

"Long sleep," she says.

I nod. "You, too? Did you take a nap?"

She kisses the air yes. She smells of sour milk. Dried flecks of hot cereal speckle her lower lip. Mother must have wanted to get some lunch into her, and a little hot cereal was all either of them could manage. I have to smile: Sophy's breath is a comfort, whether it's sweet or sour. Her breath means she is alive, never mind what the doctors have said from the day she was born. She won't live a year, the first doctor said, having dragged her with his forceps into the world. She won't make it to two, three, four, five, the next doctor said. And then it was six, seven, eight, nine, ten, and then Mother found yet another doctor, Sophy's doctor now, who says maybe twenty. She'll live to be twenty years old, that doctor thinks. If she's lucky.

We'll show him.

Sophy cranes her neck to see something, and then, "Mermaid," she says. "Please."

Mounted on the wall behind me is a plate that bears the image of the Little Mermaid from Hans Christian Andersen's fairy tale. *Den Lille Havfrue*, Mother calls her. Small and unimposing, the Little Mermaid sits on a rock in the harbor, looking out to sea. Mother and Dad gave the plate to Sophy for her tenth birthday. Sophy has always cherished it; when we moved into this apartment it was the first thing she asked me to unpack, the first thing she asked Dad to hang on the wall.

Now, for the first time since our move, she asks me to tell her the story of the Little Mermaid again.

"Now?" I'm not sure what this story will do for either of our moods.

She kisses the air.

When we were much younger, I would pull out the old, leather-bound book of Hans Christian Andersen's tales and tell the story as we turned the pages—*tell* the story, not read it, because the book, published in the 1800s, is a Danish edition. Except for our old family Bible, it is the most beautiful book we own, with richly detailed watercolor illustrations. Sophy and I especially like the picture of the Little Mermaid washed ashore, discreetly draped in seaweed. Her prince approaches her, awestruck, lovestruck, holding out his cape like a shield to cover her body.

"Do you want me to get the book?" I know exactly which shelf it's on in the front room.

She hisses, impatient. "Tell."

So I tell about the Little Mermaid's underwater kingdom, her intoxicating singing voice, her love for the handsome, human Prince. I tell how a great storm strikes, and the Little Mermaid saves the Prince from drowning. She swims away, but her longing for the Prince doesn't fade. It grows stronger. She visits the cruel and powerful Sea Witch, who strikes a bargain: *I'll give you legs, Little Mermaid, but you must give me your tongue in exchange.* So the Little Mermaid sacrifices the only life she has known—and she sacrifices her voice—for her Prince. With every step she takes on land, she feels as if she is walking on sharp swords.

I take Sophy's hand, and we hold tight to each other. We know what happens next. The Little Mermaid finds the Prince. He thinks she's beautiful. She can't speak, of course, but he loves to see her dance, which she does, though every step, dip, and sway causes her horrible pain.

I press my lips together. This story troubles me as never before. But Sophy begs me to continue, so I do.

"In the end the Prince marries another, and the Little Mermaid's heart breaks. At dawn, she throws herself into the sea, expecting death. But instead of fading away on the waves, she becomes a spirit of the air. She rises to heaven."

Sophy and I are quiet for a moment. Then Sophy says what she always says at this story's end.

"Sad."

"Yes."

"Sing."

I shrug. "Yes, she'll get to sing again in heaven. The story doesn't say that, but we'll say that."

"No!" Sophy grimaces with frustration. "You. Now."

I smile at my sister. "I think I'm a little too tired to sing right now."

"Now."

I'm not smiling anymore. "Later. You name it, I'll sing the song. Right now—I'm so tired, Sophy."

Sophy hisses.

"Sophy, I—"

Her face reddens with impatience and anger. "You . . . *Den Lille Havfrue!*"

Sophy's Danish is garbled, but suddenly I understand. I could almost sing my understanding.

She doesn't want me to be like the Little Mermaid. She doesn't want me to give up singing for a life that hurts me.

"Oh, Sophy."

I think my heart might break, the way it beats with love for my sister. I bury my head in her cottony hair. I thank her. I ask her to name the song.

SEVENTEEN

Next morning, Mother wakes me at five, all in a flurry.

"I'm late," she whispers, trying not to wake Sophy. Quietly, quickly she asks me to please pack her something to eat on the train. She can assemble some kind of little lunch at the Nygaards', but they've made it clear that she can't eat their food for breakfast, too.

There are four eggs in the icebox. I set two of them to boil, and then take a nice loaf of bread from the pantry. Mother must have brought the bread home from the Nygaards' party—with Mrs. Nygaard's permission, I'm sure. I slice two pieces. When the eggs are done, I peel and slice them, too, make a simple sandwich, wrap it in paper. Mother gives me a swift kiss, and then she tucks the sandwich into her overnight bag.

"There's a party," she says. "I won't be back until tomorrow morning."

She gives me a resolute look. There will be no more talk about the risk she's taking with her health. No more talk about

me singing instead. I give a nod. Let her take my nod as acquies-
cence. I know what I'm going to do.

I'm standing at the front door, watching Mother lug her little
bag down the stairs, when Dad, dressed in his white coveralls,
emerges from their bedroom. He goes to the kitchen. The coffee
pot rattles as I softly call one last good-bye to Mother and close
the door. It seems cowardly to go back to bed, especially as I'm
wide awake now, so I straighten my shoulders and head to the
kitchen, too. If he talks to me, I will talk to him. I make this resolution.

Dad stands at the kitchen window, staring silently out at the
El tracks, so I sit down at the table and wait for some change in
his chilly demeanor. I don't back down. I don't leave, even as the
coffee finishes brewing and he drinks one cup at the window,
then a second. I eat a piece of the nice bread. He wraps a few
pieces of the bread in a napkin, takes some cheese and meat as
well, and then he's gone, too.

The way Mother treats me you'd think I'd never sung a word.
The way Dad treats me you'd think I didn't exist at all. I go to the
bathroom, look in the mirror, and hum a few notes to remember
who I am, and that I'm here. I splash my face with water. Then I
tiptoe from the bathroom down the hallway past Andreas's
room. He must have come home after I was in bed last night; I
can hear him snoring through the closed door. Monday is his
only morning to lie about late. If I have my way, I'll have Sophy
ready and the two of us out of here before he's up and at 'em—
because up and at *me*, that's what he'd actually be.

Sophy is awake now, but she proves sluggish. I've barely
gotten her dressed when I turn to see Andreas, standing in his
robe at the bedroom door. My brother is so tall that in this

humble apartment his head nearly grazes the lintel. If he were wearing shoes, not slippers, he'd have to duck to enter the room. His long shanks are startlingly pale compared with his robe, which is exactly the bright red of his sun-damaged nose.

"I need to speak with you."

As I expected, my brother is looking at me as if he's still standing in the pulpit.

"*Den Lille Havfrue,*" Sophy whispers.

I surprise Andreas by laughing; I surprise myself, too.

"What's so funny?" he asks.

I make some crack about Danish humor, and then walk right past my brother, saying Sophy needs to eat before anything else can happen. I promised her a treat—scrambled eggs—and he's not going to keep me from following through on this. Besides, he knows how important it is that Sophy eats on time. And by the time she's finished eating, he may be gone.

But he's not. He's waiting for me by the front room fireplace, weighing Dad's bayonet in his hands.

After yesterday, I don't want Sophy to witness another argument, let alone an impaling—ha, ha—so I settle her in her chair by the bedroom window. The sun is out today, and there's no frost on the glass, so I open the window a crack to let in some fresh air. Or as fresh as it gets, given the trash cans in the alley. The children are already at school—those that aren't truant—but someone whistles a melody below. It's a song I don't know, a song I wish I knew; it's that bright and happy. I peer down and see the garbage collector making the best of his lot. I ask Sophy to try to remember the words to the song if he starts to sing them; then I leave her to listen. Tomorrow night at Calliope's I'll hum the melody, toss in any lyrics she might pick up. One of the

Chess Men will surely recognize the song and teach it to me. Maybe we'll make it our own.

"Tomorrow night at Calliope's," I say to myself as I walk down the hallway toward my brother. I remind myself of the person I am now. *I'm a singer. A vocalist. I sing with the Chess Men.* I gird my loins, as Andreas might say. In the front room, I perch on the edge of the love seat. Andreas sets the bayonet back into its rack on the wall and then turns to me.

"There's talk of another war," he says, apropos of nothing.

"Yes." I've heard stories on the radio. I've read the newspapers, too. At Old Prague, Nils said something about all his many good plans being for naught if he had to join the army. And just Saturday night, the subject of war came up between sets, and Jim, who's about Dad's age, talked about his time in the French trenches. "Nineteen-seventeen was all rats and mud and blood and gas," Jim said. "I wonder what the next years will hold over there." We all looked at Theo, then, the only man in the room who was the right age for service. "If it comes to that, there'll be no holding me back," Theo said firmly, answering our unasked questions. I can't imagine Theo bearing anything like the bayonet above the fireplace, but apparently Jim could. "You're the very man I'd have wanted beside me when the going got tough," Jim said, and the room got quiet then. The Chess Men have managed to find a way to play music together. But not even they could find a way to fight side by side on the battlefield. There are white troops and there are black troops, and that's the way it is.

Andreas interrupts my thoughts. "I know you don't remember Dad before he went off to fight, Rose—you were just a baby—but I remember him well. Dad was a different man. A kinder man. I look at him now, and I wonder what broke inside him. What weak link did he carry? I search myself for weakness all the time. When I find it, and I *do* find it, I ask the Lord if it can be turned into strength, or I ask the Lord if what appears to be weakness is actually a manifestation of Christ's compassion. But when it's weakness, plain and simple and *dangerous*, the Lord shows me, and I don't deny it. I acknowledge my flawed, sinful nature, bald as can be." Andreas taps his own balding pate, and smiles as if he's making a joke, but his eyes are deadly serious. "When that's the case, I do my best to go in for the kill." His finger is a gun now; he mimes shooting himself in the head. "I remember Dad, who he was before the Great War, who he became afterward, and I promise myself and I promise the Lord that I'll never change like that. With the Lord's help, I exorcise the weakness within myself, and I do the same for others. I don't just save people, Rose, I help them grow stronger, with the Lord's help."

My neck aches from looking up at my brother, but I am not relieved when he drags over an ottoman and sits down right in front of me. Eye-to-eye like this (the ottoman is lower than the cushion on which I'm perched), I face the full intensity of his bright blue gaze. I am more sinner than sister in his eyes. Not a few brief seconds have passed, but it is hard to remember that God is my judge, not Andreas.

"I want to help you," my brother says. "I've helped many, many people—our friend Dolores, to name one. Now it's your turn. I'll help you to be strong."

"I am strong," I say.

Andreas shakes his heavy head. "I've always known Rob had it in him to take the wrong road. Rob's like Dad in so many ways. But you, Rose—how on earth could you? You have a family who loves you. A fellow who cares. Oh, don't look surprised. Anyone with two eyes in his head can see what Nils feels for you. I've watched Nils watch you at coffee hour. I've watched him watch you when you sing during church. And that's just it, Rose. Dad hasn't really heard you, and Mother doesn't really understand, but I've been beside you at the altar when you've sung the altar call. I know that's what you were created to do, as I'm created to preach. Think of it, Rose. I could be the pastor, and you could be the choir director, and together, strong as only we can be, we could save so many. We could make so many strong."

When I was a very little girl, Andreas sometimes looked up from his books and played pretend with me. He'd be the explorer, and I'd be the Indian companion. He'd be the Crusader, and I'd be the Moorish princess. He'd be the soldier, and I'd be the nurse. If I played nurse well enough, I'd sometimes be rewarded by being allowed to be an ambulance driver instead. But only sometimes, and only if I followed Andreas's rules.

I stand and my knees bump my brother's. "Singing in church is wonderful, but it's not enough. Not for me."

Andreas narrows his eyes to bright blue points. "Yield not to temptation, Rose."

"One man's temptation is another woman's calling."

Andreas slowly shakes his head. "How did this happen to you?"

"God made me this way."

I go to Sophy then. I ask if she thinks it's about time we got out of here.

Her yes is music to my ears.

It's March, I realize as Sophy and I enter Garfield Park. The month has turned over without my knowing it. The raw, wet air holds the first hints of thaw. Garden beds float like islands of rich, black earth, surrounded by the shrinking patches of dirty snow that linger on the park's wide lawns. On the gray pond, wind stirs, widening puddles of water amid the uneven hunks of ice, which pop and crackle like small fireworks. Brave birds sing in the trees. Sophy cheers as black-capped chickadees dart and dive from bare branch to bare branch. Their jostling loosens clumps of melting snow that splat to the ground, or onto Sophy's lap (once), or onto my hair (twice).

We quickly grow chilly, Sophy and I. The Conservatory glows like a warm beacon of color on the opposite side of the park, so we head there. Not so far from us now, not much more than a stone's throw, Nils is working away at the National Tea. Monday morning, he's told me, is a particularly busy time. Not as crowded as Friday afternoon or Saturday all day, but busy. He's probably checking inventory, adjusting prices, helping Mr. Block sort out this week's specials. Or he's already behind the cash register, ringing up the first shoppers. Perhaps Mr. Block has given him some other important task, and he's behind the big window at the back. I need to talk to Nils. I want to talk to him, to apologize yet again. But Monday morning is not the time to do it; he'll be distracted by his job. He'll want to do his work. Perhaps it would be best if I waited for Nils to come to me. Yesterday, with his guard up at church, he seemed to be sending that clear message. *You've hurt me. Now give me time.*

I bow my head against shame and wind, and push Sophy's chair forward on the path. Muddy slush sucks at my shoes and the chair's wheels, and spatters my stockings. Finally we reach the

Conservatory. I push the wheelchair through the wide entrance and just inside the first room. We can go no farther now—not without help. But that's all right. The first room is the Tropical Garden. It's warm. The steamy air feels good on our skin, and light bounces off the glass ceiling and walls, making the day seem even brighter. Our escape has been made. More than an escape, Sophy considers this place another world. "Maybe this is what the Garden of Eden was like," I say, pulling up a metal garden chair to sit beside her, and Sophy kisses the air. Shame and strife were not welcome in Eden; they're not welcome here. I tell myself this until I almost believe it. Happier, with Sophy happier, too, I tell myself that all that has happened was meant to be. Things will work out for the best in the end. Not just for Sophy and me but for all of us. For Mother. For Dad. For Andreas. For Nils. For Theo.

Theo. Last time I was here, there was Theo, too.

Sophy and I count the bananas on the trees, and then the coconuts. The big purple blooms and the small red ones. There's a cage just beside us and, inside, two noisy parrots perch and flutter and squawk. When we've counted just about everything we can, we watch their antics. I haven't asked Sophy much about her time at the Nygaards' house this past weekend, so over the noise of the parrots, I do. She scowls, baring her crooked teeth. Her gums are still inflamed; apparently, Dr. Nygaard is no more gentle in his dentistry than he is in any other area of his life. But Sophy enjoyed watching Zane play tennis. She enjoyed meeting the elderly couple who hosted her for lunch. She would like more outings, more adventures with new people to meet.

I catch my breath. "I have a friend. Maybe you'd like to meet him?" I sound so eager.

Almost as eagerly, Sophy asks, "When?"

"Soon."

The parrots must have gotten comfortable with our presence, for now they start talking. They say hello. They call us pretty. They tell us we're late for dinner. We laugh, and they mimic our laughter. I remember the whistling in the alley and ask Sophy if the garbage collector ever sang the words to the song. Alas, no. So I whistle the song's melody as the garbage collector did. The parrots cock their heads and listen. Soothed by my whistling, they grow quiet, and tuck their heads under their gray wings. I fall quiet, too. We sit in the humid warmth, and next thing I know, Sophy is asleep. Her hair, always a tangle of loose curls, has coiled into ringlets. Even my wavy hair is curly now. I stretch, yawn, lean my head against the arm of Sophy's chair, and close my eyes. But I slept too much yesterday. I'm restless. I can't even daydream the time away.

The entrance is just behind me, and of course the telephone is still there. *I have a friend. Maybe you'd like to meet him? When? Soon.* Now I go to the phone, take a coin from my pocketbook, plug the phone, dial Theo's number. It's likely no one will pick up on a Monday morning. Mrs. Chastain must be at work, and Mary must be at school, and Theo might be giving piano lessons, or helping out at Hull House—that's where he was yesterday after church, I bet—or working elsewhere or practicing something or doing whatever it is that Theo does on any given Monday morning, which I wish I knew. There is still so much to know about him. I must remember to ask him as much as I can. Music is everything, but also there's more. Knowing more might tide me over when Theo and I are apart.

There's a click, and Theo says hello. "Oh!" I cry, delighted and surprised. He laughs when he hears that I'm calling from the

Conservatory again; his laughter is as happy as mine. My laughter echoes back to me from the Tropical Garden. I hope the parrots don't wake Sophy. There's no one else here to bother her; still, she might feel unsettled not knowing where I've gone.

Quickly, I tell Theo that a lot has happened in the past twenty-four hours. "Too much to say," I say, but then all in a rush I say more. I babble on about Mother's employment, Sophy's fit, Dad's blame, Andreas's judgment. Theo remains quiet. Finally I run out of breath. The time is almost up on this call. I shake my pocketbook, but no coins jingle. When the phone goes dead, we're done talking, unless he calls me back. I look for a number to give him, but there isn't one posted.

Theo is talking about piano lessons. He's only giving four lessons today. Two of them he's already given, one student just canceled, the last lesson is about to start. "If you'll just sit tight," Theo says, "I'll be by for you within the hour."

I smile. Then remember.

"And my sister, too? She's with me."

"Will she be all right? With me, I mean."

The fact that he has to ask this question makes my heart ache. "As long as you're all right with her," I say.

"It will be my pleasure."

I can hear the smile behind his words, and I remember that first night at Calliope's, the gentleman stranger in the crowd, the man whose low, courteous tone captured my attention then, and means the world to me now.

Sophy is still sleeping deeply when Theo arrives. Without thinking, I take his hand to lead him to her, then, quick as a wink, release it. Where his hand was, even this warm air feels cold against my skin.

There's no one else nearby, thankfully, so Theo and I can stand side by side, looking down at my sister. Her head droops to one side; her curls tangle in her long eyelashes and fall across her flushed cheeks and throat. Her expression is relaxed, her lips slightly parted. Her eyes move beneath her closed lids. She is dreaming, and now something in her dream tips up the corners of her mouth, and her faint, fleeting smile reveals her dimples.

"She is as lovely as you described," Theo says.

I nod. What sweet dream is she dreaming to make her so content? I hope she'll remember and tell me. We've both dreamed that we were each other. When I dream I'm Sophy, I awake sweaty and shaking, bound by sheets, barely able to move. When Sophy dreams she's me, she says she spreads her arms and flies.

Theo is watching me closely. "Clearly she's as loved as you described, too."

"Words can't say how much I love her."

Lovely, loved, love. I look at Theo. He leans close to me, and I lean close to him, and a pack of people bursts through the entrance—six dark-haired white boys, who'd probably be in high school if they weren't playing hooky. Theo and I draw back from each other as the young men charge into the Tropical Garden. Three of them barrel on down the path; the other three stop short at the sight of us. I wonder if these are the same boys who startled Rob and me, stumbling out of Garfield Park so late at night. They don't appear to be drunk; they're too alert for that. They stare at Theo and me. They stare at Sophy, too. They've awakened her. With some effort, she looks dazedly back at them.

Then she sees Theo, and her eyes widen. She isn't frightened by all these strangers, but she is startled.

"Well, well," one of the young men says, and I wonder if Sophy is frightened now, because suddenly I am. Something in the way he's looking at Theo makes me edge my way between them. "Keep back," Theo breathes, but I stay where I am. The young man's hand is in his pocket; he's fiddling with something there. There's a flash of silver as he draws the thing out, tosses it into the air, catches it. He flicks his thumb, there's a click, and a knife springs from its case. "Well, well," he says again.

"What do you think, Mike?" one of the friends says.

"Traveling circus?" says the other. They position themselves on either side of Mike, arms crossed, feet spread wide.

Mike doesn't answer. He purses his lips and gives a piercing hoot. The parrots squawk and flap their wings, shedding feathers, rattling the bars of their cage.

"Think they'll hear you?"

I don't know which of Mike's companions says this. I am too busy watching Mike, the slow smile altering his face, the chipped teeth his smile reveals.

"They always hear me," Mike says.

Feet pound the path, coming closer, matched almost beat for beat by the pounding of my heart.

Theo puts himself between Mike and me. "Driver," I hear Theo say, and, "leaving." And, "Place is yours."

Next thing I know, Theo is wheeling Sophy toward the Conservatory entrance. He looks over his shoulder, jerks his head to signal that I should follow.

"Freaks!" The insult catches up with us, and then: "Wouldn't come back if I were you."

"Oh, come on back." This is Mike, laughing. "We'll have a good time then."

Theo and I settle Sophy into the backseat of his old car, and I slide in beside her as he opens up the rumble seat and hefts her wheelchair inside. The car jounces as he wrestles with the chair and anchors it at a crazy angle. He pulls out two pieces of rope, secures the frame, and we drive off, leaving Mike and his companions behind. I hold Sophy tightly as Theo makes sharp turns down side streets. Quicker than I expect, we turn onto State Street. We drive south for a few blocks before Theo finally looks in the rearview mirror and asks if we're okay.

I nod. Sophy tries to do the same. I tell Theo she's okay, too.

In truth, it's Theo who looks most shaken. His eyes, reflected in the mirror, dart anxiously. He leans into the steering wheel, grips it hard. He can't seem to relax, not even when we pull up in front of his house. He turns off the engine, but he doesn't take the keys from the ignition. We sit for seconds that stretch into minutes as he stares out the windshield. His expression fluctuates between anger and fear and other feelings I don't fully understand.

Sophy plucks at my sleeve. "Friend?" She asks this quietly, but Theo hears her. He turns around in his seat and apologizes. "Memories," he says as if that's explanation enough, and he passes his hand across his forehead as if he'd like to wipe these memories away.

I tell him it's okay. He's okay. It's those foolish boys who are the problem. I tell Sophy yes, this is my friend, the one I mentioned earlier. "Theo's a musician, too," I say. "A pianist."

Sophy's face brightens at this news. When Theo sees the change in her, he smiles, shining his light, too, and his grim memories seem to fade.

"My mother's at home. It's her day off," he says. "She'll be glad to see you again, Rose, and meet you, too, Sophy."

Leaving the wheelchair strapped to the rumble seat, Theo carries Sophy inside. We find Mrs. Chastain sitting in a rocking chair in the kitchen, her dress hiked up around her knees, her feet soaking in a washtub. The sleeves of her dress are rolled up as well, and the collar unbuttoned. She looks at the three of us and lets out a low moan.

"I wasn't expecting company!" Mrs. Chastain pats at her hair and tugs down the apron that covers the front of her dress. She's embarrassed by her state, but she doesn't even blink at the sight of Sophy, cradled in Theo's arms. She hoists herself up and steps out of the tub, dripping. "Least I've got some nice chicken soup simmering on the stove. You two young ladies will have to stay for lunch. I'll cook up some biscuits, too."

And now I see the thick scars circling Mrs. Chastain's ankles. They are angry scars, ugly scars, and they circle her wrists, too.

Theo sees me seeing. Calmly, quickly, he tells his mother to sit back down. He'll take care of the biscuits. He'll take care of everything. She needs to rest up.

Grumbling, Mrs. Chastain complies. Her ravaged feet are back in the tub again by the time Theo and I settle Sophy on the little daybed in the corner of the kitchen. While Theo makes the biscuits, I clear and lay the table, pour glasses of water, put the coffee on. I try not to look at Mrs. Chastain's wrists, or the other scars that I see now, on her calves, knees, and forearms, and the single scar at her throat, like a broken necklace.

I hold Sophy on my lap during lunch, and the four of us eat together. Conversation is sparse, but when it comes to us we keep it light and easy. Mrs. Chastain talks to Sophy as if she were any other girl. We're finishing our coffee when Mrs. Chastain asks if I'd be willing to sing a few songs. I agree, and Sophy smiles, delighted.

With Sophy settled on one couch in the front room, and Mrs. Chastain on the other, Theo sits down at the piano. I stand beside him. We work our way from one hymn to the next, and then turn to Chess Men standards. We're halfway through "It Had to Be You" when I realize I've sat down beside him on the piano bench. I'm leaning into him. I can feel the rise and fall of his ribs as he breathes. I wonder if his ribs still hurt from the beating he, Dex, Jim, and Ira took. I need to ask him that, too. I am breathing with him, in perfect time, as I sometimes breathe with Sophy. Only this breathing is different from the sisterly kind. Theo's breathing completes mine, as his playing completes my singing. Two halves of one whole, I think, and the thought makes me light-headed. I can barely finish the last verse of the song. When I do, I look down at my hands. They're clasped tightly on my lap, only inches from his thigh, and now he lifts his left hand from the keys, and his hand hovers over mine. *Touch me.* But then Sophy coughs, and Theo draws back his hand. I see Sophy watching us, wide-eyed, and Mrs. Chastain, neither wide-eyed nor narrow-eyed but very, very still, her expression un-readable, is watching us, too.

"Thank you for the music." Mrs. Chastain speaks slowly, as if she's weighing the real meaning behind each word.

Sophy kisses the air, adding her thanks, and then flushes bright red at the sound. She looks suddenly miserable, lying there on the couch, unable to say what she wants to say, or do anything to distract us from this awkwardness. I can't bear to see her miserable.

I go to my sister and take her hand.

"It's your nap time. We should go home."

Sophy scowls. "Not tired."

She wouldn't be, I realize. She had that nap in the Conservatory. "Well," I say. I can't think of what comes next.

"If you've got nowhere to be, then feel free to stay as long as you like," Mrs. Chastain says.

Sophy and I thank her, and Theo does, too. Then he stands up from the piano and heads to the front door, saying, "Here's Mary, home from beauty school."

And indeed, here is Mary, hugging Theo as he opens the door. Mary is delighted to see me, delighted to meet Sophy, delighted to offer us both manicures. "I need the practice," she eagerly explains. I decline, but Sophy seems overjoyed at the thought of her first-ever painted nails. What Mother will say about this I don't know and I don't care, for Mary is chattering on now about various shades of pink and red, and Sophy is choosing Sunrise, and Mrs. Chastain is dozing on the couch, and Theo and I are heading toward the kitchen, readying ourselves to clean up the lunch things, and I am asking him the first of many questions.

"What happened to your mother?"

EIGHTEEN

"She was convicted of a crime she didn't commit. That's where the scars came from."

Theo runs water into the sink and adds soap, carefully submerges dishes, glasses, and cups. I pick up a tea towel and watch his hands stir the water.

"I was a sickly kid, and Mary was a sickly newborn," he says. "That's what happens during hot summers in certain wards down in New Orleans. Some bug bites you, or you drink water from the wrong tap, and next thing you know, you're barely alive. My mother lost her job, doing laundry for a big hotel there—they wanted to hire cheap Irish labor, *white* labor, instead—and there Mary was, barely six pounds, not taking milk or water, shaking with fever. And me, eight years old, not much more than skin and bones, shaking with the same. The doctor said we needed some kind of medicine. Expensive medicine. Without it we'd die. So Mother did what she had to." Theo lifts a glass from the soapy water and wipes it clean with a rag. "One night, she left Mary and me with the pastor of her church. She went down to the French

Quarter. She walked the streets. First hour out, she gets picked up by the vice squad before any vice has happened. Next thing she knows, she's in jail. Next thing after that, she's a licensed convict, working a plantation like her mother before her. Only my mother's not a slave, because slavery's been abolished. She just looks like one, feels like one, lives like one in chains for seven long years. The cheapest labor known to man." He's still wiping that same glass. Now he drops the rag into the water and begins to rinse it. "When she finally gets out, she comes looking for Mary and me. I don't recognize her. Not right away. Not with those scars. She's changed in every way. But our pastor recognizes her. Papa, we called our pastor. When our mother never came back, he found a way to get that medicine for us, and he didn't get caught. Papa never told me what he did, but he saved my life and Mary's, too, and I believe God has forgiven him, regardless of what some earthly judge might say."

I nod, though Theo hasn't asked a question.

"When I saw what they did to my mother, something snapped tight around my own neck, wrists, and ankles." He's still rinsing that glass. "I was a fifteen-year-old boy, but I started living like a crazy man—drinking myself sick and doing much, much worse. I stopped playing the piano. I started playing with knives. Papa said we had to get out of New Orleans. The memories weren't doing my mother any good, either. So she packed Mary and me up, and we headed north. Along the way, I found God again. I told you about the tent meeting. I found God there, or I let God find me, then we settled here, started a new life." Theo gives me a hard, long look. "But still, the anger stalks me, and the fear. I grow hopeless sometimes." His gaze softens as he looks at me. "But then I remember good folks like Jim and Ira. I

remember Dex, a black man like me, who somehow, by the grace
of God and his music, lives an unchained life. And I remember
you, Rose."

He sets the glass on the drying rack. I've wrapped that tea
towel tightly around my hands. He takes my bound hands in his
own. He frees my hands from the towel. It slips to the floor as he
laces his wet fingers through mine. His palms are dusky pink, my
palms are the palest pink possible, but they meet, they fit together, our hands hold fast. He bows his head and presses his
forehead to mine, and we stand together like that as time stops,
and water cools in the sink, and the glass dries on the rack. Then
he gently kisses my forehead, and I stand on my tiptoes and kiss
his forehead, too—so this is how his skin feels, smooth and soft
as silk—and we look at each other, sober and serious, *this is serious*, and then he picks up the towel and gives it to me, and we
turn back to the dishes, help his mother the best way we can, do
the work we've been given to do.

It's late in the afternoon when I finally tell Theo that I think
Sophy and I had better get home. In a couple of hours Dad will
be back for dinner, and possibly Andreas, too. With Mother
staying the night at the Nygaards' house, it's up to me to have
dinner ready. And though Sophy is having the time of her life,
she's a little worn out, I can tell. We've spent much of the afternoon listening to repeats of *The Lone Ranger* and *The Shadow* on
the radio. In this past hour, we played charades. Theo, Mary, and
Sophy were one team, Mrs. Chastain and I were the other.
Sophy had never played charades before, but she and Theo made
a great pair. With Mary's help, she acted out a famous person.

While Sophy reclined on the couch, Mary mimed lining Sophy's eyelids with kohl and painting her glossy nails Sunrise all over again. Mary fanned Sophy with a pretend palm leaf, popped pretend grapes into Sophy's mouth, and Theo snapped his fingers. "Cleopatra!" he said. "That's right!" Mary shouted as Sophy kissed the air.

Now Sophy's eyelids are drooping, and Theo agrees that it's probably time for us to go.

On the way, Sophy sleeps, and Theo and I confirm what we've already discussed this afternoon. What with Mother working and my parents' disapproval, I will have to miss rehearsals. I'll make it to the gigs, but just barely, and only if Rob can give me a ride. Who else could I ask? Zane is too unpredictable; his parents complicate things. Nils is too wounded.

Of course, the answer—the answer I want—is sitting right in front of me.

"Or maybe you could take me?" I ask, hoping.

Theo looks at me in the rearview mirror and smiles. "No maybe about it. Just tell me where to be and when, and I'll be there."

When we pull up in front of the apartment, I point out the alley, the fire escape, and the shadowy place where Rob has parked. Theo promises he'll be waiting there tomorrow night, and I thank him.

He doesn't hesitate, hoisting Sophy's wheelchair down from the rumble seat, wheeling it into the courtyard of our building, parking it in the foyer, then helping me carry drowsy Sophy up to our place. But he is carefully distant, not talking or looking at either of us along the way. I understand why. I can feel it, too. We are being watched from windows and street corners, and there are a group of kids playing in the alley who peek around the side of the apartment building and boldly stare.

Theo lays Sophy down on the love seat in the front room, then looks quickly around, taking note of the luxuries my family has managed to maintain. I feel heat rise in my face. Our cluttered pomp and preciousness stand in sharp contrast to the sparse, simple style of Theo's home. I'd say we were poor, too, that my mother has suffered also, but I know there's no real comparison to be made.

I walk Theo to the door. It's almost five thirty; Dad will be home any minute. I have to work myself up to make some excuse about Sophy's nails. I'll say a friend did them for free, which is true. And if Mother or Dad makes a fuss, I'll find a way to get the polish off. I should probably call Mary and ask her what's the best and cheapest way to easily remove it. I'll call her when Theo leaves.

For this moment, Theo and I stand at the door, stand close to each other. We take this moment, and this one, and this. And now, as Theo bends down to kiss my forehead, I lift my face to him and our lips meet instead.

Tuesday night just past ten I slide out of bed, open my dresser drawer, and slip into my blue dress. Sophy is sleeping, and Mother and Dad, too, and Andreas is not home yet. Still, I am shaking with nervousness. They've outright forbidden me to do this, and I am doing it anyway.

Then again, they forbade Sophy to wear nail polish, but she's gone and done that, and after a brief scene last night they gave in to her, didn't they? That's what I tell myself as I put on my coat and pick up my silver satin purse. Quiet as can be, I go to the window, raise it, plant my foot on the sill, climb out onto the fire escape. The wind is almost balmy, stirring the skirt of my dress. With this break in the weather, I might not have needed my coat. That's what I'm thinking as I start to lower the window, and I hear Sophy say my name.

"Rose!" Again she calls to me, loudly enough that Mother and Dad might hear.

I clamber back through the window and lunge at the bed. I do something I've never done before. I clap my hand over my sister's mouth, silencing her.

She glares at me in the moonlight.

"Will you please be quiet?" I whisper.

She gives a fierce, angry nod, and I draw back my hand.

"I'm going out," I whisper.

She glares. "Nils?"

I look at her. She looks at me.

I don't lie. I don't find a good excuse. I remind myself that this is my sister, my Sophy, and she doesn't want me to be the Little Mermaid. She wants me to sing.

I tell Sophy that Theo is picking me up in his car. Right now, he's waiting out there for me. I'm the vocalist for a band called the Chess Men, I tell her. We're going to make some music tonight at a club called Calliope's. I'm going to sing the kind of songs they play on the kind of radio stations Mother doesn't like, and I'm going to get paid. I promise I won't do anything wrong. "I'm going to be okay," I promise. "No. Not just okay. I'm going to be happy, singing."

Sophy says, "I know."

There's a sharp intake of breath—me, gasping. "You know what?"

"Everything," she says.

I clap my hand over my mouth, this time, trying to suppress a burst of nervous laughter. After a few moments I compose myself and lower my hand. Sophy watches me, smiling, satisfied that for once she's taken me by complete surprise.

"How do you know?"

She takes a deep breath. "I know more than you know," she says—the longest thing I've ever heard her say. And then, "I know what makes you happy. And who." She jerks her head and I follow her gaze to see the Little Mermaid plate on the wall behind us.

"Be happy," Sophy says.

I don't need her permission. I know that. But when I'm on the fire escape again, closing the window, and she smiles at me, I feel sweet, deep relief. Her blessing. That's what she's given me.

That night at Calliope's I look out into the crowd and see Nils, sitting alone at a table near the bar. I falter, singing, and my sense of blessing seems like an illusion. I can feel Theo watching me. The rest of the Chess Men are aware, too. Together they cover for me. They make music where my voice should be. They wait for my voice to return. I lean toward Nils. I lift my hand in a discreet wave, and I smile. He doesn't smile back.

I am faced with the choice all over again. I close my eyes and listen, and I hear God's voice, and I remember mine.

Eyes closed, listening, I work my way back into the song. Theo gives a little high trill of the keys. *Welcome back*, the trill says. I focus on the music, open my eyes to the crowd. Only when the number is finished and applause fills the room do I look back at Nils.

He's gone.

I have to walk away from the microphone. I have to take a quick circle around the stage. I have to compose myself. Once I have, I quietly ask the fellows if they're okay with us doing a ballad next. Something in a minor key. "Sure," they say. Only Theo looks worried, but he says, "How about 'Red River Valley'?" I nod. That's perfect. We've been working on old folk songs, playing with them, exploring their possibilities. This is our first time trying one out in public, and I pour all my sadness into the words:

> *From this valley they say you are going.*
> *We will miss your bright eyes and sweet smile.*
> *For they say you are taking the sunshine*
> *That has brightened our pathway a while.*

We finish the song, and the stunned silence tells me that our experiment has failed. I look away from the frozen crowd; I look toward Theo for reassurance.

"Beautiful."

Theo's lips shape the word, but I don't hear him say it. The burst of applause is too loud.

March is filled with music. Three times a week, I perform with the Chess Men at Calliope's. I've never been happier.

I talk with Theo as we drive to and from gigs, or as we walk, arm in arm, through desolate city streets—streets that once would have filled me with fear. Before Theo, my hope was that each passing stranger would prove to be an angel. Now my hope is that there will be no passing strangers at all, only shadows and safety and Theo and me, able to walk together and talk together, able to be ourselves in a place and at a time where the color of our skin doesn't matter at all.

By day while Mother works, I care for Sophy. Sophy meets with Pastor Riis now, two, sometimes three times a week. She's preparing for her baptism. Dolores is meeting with Pastor, too. Like Sophy, Dolores will be baptized on Easter Sunday morning. Dolores is often at our place these days, talking in the early evenings with Andreas. Sometimes I find them sitting in the front room, reading the Bible together. I'm glad for her presence. Andreas is so busy helping her grow stronger, he doesn't have time to think me weak.

On the third Wednesday of the month, Andreas and Dolores offer to take Sophy out shopping for a special dress for her baptism day. Dolores wants to buy one as well. They want to go to Marshall Field's and stay for dinner at the Walnut Room. It will be a special treat.

So for the first time in a long time, I find myself alone during the afternoon. I call Theo from our hallway phone this time. I tell him what Dolores and Andreas recently told me: there's a roomful of Easter lilies at the Conservatory. It's a beautiful way to mark the season. "I'd love to meet you there," I say.

Theo meets me there.

The fragrant, sun-filled room is crowded with families and friends, old people and young, and all but two others—an elderly couple who move with dignity and grace down the path, careful to wait their turn, careful not to get in the way—are white. Theo doesn't dare come close to me. From the doorway he nods hello. I stand and slowly make my way down the path. He follows me at a safe distance. We circle the great glass room, exchanging glances when it seems most likely no one will see. *Consider the lilies of the field, how they grow.* We circle the room once, twice, three times. It is like a dance, this thing we are doing. We catch each other's eyes, and look away before anyone else in the crowd can see. Sometimes we smile. Among the lilies, we consider ourselves. We are growing together, flowering in spite of, because of, a harsh climate.

It is time to leave the Conservatory. Theo inclines his head toward the exit, showing me that he understands this, too. At a safe distance, I follow him to his car, which is tucked down a nearby alley. He gets in; I wait a few moments, and when I'm sure no one is watching, I slip into the backseat.

"Where shall we go?" Theo asks, pulling out into the street.

I surprise myself by knowing. "Away from here. Far away out into the country, where no one knows us at all."

I tell him what streets will lead us out of the city to a place he's never been. I point out the route that leads west. As we drive past Oak Park, and then smaller towns, he tells me about New Orleans. He talks about spicy food, shotgun houses, the long, slow funeral marches, the brass bands that lead the mourners to the grave-yards, where weather-worn graves rise like little houses above sea level. "Someday we'll go there—you and me and the rest of the Chess Men," Theo says. "We'll follow the Mississippi south. We'll do gigs along the way." Theo and I try to imagine how we'll get there. If the five us of save our money and pool it, surely we can rent an old bus. We'll put curtains over the windows. Curtains will allow those who aren't driving to sleep through the night. And curtains will allow the driver to safely steer us past any hostility. We'll stay out of sight when we stop at filling stations. We'll avoid those towns where the KKK is known to have a strong presence, and crosses burn on lawns, and men hang from trees and tele-

phone poles. And if we can safely navigate the South, why not consider other places as well? New York, for instance. And I've always
wanted to see the Grand Canyon; from there, we could drive on to
Los Angeles. Theo's always wanted to go to Miami; from there, we
could take a boat down to Cuba. He's heard the musicians are out
of this world in Cuba. Which gets me talking about Paris—I've
always dreamed of going to Paris. And London, too.

"Aren't you curious about Denmark?" Theo asks.

"Not really."

I catch his gaze in the mirror. His eyes are puzzled. "But that's
where your people are from. You must still have family there."

I must, I realize. Funny thing is, Mother and Dad have never
said so. Funnier thing, I've never asked. It's as if in coming here,
in building this life, we've cut all ties.

I look out the car window, considering this. We are driving
through cornfields now, which are barren except for the shorn
stalks of last fall. After the long winter, spring is finally here. We are
moving forward. Soon we will pass by the institution where Donald
Larsen lives. I wonder how often Mr. and Mrs. Larsen make this
trip to see their son. Once a week? A month? On holidays only?
How much of his life, how much of their lives, are they missing?

"I would like to go to Denmark," I say.

Next thing I know, Theo has pulled the car over to the side
of the road, and then off the road into a little ditch. He turns off
the engine and faces me. His hands grip the back of the front
seat as if for dear life. He takes a deep breath and says, "I've been
thinking a lot about Denmark lately."

"Why?"

"Because I love you."

We look at each other over what divides us—this human

construction of who sits where. If Nils were the man before me, nothing would divide us. But here is Theo. Theo is here. Theo is the man before me, and Theo is the man I want.

I hold out my hands to him, and he unclasps his. When his hands take mine, I can do anything. So, like that, I scramble into the front seat. We are a tangle of limbs and laughter, and then, when we're finally untangled, and I'm settled beside him, I say it.

"I love you, too."

This kiss is different. This kiss is yes.

"In Denmark, we could be together," he says after a bit.

I look into his eyes. Look in wonder.

"It's true," Theo says. "I've heard about more than one couple like us who made a life there."

He tells me then about the stories he's heard. The black woman, a writer, who moved to Copenhagen, fell in love with a white man there, and stayed on. The musicians, mixed groups like ours, who make their homes there. And Paris, he says, is a possibility for people like us, too.

"I can't believe it."

"Believe it."

"I don't know."

I don't know if I could leave my family, my country. My family worked so hard to come to this country, and I don't know if I could leave the fact of that. It seems like such a betrayal. But I can't say that. Not now, with my hands in his. Not here—safe, together—where I long to be when I'm not.

"Let's keep the possibility in mind," Theo says.

There is no car on the horizon, and none behind us, either. I lean into him. The sun is lowering toward the earth now, casting golden light across the fields. If Mary has a nail polish called

Sunset and it is just this color, I will ask her to paint my nails with it to remind me of this night. This night will be my color. This night will be Theo's color, too.

We need to get me home, we finally agree. As we drive, we talk about other things than the future. We talk about this Sunday, his Palm Sunday service and mine. We talk about the busy week to come. Theo describes the foot-washing service at his church. I grimace at the thought of a stranger touching my bare feet, but he tells me it's his favorite service of the year, and his mother's, too, even with her scars—no, *because* of her scars. We are silent for a moment, thinking on that, and I find myself talking about Sophy—how happy I am that she will finally be baptized. I wish he could be there. He wishes that, too. We make our wishes on the flickering stars. If they don't come true (and in our hearts we know that they likely won't), I promise it won't matter. I'll tell him all about it. I'll tell him all about everything in my life. My life will become his life in that way.

We drive east past the wide, open flat fields, and then a scattering of farmhouses. Next thing we know, there's a dip in the road and the first small town appears before us. I scramble into the backseat as we approach the main street.

We pass through this town, and the next one, and the one after that. Now Oak Park is behind us, and Chicago's buildings rise above. Theo and I are talked out. We take this turn and that, driving as we must drive now to make our way safely home. And then we say good-bye.

The last Friday in March is Good Friday. There's an evening service at church, and I sing with the special choir there. We sing

"When I Survey the Wondrous Cross" and "O Love, How Deep."
Pastor Riis preaches. When Andreas gets up to lead the altar
call, he beckons to me. I put aside my reservations and go and
stand beside my brother to sing "Just as I Am." We do make a
good team, as he said. Five people come forward to be saved.
But I know, even as I put my whole heart and soul into my singing, that this isn't my calling. My calling is elsewhere. My calling
is a place Pastor Riis calls the world.

When the service is finished, I dodge members of the choir
who are encouraging me to come to the late supper being served
in the church basement and slip into the bathroom. There, I
change from my choir robe to my blue dress. Then I'm out the
door. I don't want to waste money on a taxi. I get on the El and
head to Bronzeville.

Tonight at the start of the last set, I can't help myself. I
launch into the spiritual "Were You There?" I take the Chess
Men by surprise. We've never sung this one before. For most of
the first verse, I sing solo:

Were you there when they crucified my Lord?
  Were you there when they crucified my Lord?
    Oh! Sometimes it causes me to tremble, tremble,
      tremble.

Finally Theo sets his fingers to the keys, drawing out the
minor chords. Then Dex lifts his clarinet to his lips and adds his
melancholy echo. Having been raised on songs like this, Theo
and Dex know the hymn as well as I do. Maybe better. Theo and
Dex lift my voice up and carry me forward, and then Jim and Ira
are there, too, lending their hands.

The crowd is quiet when we're done. I glance at Theo, worried. Perhaps the people are here tonight because they just want to forget about the cross, the tomb, the stone rolled away. Perhaps that's the only reason they're here at all.

But then someone in the crowd asks for "Rock of Ages," and enough people say yes, do that one, and Theo says, "Sure. Why not?"

This hymn, Jim must have been raised on, from the way he lays into his bass. Soon enough Theo, Dex, and Ira are along for the ride. We hide ourselves from the storm, take shelter in a rock cleft for us. Ira works at his drums until a roll of thunder fills our ears, and then strikes the cymbals with a clash like lightning. Less wistful and melancholy, more brooding and charged with desperate longing—that's how we shape this song:

> *While I draw this fleeting breath,*
> *When my eyes shall close in death,*
> *When I rise to worlds unknown,*
> *And behold Thee on Thy throne,*
> *Rock of Ages, cleft for me,*
> *Let me hide myself in Thee.*

When I've sung the last word, the last whisper of sound—Ira's brush across the cymbals—fades like soft wind from the room.

"How about something a little more uplifting, Laerke?"

I look down, and there's Rob, standing near the edge of the stage. He's holding a drink. He tips it to his lips, winks at me. He nudges the man next to him. "What do you think? Enough of this Holy Roller stuff?"

The man agrees, and the woman beside him agrees, too, and like that, the sentiment spreads and the crowd's mood shifts. There are cries for something fun. People want to *dance*. They want to dance as fast as they can, dance till the cock crows.

Theo says "Fun," and we dig into that:

Every morning, every evening
Ain't we got fun?

"That's the ticket!" Rob shouts. He drains his drink, sets his glass down on the stage, grabs the nearest woman around the waist, and throws himself into the crowd. The room seems to spin like the bodies before me. I keep singing. The Chess Men keep playing. We've got fun. They've got fun. And after that, "Yes! We Have No Bananas" and "My Blue Heaven" and "Toot Toot Tootsie." We've got all this, too.

In this way, we wind down the night. The crowd disperses, hot and sweaty and satisfied. Rob gives me a wild wave, and then he is gone as well.

In the dim little back room, the Chess Men talk about the last set. There's a fine balance, we agree, when it comes to managing a repertoire and arranging a program. It all depends on the night, the mood—how many risks you can take.

I pick up a piece of sheet music—"Someone to Watch over Me"—and fan myself with it. The air stirs my hair, and I agree with them.

"Tonight the risks were worth it," I say.

Then Theo drives me home, and the risks become real indeed.

NINETEEN

In the wee hours of the early morning, when the streets are empty and the rest of the world seems asleep, Theo has made a habit of opening the car door for me, extending his hand and helping me out, and walking me up to the apartment building.

He is doing just this when it happens.

As fast as lightning, it happens. As fast as the clash of a wooden stick against a brass cymbal.

A shadow lunges at us from the shadows. The shadow solidifies into a man—into a group of young men. They surround us now.

"We warned you," Mike says.

They are going for Theo now—or some of them are. Others are coming for me. They grab my arms and drag me backward. They tear me from Theo. I stumble over the hem of my blue dress. Fall. Hit the sidewalk hard. A bolt of pain flashes from my tailbone to my neck. For a moment I can't see. Then my head clears.

Theo is on the ground before me. They are hurting him. They are doing it quietly so as not to wake the neighbors.

"Teach you to lay a hand on our women," one man says as his fist swings low and hard against Theo's jaw.

I'm not your woman, I think.

His hands, I think.

Theo rolls onto his stomach to protect his hands. Boots come down on his back.

I try to scream for help. My mouth opens. But no sound comes out.

I have had nightmares like this, where my voice is lodged like a stone in my throat. Now I am my own nightmare, and Theo is, and these men on the street where I live, in this dark night where dawn may never come.

The men drive their boots against Theo's ribs as if they can kick their way through bone and muscle to his hands. "Boy," they say again and again and again, and other words I try not to hear, but I hear them. They flood my mind, my heart, like foul, filthy water.

Theo doesn't make a sound. I can't make a sound. I'd run for help, but my limbs won't move. I am a silent, stone Mermaid lying on the stone-cold ground. Theo is a knot of pain.

In the distance there's a flicker—a pale sliver of light, high above and to the right. It's the kind of light that flares when a curtain is swiftly lifted and lowered. An interior light in the night. Someone is looking out from a window in our building. Someone may see—though this brutal huddle might be anything in the darkness. A pack of dogs, it might be. And I am next to nothing in the shadows on the ground. And Theo is lost to sight.

The sliver flickers again. This time I'm able to turn toward the light. It's Dad, parting the velvet curtains at the front-room window.

"Dad!"

I call for him, my father, in a way I haven't since Sophy's birth. Again and again I call for him. *Dad, Dad, Dad.*

The curtain falls, the sliver of light vanishes. The men turn from Theo. They turn on me. Theo uncurls himself as they drag me to my feet. It takes the four of them to do it, for now that my voice is working, my limbs are working, too. I kick, claw, spit, scream. I don't stop screaming until one of the men slams his hand over my mouth. I bite down hard on his thumb and taste blood. The man grunts, slams up on my jaw with his arm. The other men hold me in other places. One man constricts his arms so tightly around my chest that I can't breathe. Little lights like white sparks dance before my eyes. Through them, I see Theo, staggering to his feet. He is bleeding, hunched. I cry out to him. "Don't!" I cry, even as Theo flings himself at the men. They bat him away. He falls, his body thudding against the pavement. Stands again. His beautiful hands are bleeding. His beautiful mouth, too. He comes at the men who hoist me into the air, though I writhe and flail. The alley. That's where they're carrying me. Theo's on them again, on the ground again. Only this time a man releases my leg and whirls around. He stoops, grabs something as round as a Roman shield, and lifts it high. A scream rises in my throat, only to be muffled by the hands on my mouth. The man is holding the tin lid of a garbage can. He hefts the lid higher. He intends to bring it down on Theo's head and crush Theo once and for all.

"Stop."

Dad's voice is loud and eerily calm, given the fact that he's standing over Theo, holding his bayonet at the ready. The bayonet's blade is pointed at the gut of the man holding the garbage can lid.

"I know how to use this. I had plenty of practice in the trenches," Dad says.

The man—Mike—drops the lid. It hits the ground with a clang as Andreas runs up behind Dad. Andreas is holding a baseball bat. At the sight of Andreas and Dad and their weapons, the men holding me hesitate. One of them loosens his grip on my mouth and I bite down hard again. There's a muffled grunt as the man jerks his hand away.

"Let her go." Theo's voice is thick with blood.

"Gently," Dad says.

The men set me on my feet. I can barely stand for the shaking. The heel is missing from my left shoe. My blue dress is torn at the waist, and there are other tears as well, at the neckline and shoulders and down the whole long side of me. I am half naked except for my underthings. I am exposed.

Holding my dress together, I wobble toward Theo, collapse on the ground beside him. I don't care what anyone says or does. I wrap my arms around him. He leans into me, rests his head on my shoulder. His blood is warm and thick on my skin, but he is alive. I kiss his hair.

"I'm calling the police." Dad is brandishing the bayonet near Mike's chest, and now Mike and his gang are running away.

"See if they care!" Mike casts this over his shoulder with a leer.

"I'll make them care." Dad shouts this as the men round the corner and vanish.

Andreas kneels beside Theo and me. "We must get him inside," Andreas says. He looks at me and winces. "You, too, Rose."

Something drips onto Theo's hair, and I realize that it's my blood, coming from somewhere I don't know.

Dad's hands are suddenly shaking. So hard are they shaking that the bayonet falls to the ground. Dad looks at me, and I see that he is terrified.

"I could have killed them," he says.

Dad's not terrified of Mike and his companions. Dad's terrified of himself.

Andreas is looking at Dad with an admiration I've never seen before. Maybe this is the father Andreas remembers from when he was a young boy, the father I can't remember from before the war. A brave, good man. A humble man who can suffer remorse.

"We've got wounds to tend," Andreas says, before either Dad or I can say anything else.

I carry the bayonet and the bat. Dad and Andreas carry Theo through the courtyard and up to our apartment. They do this with relative ease; they've had a lot of practice carrying Sophy. But the journey is painfully hard for Theo, I can tell, from the moans he can't suppress, though he grits his teeth until they grind, trying. By the time Dad and Andreas lay Theo down on Andreas's bed, Theo is out cold. Dad goes for Mother. They return quickly, Mother drawing on her robe. She leans over Theo and regards his wounds. Quietly, urgently, she asks for hot water, clean towels, rubbing alcohol. I run for these. By the time I return with them, Andreas has gone for Dolores. "I don't know what to do for him. We need an experienced nurse," Mother explains. "Dolores will know better than I whether we need a doctor, too."

Mother cleans and bandages my cuts, and then I kneel down beside Theo. His eyelids flutter, but he doesn't open them. I watch his pulse beating in his throat. I watch his chest rise and fall with each shallow breath. His blood has stained the sheets. His tuxedo pants are stained, too—with urine, I realize. Theo would be so ashamed if he knew.

While Dad paces, Mother loosens Theo's bow tie, undoes the studs on his tuxedo shirt, and gasps at the sight of the gashes and welts rising on his ribs.

"I wish you *had* hurt those men, Jacob," Mother says. And then she closes her eyes. "Forgive me, God."

Sophy calls from the bedroom. She calls until I go to her, and then she insists on knowing what is happening. I tell her, and she insists on seeing Theo. There's no use in denying her. She'll raise a ruckus. She cares for him, after all. He is her friend.

By the time Andreas returns with Dolores, Theo is stirring. He looks up at Mother and Dad, Dolores and Andreas, and his eyes turn wild. "Where am I?" he says with a gasp.

I go to him.

"Rose." His face relaxes for a moment, then the next spasm of pain takes him, and he sees the bandages on my face. "Are you all right?"

I tell him I'm fine. He will be fine, too. I promise him this.

Dolores doesn't wait long before deciding to call a doctor. When the doctor arrives, he takes one look at Theo and gravely asks us all to leave the room. Only Dolores is allowed to stay and help care for him. When I linger in the doorway, she gives me a look of compassion, and then she shuts the door in my face.

I don't sleep. None of us do. Andreas, Sophy, Mother, Dad, and I sit around the kitchen table while the doctor sets Theo's bones and stitches him up.

They don't need to ask me where I was tonight, and why Theo drove me home. Of my own volition, I tell them about the Chess Men and Calliope's. I tell them about my singing. I don't speak of my feelings for Theo, or Theo's feelings for me. *I love him. He loves me.* After all the time he and I have shared in the shadows, I won't admit this in the bright light of this kitchen. Not without Theo standing beside me, agreeing that this is the right thing to do. My family may have helped us tonight, but there was a time when any one of them, except Sophy, of course, would have done their own kind of damage to our love. I want to protect us now more than ever.

Still, explaining as I am, I can't help but say Theo's name. Maybe I linger over his name. Maybe I say it more often than I should. For whatever reason, by the time I'm finished talking Andreas is looking at me cockeyed. Dad's face is ashen. Mother hides her expression behind her hands. Sophy watches us all.

I can feel the tension building. Any minute, someone is going to say something I don't want to hear. I've got to escape, if only for a moment.

I go to the bedroom and take the money I've earned from beneath the mattress where I've hidden it. I return to the kitchen and press the money into Mother's hands.

"It's all yours. Over a hundred dollars—yours and Dad's."

Mother, Dad, and Andreas look at me, astonished. Only Sophy is not surprised.

"We told you not to do this." For once Dad sounds more desperate than angry, talking to me. He lost control of himself tonight. Or he gained control of himself. He still doesn't know which, I think. "We knew something bad would happen," he says. "And it did."

"But so much good has happened, too." I'm steeling myself to say that I'm a grown woman; I can make my own decisions. I've been called to do this. But then the doctor comes into the kitchen, drying his hands on a towel. His coppery hair has turned rust-colored with sweat. He looks tired and concerned.

"I've done as much as I can," the doctor says. "He's sleeping. Doped up. X-rays are in order. But for now, let him rest. He may sleep for many hours, and if he does, well and good. He should stay in one place for as long as possible. He should be moved only when he is ready."

"You're asking us to keep him here?" Dad shifts uncomfortably in his chair.

Mother says quietly, "He can stay with us for as long as he needs."

The doctor is almost out the door when I think to ask about Theo's hands, which are swathed in bandages. The doctor hesitates, and then pats my shoulder, where the fabric of my blue dress has gone stiff with Theo's blood. "His hands aren't broken, but there may be nerve damage. Time will tell."

I return to the kitchen. "I'm going to be with him tonight," I tell my family.

"Oh, Rose." Dad shakes his head slowly.

"You love him." Mother says it for me. She says it in a moan.

Andreas says something about weakness. He says something about my path, and its dangerous twists and turns. I feel myself bowing under the weight of my brother's words, cringing at the grim expressions on my parents' faces. But then Sophy hisses at Andreas, and he goes quiet. Sophy looks at me and her eyes say *I love you no matter*. With a single look, Sophy helps me remember my strength, my desire, myself. I turn away from the table where I've eaten almost every meal of my life. I take one step after another until I find myself standing where I want to be, need to be, am determined to be, come what may.

Theo's hands lie still on the covers. I touch where the bandages aren't. He feels cold. Carefully I cover him with an extra blanket. I sit down on the floor beside him. I will stay here until he wakes, and even then I will not leave his side.

When I wake, I'm lying on the floor of Andreas's room in a pool of afternoon light. I sit up, dazed, and see Theo, still tucked under the extra blanket, sound asleep. He hasn't moved. He's breathing still. He's alive, and I am here.

I don't kiss him for fear of waking him, but I look at him with all the love in my heart. I can do that.

Time passes. The apartment is silent all around. I am thirsty; perhaps I can get a glass of water and bring it back here without being seen.

Filling my glass at the kitchen sink, I remember that it's Saturday. Dex, Ira, and Jim have no idea that Theo won't be playing tonight. They'll be expecting him, and me, too. And then there's Mrs. Chastain and Mary. They have no idea about Theo, either.

I can't go back to him yet. I have things to take care of first.

I go quietly to the hallway phone. The numbers blur, and I realize how tired I still am. I blink and the numbers come into focus. I dial Theo's number, and Mrs. Chastain answers. I can hear the panic in her hello. When she realizes it's me, she says, "What's happened to my boy?" I start to tell her, and she interrupts me. "Is he dead?" Only when I've reassured her does she allow me to continue. I explain everything that has happened. "He's sleeping in my brother's room. He'll need to have X-rays," I finally say.

Mrs. Chastain is weeping. Mary wrests the receiver from her and begs me to explain all over again. When I do, Mary cries, too.

In the end, they agree to come to see Theo. I tell them our address. Neither of them can drive, so they'll have to take the El. They'll get here as soon as they can. And no, they don't know how to contact Jim, Dex, and Ira. Theo always called the other Chess Men. There was never a need for Mrs. Chastain or Mary to do so before.

I hang up the receiver and turn to find Mother standing there. I try to say that I have more phone calls to make, but she won't listen. She leads me into the kitchen and sits me down before a plate of food. She tells me that Dad will be working all day and into the night, and that Andreas is off somewhere with Dolores, and Sophy is taking a nap. When she starts to talk about Theo and me again—*How can you think this will ever work?*—I push away the plate. Mother holds up her hands in a truce. I agree to eat if she stays quiet. She stays quiet. I don't taste a bite, but at least I can see straight, with food in my belly again. I go back into Andreas's room and, wondering how to contact Dex, Ira, and Jim, I watch Theo sleep. He is sleeping so deeply. Too deeply. *Coma?* I think, and push that thought right out of my mind. Theo is asleep. That's all.

It's nearly six o'clock when there's a knock at the apartment door. I let Mrs. Chastain and Mary inside, thankful that Dad and Andreas are still nowhere to be found. It's easier this way. I lead Mrs. Chastain and Mary down the hallway to Theo. Mrs. Chastain eases herself down on the mattress beside him; Mary eases herself down, too. When they start to pray for Theo's healing, I leave them in privacy. In the bathroom, washing up, I realize what I need to do.

I find Mother in the front room, ironing Sophy's baptism dress, and Sophy watching from her child-sized wheelchair.

"I have to go to Calliope's," I say.

Mother keeps ironing. She won't look at me.

"I have to tell the other fellows what's happened," I say. "If Theo doesn't show up and I don't show up, they won't be able to perform. We'll lose this job." *We.* The word sounds so right to me. I am part of the Chess Men. "We can't afford to lose this job," I say. "I have to go there, Mother, and I have to sing. I have to sing for Theo, Dex, Ira, and Jim. I have to sing for me."

Mother sets the iron down on the board. She looks at Sophy for a long moment. Something in Sophy's expression makes Mother nod, and then Mother turns to me.

"Go quickly before your father and Andreas return."

Mother helps me remove the bandages from my face, arms, and hands. I can leave a few of the cuts uncovered now. Some I can hide with my hair. Others Mother bandages again as discreetly as she can.

I can't wear my blue dress. Unless Mother works some kind of magic with her needle, I may never be able to wear it again. So I put on my second-best option: the green, cape-backed dress with the long sleeves and ruffled collar that I wore to my high school graduation. It was fashionable in 1934; it's not so fashionable now. But it will have to do. Mother lends me a pair of white gloves, and I wear those, too. They hide the bruises and cuts on my hands.

I'm at the front door, ready to head out to the El, when Mary emerges from the bedroom and walks down the hall to me. She takes a deep breath and draws herself up to her full height. She holds out her hand, and I take it, and Mary leads me back to the bedroom, where Mrs. Chastain still sits by Theo on the bed.

Mrs. Chastain looks up at me. Her face is dry. She must have cried all the tears she can cry for now.

"I've never asked a white woman for a thing in my life. I want to ask you for something now, Rose. The most important thing."

I nod.

"I am afraid to move Theo before he's had the X-rays," Mrs. Chastain says.

"I understand."

She gives an impatient shake of her head. I don't understand at all.

"Will you take care of my boy until he can come home to us? Will you keep him from getting hurt again?"

"Yes." This yes feels as important as any vow I'll ever take.

Mrs. Chastain nods. "Thank you."

"I'm sorry." I blurt out the words, and the horrible thing I've not been able to say. "This is all my fault."

"You're not to blame, Rose. Not any more than Theo is." Mrs. Chastain closes her eyes and murmurs something under her breath. When she opens her eyes again, it seems she is look-ing right through me to a different time and place. "This world is a hard world. We've known this all our lives, Theo and Mary and me, and all our family, and my mother and her mother, too, and her mother before her, and all our men. I suppose you'd best know it too, Rose, if you love my boy. He'll need you to know it when he wakes up. He'll need you to understand."

"I know it. I'll never forget it," I say.

I look at Theo there on the bed, her wounded boy, the man I love.

When he wakes up.

Not if.

"Look at you, so early tonight," the coat-check girl says, leaning her elbows on her half-door and eyeing me as I enter Calliope's. I nod my hello to her and walk swiftly to the back room, ignoring the crack she's making about my new dress—something about the big, bold change I've made from blue to green.

She has no idea how much I've changed.

Dex, Ira, and Jim haven't arrived yet. I don't know what to do with myself. I circle the room, and my thoughts circle with me. I want Theo to be awake when I get home. I want him to be smiling his light. I want last night never to have happened. I want this world to be different from hard. I circle the room.

Then I see it: an unfamiliar piece of sheet music lying on the table. It's a crisp, new copy, probably fresh off the press. "Strange Fruit," written by Abel Meeropol. I open to the first page.

It's something, all right. It's like nothing I've ever seen or sung:

> *Southern trees bear a strange fruit,*
> *Blood on the leaves and blood at the root*

I finish reading the lyrics, close the music, sit down at the table, rest my head in my hands, and try to pray. No words come but the words of the song. So I send them up to God as a prayer. Only God can contain this.

Maybe an hour later, Dex, Ira, and Jim find me that way. They realize I've looked at the sheet music and quickly apologize for the harsh message of the song. We don't sing songs like that. They know we don't. Still, there's something about it, something truly powerful. Don't I think so, too?

"Lilah passed the music on to us," Ira adds. "I went to see her for old times' sake. I wanted to see how she was doing."

"Mainlining again," Jim mutters.

Ira nods sadly. "She's hooked up with some record producer. A real player, she says. He's taking her to LA to cut a single."

Jim says, "'When I Get Low, I Get High.' That'll be her single."

"Enough. She's a friend." Ira nods at the music on the table. "Anyway, she gave us a copy of this song in case we were interested in performing it. No one's even recorded it yet. No surprise, right? Lilah doesn't want to touch it, and neither does Jim. Dex and I are tempted, but we know, we know. Theo ditched practice this afternoon—the schmuck—so we haven't asked him yet. What do you think, Rose?"

"It hits hard," I say.

"Exactly," Dex says quietly. He runs his fingers over his clarinet, testing out a silent melody.

"It hits close to home." My voice falters.

But then I do what I have to do. I tell them what happened to Theo.

At first I think Jim and Ira are going to tear the room apart. They kick chairs, upend the table, scattering the sheet music across the floor. Dex takes the news differently. He goes to a corner and leans into it. I follow his example and stand in the opposite corner, the better to stay out of Jim's and Ira's way. Dex doesn't even flinch, with all the noise and mess Ira and Jim are making. He's too busy taking apart his clarinet. Only when the instrument is disassembled and back in its case does he look up at us. Then, quietly, Dex tells Jim and Ira to stop. Loudly, he tells them.

Jim and Ira turn to Dex, as startled as I would be if anything could startle me now.

Dex says, "Save your energy for the real fight, boys. If you were black you'd know to do that by now." He closes his clarinet case with a snap. "I can play the piano. Not great, like Theo. Not even very well. But I can play it. A pianist is necessary. A clarinetist isn't. I'll play the piano tonight and every night until Theo returns. I'm going to keep our spot here until he comes back, and then I'll play the clarinet again. Is anyone else going to join me?"

"Yes," I say. I will tip the coat-check girl, call Mother, and beg her to take my place by Theo's side. I want to be home with him, but he'd want me to be here. *Our music depends on it.* I swear I can hear his voice saying that.

Jim and Ira are nodding in sheepish agreement. The four of us do our best to clean up the room. And then we start trying to figure out how to hang tight, hold on, make it work without Theo. For a while. For just a little while.

TWENTY

It's the darkest hour of early Sunday morning, not nearly dawn, when I return home to find Theo awake in Andreas's bed. When he sees me in the doorway, he tries to sit up, then grimaces and falls back again. I go to him and carefully lower myself onto the edge of the bed. I am afraid to take his bandaged hands in mine, but I can't keep from touching him, so I slip my hand between the mattress and his arm, and cup his elbow instead. This part of him I've never touched. So much of him I've never touched. And now, even if we were married, I couldn't touch him. He's in too much pain. His body is, and his heart, and his spirit, too. His beautiful dark eyes have gone dull, half hidden beneath hooded lids. Again he bears the weight of those chains.

I won't cry.

"When did your mother and Mary leave?" I manage to ask.

He licks his dry lips. "Just a little while ago. They waited until I woke up."

Theo is wearing one of Andreas's shirts. His mother must have helped him change out of his torn, bloody clothes, and taken his clothes home with her. Andreas's shirt hangs big on Theo's lean frame; the cuffs droop nearly to his bandaged knuckles. I slip my hand from beneath his arm and fold up the cuffs so they fall at his wrists as they should. "Are you hungry?" I ask, cupping his elbow again.

He gives a slight shake of his head. "Your mother made dinner for the three of us." A ghost of his smile flickers. "Between the efforts of your mother and mine, I was well fed, believe you me."

I force my own ghost of a smile, and then our smiles vanish. "Are you thirsty?"

He nods. It is all I can do to keep from leaping up to *do* something for him. I go to the kitchen, return with a glass of water, tip it to his lips. He drinks his fill, and then I dab at his wet chin with my sleeve. He blinks, taking in my green dress.

"Pretty green. Pretty you." His expression darkens again under the weight of memory. "Your blue dress—oh, Rose. How badly did they hurt you? They hurt you because of me—"

"They hurt me because they hurt you. That's all." *That's enough. That's too much.* I grip his elbow so tightly that he winces. I loose my hold on him, but I don't take my hand away. "They hurt me *only* because they hurt you." My voice is calmer now. "Otherwise I'm the same as I ever was. I feel the same as I ever did—about you, about everything. I promise, Theo."

"Good." But he doesn't look relieved. He doesn't look like he believes me, either. His legs stir restlessly, as if he'd like to kick off the covers. His foot pokes out and I see that he's wearing clean socks and trousers, too. Also Andreas's, I imagine. The trousers will be far too long. Tomorrow, after church, I will hem them.

"I have to call Dex." Theo sounds fretful.

"I already talked to Dex."

His eyes widen. "And Ira and Jim?"

I nod.

"You told them?"

"Yes."

"What did they say?"

I won't tell him about the scene in the back room—not in detail, at least. "They were upset."

Grimacing, Theo pushes himself up on his elbows. "What did they tell George?"

"I don't know."

"What do you mean? They must have made some excuse."

"I saw Jim talking to George between sets, so maybe he said something then. But I didn't have time to ask, and nobody thought to tell me. We were all too busy just trying to pull the night off."

"Wait." Theo's brow furrows as he tries to understand. "Wait a minute."

"We did it for you, Theo. We pulled it off." My throat tightens, but I manage to say it. "The fellows played every note, I sang every word. For you. We told the audience you weren't feeling well. You'd be back as soon as you were able. Thank goodness they like our music so much. They were mostly only compassionate, wishing you well. No one walked out—at least not that I saw. They all stayed and listened."

I tell him about Dex at the piano, and the rest of us, making adjustments, making do. It wasn't the same, not nearly as good, but we didn't lose our spot at Calliope's. "We'll be back on Tuesday, it seems. Jim did say George would be expecting us."

"But not me," Theo says.

And now, never mind any concern, I take his bandaged

hands in my own. Gently, I hold his hands. "You're hurt. You need to rest, Theo. The doctor said so. It's how you'll get better. When you're ready to come back, we'll be waiting."

"But—"

"Everything's going to be all right. You just need to take care of yourself, and everything will be all right. The music isn't going anywhere."

"I need to take care of myself." His voice is as dull as his eyes, repeating this.

My throat tightens. I want him to be angry. Sad. Anything but this. Defeated.

"You're not alone, Theo. Your mother, your sister, Dex, Ira, and Jim. And me. Especially me. We're all here. We'll help, any way we can. Anything you need."

He turns his face to the wall. "Sounds like some kind of song."

"Maybe it is." I kiss the bandages on his hands, my lips light as a whisper. "Maybe I'll sing it for you. Tomorrow morning, Easter morning. I'll sing it for you then."

Theo closes his eyes. And now his breathing has deepened and slowed, and now he has escaped into sleep.

I write a note in case I don't have time in the morning:

Dear Theo,

Sophy is being baptized this morning. I'll be home right after church. We'll have lunch together.

Love,

Rose

I pin this to his covers so he'll be sure to see it when he wakes.

The baptisms have begun. This Easter morning, for the first time ever, we sit in the front row of the sanctuary. Mother and I support Sophy so she can easily see Dolores walking up to the baptistery. Even Dad is here, sitting beside Mother, watching. Dolores leans back in Pastor Riis's arms. Andreas stands at the head of the font as Pastor Riis lowers her into the water. When she rises up again, her streaming face is joyful.

We welcome Dolores as a child of God.

Andreas wraps Dolores in a white towel, and she steps to one side, then turns toward the congregation, her gaze seeking our family.

It's Sophy's turn.

Mother and Dad make a princess's chair for Sophy, and I follow behind them as they bear her up to the font. She has waited so long for this day. Finally she is ready in body and spirit. Pastor Riis steps aside, and Andreas takes Sophy from Mother and Dad. He lowers her into the water. A blessing she descends, a blessing she rises up. A blessing, I sing so all can hear:

> *Shall we gather at the river,*
> *Where bright angels' feet have trod?*
> *Shall we gather at the river,*
> *That flows by the throne of God?*

If only Theo were able to join our gathering. I close my eyes and sing for him, too.

I look out onto the congregation again as they join in on the last verse of the song. Dad is scowling. Then he wipes his eyes, and I realize I've misread his expression; he's not doing this at all. He's weeping, like many others. He's just trying to hide that human fact.

We sing amen. There are a few announcements to be made, and a final, beloved hymn to be sung:

> *Come, thou fount of every blessing,*
> *Tune my heart to sing Thy grace;*
> *Streams of mercy, never ceasing,*
> *Call for songs of loudest praise.*

The service is nearly finished now, but there are still a few announcements, and we can't afford to let Sophy get chilled. So Mother and Dad carry her, wrapped in her white towel, to the back of the sanctuary and down the stairs to the basement, where trays of pastries and coffee urns are already set out on the long tables. At the bathroom door, I take Dad's place, and Mother and I carry Sophy inside. We left a bag holding a change of clothes there before the service. Now we take off her wet things and help her into dry ones. Here is her new pink dress, replete with ruffles, purchased on her outing with Andreas and Dolores. Sophy beams as we help her put it on. "Happy?" I ask. She kisses the air, not just once but three times. And then she says it anyway. "Happy."

When we emerge from the bathroom, the rest of the congregation has assembled in the basement. Mother and I sit in folding chairs with Sophy, and our family gathers around us, holding all the cups of coffee and plates of pastries anybody could ever want. Rob sits beside me, preening in a blue suit I've never seen before, and a bright, Easter yellow tie. "Pawnshop?" I ask discreetly, and he shakes his head until his curls bob. "Field's," he says proudly. "Nothing like a job with a decent wage. Though I'm not abandoning the pawnshop entirely, believe you me." I smile and nod. I smile and nod at Julia and Paul, too, who are talking excitedly about all that needs to happen before their wedding. I smile and nod at Andreas and Dolores, and when Mother leans behind Sophy and whispers that there's surely a spark of romance between these two—no, more than a spark, a flame—I smile and nod at that. I smile and nod at Zane across the room, and at his parents, who are talking with Dad, and all the while I'm smiling and nodding, my thoughts are with Theo. *Has he awakened yet? Is he hungry or thirsty? Does he feel well enough to get up and take care of his own needs? Does he want me, need me, and I'm not there?* Only a few more minutes, I tell myself, and I will return to him.

Smiling and nodding, I look away from the Nygaards and Dad, and my eyes meet Nils's. I stop smiling and nodding. I return his sober gaze.

"I think someone wants to talk to you," Mother says.

"Rose," Julia says. "Come on now. Go to him."

Julia takes my place beside Sophy so that I can stand. I go to him. Balancing our cups of coffee on saucers, we say our hellos. My coffee sloshes on my hand, and Nils draws out his handkerchief and gives it to me. I busy myself, wiping up. Then I set my cup and saucer on a nearby table, fold his handkerchief so that the wet portion is tucked safely away, and hold the handkerchief out to him like a small white flag of truce.

"I saw you at Calliope's," I say.

"And I saw you." He takes the handkerchief, tucks it into his pants pocket.

"And?"

"I don't know what to say."

"Oh." I swallow hard. "Well, thank you for coming."

"I had to. I didn't have a choice. If that's who you really are, if that's what you really want, I need to know."

"I'm sorry."

His face is pained. "You can still see the light. You can still change your mind."

"I've seen the light." I think of Theo's smile. "And that's not what I'm sorry for."

He frowns. "For what, then?"

"I'm sorry for saying I was with you when I was really somewhere else. I'm sorry for using you as a lie."

"You've already apologized for that."

"I thought I'd try again."

Nils ducks his head, and his hair falls into his eyes, and this is not the right time to even think about touching his hair, or tucking it back into place. I won't think in this way, out of respect to us both.

Nils looks up at me again, and pushes back his hair.

"Nearly all my life I've known you, Rose. For the first time, you're making me utterly confused."

A sharp laugh escapes me; it sounds almost like a cry. "I confuse myself, too, sometimes. I'm just beginning to understand myself, I think. So maybe I understand what you're feeling a little bit."

"I don't know if you do." Nils presses his lips into a thin line, and I see that his lips are trembling.

Before I can stop myself, I've apologized again. Immediately, I regret it. His face has gone grim. "Please stop saying that." And now his words are distinctly, firmly articulated; he wants to be as clear as he can be. "I want to love you, Rose. I want you to let me love you."

Right here in middle of the church basement, balancing his cup of coffee on its saucer, he says this. Right here—his cup, his life, *our* lives in the balance—he leans close to me, closer, closer yet. He will kiss me on Easter morning with all these people watching, or not watching, but still they will hear about this kiss, the news will swiftly spread, and Nils and I will be a couple, and Theo will be waiting, and I need to go home to him—wherever Theo is, is my home—but Nils's lips are near my cheek now, only a fraction of an inch away, and I can feel the familiar pull of his presence, and I raise my face to him; it's instinctual, like a flower turning its face to the sun.

Nils draws back.

"I knew you were confused," he says, and there is triumph in his eyes. "You have to decide what you want, Rose. Think hard. Remember where you came from. Remember who you are."

He turns, carefully balancing his cup of coffee on its saucer, and walks away.

At last we are home, Mother, Dad, Sophy, and I. Others will soon follow and join us for Easter dinner. Andreas will bring Dolores and any leftover coffee and pastries from church. Julia and her parents are coming with Paul; their family's renowned asparagus dish will make a brief appearance before it's devoured. Rob will bring his mother, who is contributing dessert (in case the pastries prove insufficient), a cake the family calls Aunt Hulga's Strawberry Delight. And in the kitchen already there's a ham to be glazed, sweet potatoes to be boiled and mashed, rolls to be baked. On this day, even more than on Christmas or Thanksgiving, we always work hard to create a bountiful feast.

"I'll be right there," I tell Mother, and then I rush to Andreas's bedroom.

The bed is neatly made. Theo is nowhere to be seen.

I search the apartment. Only a moment it takes and I understand.

Theo is gone.

I go back to Andreas's bedroom and look down at the place where Theo was. Not three hours ago he was here. But there's not a wrinkle in the sheet, not an impression in the pillows. If it weren't for my note, still pinned to the covers, I might doubt that he'd ever taken shelter with us at all. I unpin the note, read again what I wrote. Could he have misread my *Dear* or *morning*. My *home* or *right after*? Could he have misread *together* or *love* or *Rose*?

The paper trembles in my hands. I fold it in half and then again. And then I see Theo's writing on the other side. His writing is altered for the worse by his injuries, but I can still make out the cramped words. I unfold the paper and read what he has written:

Dearest Rose,

When I woke up, I called your name, but you didn't answer. You couldn't answer. But I didn't know that then. I just knew that the quiet frightened me. I felt trapped by the quiet, and everything all around. I felt trapped by myself. And I knew that you were trapped by me, too.

We are trapped.

Then I saw your note, and I read it, and I knew what I must do.

I'm leaving. I can't shed myself, but if I go quickly before we get in deeper, I can set you free. I'm going back to New Orleans. I want to see Papa. I want to ask him who I was when I was a boy. And if I can't find him—Papa might be dead, that's the way life goes—then I can hear the music of my childhood. Every note I've ever played has sprung from the Delta, and I want to go back there and drink deeply again. Maybe I can find my way back to myself before I knew things were so bad. Maybe I can find some hope again.

So I called Dex from your phone. Dex understands. I don't mean to say you don't understand. But it's different with Dex. You and me, we're different. I'm sure you understand.

You understand, don't you, Rose?

Dex said I need X-rays, so I guess I'll try and get those before I hop a train or hitch a ride. Though who's going to give a black man with no money X-rays on an Easter morning, I don't know. But Dex and I will see if we can find that saint.

Rose, you said you'd help me any way you could. "Anything you need," you said. I need you. But I can't have you. You can't have me. Not in this world. I need to get away so we can get over the pain of that. The pain of that might kill me, which is one thing, but if it hurts you nearly as bad, well, then I won't be able to answer for my sins. Not before God or anyone.

Rose, they would have killed you and me both if they'd had the chance. I believe that.

I know your address by heart. When I know mine, I'll send it to you. Maybe by then we'll be able to tell each other that we're free.

If you write me, write me a song. Rose, keep singing. Keep singing with the Chess Men. They need you more than they need me, and once they get over me going away, they'll realize that. Someday, when enough time passes, well, maybe I'll be able to play a gig with you all again. Just one gig. A guest of the Chess Men. A visiting musician. I'd like that.

Theo

I turn to see Mother standing at the bedroom door, watching me. She takes one look at my face and says, "Oh, darling. What have you done?"

I don't taste a bite of Easter dinner. I don't say a word. I get through it for Sophy's sake.

TWENTY-ONE

"He jumped the blinds," Dex says on Tuesday night, clasping his hands tightly on the cluttered table in the back room at Calliope's.

Like Ira and Jim, I look at Dex, waiting for more.

"Hopped a boxcar in the dead of night," Dex clarifies for my sake. "It's faster than going by hand, that's for sure."

Jim says, "Dangerous, though."

"At least hitching you get a look at a fellow before you climb in his car," Ira adds.

Dex doesn't respond to this. The expression on his thin dark face is suddenly distant. There's something he isn't telling us. I lean forward and grip his arm. "Did he get the X-rays?"

Dex soberly shakes his head. "He wouldn't have it. We couldn't find someone who'd do them on credit, not even in Bronzeville. His mother was on the way to her bedroom to empty out the shoebox that holds her savings, and Theo told me he had to get out before she got back. He didn't want to take her money. So we hightailed it. We found some fellows down in Hooverville, and they told us which track to take south."

George flashes five fingers through the open door, and then he's gone.

"We've barely practiced," Ira says. "Are you sure you're up for this again, Dex?"

Dex shrugs. "I'll do my best."

"If he wasn't so beat up already, I'd give him what for," Jim says. "Jumped the blinds, stupid fool." But then his broad face crumples and tears stand in his eyes.

Dex sighs. "Do you really blame him?"

Jim presses his fingers to his eyes and shakes his head.

Ira says, "We want him back. That's all."

"Yeah." Dex picks up the piano music. "But there's even less of a chance he'll come back if we lose this gig."

"He'll come back." I have to say this. I have to make it true.

The fellows muster smiles that make me feel worse than if they'd ignored me. Then Dex heads for the stage, and the rest of us follow. I'm wearing my green dress again tonight. Mother promised she'd start working to repair my blue one just before I left for the El. As I walked down the sidewalk, I glanced back to see her and Dad standing between parted curtains at the front-room window. They knew where I was going, and what I was going to do when I got there. But they didn't say no. "Don't go to Calliope's. Don't sing. Don't lower yourself, ruin yourself, endanger our reputation." They could have said any of these things, but they didn't. "Be the young woman we've raised you to be." They didn't say that, either. Mother only said she'd try to repair my blue dress. They stood at the window and watched me walk away, and the last light of sunset glanced off the metal of the bayonet mounted on the wall behind them. The way they looked at me, and the memory stirred by the sight of that glinting metal—*Dad defended me*—briefly lifted my spirits. I turned back to the El. I walked toward it, toward tonight, all the faster.

Tonight our first number is "My Funny Valentine." It's a song from a musical that's just opened on Broadway. Dex learned it just a few days ago on the clarinet. He picked it up by ear—he's good at that—so he was to able to figure it out on the piano, too. We ran through it for the first time tonight. Our relationship with "Valentine" is fragile at best. Maybe that's why it seems so very near and dear to us, so tender, almost raw. Nobody in the crowd dances when we perform it. They stay very still as the song washes over them, listening hard:

> Don't change your hair for me
>> Not if you care for me . . .

I remember my hands in Theo's hair. I sing like my heart is breaking. It's not that hard to do. And when the song asks a sweet, funny, comic, tragic valentine to stay, I sing this to Theo. *Come back*, I sing to him. *Come back to stay*.

At the end of the night, George peers over his horn-rimmed glasses and asks me when Theo will return. Dex, Ira, and Jim—they're already backstage. If only I hadn't spotted Rob and Zane during the last set. If only I hadn't let them keep me here after the encore. They asked questions about Theo I couldn't answer, and now George is doing the same. If only I'd gathered my music and fled while the fleeing was good, like Dex and Ira and Jim.

"I don't know. As soon as he can. He's having some health problems," I say.

George sticks an unlit cigar in his mouth. "Like Lilah?" His mouth moves around the blunt brown stub, but somehow it stays put.

"No!" I draw back, startled by the suggestion. "He's not like Lilah at all."

Though wasn't he in such danger when he was younger, in New Orleans? He told me as much.

Now, in New Orleans . . . is he in danger again?

I wrap my arms around myself and hold myself tight.

George shrugs. "Didn't think that was Theo's problem. Had to check, though. The boss has been burned once too often."

Suddenly I'm angry. "Who is this boss, anyway?"

George laughs. "Believe me, sweets, you don't want to know." He lights the cigar now, takes a long draw. "Listen, tell the others that the boss says you're okay here for a while, as long as no one complains. But the sooner Mr. Chastain gets back, the better, you hear? And in case it takes him a while to solve his so-called health problems, your little quartet had better practice hard and hold your own, or you'll be hitting the streets."

"I'll tell them," I say, and I hold myself tighter.

Nights we're not performing, we practice.

Mrs. Chastain and Mary invite us to come to their house. When we do, they fix us delicious meals. After we've eaten, they sit and listen to our rehearsal, smiling, sometimes, or crying, sometimes, or sometimes with their heads bowed or their hands busy doing small chores or tasks. When we leave, Mrs. Chastain and Mary follow us to the door. They reach out, saying good-bye, and their hands linger in ours. Touching us, you'd think they were touching Theo, holding on to him, somehow, because they're holding on to his friends. Three weeks have passed— we're a few days into May—and still none of us have heard from him. Ira and Jim are matter-of-fact about this: "Don't worry, Mrs. Chastain. It takes a while to cover so many miles." Dex is reassuring: "Now, Mary, don't cry. You know he's made of tough stuff." But I look at these other women in Theo's life, his mother and his sister, my friends who feel almost like family, and I don't say a word. Their eyes, like mine, are filled with contradictory emotions. Hope and dread. Fear and courage. Doubt and resolution. Nothing is black-and-white anymore. Everything is mixed to gray.

On the nights we don't practice at the Chastains' apartment, we practice at Jim's house. Jim lives near Rob, in Austin, and when Rob knows we're there he'll stop by. Sometimes he'll bring Zane. The two of them drink more than they should, and when they get too distracting, we ask them to leave. "Save it for Calliope's," one of the other fellows will say, and I'll add, "Better yet, stop it altogether."

On Monday nights, when Calliope's is closed, we practice there. And it is here that Nils finds me, the second Monday night in May.

We're leaving for the evening when I spot him. He's pulled his car close to the curb, and though it's a warm evening, with the wind blowing balmy off the lake, he's sitting behind the steering wheel, windows up, intently watching the door. He doesn't feel comfortable in this neighborhood, it's clear. When he sees me, his eyes widen with surprise, and then narrow with confirmation. He nods, opens his door, and steps out. Dex, Ira, and Jim are gathered around me, saying good-bye, see you tomorrow night, when Jim says sharply, "Who's that, Blue Dress? You know him?" Nils is fast approaching, his face tight with concern. Ira steps in front of me, and Dex, too, and Jim stands stalwartly by my side. Only when I tell them that Nils is an old friend do they give him some room.

"Rob wouldn't tell me where you were tonight, but Zane thought you'd be here," Nils says in lieu of hello. Then he thrusts his hand into the space between Ira and Jim. Awkwardly I take it. But shaking my hand isn't what Nils wants to do. Instead, he draws me to him and starts to walk me toward his car.

"You all right with this, Blue Dress?" Jim calls to me. "I was planning on driving you home just like always."

I look up at Nils. "Are we all right?"

He says, "I'd like to talk with you again, Rose. I've been waiting for you to call me. Then I started waiting for the right time to call you. Tonight I just couldn't wait anymore, so I decided the time was now."

His big hand covers mine, hiding everything but the tips of my fingers. His long legs span the distance to his car in great strides, so that I have to jog to keep up. Trailing behind him, I feel like a little child. After the challenges of these last weeks without Theo, this feels comforting. I look over my shoulder at Jim, Ira, and Dex, and I tell them everything's fine. Breathlessly I call, "See you tomorrow night," to remind myself that I may indeed look forward to this. Then Nils opens the car door for me and I sit down in the front seat beside him.

This is the way the world is. If Nils were Theo, I'd sit in the backseat. I'd sit there happy in my discontent. Now I sit in the front, relieved to be with my childhood friend again.

We drive north toward our part of town, with the sun sinking below the horizon to our left. For a while we don't say anything. I keep my eyes out for a glimpse of the gorgeous, tumultuous sunset that flashes in intermittent bursts down the alleys between factories, and stores, and homes. We're in the vicinity of Hull House now, near the apartment where Theo first heard me sing, where he asked me to do the work I wanted to do, then took a rose-patterned rag in his hand and helped me do the work I needed to do. So I'm thinking of Theo, the way he cleaned those radiators until they gleamed, when Nils turns to me and says, "Where would you like to go? Name it. I'll take you there."

I blink the thought of Theo away, or try to. For old times' sake, I say, "Your house? I've been wondering whether you've gotten any new butterflies."

"Come on." Nils smiles wryly. "Really?"

"Really." And, really, I have wondered this. I've wondered what train tracks Theo took south, and in wondering this, I've wondered if he jumped on a freight car, and in wondering this, I've wondered what kind of freight the car carried—livestock? produce? coal? steel?—and in wondering this, I've wondered about Nils, whether he's made any recent trips to the yards and, if so, what kind of insects did he find there in the freight cars? Tarantulas? Butterflies? A creature I can't imagine, that I don't even know exists?

"I'd love to see something beautiful," I say.

Nils says, "My parents are at home. So not tonight. I want to talk without interruption."

I blink. "Oh."

"So. Where?"

"Let me think a minute." I open the car window and look

toward the lake. I smell water on the wind and, fleeting as a bird's call, I hear the bell-like clanging of sailboats anchored in the closest harbor. Yearning fills me. Maybe I've inherited Dad's love of the sea. If I'd been a boy living in Copenhagen, maybe I'd have been a sailor, too. I wouldn't have been a little mermaid, that's for sure.

I want to see the water.

And now I'm remembering the sweet, comfortable night with Nils at Old Prague, and the way I imagined things would go when he said he had something he wanted me to see. Almost that night seems a lifetime ago. Almost I was a different girl, not even a young woman yet. Almost I miss her, that girl, myself.

I look at Nils. His fine profile, that shock of hair, are distinctly familiar against the purpling sky.

"Let's go to Adler Planetarium and sit by the lake and look at the stars," I say.

Nils parks, then we walk through growing dark toward the immense round building that is Adler Planetarium. I can hear waves slapping against the stones that line the lakefront, and a bright crescent moon hangs just above the planetarium's dome. Starlight pricks the sky. Nils doesn't catch hold of my hand; he keeps a respectful distance. For that I'm grateful. When we pass through the puddles of light cast by streetlamps, I can see the expression on his face. I may feel comfortable with him, but he looks anything but that with me. He chews worriedly at his lip, and his gaze is focused intently on something I can't make out. It could be the planetarium's granite facade, but I think it's more likely the future.

"Sophy desperately wants to visit the planetarium," I say for something to say. "As soon as I can save up a little extra money, I'm going to bring her."

"Good." Nils sounds distracted because he *is* distracted, still staring off at something I can't see. He is walking quickly now, even for him. No jogging about it; I have to run. In the next puddle of streetlamp light, I look up at him and see the back of his head. He's leaving me behind. Did Theo leave me behind? Is that what's happened?

I'm about to call *Slow down, please!* when Nils whirls around, lopes back to me, swoops me up in his arms, and runs, runs, runs toward the lake. I feel small in his arms, which feels all right for a moment—*this is how it's supposed to be, this is what I was raised to expect, this is what dreams are made of, being cradled like this, being carried over the threshold*—but then he stumbles and my head whacks against his shoulder, and I come to my senses. "Put me down," I say, but he doesn't hear me. Or he won't. He runs on, cradling me in his arms.

I am frightened. I fling my arms around his neck, lest he drop me. He must take this as a sign that I am where I want to be. He runs on. We pass the planetarium and in its massive shadow the air turns cool. Then we are by the water. Nils leaps down to the first tier of stones, jarring me; he leaps to the second tier, and I feel the bones of his arms, his shoulders, and his ribs, jarred by the impact of his landing. He staggers, and then leaps to the third and final tier. We are just above the water now. He walks to the stones' edge. For one horrible moment, I wonder if he's going to throw me in just so he can save me, little woman that I am in his arms. He's struggling to catch his breath, struggling, I realize, as the moonlight illuminates his face, not to cry.

But he doesn't drop me into the choppy water; not yet. He bows his head. "Save us," he says to someone I imagine must be God. Then he sets me down.

When my feet touch stone, I gasp with relief. I look at Nils and he looks at me.

"Marry me, Rose," he says.

I close my eyes. In the darkness, I gather my thoughts. I open my eyes. I tell him yet again that I'm sorry. He is a good man, a great man—the best of the Old World in the New, and even more than that. But I'm not the girl he used to know, not entirely. And I'm not the young woman he wants me to be. I'm someone different from that.

"I'm called to be someone different," I say.

"And with someone different."

"Yes."

I push back the shock of hair from his eyes, and hold him as he collects himself. How can it be that a man this tall can weep like a small child in my arms? The single shadow we make breaks and mends again on the waves.

TWENTY-TWO

Next afternoon while Mother and Dad are at work, I sit with Sophy on our bed, reading aloud from *Gone with the Wind*. It is not the kind of book Mother would want us to read, or Dad either, probably. Dad likes manly stories where women play a certain part. Mother likes the Bible. I know we're playing outside the fence, reading this kind of romance; Sophy knows it, too. But ever since I heard people talking about the book at the Nygaards' party I've been curious about it, and this morning, when Sophy resisted every book I pulled from our shelves, we decided to take a trip to the library, and there it was on display. When I told her what I knew about *Gone with the Wind*, Sophy was as eager to read it as I was. In the hours since, we've been unable to put it down. A deep pleasure—the book is this and more. I am dismayed by Scarlett's selfishness. I admire her spirit. I linger over the descriptions of the slaves, wondering again and again what Theo would say if he were here to read them, too.

The day is warm and sunny, the window is open, a breeze stirs the curtains, and for these hours, Sophy and I are not in

Chicago. We are not even in this century. We are captured by the book, we've escaped through it, and, for our different reasons, we're grateful.

Then Andreas walks into the room, holding an envelope in his hand, and thrusts the envelope in my face.

"For you," he says.

I set the book down, take the envelope from Andreas, look at the handwriting there: the full curve of the *R* that marks the beginning of my name, the particular slant to all the letters that follow. I remember the note he left so many days ago now, the phone number he wrote on the church bulletin so many weeks—no, months—before that. Tracing the indentations made by his pen, I read the return address. It's an unfamiliar number on an unfamiliar street in the unfamiliar city of New Orleans. Then I trace and read the address he knows by heart: mine.

I am back in this time and place, and he is here, too, as best he can be.

"It's from him, isn't it?" Andreas says.

"Yes."

Sophy says his name. "Theo," she says, and her voice is happy and relieved. "Open it!"

"Rose." Andreas's voice is heavy with warning. I look up at my brother. The sudden fury I feel surprises me. It's true what they say: my blood is boiling. It must be, to make my scalp prickle so, and my neck, too.

"Dolores is a Catholic," I say.

"*Was*, not *is*. Dolores changed that," Andreas says. "Some things can be changed. Some things can't."

I think about the way I was raised. I remind myself that I was raised to be a fine Christian woman, a lady. My blood may be boiling, but I am still the woman I was raised to be—at least in this way. And I still have a calling that's important to me, no matter what Andreas says. I draw back my shoulders and sit up straight. Calmly, regally, I thank Andreas for bringing Theo's letter to me. "You may leave now," I say. "Or I will."

Andreas turns on his heel and storms off, and Sophy laughs and gives me an appreciative look. She loves Andreas. But she grows weary of his judgments, too.

I don't laugh. Andreas's words made me angry because they are, in part, true.

I tell Sophy I need to stretch my legs. I'll be back shortly, as soon as I read my letter. She nods, understanding. "Tell me," she says. I promise I will tell her all that I'm able to tell about Theo. I help her into her chair by the window. Then I put on my shoes, take Theo's letter, and slip out the back door so I don't risk running into Andreas, who is preparing next Sunday's sermon in the front room.

I walk to Garfield Park. Though my memories of Theo draw me toward the Conservatory, I decide to stay outside in the sunlight. There's an open bench by the lagoon, and I sit down there. I watch the happy couples paddling about in the swan boats. At Julia and Paul's suggestion, Andreas and Dolores tried boating here just a few days ago. "We had the time of our lives!" Andreas said afterward and, from the smile on Dolores's face, I believed they did. If things had worked out differently, if life had been different, Nils and I might have taken out a swan boat this summer. It will only be a matter of time before Nils enjoys boating here with someone else, I'm sure.

I press Theo's letter to my heart, press down the pang of envy that I feel for Andreas and Dolores, Julia and Paul, Nils and someone else. If life had been different, if the world were different, Theo and I might have found ourselves enjoying the lagoon on this beautiful day, but life isn't different, the world is what it is, and Theo and I never will sail across the smooth, green lagoon, splashing water at each other and laughing, or opening a picnic basket and sharing a lunch, or talking together quietly, making plans for the future right out in public, where anyone can see. We won't sit together on this bench, watching others in swan boats do the same. We won't be together, *truly* together, in the naked light of a Tuesday afternoon. We won't.

But we might someday, mightn't we? One can always hope. I can always hope. He can. We can, together.

I can't wait any longer to know his hopes and fears. I slide my fingernail under the envelope where Theo's tongue perhaps touched, and I take out the letter, a single page, carefully folded by his beautiful hands into thirds. I open it:

Dearest Rose,

If you are reading this, then you know I couldn't keep from writing you. If you aren't reading this, then I think you may have done the reasonable thing and thrown my letter away.

There is a garden I would like to show you here in New Orleans, a garden as beautiful as our Conservatory, only it is out in the open air. If we visited this garden in the night we would walk together at our risk, as we walked the dark streets of Chicago. In New Orleans, as in Chicago, we would be expected to keep our lives separate.

But there is a chance in this city if we were wealthy enough that one of us could buy a house built around a hidden courtyard. That is the beauty of some of the homes here. They offer private gardens where people can be alone, hidden from the world.

Papa lives in a shotgun house where any passerby can stand at the front door and look straight through to the back. There is no hiding here.

This is where I am.

After days of jumping from one train car to the next, I got off in New Orleans. After a few more days of searching this city, I found Papa. Now I live with him, and we walk and talk and pray. I listen to music, and we walk and talk and pray some more. On days when there's a funeral, I walk with the mourners, and I mourn with them.

Here I am again in my first home, only to realize this place is no more home than anywhere else.

I still love you, Rose. I haven't stopped. Not for a moment. But I cannot offer you a life of homelessness.

This is what I tell Papa, what I am writing you now.

And this is what Papa says. He says on this earth we are all homeless and searching, though we may fool ourselves into thinking otherwise. He says it doesn't matter, the color of our skin. We are traveling through this world, seeking another home. Of course, even Papa has to acknowledge that the color of our skin often dictates the nature of our travel, the quality of our journey, and our companions along the way. But still, Papa says, none of us is so different from the other in our searching.

We are not so different, Rose, and our differences only complement each other. I believe that. God knows, I believe that.

But until the rest of the world believes that, how can we be together? If I returned to Chicago, would I build us a little house with a courtyard, our secret Eden, and would we marry and live in our little house and love each other in our hidden garden, and only those who believed in us—my mother, sister, and Papa, your sister, the Chess Men, and Rob, and others we may meet along the way— would only they join us there? Would we make music only there? Would we eat of every good fruit, but only there? Only there, would we be safe and sound and happy and whole and complete in each other? Or would we be trapped in the garden of our making? Would you become a caged bird that couldn't sing?

These are the things I'm thinking about, Rose, and talking about with Papa, and praying about, too.

Meanwhile, I am hearing all the great good music that this place holds. I long for you to hear it, too. I long for you.

Theo

I write Theo back. I tell him to keep thinking, talking, praying, and please, oh, please, I tell him, please keep writing to me.

We can make a home out of homelessness, traveling with Jim, Ira, and Dex, making music wherever they'll have us. I'll send money home—every penny. If we drive far enough, long enough, in the right direction, maybe we can find a place to settle down.

I write this.

And I pray that we'll be able to find the strength, the spirit, to travel through life together and find that place. And if he says no, he can't take that journey, I pray for strength and spirit, too.

I write Theo about the time that is passing, the weeks that fold one into the other. I write about the Chess Men, how we are getting by, holding on, playing each and every set, waiting for his return.

He writes back.

He tells me about the music he's been listening to, and playing as well. He's been sitting in with bands. *Swing bands are hot in the Crescent City, like everywhere else,* he writes. *So I've been playing my fair share of swing. Hoping it helps my playing. Thinking it will. We are good at this, but I think we can be better. Look at that. You are my we. You and the Chess Men. I miss you, Rose. I miss you all. The people I've been playing with, the music I've been playing—it only shows me how important you are. Papa is telling me to pay attention to this fact. "Home isn't always a place," Papa says.*

Labor Day and Julia's wedding weekend are fast approaching, I write to Theo. I'll be her maid of honor. Aunt Hulga has done a beautiful job on both our dresses. My dress is gray lace, which sounds plain, but it isn't. It's like spun silver. When the wedding is done, I'll be able to wear mine to sing. Mother fixed my blue dress, but I am eager for other options. *We are holding on at Calliope's, the fellows and I. I am holding on. But I'm hoping I can let go soon, and just hold your hand instead.*

I allow myself to come right out and say this on paper. And then I send the letter off.

I hope that, too.

That's all that Theo writes in his letter when he writes back. A few days later, he writes more:

I'm coming home to you. Papa and I have been pray-ing for guidance, seeking wisdom as to how I should return. I don't want to run back to you, Rose, hopping trains to make the journey. Doing that makes the way long, hard, and unpredictable. I want to look at a map and chart my way safely. Already I've mapped out a few clubs here where the Chess Men will be well received, should we choose to come to New Orleans. Turns out there are owners who are interested in varying their line-ups. Swing may be king, but it'll abdicate for a couple of nights. Of course, it'd be like Calliope's. We'd play off-nights or between sets or after hours. But at least we'd have some new places to play.

At the last minute, Julia has decided to change the lo-cation of her wedding, I write back. *Paul's church flooded in a summer storm. Julia and he had a long talk, and now the wedding is going to happen at Aunt Astrid's farm—the very place where Andreas, Sophy, and I were born, and Julia and Rob, too. It's Julia's favorite place in the world, and I've got to hand it to Paul and his family*

and friends: the thought of being married there has made Julia so happy, they've agreed to drive the long hours and make a weekend of it. Aunt Astrid and her friends in Luck are opening up their homes to the guests, and some people will rough it by camping on Aunt Astrid's land. We'll all get a little vacation out of it.

I have to confess something, I write. When I first met your mother, her still-waters-run-deep spirit reminded me of the lake at the edge of the spruce forest on Aunt Astrid's farm. Julia wants to be married by that lake. If only you could be there, Theo. She's asked me to sing a song. If only you could play it on the piano, the way only you can.

Theo writes that he is leaving New Orleans.

He's decided to drive up the coast to New York. He'll stop in a few cities along the way, but his real destination is Harlem. *There's got to be a club in Harlem that's like Calliope's. There's been so much going on in Harlem. It's a renaissance, people are saying. I want to be a part of it. I want Dex, Ira, Jim, and you, most of all you, to be a part of it, too. Oh, Rose. I hope. I have hope again.*

I slide this letter back into its envelope, and put it under my pillow with the others. When I rest my head on my pillow at night, the paper rustles like a whisper. *I'm coming home to you.* That's what his letters say.

TWENTY-THREE

The Saturday before Labor Day, I walk across a freshly mown field to the still-waters-run-deep lake on Aunt Astrid's farm, a bouquet of black-eyed Susans, baby's breath, tiger lilies, and roses the color of sunset in my hands. The spruce forest rises on the other side of the lake, and as I approach the water, wind stirs the pointed tops of the trees, and they bend and bow and beckon gently to me: *come closer, it's time.* Julia and Paul's guests, many of them my family and friends, flank me on either side, and as I pass, the children wave, the women smile, the men nod. Close to the front, Sophy catches my eye. If she'd been able-bodied, she would have been a bridesmaid, too. As it is, Dad pushed her down this path before me, and Mother walked beside her, strewing flower petals with each step. Sophy beams at me now; she's content with her role. If Theo were here, my happiness would be complete.

I walk up to the gazebo that we spent much of yesterday building at the edge of this field, right beside the lake. Constructed of scraps of wood and cast-off pieces of tin, decorated with dried grapevines and thick chains of wildflowers, the gazebo is another kind of hidden garden, a shelter from the elements, a beautiful testament to Julia and Paul's love. We erected an altar inside the gazebo, too—a simple piece of flat fieldstone, set up on four thick logs of a recently felled oak tree. Rob was the one who found the two long iron nails, pulled from railroad ties, in Aunt Astrid's barn. He bound them together with twine to make a cross, then hammered the point of the vertical nail into a plank of wood and set it on the stone. Paul and his best man stand to one side of the altar and that cross now. Andreas stands before the altar. He's positioned himself so that everyone walking down the aisle can see the cross, and I keep my eyes on it as I step into the gazebo's shade. My gaze briefly meets Andreas's. My brother smiles at me—his old, tender smile, the one I remember from childhood when I was playing the right way; this smile is not burdened by judgment. I smile back at him, and then I turn to look at the bride. With her arm hooked through her father's, Julia slowly draws near, her sandaled feet gliding gracefully through the shorn grass, her butterfly sleeves fluttering in the gentle wind. I hear Paul sigh. He is as radiant as Julia, and as ready for this day.

Julia pauses beside me. "I love you, cousin."

"I love you, too," I say.

She holds out her bouquet of roses and lilies and, taking it from her hands, I spot Nils in the crowd of guests. Like everyone, he is standing (to save energy and time, we left all the chairs under the reception tent, which is nestled a little farther back in the field, on a rise of land that will allow us to enjoy a view of the sunset and stars). Nils drove up yesterday with a group of friends from our church; he stands now by a young woman I don't recognize. Perhaps she is someone he met back in Chicago, and invited here; perhaps she is a local girl. Regardless, they look happy together, and Rob, standing in the row just in front of them, looks happy, too. Rob wears another new suit. This whole weekend he has tormented me by saying that he's going to spike the punch at the reception later; however, I don't think any of the aunts, let alone his mother, will let him get away with that. And I don't let his teasing get in the way of my high spirits. As far as I can tell, he's drunk nothing but Coca-Cola so far this weekend. His gray-green eyes are still clear and serene.

Satisfied, I step closer to Julia and enter into the service. Andreas's message is simple and sweet. When the vows have been exchanged, I turn back to the guests. Without any accompaniment, I sing "At Dawning," as Julia and Paul requested:

When the dawn flames in the sky I love you;
   When the birdlings wake and cry, I love you;
When the swaying blades of corn
   Whisper soft at breaking morn,
Love anew to me is born,
   I love you, I love you.

The song would sound so much better with Theo playing beside me. But I won't let myself dwell on this.

Julia and Paul fairly glow with love for each other, for all of us, as we gather under the reception tent. And when Julia lobs the bouquet directly at me, I allow myself to catch it.

After the wedding reception, true to Julia's wishes, we extend the celebration to dinner. As the heat of the day fades, the night proves balmy and clear, so we decide to leave the tent behind and lay out a feast in true Danish style by the lake—a *smørrebrød* with all our favorite foods. We eat and laugh and lounge and talk, and someone carries out Aunt Astrid's gramophone, winds it up, and we play one wax cylinder after the next, one wonderful old song after another. These are the songs of our parents' youth. This music makes everyone happy.

The nights are long this far north, and this night stretches even longer. It may be nearly nine o'clock, the sun may be lowering on the horizon, but the party shows no signs of winding down. Sophy is nodding off in her wheelchair, but she doesn't want to go lie down on her bed in Aunt Astrid's house. Sophy never wants to miss out on a party, and parties where all of our family are gathered together are rare. So she asks that I simply push her over to sit beneath a willow tree that rises beside the lakeshore. Here, we're only a stone's throw from where the others have gathered. She can watch the revelry from this vantage point, but she can look out at the peaceful stillness of the lake as well. She can rest as she needs.

When I've settled Sophy in a favorable position, I realize that I'm tired, too. It's a relief to put so much activity at a distance for a moment. I am with my sister. A loon calls, and the haunting sound echoes across the water. The willow's branches whisper back and forth above us; some of the longer branches touch the ground, and when the wind stirs they make a rustling sound. The longest branches of all trail across the skin of the lake and trace patterns there. Sophy dozes in her chair, and soon I'm swaying a little on my feet. A good kind of tired, that's what I am. We keep a blanket in a basket attached to Sophy's chair, and I take the blanket out, spread it on the ground. I sit down on the blanket. In a matter of hours, somewhere in Harlem, Theo will be listening to music, or playing it. *More than New Orleans or Chicago, Harlem seems a good place for the Chess Men to be right now,* he wrote. *There are clubs that will headline us, I think. I can't wait until you see this place, Rose. I long for you to be here. I long to be with you.*

I lean against Sophy's chair and close my eyes. I try to imagine what song I'll sing when Theo and I come home to each other.

It's coming on October. Chrysanthemums bloom in the Conservatory. Through the brilliant leaves of maple trees, I glimpse the building's glass walls, a kaleidoscope of garnet, amethyst, and amber, as I walk alone through Garfield Park this late Saturday afternoon. Sophy has gone out for ice cream with Dolores and Andreas, Mother and Dad are working, Rob is readying himself for a date with a girl I don't know—*She's the real deal, Rose! You'll see what I mean when you meet her at Calliope's tonight!*— and Theo still hasn't returned to me. His letters say he is figuring out how to do just that. *My hope is growing ever stronger,* he writes. But sometimes, walking alone like this, watching couples enjoy their last swan-boat rides of the season, I wonder if my own hope is fading. The cottonwoods have shed their brown, heart-shaped leaves; they lie brittle and broken at my feet. I wonder if my hope is like that.

If I keep walking I will reach the National Tea. Soon Nils will be loosening his black bow tie, hanging up his green apron, calling it a day. I could be waiting for him outside. But Nils has a girlfriend now, and from the way they sit side by side in church, she seems the real deal, too. Why tamper with this? Why confuse my own feelings further? Why doubt my hopes? Why not doubt my doubts instead?

I turn and walk back to the apartment, where my dress from Julia's wedding hangs in the closet, filmy and delicate, a sheath of silvery gossamer with capped sleeves. I put it on, and the dove-gray shoes from the wedding, too. I fix my hair and apply the little bit of makeup I wear on nights like this—just a hint of the face paint I wore that first night in the DeSoto, when Rob offered me a blue dress, a silver purse, be-still-my-beating-heart red lipstick, and the city on a half shell. The night I entered a place I'd never imagined where a gentle man I'd never dreamed of first learned my name.

I gather my things, lock the apartment door behind me, and take the El to that place once again.

I want to sing a new song. We've been practicing it, trying to get it right, and tonight Dex, Ira, and Jim agree to spring it on the audience during the second set. "Sing your heart out," Dex tells me on the downbeat, but there's no need for him to say that. Every word of this song will hold the heart of me. "Autumn in New York"—I'll sing my heart there.

Dex plays the opening refrain on the piano—he keeps his playing simple so he's less likely to make a mistake—and I sing a question. *This city, this season, why do they seem so inviting?* I close my eyes and sing like I don't know the answer. I sing wonder and longing, promises broken, promises kept. I sing Central Park, lovers blessing the dark. I sing dreams. I sing crowds and clouds among canyons of steel.

They're making me feel I'm home.

I sing all this. I share my heart. And there is the piano, returning to me. Notes flare from the keys; they lift my heart up.
Notes cascade, and they return my heart safely.

Dex doesn't play like this.

I open my eyes and turn from the microphone. Theo sits at
the piano, playing his heart out. Playing his heart out for me.

We look at each other across the narrow space that divides
us. I see nothing but the light in his eyes, the light in his smile. I
see nothing but him.

I go to him. The distance between us seems to lengthen instead of lessen with my every step, but somehow he is lifting
his hands from the keys now, and my hands are meeting his.
Our hands clasp tightly, never mind the crowd. Theo must
have brought Dex his clarinet, for there is the instrument's
haunting sound, weaving the comforting pattern of melody
around us. There is Ira weaving rhythm, and Jim weaving harmony, too.

The song ends. People are applauding.

"I'm home," Theo says, holding my hands.

"Me, too," I say, holding his.

"Should we finish the set?" he asks.

I nod.

I sing about things deep inside that can't be denied. I sing
about valentines and heaven and home. I sing for him.

Between sets in the little backstage room, Dex, Ira, and Jim
welcome Theo back. When George flashes ten fingers—*Glad to
see you're finally all here, Boss is glad, too!*—Theo turns to me.
The other fellows seem to understand. They need to take care of

a few things onstage, Jim mutters. Then they're gone, and we're in each other's arms.

We gather around the table at the end of the night, Theo, the other fellows, and me. We talk until the wee hours. Theo tells us about New Orleans and Harlem, and the gigs he's got in places for us there in the months to come. "Nineteen thirty-eight looks hopeful," he says. His smile is guarded, saying this—this world is a hard world, after all; none of us can deny it. But he didn't run away from that fact. He made a necessary journey. He didn't simply return to us; he also returned to himself. If he can make that kind of journey once, he can do it again, if need be. And we can do it, too. We can make the necessary journey. We can be the better for it. All of us, gathered here.

"Papa got a new bus for his church, and he let me buy the old one," Theo tells us. "That bus carried me back here just fine, much faster than a train ever could, and more safely." He gives me a long look. "That bus will be our garden. It will take us where we need to go."

We talk a little longer. After so much time apart, Dex, Ira, and Jim don't want the night to end. But finally even they can barely keep their eyes open. So we say our good-byes, and then Theo asks if he can drive me home.

"We *are* home," I remind him as he draws my arm through his.

The bus is parked in the back alley. It's purple, with *Children of God Church* painted in big red letters on the side. Theo sits in the driver's seat. I sit just behind him. It's not so noticeable in this big old bus with the tattered curtains on the windows—*I'll start sewing new curtains first chance I get*—that he is there and I am here. It is the way things go in buses with drivers and passengers. And someday if we keep hoping, if we keep the faith, we'll be able to sit anywhere we want, no matter the color of our skin. Surely that is the future we'll share.

It's almost dawn. Theo turns the bus toward Lake Shore Drive and asks if I'm up for a bite of breakfast.

I laugh. "Where would we go?"

At this hour, I mean. But of course I also mean: who would receive us?

"We'll find a place," Theo says.

I expect him to drive north on Lake Shore, because that would be the quickest way back to my neighborhood. Perhaps we'll grab rolls and coffee from a street vendor near Garfield Park and take an early-morning picnic in some discreet place there. The gazebo where Sophy and I stopped and talked on that cold, hard winter's day, maybe. I'd like that. Or even better: a cluster of trees by the lagoon. The Conservatory will be closed at this hour, but we can look through the windows and see the chrysanthemums inside.

But instead Theo drives south. We must be going to his mother's place. I know how much he loves her Sunday-morning biscuits and gravy. Now I'll finally be able to taste them, too.

We're nearing his neighborhood when I remember another place that will receive us. How could I have forgotten? I lean forward and rest my hand on Theo's dear, strong shoulder.

"Mahalia Jackson," I say. "Let's hear her sing. Today."

Theo laughs, and his laughter is joyful, its own kind of music. The sound says *yes*. To my surprise, he turns the bus in a new direction, away from his mother's house, coffee, and the only real breakfast we can partake of together in this city. He steers the bus purposefully down bumpy, narrow streets. And I keep my hand on his shoulder all the while.

We veer onto a wide boulevard I don't recognize and pull up in front of an unfamiliar stone church. Theo shuts off the bus's engine and turns to me, smiling. He just might laugh again, which would be fine by me, because now I'm laughing, too.

He takes my hand in his. "All nations and races are welcome here."

I remember similar words, printed on the poster I saw outside the public library, so many months ago now.

"Mahalia Jackson and her choir? Already?" I look at the dark sky, the rosy dawn faintly tinting the low horizon. "Isn't it a bit early?"

"It is indeed." Theo lifts my hand, and his lips brush my fingertips, and then he kisses my palm, and the calluses there, from all the buckets I've carried, mops I've pushed, scouring I've done. When he looks at me again, his expression is triumphant. "The last Sunday morning of every month they offer a sunrise service here, and a breakfast afterward. Today's the last Sunday. Isn't that something?"

"It's something all right."

I leap from my seat and throw my arms around Theo. He stands, the better to hold me.

"And guess what? They invite the congregation to join them, Rose. You can sing with them if you like."

"It's what I've always wanted," I say.

And this, I think, as we walk hand in hand toward the church. I've wanted this. And this, I think, as hand in hand we step inside.

They stand on the stage in their golden gowns, the men and women of the choir, glowing and shimmering like the stars that have just vanished from the sky. And there's Mahalia Jackson standing in front, the brightest star of all. Theo and I slip into a pew near the front, and no one protests. Soon the pews are crowded all around us, and still we are welcome where we are.

Then she sings, and thank goodness there are kneelers, because, yes, she brings me to my knees.

At the end of the service, we are called to come up onstage. We join many from the congregation there, pressing close together so that everyone who wants to sing with the choir is able. There are other white faces in the crowd, but mostly the faces are all shades of rich color. *Children of God Church*, our bus says outside, and soon we will start that new journey, but now, in this moment, our family is here. We are home. And as we raise our voices with Mahalia Jackson and her choir, I know that this is what I've wanted from the beginning:

> *Precious Lord, take my hand*
> *Lead me on, let me stand*

This—our hands clasped, music all around and inside us, the family we make together—I will sing to the end.

ACKNOWLEDGMENTS

In 1995, I started working on a story that evolved into this novel. The fact that this book exists and that you are reading these words is a testament to the many good people who supported and encouraged me along the long and winding way of writing. It is an honor to have the opportunity to thank them now—and a daunting task, because, honestly, do words ever suffice? If nothing else, let the following hint at what my heart holds.

Thank you, Sandra Bishop, for acting as my agent. You are a warrior for good and growth, and a wise guide for the writing life. Plus, you understand about the dark chocolate of the soul. Your laughter lifts the heart. And you've got the kind of fearless moxie that inspires me, for one, to be brave.

Beth Adams, I have worked with numerous editors over the years, and you take the cake for *withness*. Your vision and understanding for the shape and needs of this novel took my breath away more than once and left me humbled in the best possible way. I am so grateful to have shared in the experience of writing and revising with you, Beth. Reared on stories of writers working with the likes of William Maxwell, I now feel, after having worked with you, that I have my own stories to share.

Amanda Demastus, when Beth framed her revision letters, she wrote "Amanda and I feel/think/wonder" so often that I fully understand what an editorial team the two of you make. You are an incredible editor in your own right, Amanda (just look at the great books you have edited on Howard's list). It was such a comfort to know that you were lending your editorial scrutiny to my work. Thank you for responding to all my questions and for telling me not to overthink things. I needed to hear that.

Thank you, Becky Nesbitt, for agreeing to take on this book when I was a first-time author in this particular cosmos of publishing. When Sandra called to say that you'd optioned *Sing for Me*, I was at Calvin College's Festival of Faith & Writing. One moment I was standing on the sidewalk; the next moment, upon hearing the news, I stood atop a stone outcrop—a landscaping feature that I somehow scaled in a burst of joyful adrenaline. I don't remember how I turned mountain goat. I do remember being exquisitely happy. And grateful to you.

On that note, I want to say how thankful I am to the whole Howard Books/Simon & Schuster family, and especially to Bruce Gore, who asked for and received my thoughts on the cover image and transformed the mishmash I sent his way into something truly beautiful and memorable—his own distinctive work. Bruce, thank you again for what you do and who you are.

When I first wrote the story on which this novel was based, a fellow doctoral candidate at the University of Illinois at Chicago, Beth Franken, read and edited initial drafts like nobody's business, and basically steered the final version toward publication. She was my dear friend, lo those many years ago, and she's my dear friend today, and I am ever more grateful to her.

Jenine Gordon Bockman and Jeffrey Michael Gordon Bockman took that story out of the slush pile, gave it a prize, published it in their wonderful (still thriving online) journal, *Literal Latté*, sent it on to Bill Henderson, publisher and editor of *The Pushcart Prize: Best of the Small Presses*, who said *yes, this one, too*, and included it in his anthology. These three folks helped me believe there might be more of a story to tell in the future.

Getting to the future takes a while. From 1996 to now, I encountered people like Fred Shafer, whose brilliant teaching inspired me within the context of one of the best workshops I've ever taken, set in the lovely house of the gracious writer Susan Gilbert McGuire. Fred, you taught me so much—and you continue to do so. I'm grateful.

Sara Crowe said, "There's good stuff here, but maybe it's not young adult?" And her insightful, gentle prodding encouraged me to try something new, which turned out to be the thing I've been wanting and needing to do all along. Thank you, Sara.

Friend and audiophile (and maker of keep-them-for-a-lifetime wedding mixes) Jeff Arena connected me with the incomparable David Whiteis, a writer, researcher, and investigative journalist living in Chicago, whose emails to me are worth a book in and of themselves. In case that doesn't happen quickly enough, however, you can read David's actual books, *Chicago Blues: Portraits and Stories* and *Southern Soul-Blues*, or check out any of David's articles and reviews in the *Chicago Reader*, *Chicago Tribune*, or *DownBeat* and *JazzTimes* magazines, among others, or delve into his liner notes for numerous blues and jazz albums and CDs. David, you rock (to mix genres).

In addition to thanking David for his dense, compelling, and illuminating emails (and his patience with my many questions), I would like to thank these authors for writing the following books that so helped me in my research for *Sing for Me*:

William Howland Kenney, *Chicago Jazz: A Cultural History, 1904–1930*; Sandor Demlinger and John Steiner, *Destination Chicago Jazz*; Dempsey J. Travis, *An Autobiography of Black Jazz*; Chad Heap, *Slumming: Sexual and Racial Encounters in American Nightlife, 1885–1940*; Anita O'Day with George Eells, *High Times, Hard Times*. It probably goes without saying, but these folks know their stuff, and any factual errors are my own.

My cousin Sharon Wiens McAllister Willett answered my questions and shared family photographs as I wrote my way deeper in. While this fictional story and its people are very different from your memories, Sharon, I am so grateful to have received your generous perspective on the past.

Amy Simpson, Helen Lee, Keri Wyatt Kent, Jennifer Grant, Caryn Dahlstrand Rivadeneira, Tracey Truhlar Bianchi, Anita Lustrea, Arloa Sutter, Melinda Correa Schmidt, Suanne Ashcroft Camfield, Angie Cramer Weszley, Shayne Moore, and Margaret Philbrick: you have cheered and prayed me forward on so many levels, in so many ways. Thank you.

Carmela Martino, you are a writing companion I can't imagine working without. Thank you for being so present in the words.

Tim, Sherrie, and Temma Lowly, your family has been present with me from before the first word, and inspiring me to the end. I'm so glad we're friends, making stuff together, in it for the long haul, finding our way.

Thank you, Joni Klein and Jan DeVries, Amy and Geoff

Baker, Candy and Bill Crawford, and Meg Fensholt and Kirk Anderson, for being the village that it takes. I am grateful we share Zip Codes, and meals, and conversations, and memories. I am grateful we share.

Cheryl Hollatz-Wisely, you are the best reader, friend, and all-around life coach a girl could have had since she was a baby girl. Literally. Thank you for whisking me away when the deadline loomed. Thank you for the first (possibly last) facial I ever had. Thank you for hanging in there with me for half a century. I pray for decades to come, linking arms with you.

Randi and Mark Woodworth, thank you. Thank you. Thank you. You have helped my family and me weather storms. Grace abides in you, and you in grace.

"Tell me another story," I'd say to my father, as we sat around the table after dinner. And he would. "Tell me about the National Tea," I'd say, and he'd tell about that. Austin, Chicago, the Stockyards, the farm in Wisconsin—he'd tell me about these places, too, and his escapades in them in the 1920s, '30s, and '40s, shared with friends who became as real to me as my own. I am so grateful to you, Dad, for giving me the great gift of your stories. You had such a voice; you still do, I know.

My mother and father raised me in music. They filled our home with it; they filled churches, and classrooms, and cars, and if there was lack, they took me to concerts and recitals where there was more. Thank you, Mom and Dad, for teaching me not just to hear but to listen, and listen deeply.

Magdalena and Teo, my dearest ones, thank you for understanding that I am a mom and a writer, too. Truth be told, I'm not sure I would still be a writer if I hadn't also become a mom to you two. You both inspire me every day to keep the work alive, to do my best (even when my best is broken). You have taught me that time is fleeting and precious, and love is powerful and expansive. You have brought me out of myself and taught me about sacrifice, and when I'm not with you, then I want to be doing something you'd be proud of. I love you, Magdalena and Teo. Thank you for that fact, most of all.

Greg, you know better than anyone else in the world who I am and what I do and why I do it. You have walked with me through it all. I will never, ever be able to thank you fully for being my husband, comrade, soul mate, watchman, except by learning, every day, how to better walk with you. Thank you, Greg Halvorsen Schreck, for taking my name as your own, and for giving me yours. Now, let's go play some Ping-Pong.

A CONVERSATION WITH
KAREN HALVORSEN SCHRECK

1. Who or what inspired you to write *Sing for Me*?

I was originally inspired by the stories my dad told me about growing up as the child of Danish immigrant parents in Chicago during the early part of the twentieth century. My love for music inspired me, too.

2. You are not only an author but also a teacher of writing and literature. How does this, accompanied with your educational background in English and creative writing, influence your writing and storytelling process?

What doesn't influence my writing and storytelling process? Maybe that's more the question. I clean my house, for example; I get down on my knees and scrub the floor. Because I do that work, I'm better able to write about Rose's experience in *Sing for Me*. Washing the floor is a creative act that inspires and contributes to my storytelling process. I honestly believe this. In fact, I've made a recent resolution to embrace this more unified way of looking at experience. Increasingly, I want to break down the divisions between work and play, between productivity (of a certain nature) and creativity (of a certain nature). Doing so sure makes washing the floor a happier time.

So back to the original question about my teaching and studying literature and writing: as with cleaning the house, my time in academia has absolutely influenced and contributed to my storytelling process. I've spent so much joyful, challenging time reading and reflecting actively and deeply on all kinds of writing. Whether the work is traditionally published or that of my students, I learn an immense amount about writing, story-making, *life* from so much of what I read. Cliché as this may sound, I never stop learning. It's a gift really, and like cleaning the floor, teaching and studying writing and literature feeds a single fire.

3. Who is your favorite character? Why?

I've heard other writers say this, and I'll concur: I simply can't answer this question. If I were to try, it would be a bit like my saying that I favor my daughter over my son, or my son over my daughter. The truth is my children are very different people, and I love them equally. This goes for my characters, too. As I write my way forward in a book, I get to know the people who populate the pages; I enter into their lives, hearts, and minds, and they enter into mine. The more time I spend with them, the more I come to care for them in all their complexity, and this goes for the more "minor" characters, too. In the end, I find myself thinking about each and every character: *Oh, you have such a story to tell, too. I want to write your story! Tell me. I'm listening.*

4. A large portion of *Sing for Me* was written during your Metra train commutes to Chicago for work, along with various other nooks and crannies in the city's centers. Describe your favorite writing location or room.

I read Virginia Woolf's *A Room of One's Own* at a formative age. I had wonderful teachers and read wonderful writers who said things like: *A window works best for me at this level in my writing room, and I make a practice of handwriting my first drafts in pencil on lined paper always, and I keep my desk bare except for my paper and pencil and the coffee I made the night before and put into a thermos because I only write in the morning hours, starting before dawn so that I enter the page in a kind of dream state.* I thought that kind of practice was wonderful way back when, when I first read and heard such statements. For years, I tried to emulate them.

Then I had kids.

And then the basement room where I worked in our current house flooded and became unusable as a writing space.

And then I took an extended freelance job that had me commuting regularly.

Luckily, at some point, I also read the amazing poet Lucille Clifton, who said, "The best conditions for me to write poetry are at the kitchen table, one kid's got the measles, another two kids are smacking each other. You know, life is going on around me."

I found the essence of Lucille Clifton's statement both convicting and liberating. Never mind the ideal scenario, I needed to get the work done, and I could and would find a way. Look at Lucille Clifton. She did.

Thus, writing on the train, where every morning and evening (if possible) I'd alight on one of my two favorite perches: an upper seat by the window at the back of the blessed quiet car, or a lower level seat by the window at the back of the blessed quiet car. I loved (and still love) writing on a train, the miles rolling by beneath me. I think it helps me with things like pacing and plot—all that momentum and motion I'm feeling in my body get carried over onto the page.

I also love the Silent Reading Room in the Wheaton Public Library; my kitchen table; my couch, especially if it's winter and there's a fire in the fireplace; my son's bedroom, because the WiFi's best there; and a particular friend's third-floor upstairs' study, where I did a fair portion of solid revision over the course of a week. Cafés, not so much anymore. The music. The noise. I drink too much coffee and then I can't focus, and then I smell like coffee for far too long after. But most any other place: give me a quiet place and I'll do my best to get the work done.

By the way, Lucille Clifton also said this: "Every pair of eyes facing you has probably experienced something you could not endure."

Amen.

5. This novel is steeped in historic detail of Depression-era Chicago. What was your research process like?

With his stories, my father gave me an incredible understanding of Depression-era Chicago—an understanding that became so much a part of me at an early age that I almost felt it was my history, too. But in addition, I did research by reading a lot of books—nonfiction and fiction—about Chicago, the Depression, jazz, the African American experience, and the immigrant experience. (In fact, two of my areas of study for my doctoral exams were literature of the immigrant experience and African American women writers.) I interviewed journalists who write about the Chicago jazz and blues scene. I listened to the music that I included in the novel (such a pleasure). Watched movies made during that time or set in that time, and other people's very old home movies from the 1930s, which, God bless them, they'd posted on YouTube. I also explored historically focused websites and, yes, Facebook groups—you'd be amazed at how much I got out of one particular website that was completely devoted to antique postcards.

6. What would you describe as the main theme(s) in *Sing for Me*?

This is what I believe about theme, and because I can't say it any better than Flannery O'Connor, I'll let her say it for me:

> *I prefer to talk about the meaning in a story rather than the theme of a story. People talk about the theme of a story as if the theme were like the string that a sack of chicken feed is tied with. They think that if you can pick out the theme, the way you pick the right thread in the chicken-feed sack, you can rip the story open and feed the chickens. But this is not the way meaning works in fiction. When you can state the theme of a story, when you can separate it from the story itself, then you can be sure the story is not a very good one. The meaning of a*

story has to be embodied in it, has to be made concrete in it. A story is a way to say something that can't be said any other way, and it takes every word in the story to say what the meaning is. You tell a story because a statement would be inadequate.

(Flannery O'Connor, "Writing Short Stories," *Mystery and Manners: Occasional Prose* [New York: Farrar, Straus and Giroux, 1969], 96.)

7. What do you want readers to experience or take away from this novel?

Hope, in spite of, because of.

8. This story, or at least a version of it, has been on your heart since 1996. Though likely different from Rose's factors and risks in pursuing her dream, what factors prolonged your completing this novel?

I couldn't get the words right. Really. I tried many different times and ways to write this book, but I just couldn't get the words right. Or the characters and plot (especially the plot).

Also, other stories possessed me, and I felt called to tell those stories, too. "Write where the pressure is," the great writer Larry Woiwode once said to me, and the pressure was with those stories in those seasons.

And then there were seasons when life, for better and worse, simply demanded all of my attention.

9. A line from your blog reads, "Sometimes writing feels that way to me, a journey from empty to full, from loss to reconciliation, from mystery to simply story, which doesn't answer the unanswerable questions, perhaps, but makes them bearable."

BT
4/28/14

How has your own journey of making the unanswerable questions bearable played out in this story?

The act of imagining, of laying down words and then revising those words—re*visioning*—is healing for me. Writing stills my soul as prayer does. There's a kind of emptying process that goes on, a kind of release, that leads to not just fullness but fulfillment. Plus, writing keeps my head clear. "How do I know what I think until I see what I say?" E. M. Forster wrote, and for me that's true, too. Specifically with *Sing for Me*, I was emptying out a bucketful of questions about discrimination and equality, ability and disability, community and calling, among other things. There were all those questions before me, made flesh in character, infused in setting, played out in scene. What a relief to give shape and make meaning from the mess of questions in my mind.

10. An excerpt from one of Theo's letters reads, "None of us are so different from the other in our searching." Is this an idea that you would like your readers to grasp? Why?

I work to grasp Theo's statement every day myself. Often I fail. But when I remember what I believe is a fact—that we have so much more in common with each other than we have with what divides us—when I *live* like this, then I am more reconciled with the world and the world is more reconciled with me. Bridges get built, chasms crossed.

11. Can you envision a sequel to *Sing for Me*?

Yes, I can. But I will carry these thoughts quietly in my heart (thank you, dear Gospel writer). If I was able to wait for the right time to write this book, surely I will be able to wait for the right time to write the next one.